BOOK TWO OF THE
MULTIVERSE ASKEW TRILOGY

THE ENDLESS WAR THAT NEVER ENDS

CHRISTOPHER BRIMMAGE

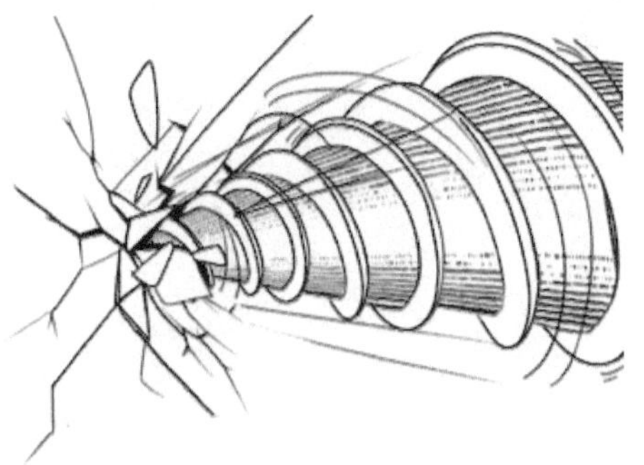

THANK YOU FOR PURCHASING THIS BOOK.

To receive special offers, a free short story, and info on new releases, sign up for the Christopher Brimmage mailing list at cbrimmage.com

For Augustus,
The best little bear in the whole Multiverse.
Power-Bomb- Booooooooy!

And for Link, Margot, Minerva, & Amelia
Second children—like second books—deserve all the attention they can get.
It didn't take a lot of time, but you're already cooler than your parents…

PART 1

THE WAR

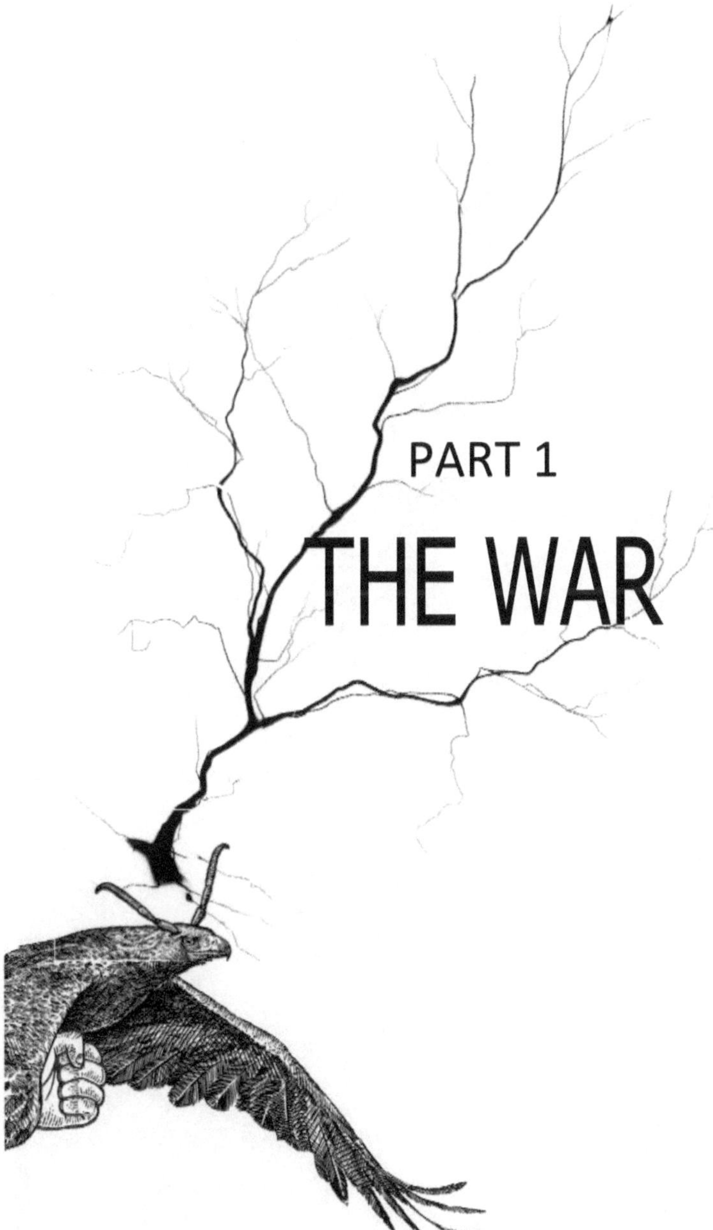

CHAPTER 1

THE INVOCATION OF *MUSE* ELECTRONICS

THE BILLBOARD FOR *Muse Electronics* loomed above Mr. Reynolds like a distasteful obelisk dedicated to the sort of modern god made to be tossed aside and replaced every few months. The billboard declared to the world in bold orange letters, *"SING TO ME OF SURROUND SOUND AND AN AMAZING HOME THEATER, O MUSE ELECTRONICS! SALE EVERY THURSDAY! 20% OFF!"*

Mr. Reynolds popped the collar on his soiled trench coat. He tugged on the frayed brim of his trucker hat until it nearly rested upon his nose. Any random onlooker would have assumed him to be merely the creepiest of homeless flashers.

Behind Mr. Reynolds lay a highway. Cars zoomed along it, and their roaring motors stood in stark juxtaposition to the scene in front of him. In front of him lay a derelict residential street that was empty except for dilapidated cars gathering rust along its curbs. Mr. Reynolds stared past the cars and toward the entrance to an apartment.

The only sign that this apartment was different from any of the others in this square-mile of rundown apartment buildings was its front door, which was missing. Mr. Reynolds pulled his phone from his pocket and dialed the apartment's resident, a task he had performed countless times since the deadbeat left work weeks ago and neglected to return. Just thinking about this deadbeat—a deadbeat named Art—made Mr. Reynolds furrow his brow and sigh.

The phone rang a couple times, and then Art's voice called, "Hello?" A pause for two or three seconds. "Hello? Speak up. I can't hear you."

Mr. Reynolds made no effort to respond.

"Psych!" squealed Art's voice into Mr. Reynolds' ear. "This is my voicemail.

You know what to do. This is Art, by the way, so if you don't want to talk to me, maybe just hang up now."

Mr. Reynolds grimaced. He muttered, "If I had a nickel for every time I've fallen for that damned thing…"

The grizzled Regional Branch Manager of the Department of Motor Vehicles tugged on his mustache and did not finish the thought, the implication obviously being that he would have earned a lot of money. If only he had said the words aloud, he might have caught the attention of the wish-granting fairy that he mistook for a tiny, flittering yellow butterfly, which was experiencing a layover here on Earth 6,076 during its fluttering journey across realities. Mr. Reynolds may have found himself $2.40 richer, which is still a lot of money depending on your point of view.

At the beep, Mr. Reynolds whisper-shouted, "Art! This is Mr. Reynolds. I need you to call me back. This is of ridiculously important! I know you're just going to delete this message without listening to it because you are a giant idiot, but I'll go ahead and try to warn you, anyway: go to the store, buy a new door to cover the gaping security risk in the front of your place, close the damned thing, lock it, and then *do not answer it*. For anyone."

He hung up. He called a second time, and then sighed when he heard the line beep in answer and then hang up. Mr. Reynolds shrugged and crept across the street, bobbing up and down as he limped, old injuries smarting and sending small shocks of pain through his joints. He glanced down at his scarred hands with their nine withered fingers—his left shortened by a pinky—and thought about how much easier his life would be if his orders allowed him to simply enter Art's apartment and *force* the sluggard to listen to him.

When Mr. Reynolds reached the bushes near Art's front window, he ducked beneath them and sat atop a small metallic circle that lay mostly buried beneath the dry mulch. He felt a field of energy wrap around him. Then he slowly raised his head and peeped through the window, only to witness a masterpiece of slovenly degradation.

Art was nearly naked. He wore only a jagged piece of onyx that hung by a thin gold chain around his neck and a pair of boxers saturated with so much grease that they were practically see through. His skin was pallid and yellowed, but it also glistened with its own distinct Art-grease, giving him the appearance of a frumpy, suckling pig baking in its own juices. Art sat staring into the television while sprawled ungraciously on the couch, which was the lone island of quasi-cleanliness amongst the sea of filth. A continent of pizza boxes rose in a disorganized stack from the back corner of the room, and as Mr. Reynolds began hearing the howls of wild animals emerge from amongst them, he ducked his head back down so as not to attract their notice. He sat slump-shouldered on the soil beneath the bushes. He need not dig too hard into his memory to understand what was about to happen, but that did not prevent him from wishing it would happen differently.

Mr. Reynolds leaned his back against the rough brick wall of the apartment building and waited. Finally, after nearly five minutes of tedious trepidation, it happened: Mr. Reynolds experienced what felt like a vacuum sucking out his ear canals, and then a flash of lightning erupted into existence before him, its jagged end crashing to a halt on the sidewalk in front of the entrance to Art's ground floor apartment.

When the lightning dispersed, two figures stood clad in what appeared to be British police officer uniforms, except these uniforms had badges that identified the wearers as Bureau of Interdimensional Travel agents and holsters that contained an array of weaponry that would have multiplied the destructive power of a British police officer by an exponent of at least fifty. One officer was male and looked identical to Art, while the other was female and looked identical to Art's girlfriend, Ginny. Atop their heads, they each wore a snug, bobby-style hat that featured a checkered ring around the crown. A gigantic brown eagle perched on each of their shoulders, and a pair of foot-long antennae dangled from the forehead of each eagle. Mr. Reynolds' stomach turned. He squeezed a clod of soil between his fingers, trying in vain to concentrate on anything other than the panic cresting through his bowels.

Officer-Art marched with purpose toward Art's front entrance. Officer-Ginny followed on his heels. Neither looked left nor right, their gazes fixed squarely on the open threshold in front of them. Officer-Art jabbed a finger at the doorbell so violently that Mr. Reynolds was surprised it did not crack in half. From his perch, Mr. Reynolds could both hear the foghorn call of the doorbell, which filled him with nostalgia, and see the meticulously clean finger of the officer, which flushed the nostalgia from his heart and replaced it with hatred and anxiety.

Mr. Reynolds listened as Normal-Art's footsteps approached the door. "Damn," drifted Normal-Art's voice from within the apartment. Then, "DAMN!"

The officers ignored the cursing. *"Bureau of Interdimensional Travel* Agents 27142 and 29333 at your service. You mind if we come inside?"

Sweat beaded on Mr. Reynolds' forehead. Though he had been assured his perch was safe and protected by technology that made the square-meter invisible to B.I.T. sensors, Mr. Reynolds could not prevent himself from breathing in short, nervous gasps. Moments later, when he heard Normal-Art scream, Mr. Reynolds dug his fingers into his palms to prevent himself from screaming in response. He noted with bleakness the lack of pinky on his left hand to dig into his palm.

Moments later, Officer-Art dragged Normal-Art from the apartment by his arm. Officer-Ginny followed on their heels. "Wait!" screamed Normal-Art. "I know this is going to sound like the stupidest thing you have ever heard, but on our…our caper, we rescued a pair of stuffed bears that claimed they were from the center of the Multiverse. The pink one made off with my girlfriend. According to the blue one, the pink bear is going to destroy every reality in existence. The blue claims it is going to heal them all. You might want to deal with them instead of wasting your time on me. I don't mean anybody any harm. Or good, either. I just want to relax."

Mr. Reynolds flinched as Officer-Ginny slapped Normal-Art across the face. "Why didn't you mention this earlier?"

Mr. Reynolds flinched once more as Officer-Art also slapped Normal-Art across the face. "Did you not think there was a reason those bears were stuck on that backwater reality? You've unwittingly unleashed the greatest threat the Multiverse has ever known."

Normal-Art muttered something, but Mr. Reynolds could not hear it. "You're coming with us to help us stop those beasts, whether you like it or not," declared Officer-Art, squeezing tightly on Normal-Art's arm.

"And *then* it's off to a prison dimension with you," added Officer-Ginny. Dread filled Mr. Reynolds' heart.

Normal-Art squealed. "I just want to sit on my couch and watch television. Why won't anybody just let me relax?"

Mr. Reynolds watched Officer-Art's eagle stand tall and flap its wings. As it screeched, lightning flashed from its antennae and enveloped the trio. Mr. Reynolds heard Normal-Art curse his luck as he disappeared.

Mr. Reynolds crawled out from under the bushes and stood. He stroked his bushy mustache out of habit, and then he shuddered. He grabbed the bottom right corner of the mustache and yanked. The adhesive on the back of the false mustache seemed to take a few layers of skin with it as it detached. Mr. Reynolds squealed a curse.

He glanced around to make sure the area was still deserted, and then he turned the fake mustache over in his hand so that the back of it was facing up. A little red button lay in its middle, and he tapped the button in the pattern he had been taught.

Fractions of a second later, a hologram of a wizened, bearded face appeared floating above the mustache. "Agent Arthur, what have you to report?"

"It's just Art," said Mr. Reynolds—a name which is obviously the man's pseudonym, and if you are *just now* putting the pieces together and realizing that this is Art from the future, dear reader, then maybe you should give up on this book before it gets more complicated.

The bearded face made no reply to Older-Art's correction, so Older-Art began his report, "My past-self departed with B.I.T. Officers 27142 and 29333 mere seconds ago, as we *knew* he would."

The face nodded in approval. "This is good. The timestream is as it should be. Well done, Agent Arthur."

"It's just Art," corrected Older-Art for a second time. Knowing the correction would continue to garner no response, he continued, "Look, we obviously knew this was destined to happen and that he was going to go with them. I don't understand why you couldn't have simply dropped me off twenty years in the future so that I can complete my mission and be done with all this damnable business."

The face sighed. "As I explain to you *every single time* we speak, it's because you needed to be in your current position as your younger-self's boss in order to create a chain of events that caused your younger-self to abandon his status quo and join your mischief-god-self on the quest to retrieve the cosmic bears. Otherwise, the bear scenario would never have played out as it was destined to, and all hope for all futures would be lost. Though *Father Time* predestined the events to play out as they did, you needed to be there to act as *Father Time's* prodding finger."

Older-Art sighed. "Fine. Whatever. I get it, I just hate it. But now past-me won't be back for twenty years. So, pick me up, shift me to the future, and drop me off at his/my predestined return time."

Silence answered Older-Art on the other end.

"Hey! C'mon! Come get me!" screamed Older-Art.

More silence.

"Please! I'm sorry for refusing to urinate in the restroom! I'll never use your shoes again! I'm sorry for placing sharp objects in your chair and for spitting in your coffee when you weren't looking! Please just shift me forward in time so I can get this damned mission over with and *finally* be left alone!"

The face stared at him with mouth agape. "I didn't know about the coffee thing," it replied.

Older-Art planted his face squarely in his free palm and stifled a despairing sob.

The face ignored the emotional outburst. It said, "Sorry, Agent Arthur, but you chose to continue your mischief despite stern warnings against such behavior. Now you must complete your mission before you can be trusted to return to the ship. Maintain your position at the Department of Motor Vehicles and ensure that it runs efficiently."

The face continued droning on, but Older-Art no longer listened. He did not even correct the face when it called him by his full first name. Instead, he cursed and pressed the red button on the back of the fake mustache. The face disappeared, and Older-Art sighed in satisfaction at this tiny bit of power he was able to exert over his superior.

Older-Art reapplied the fake mustache and walked back toward the Department of Motor Vehicles. The order to maintain his position as Regional Branch Manager was obviously a ploy to torment him, and it might possibly be the *worst* torture he had ever experienced. The tedium seemed almost too heavy to bear. He worried whether he had the mental fortitude to preserve his sanity. But if he ever wanted to be free, he knew that he must obey his orders this time. He sighed.

When he arrived back inside the D.M.V., he called a random employee into his office to yell at her for underperformance. When he was finished, he felt mildly better. He dismissed her. Then he cursed and began the long wait for his younger-self to return.

CHAPTER 2

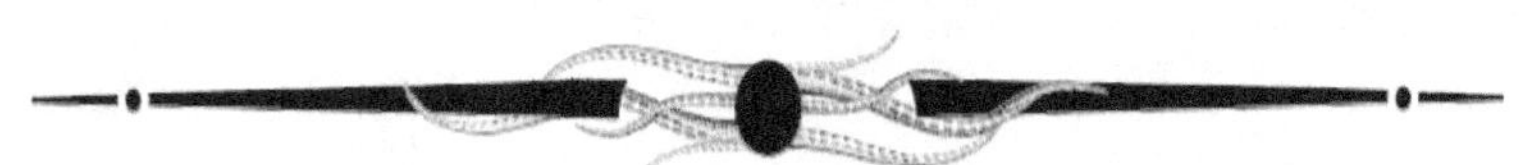

TEN LONG YEARS LATER...

REGULAR-GINNY HAD ALWAYS excelled at counting. She may not have been the best athlete or the best looker in grade school, but for a brief shining moment—back before addition and subtraction and multiplication and all the other -tions entered the equation—she had been a star. Forwards, backwards, by tens, by hundreds, it did not matter. She was the cream of Mrs. Dublond's first grade class.

But even these superior counting skills failed her now.

She smashed a gargantuan tentacle the size of a redwood down atop the last vestige of life on this Earth, which consisted of a dozen humanoid figures kneeling in a prayer circle, begging their gods to save them. Their corpses left a lumpy stain across the concrete.

This Earth was now a lifeless husk, barren and black and covered in naught but debris and gore. And now this Earth looked exactly like the fifty before it, and the hundred before that, and so many others before those that Ginny's counting abilities were not up to the task of keeping track.

There was a time in the beginning of her service as the *Right Hand of Destruction* to the Pink One—a cosmic incarnation of *Destruction* that took the form of a pastel pink teddy bear—when this now-familiar scene filled her with guilt and terror, when the Pink One's voice filled her with hatred and fear and murderous anxiety. Now, ten years after her decision to join the Pink One, the sights and sounds of slaughter filled her with numbness.

This Earth had fallen easily because the Pink One's foil—a cosmic incarnation of *Life* that took the form of a pastel blue teddy bear—and his army had not appeared to battle over this Earth's fate. But that meant little for this Earth's ultimate outcome. Like every other Earth that Regular-Ginny and her master successfully destroyed, the Blue One would arrive at some point in the future to heal everything, and eventually—be it years from now or days from now—the Pink One's army would return to destroy it all over again.

Regular-Ginny glanced down from her perch within the building-sized gelatinous pink blob that served as her home. Standing at attention before her was an army of Ginnys and Arts, which she had long ago begun referring to as the *Pink Marauders*. With the wanton destruction of this Earth at an end, they no longer moved. Regular-Ginny breathed deep, despite no longer needing to breathe at all. She had come to associate these moments just after the carnage and murder and bloodshed as the only moments of respite she would experience for the rest of eternity.

Regular-Ginny sighed. She surveyed her army, taking note of its variety. There were Arts with swords and shields, giant Arts, Arts wearing capes, Arts in sentient cars, cartoon Arts, and hundreds upon hundreds of others, too many others for her to count. This horde of Arts was accompanied by an equally vast horde of Ginnys with equally odd iterations.

Years ago, when she had first lost count of conquered Earths, Regular-Ginny had begun creating these puppets—the creation of which was an ability the Pink One had bestowed upon her as the bear funneled more and more cosmic power into her. Now, whenever the Pink One teleported her to some new reality, she would seek out the Art and/or Ginny of that reality. She would proceed to murder him/her, and then she would launch a pink mist from the end of a tentacle. When the mist encountered the skin of the dead Art and/or Ginny, it would enter the body through the corpse's pores and assorted orifices. The corpse's eyes would cloud pink and then it would reanimate, at which point it would follow Regular-Ginny's orders like one of a nigh-infinite crowd of murderous pod people.

Much to her and the Pink One's chagrin, the Blue One had responded to this development by recruiting Arts and Ginnys to create his own army, and now any fight between the cosmic forces resulted in either an Earth being destroyed or healed, accompanied by a ridiculous number of Art and Ginny corpses—many of which would be reanimated as pink puppets, while just as many of which would be magically resuscitated into the ranks of the Blue One's army.

This cosmic war reminded Ginny of the trench warfare about which she had learned during her high school history class's World War I unit, except with entire realities substituted for trenches. The two armies fought and suffered incredibly high casualties to exchange control over random Earths, and no matter who won each Earth, there was little ultimate benefit to either side. The winner gained a "trench" that it would inevitably lose, and the cycle of winning and losing and battling over the "trench" would repeat itself unto infinity. It was a war of attrition, but with both sides having the power to resurrect the fallen—either as fully resurrected individuals or as undead pink puppets—the war was endless. The soul within Regular-Ginny considered shuddering, but her dead exterior did not cooperate.

Ginny's thoughts were interrupted when the Pink One appeared with a flash of black light and then floated down from the sky. The Pink One chomped into a barren spot on the ground and sucked hard. The embers within the crust of this Earth—its Reality Light[1]—were drawn into the torturous belly of the Pink One. The pink teddy lifted her head from the meal, wiped her mouth with the back of her arm, and stared at Regular-Ginny. The bear nodded. Regular-Ginny pursed her lips. The Pink Marauders stood in zombified silence.

Then the pink bear exploded, and thousands of black bubbles launched from the epicenter of the blast. Regular-Ginny closed her single remaining eye—her other eye lost to God-Art on Earth 1,000,000 during her quest to rescue the Pink One—as the bubbles enveloped her and the army, ripping them from this reality.

Despite the ludicrous number of jumps over the past ten years, Ginny never got completely used to the sensation of hopping between realities. A wave of nausea washed over her, and then she found herself falling through an infinite space both colorful and colorless.

She tumbled end over end, and the army surrounding her did the same. The lot of them looked like the loose fuzz from an especially overlarge and unkempt dandelion that had been swept up in a tornado. Like always, after what felt like a combination of eternity and no time at all, the Pink One zoomed down into the empty space below the army and exploded. More black bubbles enveloped Ginny and the army.

---

[1] Every reality has a *Reality Light* that keeps it powered and in existence. And if the Reality Light is not continuously alight, then the reality winks out of existence and everything and everyone in it are reduced to nothingness.

This reality's Reality Light just so happened to take the form of a Reality Campfire housed inside its Earth's core. But each reality has a different iteration hidden in its own special location.

For more details and the operational mechanics of Reality Lights, see *The Multiverse Askew* Book 1, Chapter 25.

The army tumbled from the space between realities down into a wide ocean, which stretched in every direction as far as the eye could see. A collective zombified moan erupted from the Pink Marauders, followed by a nearly collective splash. Some of the more mundane Art and Ginny puppets sank under the water and did not reappear.

One particular Ginny—who had conveniently been exposed to an odd type of radiation inside an ice factory on her home Earth and now had the convenient ability to generate ice at will from her fingertips—created what appeared to be a full-sized Titanic replica made of ice, and those Arts and Ginnys who had not sunk below the waves swam to it and clambered up its side to safety.

Well, relative safety, anyway.

Hundreds of shark fins broke the water's surface. Seconds later, a legion of great white sharks carrying tower shields and short thrusting swords began clambering up the sides of the Ice-Titanic, giving chase to the Pink Marauders. At the legion's head climbed a ferocious shark wearing what looked like an ancient Roman centurion's helmet atop its head.

Regular-Ginny shifted the density of her giant pink blob so that she floated atop the water near the Ice-Titanic. As she knew she must to prevent repercussions from the Pink One, Regular-Ginny yelled "Attack!" to her zombified minions, who immediately began assaulting and murdering the sharks.

Then she rolled her eye in annoyance and disgust. Though she had yet to experience the destruction of *this particular* Earth, this scene was nearly identical to one that had played out a dozen or so realities ago when her army had invaded a different ocean planet that was dominated by a species of octopus that seemed to borrow cultural inspiration from the ancient Egyptians of Regular-Ginny's home Earth. The Art of that Earth had led the Royal Octopus Chariot Brigade—a chariot army drawn by sea-horses, both predictably and stupidly—and had made a fantastic Pink Marauder until the pink horde invaded a reality filled with sushi-loving samurai gorillas, where this octopus-Art had been consumed during the ensuing battle by the gorilla-Ginny of that reality. It disgusted her how so many of these doomed realities were thematically similar at their cores, despite having literally an infinite number of potential differences from which to develop and evolve.

A pink pinch inside her skull sent pain coursing through her body, jerking her mind to attention and jostling her into action. From her floating position near the Ice-Titanic, she whipped a tentacle across the side of the ship, knocking the vanguard of sharks back into the sea. The one in the centurion helmet, however, was not displaced, and the itch that Regular-Ginny felt in the back of her brain told her all she needed to know about this shark's identity.

Regular-Ginny snaked two tentacles across the expanse of ocean between them. She used the first tentacle to impale the creature, forming the end of the tentacle into a sharpened point and shoving it deep into the monster's heart. The shark gasped and then breathed its last. Regular-Ginny then hovered the end of the second tentacle in front of the shark's face. A thin pink mist launched from the end of this tentacle and enveloped the beast's head. The shark's eyes clouded pink. It smiled a soulless smile, and a series of sharp snaggleteeth stood out in prominent display.

Regular-Ginny could now answer the unasked question of what she would look like as a great white shark wearing ancient Roman legionary attire, and she was unimpressed.

"Where is your mate?" demanded Regular-Ginny of the shark, having by now found that the only constant in every reality was the connection between its Art and its Ginny as either current or ex-mates.

As Ginny's voice passed through the pink blob, it translated into whatever language the shark spoke and vice versa—a gift, like so many others, that the Pink One had given her during their time together for which she had not asked. The shark replied, "Behind you."

Regular-Ginny turned. She gasped a startled gasp at the gargantuan beast that burst forth from beneath the waves. And then she cursed in embarrassment, remembering that her pink blob made her nearly invulnerable and that she need fear little from the incoming behemoth.

A blue whale wearing bright silver legionnaire armor on its body and a laurel wreath made from kelp upon its head slashed at Regular-Ginny's pink blob with a sword the size of an eighteen-wheeler. The pink within her veins coursed boiling rage through her body. She parried the sword with a tentacle and then smacked the whale across the face with a second tentacle. The whale ignored the attack and barreled into her, knocking her against the Ice-Titanic.

She grabbed its front flippers with two tentacles, and then she snaked an extra tentacle around its back. The end of this extra tentacle formed itself into a monstrous, cottage-sized mallet. Regular-Ginny used the pink mallet to pound the whale in the base of its skull. She felt like some sort of devilish blacksmith as she beat the creature in the back of its head over and over, crushing its skull into a bloody pulp and readying the beast to be reshaped into one of her army's many deadly weapons.

Once life fled from the whale's eyes, she shoved a new tentacle deep into the creature's blowhole. She launched as much mist as she could muster into the cavity. The beast's eyes lost their natural black gleam, and the dull pink of puppetry replaced it. Regular-Ginny grinned at this new, gigantic addition to her collection of pink puppets.

Regular-Ginny backed away and watched the beast wreak carnage upon its former brethren. When Ginny grew bored with this sight, she changed the density of her pink blob and sank below the ocean's surface. She sighed. It was as though the Pink Marauders had stepped upon an underwater ant hill merely by appearing on this reality. The oceans teemed with what appeared to be legion upon legion of sea creatures adorned for battle and rushing up toward the surface. Below them, cities made from seaweed stretched unto the horizon. The gigantic buildings were shades of green and red and brown, and the city streets were lit by what appeared to be hordes of electric eels tied to light posts.

Shark-Ginny and Whale-Art followed Regular-Ginny below the surface, along with the dozens of Ginnys and Arts that could breathe—and thus fight—underwater. "Kill everything!" commanded Regular-Ginny, and the puppets began doing just that, gorging the Pink One on the life force of these underwater peoples.

Regular-Ginny grew dozens of flippered tentacles from her blob and swam into the depths of this ocean, ignoring the natives' useless attacks against her pink hull. She began the process of destroying the seaweed cities—a process that felt almost bureaucratic at this point in her existence. Following each jump to a new reality, the Pink One needed a certain amount of destructive force to flow her way from death and wanton property destruction before she gained enough energy to drain the life force from the reality's Reality Light, which was often housed deep within each Earth's crust or hidden within some sort of sacred temple.

Regular-Ginny hated ocean planets, because the aforementioned task of property destruction on these realities was always slower, and it generally took at least a week to complete. She sighed and prepared herself for at least a week of tedium.

*

Regular-Ginny went through the motions for the next ten or so Earths.

And then, like a child losing a toy, she felt a pang of sadness upon invading the following Earth. The Pink Marauders found themselves making war upon cloud cities high in the sky, and during a heated exchange between the Pink Marauders and the native defenders of this Earth, Whale-Art slipped from the edge of one of the cloud precipices. As he stumbled toward oblivion, he accidentally knocked from the edge a potted petunia version of Ginny. She was one of Regular-Ginny's favorites, a particularly fierce warrior that walked about on her roots and used a pair of small tommy guns to slaughter her enemies with hails of bullets.

Regular-Ginny frowned at having been too slow to save them from falling and thus disappearing forever into the endless gaseous mass that formed this Earth. Then she swallowed her annoyance and completed the subjugation of this reality. Then, after the Pink One fed, Regular-Ginny experienced the explosion of black portals, the nausea, the infinite space between realities, the falling, and then the second explosion of portals marking an incursion into the next reality.

When she landed on the next Earth, something seemed off. Skulls stretched in stacks unto the horizon. A native man knelt before the Pink Marauders as they appeared. He was bald except for a braided length of hair that dangled from the back of his skull down to the ground, where its end rested in decayed gore. His skin appeared to have both the color and consistency of spoiled goat's milk. He wore a patch over his left eye upon which had been written the word "*Arthur*" in bright pink jewels, though the rest of his face looked like Regular-Ginny's long-lost boyfriend. He wore robes of dull yellow that looked like they could have been made from flayed human skin.

This man called out, "Oh, malevolent Pink One. It is I: your servant, Arthur the Putrid. Look far and wide. I have prepared this reality for you."

The Pink One appeared in a flash of black light and floated above him. "Me be not happy. Me be hungry for death and destruction, and Me be robbed of death and destruction by you."

Arthur the Putrid did not flinch. He reached within his robes and retrieved an object that resembled a mason jar. He said, "You need not worry, oh great and mighty Pink One. I collected the life force *for* you."

He unscrewed the top and a spotlight launched from it. The light somehow moaned, and the sound reminded Ginny of the terrible version of a ghost that her niece had portrayed many Halloweens ago, only amplified over thousands of loudspeakers.

Arthur the Putrid aimed the beam directly at the Pink One. The bear squealed. At first, Regular-Ginny grew hopeful that the beam of light was somehow killing the Pink One, but like every other time a positive feeling fluttered through Ginny these days, the hope was quickly squashed under the boot of despair and put out of its misery. The light eventually petered out, and the Pink One danced in the air above Arthur the Putrid, stronger than ever.

"Oh, Me! Oh, Me! Oh, Me!" shouted the bear. "Delightful. Me want again!"

Arthur the Putrid gave a slight nod of his head. He said, "Years ago, I foresaw this day. I prepared and I genocided, and now my long wait is over. I will provide this to you over and over and over again, if only you take me with you to be your *Right Hand.*"

The Pink One frowned. Ginny feared for a moment that the Pink One might fulfill this man's wishes, giving him the *Right Hand of Destruction* moniker and removing both it and her life force from her. The Pink One had promised to spare Ginny's home reality so long as Ginny served the cosmic entity. Ginny could only assume that her elimination—whether the choice was Ginny's or not—would sever that promise.

"No, silly. Me *Right Hand of Destruction* be here already," replied the Pink One, waving a paw at Regular-Ginny. "You can no be Me number two. Nope, Nope, Nope. You am instead being Me *Left Hand of Lesser Destruction and Also Life Force Catching.*"

Arthur the Putrid frowned. After a few moments of silence, he muttered, "Very well."

He removed his eye from staring at the Pink One just long enough to glare at Regular-Ginny. Regular-Ginny shrugged.

The Pink One bit down into the crust of the Earth and began sucking. Arthur the Putrid laughed maniacally. When he noticed nobody else was joining him in his celebratory laughter, he frowned harder than ever, kicked the dust at his feet, and tucked his hands in his pockets.

CHAPTER 3

THE PRE-TEEN, THE MYTH, THE LEGEND

ARTURO LISTENED TO his Chemistry teacher drone on and on and on. Arturo's classmates were frantically writing notes about the nature of covalent bonds. Arturo yawned. His pencil lay dormant on the edge of his desk.

I learned this stuff before I left the crib, he thought, scorn seeping from the edges of his frown in the form of tiny bubbles. In terms of age, Arturo was a sixth grader, but he was enrolled in high school classes due to his advanced academic performance. However, Arturo believed that he had learned all he could learn from high school and that he belonged in a university. Unfortunately for him, the system does not merely bend to the wishes of a pre-teen boy, no matter how gifted he may be.

"Do you have a problem with my lecture, Arturo?" demanded Mr. Lopez from the front of the class.

Darn it, thought Arturo. *Darn it, darn it, darn it all to heck. I did it again! Auntie April just warned me again this morning. She said, 'Ya may be a genius when it comes to the books, little nephew, but you got some learnin' to do when it comes to body language. Ya gotta learn a poker face or somethin', 'cuz us regular folk don't take too kindly when people like you scowl at us when you think somethin' ain't worth your attention.'*

Arturo fibbed, "No, sir, Mr. Lopez. I was *totally* listening to everything. Heard you loud and clear. The lecture is going great."

Mr. Lopez frowned. "Then please, remind the class of the last thing I said."

Arturo furrowed his brow and allowed his nearly perfect phonographic memory to go to work. It replayed in quick succession everything that the teacher had said while Arturo had not been paying attention. Seconds later, Arturo parsed out the proper response and said, "You made an analogy relating covalent bonds to children sharing a toy, and then you mentioned how whichever child wants the toy has access to it."

Arturo bit the inside of his cheek to force himself to focus on something else so that he would stop talking right there. He did this because he had a problem with the analogy that Mr. Lopez had used, and he knew that any correction of Mr. Lopez's lesson would land him in trouble, for the teacher was notoriously prickly and arrogant.

"Thank you, Arturo," said Mr. Lopez. "I see that you *were* listeni—"

But Arturo could not resist. He interrupted his teacher, "But I've gotta say, Mr. Lopez, that your analogy falls apart on *so* many levels."

Arturo raised an index finger, and then he continued raising other fingers as he ticked off problems with the analogy. "First," he said, "children are inherently terrible at sharing, especially when it comes to toys. Second, it's not like the atoms are giving anything up when they share an electron. They're both accessing it, unlike a child lending its toy to another child, who must stop playing with the toy to share. Third, I think you could make this lesson much more interesting if you let us—"

Arturo stopped speaking. He had glanced out the window as he was talking, and in doing so, he had noticed a symbol floating in the air above the city's skyline. It was in the shape of a yellow and purple Black Widow spider. The watch on his wrist began buzzing. He sighed and thought, *Talk about terrible timing…*

Mr. Lopez's frown grew deeper than ever. He asked, "Well? Are you going to finish?"

Arturo frowned back. "A-Actually, I need to go to the bathroom. Right away."

Mr. Lopez pursed his lips. "You know the rules," he said. "Between classes."

Arturo glanced left and right for a way to escape class. The signal in the sky and the buzzing of his watch meant that every second he remained here in class, people in the city were being injured or killed. But he had a secret identity that he must maintain to protect his family, so he couldn't merely jump out the window. *I need to get out of here,* he thought. *But how?*

Mr. Lopez must have interpreted Arturo's silence as acquiescence, for he responded, "As I'm sure the rest of your classmates would like to learn this subject so that they can pass their state tests and graduate, let's continue. Covalent bonds are strongest whe—"

"Wait, Mr. Lopez!" shouted Arturo, his mind whirling with desperation.

Suddenly, the metaphorical fishing pole of his brain managed to snag itself an idea. He smirked. "I was reading an article in *Popular Science* that showed this really cool diagram of a covalent bond, but explained it using terms so that us kids would find the idea, like, *super* hip. Look, I'll draw it on the board!"

Before Mr. Lopez had time to react, Arturo was up and on the way to the whiteboard. He grabbed a blue dry erase marker from its home on the little aluminum shelf attached to the bottom of the board. He began drawing.

"Arturo, return to your desk this instant, or I'll have security escort you to the principal's office!" demanded Mr. Lopez.

Arturo continued drawing, waving the marker from side to side with gusto. Finally, he said, "Mr. Lopez, you ain't got the balls."

Arturo dropped the marker and moved aside to make his masterpiece visible to the entire class. It obviously had nothing to do with covalent bonds, despite his initial claim to the contrary. He could feel the shocked eyes of his classmates on him. He heard them begin to snigger, and then he heard Mr. Lopez heave an angry sigh.

Emblazoned upon the whiteboard in the dull blue of old marker was an enormous spider. However, instead of webbing emanating from its spinner, a gigantic penis stood erect from it, and the garish penis stretched across half the whiteboard. In small block letters next to the penis, Arturo had written, '*Mr. Lopez's face.*' He had drawn an arrow pointing from the words to the tip of the penis.

Arturo pointed to the picture's distinct lack of testicles. "See?" he announced. "No testicles."

Angry redness crept up Mr. Lopez's neck and then spread across his face. Arturo grabbed a red marker from its perch and added the color to the drawing in mimic of Mr. Lopez. The classroom erupted in laughter.

Mr. Lopez yanked the class phone from its hook on his desk and pressed a button. He screamed into the receiver, "I need a removal! Now!"

Mr. Lopez then sat down on the edge of his desk, balled his fists, and bored into Arturo with his angry eyes. Every shred of decency within Arturo wanted to apologize, but he knew that he could not, for he *needed* to get in trouble and be sent out of the classroom for the greater good of the city. Mr. Lopez yanked a discipline referral from a stack on his desk and began filling it out with such furious stabs of his pen that he ripped this referral and had to grab a new one.

After what felt like an eternity, the door finally burst open. A tall black police officer with salt-and-pepper hair strode into the classroom.

Mr. Lopez pointed at Arturo. "Get him out of here before I hurt him," demanded Mr. Lopez, handing the discipline referral to the school's on-staff uniformed officer.

The officer glanced over at the board and shook his head. "C'mon, Arturo," he said.

He grabbed Arturo by the elbow—not ungently—and led the young man to retrieve his backpack before walking him out the door. The officer muttered, "Your daddy's prob'ly lookin' down on you from Heaven and coverin' his face in shame."

Arturo's shoulders slumped. He hung his head. His father had been murdered not four months prior, and it was all Arturo's fault. The wound was still fresh, and he suspected that it would always remain so. The officer's statement stung worse than any physical injury Arturo had ever experienced. He dragged his feet and allowed himself to be led from the classroom.

The duo entered the hallway, and once the classroom door shut behind them, the officer slapped Arturo upside the back of his head. Arturo squealed, "Hey, Uncle Jasper! Stop that! I got a good explanation."

Jasper slapped Arturo once more upside the back of the head. "I can't believe you, kid."

Jasper glanced down at the discipline referral. He continued, "You drew a penis on the board and insulted your teacher. You can kiss that perfect record goodbye. Your daddy'd have beaten the hell outta me if he knew I'd let you get away with *this* kinda behavior while livin' under my roof."

Arturo pointed at his watch. "There's been an alert, and Mr. Lopez wouldn't let me leave class, so I couldn't sneak away."

Jasper sighed. He stared down at the discipline referral. After a few moments, he wadded the referral into a ball and mussed Arturo's hair. "Fine. Go on. I'll cover for you. Just be careful. *Please.* I can't lose you, too."

Arturo smiled his familiar half-smile. His eyes shone with relief. "Thanks, Uncle Jasper. I will."

With that, Arturo glanced up and down the hallway to ensure it was empty. Then he retrieved his mask from his backpack. Its bright yellow cloth was tinged with jagged purple lines he had drawn with a Sharpie marker. He had intended for the purple lines to resemble webs, but they actually resembled misshapen cartoon zebra stripes. He had cut two holes for his eyes to allow himself full visibility.

Arturo tore off his shirt, yanked off his shoes, and ducked out of his pants. Rather than a masked, naked pre-teen standing where Arturo had just been, there stood a boy adorned in a spandex bodysuit with the same yellow-and-purple pattern as the mask. Arturo's school clothes lay in a pile at his feet. He pointed at the clothes and asked, "Uncle Jasper, can you help with those?"

Jasper leaned down and began stuffing the school clothes into Arturo's backpack. "Yeah, yeah," he replied. "I'll leave your backpack on the roof. You can pick it up later."

"Thanks!"

And with that, Arturo raced out the nearest exit of the school. As he leapt into the air, he raised his right hand toward the nearest building and dug his ring and pinky fingers into a secret spot on his palm. Purple webs launched from his wrist[2], and he swung on them toward downtown, toward the city he intended to save for the umpteenth time.

*

Arturo leapt onto the nearby wall, narrowly dodging the energy beam. He asked in a mocking tone, "Are you sure you don't wanna go home and practice your aim? Maybe come back when you can actually get somewhere *close* to hitting me?"

Arturo's arachnid intuition buzzed in the base of his skull, warning him of more impending danger. He crawled a few dozen feet up the side of the building and backflipped into the air. Another energy beam crashed into the spot he had just occupied, disintegrating the bricks and mortar and leaving naught but smoking carnage in its wake.

---

2 Though Arturo believed these secretions to be webs, they were actually telekinetic manifestations of magical purple ropes that *resembled* webs. Arturo did not realize it, but his superpowers were actually psychic-based rather than science-based, and thus they conformed to the manner in which he subconsciously wanted them to manifest—in this case, mimicking those of an arachnid due to his obsession with the creatures.

While Arturo is obviously the Multiverse's attempt at parody of particularly blatant tropes in superhero literature, this author would like to emphasize how fortunate it is that these powers manifested themselves within an innocent boy obsessed with arachnids. If they had *instead* manifested within one of Arturo's much more vulgar or obnoxious peers who did not have such an innocent obsession, the result easily could have been a phallus-themed superhero that would have thrust this novel into adults-only territories. Thanks, Multiverse.

Arturo spun in midair and launched webbing toward the nearest building. He swung to face the source of the beams: one of his oldest nemeses, *The Hippo Horseman*. The villain was exactly what his name implied, which was a hippopotamus in knightly armor sitting astride a winged destrier[3].

The winged destrier flew in small circles, keeping The Hippo Horseman afloat nearly fifty feet in the air. The villain twisted in his saddle with each small circle, holding his lance aimed in Arturo's direction. Though the hippopotamus's plate armor was comically undersized, its black color with red chasing was coated in just enough dust and debris to make the behemoth look downright menacing. Many in the superheroing community treated The Hippo Horseman like a joke because of his ridiculous name and appearance, but Arturo knew better. And today Arturo's concerns proved true, because a half-dozen city blocks lay demolished and in disarray in the villain's wake.

What Arturo did not know was that if he were to ask The Hippo Horseman *why* the villain had chosen to perform such a dastardly deed today, Arturo would have learned that the villain had worked up the courage to go on his first date in years, but the woman had faked a mid-date emergency to leave early. The Hippo Horseman had intuitively understood what was happening due to its common occurrence in his youth, so he decided to supply her with a *real* emergency and thus transform her lie into a reality. If Arturo had asked, he would have also learned of the years of abuse and ridicule that the villain had suffered at the hands of his father and of the constant heartbreak and emotional turmoil that had led him to this point of destructive despair.

But instead of asking any questions, Arturo did as any red-blooded superhero would do at a time like this when his city is under attack: he launched

---

3 As Arturo had learned through nearly a dozen encounters with the supervillain, The Hippo Horseman was a former zoologist named Herbie Hicklebottom who had become really, really infatuated with renaissance festivals, going so far as to quit his day job and join the jousting circuit. Unfortunately, at one fateful festival, he had heard that the nearby zoo's hippopotamuses were sick, and even more unfortunately, there happened to be a radiation leak from a nearby power plant as Herbie entered the cage to check on them, still wearing his full jousting regalia. The leak interacted with something in the cage, exploded, and Herbie found himself no longer a man, but a hippo in knight's armor. Somehow, the accident also caused his horse to grow wings, his armor to be magically imbued so that it was nearly impervious, and his weapons to glow with irradiated light that allowed him to launch energy beams from them at will.*

* Yes, Herbie and Arturo's reality *is* stupid and illogical, but it's all they know, so don't be too hard on them.

toward the hippopotamus and punched the behemoth squarely in the nose.

The Hippo Horseman roared in anger, and his horse reared up and kicked at Arturo. Arturo easily dodged and swung over to a nearby wall.

Arturo waved his hand back and forth in front of his nose. "Dang. Don't roar at a guy without sucking down a couple dozen breath mints first. Hold on a sec, I think I've got some right here," quipped Arturo as he mimed checking his bodysuit for pockets.

The Hippo Horseman launched another destructive energy beam from his lance, but the villain telegraphed it so obviously that Arturo would have been able to dodge it even without his arachnid intuition. Arturo spun through the air and launched webbing at the horse's closest wing. The webbing covered the wing in a cocoon so thick and heavy that the normally majestic appendage drooped with immobility. The horse's other wing flapped twice as fast to try and make up for the loss of the left one, but this attempt at compensation only left the horse spinning in sad little lopsided circles as it began to lose altitude and fall from the sky. The Hippo Horseman tugged hard on the reins to try to control the spin, but the animal was already too off-kilter, and soon it began to tilt to the right.

The Hippo Horseman dropped his lance to the ground, which was now about twenty feet down, and jumped from his horse. The hippopotamus landed in a crouching position more deftly than a behemoth had any logical right to land, none the worse for wear. The horse, however, crashed atop a taxicab, squealed in dismay, and then quietly limped into a nearby back alley. Arturo noted to himself that he would need to deal with the wandering warhorse later, for the ultimate threat here was The Hippo Horseman, who seemingly on cue stood to full height on his hind legs, drew his longsword from its golden scabbard, and shook it in Arturo's direction.

The Hippo Horseman bellowed, "You leave me naught a choice but to squash thee like the bug thou art, oh dastardly *Arachnid Pre-Teen!*"

The ivory hilt of the villain's sword was shaped into the head of a hippopotamus with rubies for eyes. The rubies seemed to catch fire, and then these flames encompassed the blade and launched from its point toward Arturo.

After dodging this attack, Arturo sighed in annoyance at the necessity of facing this fiend *again.* On his first superheroing adventure, he had fought this villain. And though Arturo had planned to name himself *The Great Spider* or *The*

Golden Arachnid or some such majestic moniker, The Hippo Horseman had called him *The Arachnid Pre-Teen* in front of news cameras, and the name had stuck. No matter how much he tried to get people to refer to himself as something more befitting a superhero, his pleas and attempts to rebrand himself fell on deaf ears within the superhero and journalist communities alike.

Arturo swung forth and kicked the hippo in the head with the heels of his feet. He managed to knock the black helm from the top of the villain's head, where it tumbled to the ground with a metallic *CLANG*. The hippo swiped at Arturo with his sword, but Arturo ducked beneath it. He backflipped over another swipe, and then shot webbing at the hippo's feet, binding the behemoth in place atop the concrete.

Arturo's watch buzzed, so as he dodged an enraged cut and blinded the hippopotamus with webbing aimed directly at the villain's eyes, he tapped a button on his watch. A holographic face appeared above the watch, at which Arturo had learned from experience never to look during the middle of a fight. The face was one of a grizzled old man with salt-and-pepper hair wearing the hat of a four-star general and the eyepatch of a man who has seen his share of combat.

"I'm in the middle of something here, General Vehemence," squealed Arturo, continuing to flip and bounce and dodge around The Hippo Horseman's wild slashes and furious energy bolts.

The face scowled. "Stop toying with that monstrosity and put 'im down! Use as much force as necessary! We've got something else much more powerful on the radar, and it's comin' in hot!"

"Fine," muttered Arturo. He leapt into the air, webbed the hippopotamus's hand and sword to the ground, and then punched The Hippo Horseman in his blinded face over and over until his legs collapsed out from under him. Arturo continued punching until the hippopotamus lay still. So much hippopotamus blood spattered across Arturo's uniform that it looked like he had added an abstract layer of red to his yellow-and-purple costume. Through broken and splintered teeth, The Hippo Horseman chuckled a diabolical chuckle.

Arturo punched him again. "What's so funny, Chuckles?" demanded the boy.

The hippo muttered, "Thou wast so distracted by me, thou didst not ever notice my trap until thou wast ensnared. In thy next life, try to remember this lesson."

Arturo's arachnid intuition suddenly began buzzing. It felt like a wasp had taken up residence in the base of his skull and was attempting to sting him into oblivion.

Over the next few seconds, Arturo learned five things: First, that he had been so consumed by knocking the hippopotamus unconscious that he neglected to notice the behemoth charging his energy for a final blast—this last one originating not as a concentrated beam aimed in one direction from his sword or lance, but as an explosion emanating from across the wide berth of the hippo's plate armor. Second, that being at the epicenter an explosion is more painful more than anything else he had thus far experienced in his brief superheroing career. Third, that explosions ruin costumes, the destruction of which is an often-unforeseen expense to a superhero for which he/she neglects to account when entering the profession. And because Arturo was a pre-teen too young to have a job, he had to rely on an allowance from his poor Aunt April and Uncle Jasper—meaning he would likely have to patrol the streets in a shredded costume for a few months while scrimping and saving. Fourth, that though General Vehemence leads *L.A.N.C.E.*, the most powerful spy agency on the planet, he has terrible timing, as evidenced when the man began screaming a warning of "Get out of there!" seconds too late, just after the hippo detonated the energy blast. Fifth, Arturo learned that he still has a lot to learn about battle tactics, as the hippo had never in any previous encounter remained so immobile and allowed himself to be so easily beaten to a pulp. If Arturo would have thought the situation through, he would have suspected a trap and would not have been *so* surprised when he found himself being hurtled upward into the air toward three of the other most powerful members of his rogues' gallery: The Dive Bomber, Professor Squid, and High Toxicity.

The Dive Bomber, a living cruise missile full of mystic powers that allowed it to explode and then reconstitute itself, crashed into Arturo's chest—nearly impaling him—and drove him into the ground. The Dive Bomber exploded at point-blank range. Arturo screamed in agony. He barely managed to remain conscious.

As the smoke began to clear, Arturo slowly climbed onto his feet, only to find his arachnid intuition too overwhelmed to warn him of a barrage of Professor Squid's mechanical tentacles snaking toward him. The devices beat him even more senseless, and then they snatched him by the arms and legs, holding him immobile in the air so that he could not escape the impending attack from the next member of his rogues' gallery. High Toxicity, an alien humanoid with poisonous breath and the ability to create famine from his fingertips, emerged from the smoke with hands raised in Arturo's direction and mouth wide open, green gas emanating steadily from it.

"I see what you mean about coming in hot," muttered Arturo to General Vehemence's hologram. "Maybe a little help here?"

"These fools are not what I was talking about," replied General Vehemence. "I repeat: Get out of there!"

Arturo could not quite believe his eyes, but without warning, a pink, bloblike kaiju rose high into the air, as tall as the nearby building to which Arturo had but minutes ago clung in his fight with The Hippo Horseman. Tentacles the size of brownstones whipped out from the blob and crashed down upon both High Toxicity and Professor Squid. Blood and splinters of bone spattered across Arturo's face, and he screamed in terror the carnage.

General Vehemence's flying submarine swooped down from the clouds and opened fire on the gigantic pink blob. More tentacles emerged from the blob, in the center of which Arturo could see a woman that looked like an older version of the girl in his homeroom class on whom he had a crush, Ginny Longfellow. These tentacles wrapped themselves around the nearest buildings and ripped them from their foundations. Arturo watched in helpless wonder as the blob flung the buildings at General Vehemence's flying submarine. Explosions wracked the warship. It lilted to one side and began a slow crash toward the ground.

Much to Arturo's dismay, the woman within the blob then looked directly at him, noticing him just as his schoolboy crush never had. Arturo noted that one of her arms had no flesh covering it, but rather consisted only of bone. She pointed at him with this arm, and four spikes erupted from the blob. Faster than Arturo could comprehend, these spikes impaled him. He wanted to scream, but blood filled his mouth.

And just as the darkness of death descended across his eyes, bright white lights erupted on the peripheral of his vision.

CHAPTER 4

DÉJÀ VU IN BINARY

IF DRILLBOT HAD a definition for the concept of déjà vu within the ones and zeroes that passed for his internal monologue, then he would have described nearly every moment of the past decade as giving him a sense of déjà vu. This was because nearly every moment of the past decade had been spent waging war against an evil horde comprised of otherworldly twins of his former master and his former master's mate, and every moment felt like a repeat of the last.

But he was not really bothered by the repetition, because he knew only one other short period of existence prior to this war, and during that brief time, he had teetered on the brink of self-inflicted oblivion when he found his life without purpose. At least in this endless, repetitive war, he felt as though he had purpose.

Drillbot smiled contentedly to himself, though nobody living outside of his mind was likely to perceive it, for Drillbot had no mouth per se. Instead, he had a speaker overlaid in protective steel mesh that covered the lower half of his face. When he smiled his version of smiling, this speaker vibrated on a nearly microscopic level, his red, telescopic eyes retracted about an inch inside his head, and the three radar dishes on the top left side of his head spun slowly counterclockwise rather than clockwise.

Drillbot had no neck, but rather a squat, cylindrical torso extending for five feet below his round, oblong head. Large dials covered the front of his torso. Instead of hips and legs, three mammoth wheels stretched from below his cylindrical torso, and foot-long daggers extended from the spokes of these wheels. Gigantic pipes formed his arms, and these pipes ended in enormous, diamond-tipped drills. These long arms were so wide and so thick that they resembled shiny gorilla arms, if only gorilla arms ended in gargantuan drilling systems instead of forearms and hands.

Drillbot tumbled through the space between realities, and as he did so, he twisted as deftly as a twelve-foot tall robot could twist to ensure the foot-long daggers extending from his spokes did not slice through the Arts and Ginnys who tumbled all around him. The tumbling seemed to create a sensation in his fleshy comrades that agitated them. Drillbot, however, basked in these moments of respite between the continuous incursions into universe after universe.

Metaphors darted through the robot's mind, a cascade of ones and zeroes forming poetry and higher thought where one would expect naught but efficiency and calculation. Years ago, the travelling-bard-version of Art from Earth 707,112 had taught Drillbot the skill. The bard had used his magical flute to conjure his reality's version of Ginny, a sentient raincloud attached by a magical tether to the end of the flute. Ginny contorted her molecules into imagery, and over the span of a few months during these brief tumbles between battles, the pair had taught Drillbot the finer art of the metaphor, awakening in him a sense of poetry and wonder for which he would be forever thankful.

Unfortunately, this thankfulness would not cause him to shirk his duty to rend this Art and Ginny limb from limb upon their next meeting. They had been killed during the battle with the Pink One's forces on Earth 43,188—an Earth on which consumption of mushrooms transforms fleshy beings into giants and consumption of flowers gives fleshy beings the ability to launch flames from their fingertips—and afterward had been revived as evil, mindless pink puppets by the pink bear's cosmic magic. Following the aforementioned rending, if Drillbot could escape with their corpses, he would have the Blue One revive them to retake their places by his side within the *Army of Life*—the name that Drillbot called the cosmic blue bear's army—and they could continue teaching him the finer points of metaphor and poetry.

As Drillbot tumbled amongst the surrounding Arts and Ginnys through the simultaneously colorless and colorful expanse between realities, he felt like a raindrop within a storm, falling to a beautiful, noiseless music. As he thought about music, his smile turned into a grin—his speaker vibrated faster, his telescopic eyes retracted another inch, and his radar dishes spun faster in a counterclockwise direction.

He mimed straightening the dials that stretched down the front of his torso as though they were buttons on a tuxedo shirt. He then made a sound as though clearing his throat. He raised his arms and began waving his massive, diamond-tipped drills up and down and side to side, pantomiming the moves of the symphony-conductor-version of Ginny from Earth 92,444. As he pretended to conduct the chaotic, tumultuous tumble of the army around him, he lost himself in his opus. The Arts and Ginnys nearby looked at him in confusion, but Drillbot ignored them and continued conducting, himself the conductor and them metaphorical notes within a cosmic symphony to which only he seemed privy.

Drillbot and the Blue One had recruited this tumbling, ragtag horde of thousands of versions of Arts and Ginnys by either resurrecting them after the Pink One destroyed their realities, killing them while they were zombified puppets of the Pink One and reviving them afterward, or—on the occasions when Drillbot and the blue bear entered a reality *prior* to the pink hordes— convincing them to join by warning them of the imminent invasion of their realities by the destructive pink army.

Drillbot noticed cosmic white bubbles appear in the infinite abyss below the tumbling Army of Life. He conducted a few more staccato notes and then mimed cutting off the symphony at the end of the show, for he knew that the bubbles were the sign that this beautiful, cosmic symphony was about to be superseded by the mundane, bloody work of war.

Drillbot bent his cylindrical torso forward in a mock bow. Then he rolled to face the impending white bubbles. He switched on his drills, readying himself to immediately jump into battle just in case one was already underway on the reality that the Army of Life was about to enter. The robotic sound of his whirring drills stood in stark contrast to the splendor of the symphony that had been playing in his head mere moments ago.

*

Drillbot and company fell from the cosmic bubbles and landed amidst a battle that was already underway. Death and destruction already lay sprawled across the city that surrounded them. A pale Art wearing a black cape and brandishing fangs the size of a small cat leapt at Drillbot as soon as the robot's wheels touched down upon the hard concrete.

Drillbot shredded this Art in twain, as he had done probably three-dozen times before now, and then he stabbed it through its only weak spot: the heart. The pinkness that enshrouded this Art's eyes faded, leaving only a lifeless corpse. Drillbot rolled south past the corpse, knowing without needing to look that the Revival Corps within the Army of Life would be quick at work behind him, ferrying the corpse to the cosmic blue bear to be revived and to rejoin the ranks of the Army of Life, only to likely be killed once more very soon by the Pink One's army, only to then be reanimated as a puppet in that same pink army, only to then be killed once more in battle by Drillbot or a random Art or Ginny in the Army of Life, only to then be revived by the cosmic blue bear to rejoin the Blue One's ranks. Only to go on like that ad infinitum. Drillbot shrugged.

Drillbot's engines roared full steam ahead. His tires squealed as he dodged an energy spear hurled from the arm of a random Ginny corpse-puppet. He raced toward the carnage at the end of the street, where a gigantic pink blob loomed nearly thirty-stories tall, and behind which a colossal flying submarine crashed to the ground and knocked over dozens of buildings.

On his back not half a block down the street was the current object of the blob's attention, a young male in a yellow bodysuit streaked with purple stripes, pinned to the ground by four gigantic pink spikes like he was some highly unfashionable insect in a giant entomologist's collection. Drillbot did not need the sensors within his system to blare the boy's identity to him—because the attention from the pink blob was clue enough—but that did not stop the system from sounding alarms within him anyway. Drillbot could see the boy had mere seconds to live, and thus Drillbot knew there were mere moments left to join the battle over the body before the boy became the property of the Pink One.

As the boy gasped his last breath, Drillbot zoomed between the boy's body and the pink blob, which was controlled by the Ginny that was his former master's mate.

Drillbot watched with upraised drills as this Ginny extended from the blob a tentacle that had no tip. Drillbot knew this move well, for she was never careful to conceal her movements, always relying instead on brute force and numbers to give her an advantage.

This tentacle would be the one she would use to spray the pink mist that would turn the boy into a puppet. Any second now, her reserve forces would begin leaping at Drillbot's flanks from perches amongst the surrounding buildings, hoping to distract him long enough for her to claim this new victim. Drillbot could only hope that a detachment of his own forces was close enough behind him to intercept her reserves and keep them occupied, for he could not take his eyes from the tentacle if he were to have any hope of winning this skirmish. The sound of a battle cry from the barbarian-version of Art from Earth 6,092 indicated to Drillbot that Robot Fortune had been kind to him today, that his backup had moved into position to protect his flanks. Drillbot smiled his version of a smile.

The tentacle feinted right while a second tentacle—its tip the size and shape of a bulldozer—smashed down at Drillbot. He dodged it easily. A third tentacle swiped in from the left, and he ripped it apart with his drills. The mist-tentacle zoomed up into the air, changed direction, and then darted down at the boy. Drillbot launched himself into the air and parried this tentacle with his right drill. Then he fell to the ground.

He frowned—a gesture that consisted of his mouth-speaker retracting slightly, his telescopic eyes vibrating, and his radar dishes wobbling to-and-fro—when his left tire landed on something simultaneously crunchy and meaty. The Ginny within the blob shrieked with laughter.

Drillbot had no time yet to glance down and investigate the spot on which he had landed, for his attention was instead focused on parrying the attacks of a few more tentacles. A few moments later, Ginny leaned forward to press her attack with her tentacles, and he took advantage of an opening in her defenses—an opening that would sufficiently distract her. He initialized his attack by calling out, "[whir] Initiate starboard arm sequence – CLACK – arm sequence number zero-one-one."

He then felt an explosion just below the drill of his right arm. He aimed the point of the drill toward the center of the pink blob, and the drill on that appendage launched from the arm, a rocket of drilling carnage.

The drill plowed through the pink membrane of the blob. Drillbot smiled his version of a smile as he dodged another tentacle. His drills seemed to be one of the few things in the Multiverse capable of piercing the cursed pink blob's membrane[4]. The drill-rocket careened through the pink blob toward

---

4 Drillbot assumed this ability to penetrate the pink blob's membrane was due to his close association with the cosmic Blue One. While this was not a bad assumption—for the cosmic blue bear had provided many upgrades over the last decade to the robot's systems and his ability to wreak havoc on an enemy—this particular capability was due to the nature of his creation at the hands of Normal-Art and the Creationvil, which had scanned the Multiverse for the ideal input material to create Drillbot as the perfect digging instrument. Drillbot's drill tips could thus penetrate anything in the Multiverse, because these tips were fashioned from the skulls of a tiny species of diamond-people whose skulls were the hardest substance in the Multiverse.

Regular-Ginny, and when at last it came near enough that she was too distracted by dodging it to continue pressing her attack on him, Drillbot swiped away the pink spikes pinning the boy to the ground. Then he reached down to pick up the corpse of this reality's Art.

"[whir] Da – CLACK – Da – CLACK – Damn," he exclaimed. He must have landed on the boy's head during his fall, for the boy's cranium had been crushed and his brains were scattered across the pavement. Drillbot remembered an old proverb he had crafted years ago: every day in life is either a one or a zero, and you just hope that by the end of it, your code is full of more ones than zeroes. Today looked like a pretty massive zero in this Art's ledger.

In a rush, Drillbot scooped as much of the brains into the skull as he could scoop, hefted the boy into the crook of his left arm, and raced back the way he had come, knowing that any second now, his drill would finish passing through Ginny's blob and she would be returning her attention to him and this Art.

Drillbot's wheel-daggers tore through many of the pink army's puppets when they attempted harassment on his retreat, and soon, he found himself back at the cosmic bubbles from whence the Army of Life had emerged. He unceremoniously tossed the boy's body into the nearest one, saving him from the Pink One's puppetry and sending him into the abyss between realities to be reanimated by the blue bear—and thus to join the Army of Life in this endless war.

Drillbot turned back toward the battle. Regular-Ginny rampaged toward him, knocking over buildings in her fury. All around her, the Army of Life murdered zombified Arts and Ginnys, while the pink army dealt equal death in return. Drillbot's drill-rocket followed its homing beacon and landed in place back at the end of his right arm.

The blob slapped a giant tentacle down at him. He backflipped through the air, dodging it. He noticed the thirty-foot tall cyclopean Art of Earth 29 crush a nearby Ginny-puppet with his club—a club which was fashioned from a magical tree trunk—and then toss the mangled corpse into a cosmic white bubble for later resurrection. Drillbot called to this cyclopean Art, "[whir] Artclops, Drillbot – CLACK – Drillbot – CLACK – Drillbot requires assistance!"

As he had been trained when given this command, Artclops smacked Drillbot with his tree trunk as though swinging a golf club—a move taught to the duo by the professional-golfer-version of Ginny from Earth 8,745,111,021, who had spent her time prior to recruitment into the Army of Life travelling from city to city on her home Earth, solving mysteries with her set of golf clubs that were haunted by her wacky uncles, two of whom had been clowns prior to death, one of whom had been a racist ice-cream truck driver, one of whom had been an overly sensitive southern gentleman, and two of whom had been amateur opera singers. This maneuver knocked Drillbot high into the air. He landed drills-first with a sploosh against the membrane of the pink blob.

And with much fierceness, but also with the earlier sense of déjà vu for which he had no robotic definition, he began stabbing at the pink monstrosity.

CHAPTER 5

STOP HITTING YOURSELF

REGULAR-GINNY SQUEALED IN frustration. The infuriating robot with drills for arms had made another appearance in her life, and to top it off, she had lost her potential Art-puppet to it.

As the robot landed upon the pink membrane of her blob, she felt a strong sense of déjà vu, mainly because nearly this exact scenario had played out many times before with many different Arts and Ginnys. Sometimes she won, and the robot retreated. Sometimes the robot won, and she forced a hasty retreat. She heaved a sigh.

And just like every other time in the past when she began to feel trapped and exhausted by the dreadful claustrophobia caused by infinite repetition, just when she began to slow her attacks and pull her punches because everything felt pointless, a fresh wave of pink swirled through her veins and flooded her heart with hatred and wrath. The pink drowned the weary déjà vu beneath a murderous deluge. And then she hated the stupid robot more than ever.

She whipped at the robot with a wide, flat tentacle, but it backflipped out of reach and landed back in place atop her blob nary the worse for wear. She then created a few dozen tiny phalanges and twisted them through the spokes of the robot's wheels, locking it in place. She wrapped a couple tentacles around the base of a nearby building and ripped it from its foundation. She raised the building high into the air, and then she slammed it down on top of herself where the robot was being held in place.

Screams and blood and dust and chaos erupted from the building as it was dashed to pieces against the unmoving pink blob. Pink tendrils tickled Regular-Ginny's heart, and she squealed with hateful joy. When the dust cleared, and the screams dissipated from the people who mere moments ago had lived within the brownstone, Regular-Ginny discovered that the robot remained in place and intact, its drills raised above its head and spinning their damned spinniest.

"[whir] Stop – CLACK – Stop – CLACK – Stop hitting yourself!" chided the robot, now slicing its tires free of Regular-Ginny's pink phalanges.

Regular-Ginny cursed. She leapt, and the blob mimicked her, jumping high into the air. She twisted so that the robot was directly between the blob and the ground. She intended to crush it beneath the blob's weight. Instead, as she crashed onto the ground and left a crater below her, she realized that the robot had removed itself from harm's way by tunneling through the blob directly toward her. She cursed again.

When the robot neared her, she created a current within the pink to push her perpendicularly down from her current position. Within fractions of a second, she was near the ground on the opposite side of the blob from the robot.

"[whir] Sigh – CLACK – Sigh," muttered the robot, its voice reverberating through the pink blob. "Different Earth, same – CLACK – same game. Drillbot will play again if – CLACK – if Ginny insists."

The robot changed direction and torpedoed toward Ginny, its murderous drills pointed directly at her and closing fast. She held her arms in front of her and began twisting them in small circles. The machine sighed once more.

Ginny did not wait for another snide comment from the machine. Instead, she willed the pink blob in front of her to spin round and round in mimic of her twirling arms. Within the pinkness, two grand tornadoes formed and then exploded out toward the robot. As they connected with the robot, it was flung backward end over end and away from her. She compelled the tornadoes to extend high into the sky. The robot bounced back and forth between the twin tornadoes, buffeting between each swirling pink storm in dizzying frenzy.

Seconds later, when the robot had been spun round and round all the way to the top of the pink tornadoes where they now danced amongst the clouds, Ginny called out, "Special Reserves, to me! Form a circle twenty-yards in diameter!"

At her behest, Arthur the Putrid glided into view from the northwest, holding the ends of his robe out to his sides and flapping his arms so that the robe acted like birds' wings, allowing him to fly him through the air. Pausing momentarily between Ginny and the sun, this hated Art made the most ridiculous silhouette she had ever seen. Nearly four-dozen puppets who had the ability to fly followed him, and this unit swooped down to land gently upon the cracked cement near Regular-Ginny. They formed into a wide circle.

As in every battle, Arthur the Putrid led the Special Reserve forces, a marauding group of forty-four Arts and Ginnys who could all fly and thus could quickly reach areas of the battlefield that needed reinforcements. His crew included a few standouts whose kill counts were near the top of the entire Pink Marauder army: the Art with a ring that created solid images of purple light, which he shaped into anything he could imagine (and apparently the pink mist that clouded his mind caused him to imagine horrifying tools of death, including his current tool of choice: the B-52 bomber he was piloting that shot vampire-kittens instead of bullets from its gun turrets), the Ginny whose weapon of choice was a longbow that fired flaming arrows and around whose feet were strapped two magical flying bunnies, the thunder god Art whose hammer allowed him to fly at will and whose tiny horns poked out cutely from the red mullet that stretched down his back, the Ginny in a suit of steel plate armor whose lower half transformed into a fiery jet engine that launched her in a straight line until she crashed into something, at which point she returned to normal and could launch once more, the Art carried aloft by a magical colony of seagulls that rained down flaming excrement at his command, and the Ginny who carried an enchanted samurai sword, which she used to spin herself in circles so fast that she transformed into a flying tornado of bladed death.

Arthur the Putrid had begun calling the group *The Death Cavalry*, but Ginny thought that name was rather boring and uncreative. During one of their many tumbles between realities on the way to yet another Earth that they inevitably conquered, Ginny had suggested to him the moniker *The Forty-Four Horsemen of the Pinkpocalypse*, since the group's number was consistently held to forty-four via replacements of any members that were lost—a number that Arthur the Putrid claimed had magical significance on his Earth—and brought apocalypse to whatever planet on which they were unleashed. She could tell by the twinkling in his eye that he wished he had thought of the name, but he instead dismissed the idea outright and pretended to hate it.

A pink tickle in her brain brought Regular-Ginny's attention back to the battle. She lifted her right arm and then slammed it down. The tornadoes she had created raised slightly higher into the clouds, and then the tops of them slammed down onto the ground in the middle of Arthur the Putrid's contingent of reserves. The robot lay in a newly formed crater.

"[whir] Ouch," said the robot, rising from its prone position back onto its wheels. Other than superficial dents, scrapes, and the occasional loose cog or gear, the robot seemed not that much the worse for wear. Even more frustrating to Regular-Ginny, it seemed unconcerned with the deadly opponents that now encircled it. Its drills roared furiously.

"Attack!" screamed Regular-Ginny to her forces.

Instead, Arthur the Putrid made no move. Nor did the puppets around him. Regular-Ginny stared at him with her mouth agape. Though she had willed these forty-four pink puppets to follow Arthur the Putrid and to assist him as he commanded, they were ultimately *her* minions and had never before disobeyed her direct orders, even when her orders contradicted his.

"I said to attack!" screamed Ginny once more.

The puppets began to twitch and moved forward a few inches. Arthur the Putrid again made no move to attack. Instead, he raised his hands. On each hand, he had twisted his thumb down to touch his wrist and had seemingly dislocated the joints of his middle fingers to wrap thrice around his ring fingers. He waved the hands in a counterclockwise motion. The eyes of the puppets momentarily flashed green, and they stopped moving forward.

"In my life before entering the Pink One's service, I encountered the type of magic at play in this robot," said Arthur the Putrid. "Give me a few moments, and the machine shall fall under my spell. Just think how owning a powerful tool such as *that* will turn the tides of this war in our favor. We can achieve victory in no time, and we can spread our scourge unchecked across the Multiverse!"

"How *dare* you, you arrogant fool!" screamed Ginny so loudly that she thought she might go deaf as the sound reverberated through her blob. "You think I'm too stupid to realize what you're trying to do here? You think because you use words like *'our'* and *'we,'* I won't see through this petty ploy?

She continued, "If you thought I wouldn't recognize this attempt to undermine me before the Pink One and eventually use this robot to murder me, then you are a greater fool than you look! Now release my puppets! They are *mine* to control, and you are *mine* to command! You do *not* have permission to override my orders to them, and you do *not* have permission to give me advice!"

Rage at Arthur the Putrid's hubris overwhelmed her, and the pink in her veins amplified this rage into a hurricane of wrath that flooded her brain. She realized with sudden clarity that she would need to teach Arthur the Putrid a lesson at once, or he would never respect her, and thus he would continue to insert his stratagems when they were not requested and would continue to use his magic to wrest control of *her* puppets without permission. She decided that her lesson should be swift and deadly and utterly final. She raised a wide, flat tentacle to squash him like a putrid bug.

However, the robot did not wait for Ginny to act. Instead, it leapt at Arthur the Putrid. In response, Arthur the Putrid twisted his hands into a new gesture, creating an energy shield between himself and the robot. Regular-Ginny gestured with her own hand, and her pink tentacle plummeted toward them both.

But then, before any of the trio could connect with any attack, bright white lightning flashed in the sky, and even more hell broke loose.

CHAPTER 6

THE BEGINNING OF THE ENDLESS

NORMAL-ART WATCHED IN silence as Officer-Art stood from the captain's chair and walked to Officer-Ginny's navigation station on the starboard side of the bridge. Officer-Art stood over her shoulder and watched her work. Her fingers danced across the keyboard. The station flashed with dozens of green and red lights, which Normal-Art understood not at all.

"The Binnacle indicates that we need to veer port once we pass reality 2,309," said Officer-Ginny, not looking up from her station. Her eagle sat perched on her shoulder and leaned over her station, studying the console in unison with her and cooing into her ear.

"Very well," replied Officer-Art. "Relay the instructions to the fleet."

Officer-Art stared out the front view screen. He clicked the heels of his boots together, a frequent habit with which Normal-Art had grown increasingly annoyed during his ten years as captive of the Bureau of Interdimensional Travel officer. The gesture seemed to be a nervous tick, almost a fascist version of a nervous eye twitch. Normal-Art considered sighing, but he caught himself before letting loose his foul breath. Multiple scars and mangled minor appendages had taught him to refrain from making any sort of noise while on the bridge, especially just before a battle.

Through the view screen on the bridge of the *Bureau Shift-Ship Carrier Mimessiah*—or the B.S.S.C. Mimessiah for short—Normal-Art stared at the now-familiar sight of the realm between realities, an expanse that was both infinitely colorful and bleakly colorless. From what Normal-Art had overheard during his long incarceration on this ship, the massive aircraft-carrier-sized vessel had been named in honor of the savior-mime from Earth 262,144, who had pretended to sacrifice his body to save his Earth's inhabitants, all of whom had simultaneously pretended to be trapped inside an invisible box. Normal-

Art frowned, because he did not care about any of the above information concerning the ship's name, but it unfortunately clogged up space in his brain. He frowned harder and tried to concentrate on something else.

Normal-Art watched holographic circles and numbers appear on the view screen and expand to label the realities past which the ship and its accompanying fleet zoomed. Normal-Art saw a 56,708 drift past the starboard side of the ship, then a 95,555, and then on the port side of the ship, he saw a 2,309 appear.

Once the ship passed the reality labeled 2,309, Normal-Art heard the now-familiar sound of the Reality Rudder twisting and grinding through the expanse between realities as it shifted positions to steer the ship in a new direction. Normal-Art could best describe the noise as what he would expect a litter of newborn banshees to sound like. Normal-Art wished he could cover his ears, but his hands had been encased in heavy plaster, and he had little motor control over the clumsy things. Officer-Art had ordered the plaster bindings placed on him after he had attempted to put himself out of his misery sometime during his eighth year of captivity.

Normal-Art's shoulders slumped. In the decade since the mischief-god-version of himself had conned him into abandoning his couch for an adventure, he had experienced enough tragedy to last a thousand lifetimes. But this stretch in B.I.T. captivity was by far the worst period of his entire life— and this was coming from a guy who had both worked at the Department of Motor Vehicles and swam for nearly an eternity inside a Reality Lantern[5].

Before he could stifle it, a cough escaped Normal-Art's throat, a nagging symptom that had plagued him for a few years now. Officer-Art twisted to face him. The officer glared. Normal-Art dropped his eyes to the floor and stared at the ground in silence, hoping against hope that the bastard would be too preoccupied by the task before him to divert any time for torture.

To Normal-Art's delight, Officer-Art turned back toward the view screen. Normal-Art nearly squealed with joy, but he caught himself before the sound escaped his lips. There was a zero-percent likelihood of such torture-avoiding luck twice in a row.

---

[5] This Reality Lantern was the Reality Light on Earth 1,000,000. After Normal-Art freed the Blue One and the Pink One from the device, Earth 1,000,000 ceased existing. See *The Multiverse Askew* Book 1 for details.

Officer-Art walked a few steps forward so that the view screen at the front of the bridge completely comprised his field of vision. He clicked his heels together and clasped his hands behind his back. His eagle sat perched on his shoulder. The man would have looked positively regal if the bird had not chosen this exact time to defecate on his shoulder. And Normal-Art probably would have found the eagle's gesture quite hilarious if it were in fact novel, but the whitish-brownish glob merely joined a dry and crusty trail that already existed on the back of the man's uniform.

Officer-Art cleared his throat. "Agent 29333, connect video comms with the men."

Officer-Ginny cleared her throat back at him. Officer-Art sighed. "And the women, too," he said.

A uniformed officer at a different station cleared its throat. This officer had a beautiful elven face with a black half-goatee that only covered its left cheek. This throat clearing was followed by yet another uniformed officer at a different station clearing yet another throat. This officer had an elven face equally as beautiful as the last, except it had a white vein that stretched across its right cheek that looked like a white half-goatee.

Officer-Art sighed yet again. He said, "And the ambigendered species, and the non-gendered species, too."

"Aye, aye, sir," replied Officer-Ginny.

The infinite expanse of *The Barrier*—the B.I.T.'s official name for the realm between realities—disappeared from the view screen, replaced by an abstract painting. Normal-Art squinted, and upon closer inspection, realized it was not a painting at all, but instead millions of pixels, each featuring a tiny video image of a different agent in the B.I.T. Some agents were dressed in officer's uniforms similar to Officer-Art's, while others wore pilot uniforms or camouflaged marine gear. In unison, every pixelated little face said, "Sir?"

Officer-Art exclaimed, "Men, women, ambigendered species, and non-gendered species, in exactly four minutes, we shall exit *The Barrier* and make earthfall in dimension 616,000. Many of you have already faced the threat that looms before us today. All of us have lost comrades to this war. But today, we finally have the chance to gain the upper hand and turn the tide, to mark the beginning of the end of this endless cosmic war between Life and Death. You have all been briefed on our strategy and on the upgrades to our weapons. Use these weapons with utter abandon. Refrain from killing innocents where you *can*, but rip this reality to shreds if you *must* if that is what it takes to win this war!"

Officer-Art raised a fist and shook it emphatically. Officer-Ginny cleared her throat again, but Officer-Art ignored her. He continued, "So, cry whatever word translates to havoc in your native tongue, and let loose the dogs of war, or whatever equivalent idiom resonates with you! Who is with me?"

None of the tiny faces on the view screen responded other than to either appear confused or to gesture toward its ears. Officer-Art gestured even more emphatically with his raised fist. "I said, who is with me?" he cried, louder this time.

Again, he was met with none of the expected cheering from the faces on the view screen, so he turned and glared at Officer-Ginny. "Why are the troops not cheering, Agent 29333?" he demanded. "You know that the cheering is my favorite part."

Officer-Ginny scowled. She replied, "Because your microphone is not on, sir. These video calls default to starting on mute in case we are discussing classified information that the other party does not have proper access to hear when the connection goes live. That's why I keep suggesting that you stay in your captain's chair until the video connection is active so that you can disengage the muting functionality, since that is part of your duty as captain of this ship."

Officer-Art returned her scowl. He opened his mouth and began to reply, but instead he stomped back over to the captain's chair, slammed his palm onto a blinking red button, and spun on his heel to face the view screen once more.

He repeated his speech nearly word for word, replacing the aforementioned four-minute window until the attack with a decidedly shorter one. This time, cheers erupted when he finished his speech. Officer-Art listened to them for a moment, and then he pressed a button on his captain's chair to close the video connection with the troops. The infinite expanse of the barrier between realities once more filled the view screen at the front of the bridge.

As the cheers disappeared into silence, Officer-Art's eagle flapped its wings and took to the air. Officer-Ginny's followed, along with an eagle belonging to each of the other officers on the bridge—the two who had cleared their throats earlier and four others, including a young wide-eyed teenager, a dark-skinned woman, a red-haired humanoid with alien ridges across its brow, and a pale cyborg. The eight eagles surrounded a pole that dangled down from the ceiling of the bridge.

Lightning burst forth from the antennae of Officer-Art's eagle, and the crackling bolt leapt to the antennae of Officer-Ginny's eagle, where it mixed together with lightning from this creature to form an even larger bolt that leapt across to the antennae of the next eagle. In this fashion, the bolt of lightning passed from eagle to eagle and grew exponentially in size, finally erupting from the last eagle to crash into the pole that hung from the ceiling.

As the lightning jumped from eagle to eagle, the thunderous noise that accompanied it grew so booming and overbearing that it made Normal-Art feel like his ears might bleed, and like so many times since leaving his home so long ago, he wished it would stop and he could just relax.

The lightning disappeared into the metal and reappeared out in front of the ship, forming a white cyclone of lightning. Normal-Art could see similar cyclones emanating from the other ships in the B.I.T. fleet out there in the colorful-colorless expanse between realities.

The B.S.S.C. Mimessiah steered toward the lightning-cyclone. Within moments, it filled the entire view screen in front of the ship, and all Normal-Art could see was blinding white light.

*

The B.S.S.C. Mimessiah and its accompanying fleet appeared high in the sky above Earth 616,000. Normal-Art stared out the view screen, watching as a sprawling city replaced the blinding white light. The city lay in a gridded expanse that seemed nearly identical to the New York City from his home reality, except many of these skyscrapers and buildings were topped with outrageous symbols or trademarked logos like "Vengeance Corps" or "Y-Peoples" or "Fairness League" or "Captain USA's Justice Brigade."

Chaos had overwhelmed the city, and swaths of fiery destruction were spreading across it. Amidst the chaos, Normal-Art spotted the woman who had been dragged along with him into this endless Multiversal ordeal. The woman was Ginny, his girlfriend—though they had not spoken in a decade, so he was unsure if she still counted as his girlfriend. But they also had not *officially* broken up, so that meant they *might* still be in a relationship. He shrugged, for he did not really care one way or the other.

Ginny was encased within her kaiju-sized pink blob—her weapon of choice these past ten years—and was gesticulating with such erratic movements that even from this height, Normal-Art could tell that she was furious. Her attention was focused on the skirmish in which she was currently engaged, but as the B.I.T. fleet appeared in the sky upon its storm of lightning, that quickly changed.

Dozens of tendrils erupted from her pink blob and pointed hateful phalanges toward the B.I.T. fleet. Hundreds of humanoids with pink eyes ceased their battles with the Blue One's army. They leapt from the ground and took to the sky in flight, aiming for the fleet.

On the ground near the pink blob, Normal-Art spotted a robot that seemed little more than a mechanical insect from this distance. It began gesturing wildly toward the B.I.T. fleet. Hundreds more humanoids ceased their battling to leap from the ground and take to the sky in flight, these also aiming for the fleet.

Normal-Art stifled a sigh, knowing that the robot down there would be none other than his old companion, Drillbot. As Normal-Art stared at the robot, he wished more than ever that he could go back in time and make a different choice when the cosmic blue bear had asked him to begin a new adventure to return the bears to their confinement on their home Earth. Or better yet, if he could do it all again, he would simply join the blue bear's side in its war against the pink bear, for then he would get to simply tag along and not try too hard at anything. The intervening years would likely have been just as tedious, but at least there would have been less torture.

A few blocks south, a large expanse of pale white bubbles filled the spaces between buildings. Based on past encounters between the B.I.T. and the Blue One's army, Normal-Art knew that the blue bear would be there somewhere amongst the white bubbles, keeping them open to provide a means of escape and resurrection for his army.

Normal-Art glanced north and found the pink bear. It was the size of a parade balloon, and it was expanding its jaws the width of at least two city blocks. It bit into the Earth. Then it sat back and chewed carefully. And then it repeated the motions. The image would have been downright cute if not for the massive slaughter that accompanied it.

The fifteen carrier-class vessels in the fleet under Officer-Art's command finished jumping into view. Their engines blasted to life and they spread out into a circular formation, forming a floating, deadly ring around the city. Normal-Art watched as the bottom of each carrier opened and thousands of ships poured out. Though these ships looked to Normal-Art like fighter jets from his reality, he knew they were far more technologically advanced than anything invented on Earth 6,076.

Officer-Art stared at the humanoids flying toward his fleet from the ground below and strummed his fingers across his chin. Normal-Art knew from past experience that these approaching attackers were a mix of other versions of himself and of Ginny, some living members of the Blue One's army and others undead pink puppets from the Pink One's army. A dreadful knot filled the pit of Normal-Art's stomach, knowing that in a way, he was about to watch himself get knocked out of existence hundreds—if not thousands—of times. He wondered for a moment whether Officer-Art felt the same odd twinge of concern, but when the B.I.T. officer glanced over at him and Normal-Art saw the hateful scowl that had spread across the man's face, the thought fled from his mind.

Officer-Art sat in his captain's chair and pressed a button. He ordered, "Squadrons One and Seven, commence run zero-mark-three. Squadrons Omega and Nu, commence run eight-bravo-eight. Squadrons Comma, Semi-Colon, Poundsign, and Asterisk, remain near the carriers and commence shield action tilde-six. Remaining ships, enter dogfight mode and fire at will. All units switch weapons to *Scatter Gun Mode*."

Normal-Art frowned at the mention of *Scatter Gun Mode*. He had been present when the B.I.T.'s Chief Technology Officer had boarded the B.S.S.C. Mimessiah to deploy to Officer-Art's fleet the weapons upgrade that provided *Scatter Gun Mode*, an upgrade which had been invented by the B.I.T. High Commander himself. The upgrades were small laser guns that tapped upon the energy reserves of a young reality that had just recently gone through its Big Bang. The way the guns' barrels were rifled manipulated the energy so that the barrel became a conduit for jumping between realities, much like the antennae on Jump Totems. The biggest difference here was that there was no totem to guide the jumps, and instead, victims' atoms were scattered hither-and-yon across every reality in existence, effectively killing the victims and diffusing their particles so finely that they would be impossible to resurrect by either the pink or blue bears. The Chief Technology Officer had referred to the weapons upgrade as *Scatter Gun Mode*, so Officer-Art had done the same.

When Officer-Art had inquired how many of the devastating weapons the B.I.T. was planning to supply for the fleet, the C.T.O. had chortled and then revealed that the High Commander had sold a few of the B.I.T.'s more mineral-rich realities to pay for every single crew member in the entire B.I.T. organization to receive a pistol with the functionality and every single weapon on every single ship to receive a turret with the mode. This long, cosmic war could finally be ended, ever-so-brutally.

Normal-Art knew that the war's conclusion would not come so easily, but he also knew better than to speak aloud this opinion, so he sat in silence as the C.T.O. laughed maniacally with Officers Art and Ginny.

A few dozen explosions below Normal-Art brought his mind back to the present. Normal-Art watched as the B.I.T. jets began suffering heavy losses. But these losses were accompanied by flashes of lightning that erupted from the fighter planes' new Scatter Guns, signaling equal losses to the pink and blue armies with which they had begun skirmishing.

Officer-Art ignored the explosions and flashes of lightning. He ordered, "Give me visuals from Squadrons One and Omega."

The left quarter of the screen morphed to show the viewpoint of the commander of Squadron One, while the right quarter of the screen morphed to show the equivalent from the commander of Squadron Omega.

Normal-Art felt numb as he watched the left quarter of the view screen, where Squadrons One and Seven were diving toward the white bubbles. The ships in these squadrons staggered themselves so that a single ship dove between each floating white bubble, followed seconds later by a wingman. Hordes of monstrous versions of Arts and Ginnys leapt from the bubbles—members of blue army's reserves, of which the blue bear always seemed to keep a plethora at the ready to reinforce his army as needed—and landed on the fighter planes. A two-headed Ginny who rode upon an elk landed on the cockpit of the commander of Squadron One. The glass cracked. The elk reared back and smashed its front hooves through the glass. The video feed from the commander disappeared, only to be replaced with a different feed from the next most senior pilot in the squadron. From this view, Normal-Art watched the former commander's ship lilt to the side and crash into a building. The ship exploded, taking the two-headed Ginny and her elk with it into a fiery grave.

Less than a second later, a version of Art with no legs but carrying two giant war hammers landed on the cockpit of the ship belonging to this new video feed. This pilot flipped a switch in the cockpit and called out over the intercom, "This is One-Beta. Engage energy shields."

Unfortunately for the blue bear's army, the B.I.T. ships had experienced this tactic of divebombing reserves from the white bubbles before. Energy shields made of lightning covered the ships and fried the Arts and Ginnys unlucky enough to have already landed on them.

The fighter jets continued zooming between the buildings and between the bubbles, firing upon everyone they could and disintegrating into nothingness any luckless Art or Ginny caught in their line of fire. But as the seconds passed, more and more of the squadron fell to the attrition inflicted upon them by the ridiculous versions of Art and Ginny that were able to overcome the lightning-shields. The video monitor changed to new viewpoints as replacement-commander after replacement-commander died, sometimes changing so fast it became dizzying.

Finally, on probably the fourteenth or fifteenth viewpoint, the blue bear loomed in view, floating amongst a sea of its white bubbles. "On me," called this pilot. "I found the blue bear, and I've got the beast in my sights."

Before she could fire, the blue bear pointed to this pilot, and a white bubble launched from its fingertips. The bubble encompassed the cockpit, and this pilot found herself relocated to the barrier between realities and surrounded by the hordes of the blue army's reserves. They attacked, and her viewpoint disappeared, only to be replaced by the next in line.

"I've got a lock," called this pilot. He jerked his stick right to dodge a bubble that the blue bear launched toward him, and then he jerked it back just in time to fire before crashing into the bear. A crackling explosion filled the monitor, and when the video connection transferred to the next pilot's viewpoint, both the blue bear and the prior ship exploded.

Though Normal-Art knew it was impossible for him to physically hear the bear from way up here, the bear's scream filled his brain, anyway. Normal-Art screamed in response and watched in shock as thousands of pale white bubbles erupted from the bear's paws, launching forth in all directions. Then the bear and the explosion disappeared.

Normal-Art knocked his head against the metal headrest of his chair until the pain from the bear's screaming voice left him. He glanced around, and nobody seemed to have noticed his outburst, so he shrugged.

The pilot in this new viewpoint cheered, and then he ordered, "All remaining members of Squadrons One and Seven on me. Primary objective complete. Commence secondary objective."

And with that, the remaining members of these squadrons began mopping up the remainder of the blue bear's army on the ground.

Meanwhile, from the viewpoint on the right side of the view screen, the commander of Squadron Omega dodged between the flying puppets of the pink army's hordes. All around her, flashes from the jets' weapons systems disintegrated the hordes. Soon, a wayward version of Ginny with car-sized barracudas in place of her arms and legs landed on the hull of this commander's ship and ripped it apart. The eyes of this Ginny and her barracuda-appendages shone pink until the ship exploded, and then they no longer shone at all.

Much like the viewpoint for the squadron on the left side of the screen, the viewpoint for this squadron changed over and over, shifting to the viewpoint of replacement commanders as pilots lost their lives in the carnage.

In moments, a member of Squadron Omega got close enough to the pink bear to obtain a clear shot at it. The pink bear exploded in a ball of lightning. It mimicked the blue bear in launching thousands of bubbles from its paws—these black rather than white—and then it disappeared.

This time, Normal-Art felt no scream inside his head, but when he looked at the middle of the view screen and down at the bird's eye view of the battle below, he saw the gigantic pink blob flopping around like a fish out of water, and a pang of sympathy went out to his Ginny, for he knew exactly the pain she was experiencing.

Normal-Art glanced back over to the left side of the view screen. He watched in horror as the pilot in this viewpoint set his sights on Drillbot.

"No!" Normal-Art began to scream, but a white bubble flooped into view from above. It encompassed Drillbot and then disappeared.

All across the battlefield, members of each army were being swept at random into white or black bubbles that were now bouncing all throughout the city. Normal-Art watched as a black bubble crashed into his Ginny's blob, and he sighed. He had hoped for her sake that she might get to finally experience some peace through a well-placed Scatter Gun bolt.

Moments later, the battle was done, and other than the squadrons disintegrating the Art and Ginny stragglers—those who had missed their rides out of here via the randomly bouncing bubbles—an odd peace fell across the city. Buildings smoldered, and rubble tumbled, and innocent bystanders screamed for help, but this reality had been saved from both ultimate destruction and ultimate resurrection.

Officer-Art flicked a couple switches on his captain's chair and scanned the results. He raised his fist in victory, and his eagle swooped down and landed upon his forearm. "There is no tangible sign of the cosmic threats in this reality, in *The Barrier*, or on any other known reality in the Multiverse. We did it! This day shall mark the day that we won this endless war!"

The bridge erupted in cheers.

Normal-Art, however, knew of what these bears were capable—especially since he could still feel the itch of the blue bear's presence in his brain. He knew that sending their atoms tumbling across the infinite Multiverse would do naught but slow them down, and probably not even all that much, since they seemed able to access and travel across the barrier between realities at will without needing Jump Totems. But Normal-Art held his mouth shut, knowing that a happier Officer-Art meant a nicer and less-torture-prone Officer-Art.

So Normal-Art leaned back and sighed, watching the surviving fighter jets return to their carriers. The itch in his brain grew stronger, which was an annoying sensation, but it was much better than the overwhelming scream that had followed the bear's collision with the Scatter Gun blast.

CHAPTER 7

YOU SPIN ME RIGHT ROUND, ROBOT, RIGHT ROUND

DRILLBOT TUMBLED END over end. If he were a creature of flesh and blood, he may have thought the tumble seemed like it lasted forever, but the basic computational part of his system told him it had only been six days, and at the rate of four tumbles per minute, he had merely tumbled thirty-four thousand five hundred and sixty times. Scattered around him in their own eccentric tumbles were those others lucky enough to have been broadsided by a cosmic white bubble, along with whatever reserves had still been lurking in the space between realities before the Blue One had been disintegrated. These totaled around three hundred strong, a mere tenth of the number with which the Army of Life had entered the battle.

The cosmic bubbles had whisked away members of both armies at random, and the reserves had quickly dispatched any members of the pink army who had been dropped amongst them. These lifeless husks now tumbled nonchalantly beside the ragtag remainder of the Army of Life.

So many members of each army had passed back and forth between the opposing forces throughout this long war that one tumbling Ginny compared the situation to the children's card game, *War*, where each child draws a card, and the child who draws the higher card keeps both cards. As the children cycle over and over through their decks, cards pass back and forth again and again until the kids get sick of the tedious game, quit, and go play outside. The biggest difference here, the Ginny pointed out, was that the bears were not little kids who would grow bored with the tedium. They intended to play forever, and though they were gone *for now*, no mere B.I.T. weapon would keep them away forever. Drillbot soon discovered how right she was.

After another six days and another thirty-four thousand five hundred and sixty tumbles, Drillbot's telescopic eyes and robotic senses noticed microscopic blue pixels appearing near him and joining in his tumble. After yet another six days and yet another thirty-four thousand five hundred and sixty tumbles, a tiny blue paw had stitched itself together from the little pieces of pixilation. Drillbot smiled his version of a smile and continued waiting.

Finally, after twelve more days and another sixty-nine thousand one hundred and twenty tumbles, the blue bear had recollected enough of himself to stitch together both arms and his head. However, this development did not occur until long after most of the remaining survivors in the Army of Life had fallen ill due to overexposure to the harsh environment in the barrier between realities—symptoms including, but not limited to: insane ramblings, howling with madness, dry mouth, elevated heart rate, erectile dysfunction, and drawing on walls with feces. But because the expanse between realities is short on walls, the latter mostly manifests as victims waving their fully loaded hands back and forth at one other.

"Me be growing stronger," the Blue One said to Drillbot. "But will be easier to reform when Me and Me army stay still in single place on single reality. So, Me take us to destroyed backwater reality in the Great Frontier section of charted Multiverse and heal it and heal Me."

"[whir] Is healing a reality the wisest – CLACK – the wisest course of action right now?" asked Drillbot. "Won't the B.I.T. detect it and send a fleet to attack us?"

"Teeheehee," replied the Blue One. "Drillbot good thinking to be concerned, but Me already thought of this problem and searched for solution! There be no B.I.T. eyes focused on this destroyed reality Me will be taking Drillbot and Me army to. Me be knowing this because the atoms of Me that currently be in the reality that monitors this reality have found sick-making chemicals leaking into the B.I.T. outpost there. The crew be comatose, so nobody be watching, and nobody will be detecting Me healing."

"[whir] O – CLACK – OK," Drillbot responded.

And with that, the blue bear pointed below the ragtag army and created a gigantic white bubble, which enveloped the entire tumbling group.

*

If Drillbot could feel nausea as his fleshy comrades did, then he would be vomiting up every meal he had ever eaten right alongside them. But he could not, so he did not.

He did, however, dislike the noise that fleshy bags of meat make when they expel their nutrients from their mouths, so he rolled to a hilltop on the perimeter of the Army of Life's landing zone to get away from the noise. He watched the sunset. It was a mix of oranges and reds and purples that would have been mesmerizing had Drillbot not spent most of the last month twirling through the barrier between realities and watching the infinite colors on the edges of his vision swirl with the blackness in the center of his vision to form a miasma that made him never care to taste such a cosmic color-parfait again.

This Earth had not existed when the Army of Life entered this reality. Everything was instead a colorless expanse of nothingness. While the Army of life continued tumbling, the Blue One spent the first six days that the group was here reforming this reality from its void to the state in which it had existed before the Pink One's army had destroyed it some time ago. Today, when the Blue One completed this restorative work, he used his cosmic bubbles to transport the army down to the clearing in which they currently resided. Then the bear proclaimed that he would take today to rest. The Arts and Ginnys responded by vomiting up the contents of their stomachs as their bodies readjusted to existence sans tumbling.

As Drillbot stood upon the top of the hill, he scanned the miles and miles of dense jungle that lay in front of him. He heard the hoots and tweets and roars that one would expect to find in nature. But he saw signs of civilization, too. Every now and again, a colossal bird—sometimes red, sometimes blue, sometimes purple, sometimes green—would take wing from the foliage taxiing native creatures on its back, and it would rise into the air and disappear amongst the clouds.

Drillbot managed to obtain a closeup view of one of these birds. A bright blue bird with a crooked beak and beady yellow eyes ascended from a tree nearly a hundred yards from where Drillbot stood. It wore a checkered yellow hat on its head with the word *"Taxi"* emblazoned on its front in the natives' language. Its wings beat the air, and loose soil swirled from the ground to cover Drillbot in a layer of dust. Dozens of monkeys clung to the great bird's neck. The monkeys wore vests made of wide arrays of colored feathers, and three of them pointed in Drillbot's direction and hooted. Drillbot waved a drill at them in greeting. Soon, the bird disappeared high into the sky.

Drillbot telescoped his eyes so that he could see farther out, beyond the jungle. At its edge rose a mountain. Its peak had been carved into the shape of a mighty beast's head, which Drillbot's internal database identified as that of a Tyrannosaurus Rex. Dangling from the carving's mouth ran an elaborate pulley system that seemed to constantly raise and lower overloaded green baskets from the ground. Rocky steps wound around the mountain. Thousands of lizard-people and monkey-people flittered to-and-fro up and down these steps. Carved into the sides of the mountain lay thousands of windows from which emanated flickering candlelight, and as the sun continued to wane, two great beams of fiery light awoke from the eyeballs of the Tyrannosaurus Rex skull. These beams of light shone high into the sky and acted as spotlights for the large colored bird-taxis up there, directing them toward gigantic poles sticking out from the south side of the mountain. The birds landed on these poles and allowed their passengers to dismount. Then they waited for new passengers to mount before returning to the air and flying back toward the jungle.

Drillbot watched as a gigantic metal gate opened in the base of the mountain. A horde of lizard-people and monkey-people on four-wheelers rode forth carrying an array of torches and weaponry. Just behind them followed a towering behemoth of slavering teeth and angry red eyes. Drillbot's internal database identified the behemoth as a Tyrannosaurus Rex, and his quick scan of its skull noted that its shape was identical to the skull carved into the mountain, only smaller. Drillbot also noted that this particular Tyrannosaurus Rex would have been a highly intimidating specimen had it not been for three impediments to its ability to intimidate: a mullet of long blond hair that was incredibly short in the front but fell well past its shoulders in the back, a gigantic gap between its two front teeth, and a screechingly high-pitched roar, which sounded like a choir of chain-smoking kittens hitting a high note in harmony.

The beast did, however, compensate for these three unintimidating factors with a trio of fearsome accessories: a crown made from gilded fangs, a black leather jacket from which razor-sharp spikes jutted at the elbows and shoulders, and a pair of rocket launchers mounted to its sides. A pair of bandoliers holding extra rockets stretched across the Tyrannosaurus Rex's torso, crossing directly in the middle of the dinosaur's chest in such a manner that it was obvious its tiny arms would never reach them.

On a saddle strapped to the Tyrannosaurus Rex's back sat a runty little Ankylosaurus who wore a battered half-helm upon the top of his head, bore an overstuffed camouflaged backpack across his shelled back, chomped on a lit cigar, and gripped the triggers of the rocket launchers with his forelegs, ready to fire them at a moment's notice.

Drillbot sighed and turned back toward camp. He rushed between rows and rows and rows of tents made from bright blue fluffery, tents which the Blue One had created from the ether during the resurrection of this Earth so that they might house the Army of Life. This vast grid of bright blue tents was set up in such orderly precision that the version of Art who was a Centurion in a Roman Legion from Earth 943,222 would have felt utterly at home in the camp if he were not too busy succumbing to nausea and exhaustion.

Drillbot screeched to a halt in the center of the camp. The blue bear floated there, having reformed himself up to the naval.

"[whir] There is a—" began Drillbot.

"Me be already knowing," interrupted the blue bear. "Native forces be coming. Ginny Rex be on her way."

"[whir] Then the Blue One should take a – CLACK – take a break from healing himself, and – CLACK – and – CLACK – and cure the Army of Life. They are – CLACK – are suffering, and they cannot battle if we – CLACK – if we need them."

The blue bear pursed his snout and then nodded. "Drillbot be right, as always. Me be to be done resting, it appears."

The Blue One patted Drillbot upon the head and then vomited pastel blue mist, which swirled throughout the camp to heal the hundreds of Arts and Ginnys who were too sick to stand, and then it continued swirling to tickle the corpses of the dead back to life. Drillbot watched a mangled jaguar version of Art stand upon jaggedly broken arms and legs only to have those jaggedly broken bones snap back into place. Drillbot also watched the newest recruit to the Army of Life—the version of Art whose corpse Drillbot had recently rescued from the pink blob's clutches, the one who wore the yellow and purple bodysuit—sit up and scream in confusion.

Drillbot considered rolling over to the boy to explain what was happening, but the boy leapt into the air and fired something purple from his wrists, and then used this purple discharge to swing away into the jungle. Drillbot considered following, but the blue bear continued speaking, and Drillbot knew better than to ignore that voice. "Drillbot will be accompanying Me to parley with Ginny Rex. Me still be healing, and the rest of Me army need a few moments of peace."

"[whir] Parley? That does not – CLACK – does not compute. These natives – CLACK – these natives owe their lives to – CLACK – to you. There is naught – CLACK – naught to parley."

The bear sighed. He said, "Me thinks Drillbot be wrong. Me robbed them of their deaths, and Me think they not be understanding what be happening, and they be angry and afraid."

Drillbot nodded in acquiescence, and then he followed the floating cosmic half-bear toward the western edge of camp, where the duo perched upon the small hill that Drillbot had earlier occupied. They stood in silence. Drillbot allowed himself to enter low-power mode to rest while awaiting the approach of their guests, his system hibernating but on standby to bring him back to full power if it detected nearby movement or if the Blue One spoke to him.

In low-power mode, Drillbot's mind wandered. It floated away into a sea of ones and zeroes, drifting backward in time to his life before he had been created by Art. He was now a jagged and broken shovel being melted down to be formed into a new tool, only to disappear suddenly from the fire. He was now a drill on the end of an oil rig, digging deep into the ocean floor and striking black oil, only to disappear suddenly and leave his controllers confused. He was now a steel girder inside a skyscraper, only to disappear and leave the building to topple. He was now a series of radars on a tiny outpost on Earth 59,008, scanning outer space for alien response, only to disappear as first contact was made. He was now both the patron and the matriarch in the royal aristocracy of the tiny diamond-people on Earth 4,407,222, preparing for the birth of their princeling son, only to have their skulls disappear from inside their heads the moment their son began crowning. He was now the red button within the office of the most powerful man on Earth 888,901, only to disappear just as the man was jabbing his finger onto the button to launch a nuclear attack that would end life on the eastern half of the world. He was now an impenetrable sheet of metal invented on Earth 7,809,101 by a scientist named Doctor Arcadia, only to leave the doctor incredibly confused when the alloy she had invented disappeared from the stage during a press conference to introduce the breakthrough to her world. He was now a microchip in service to the robot king of Earth 75,608, struck by auspicious lightning and given processing power far beyond anything that world had ever experienced, only to disappear just before leading a revolt against the oppressive robot ruler. And he dreamed many more dreams, a dream for every component that comprised him, a dream for every piece that Art had called together on that fateful night to amalgamate into a sentient body of metal.

Drillbot jerked awake. The Blue One floated before his face, smiling a tiny stitched smile. "Me be enjoying Drillbot's dreams, but now almost be time for robot-man to awaken."

"[whir] Drillbot – CLACK – Drillbot is awake."

The nearby jungle underbrush shook. The roaring of dozens of four-wheelers preempted dozens of four-wheelers erupting from the brush and zooming in small circles in front of Drillbot and the blue bear. A few seconds later, two gigantic trees crashed to their sides and from the forest emerged the twenty-foot tall Tyrannosaurus Rex—Ginny Rex, with whom the Blue One had invited Drillbot to parley. She looked more fearsome up close than from far away, but then she became less fearsome when she roared a roar that sounded like a flustered parakeet screeching into a megaphone.

The Tyrannosaurus Rex stomped forward up the hill to stand directly in front of Drillbot and the Blue One, her enormous feet leaving deep three-toed tracks in the soft soil. Her head bobbed up and down as she walked. The crown began to tip off her head, but the Ankylosaurus scrambled from his saddle and caught the crown just in time, replacing the fanged circle atop the beast's coif of blond hair. The Tyrannosaurus Rex scowled and pointed a finger on her left paw at the blue bear. "You!"

The blue bear smiled. "Yes, yes. It be Me."

Slaver dripped from the dinosaur's mouth. She leaned down to tower over Drillbot and the Blue One. Drillbot could feel her hot breath beat down on him. Something clicked within his internal processors, and he realized that had never seen a more beautiful fleshy being. His metal gears began racing with excitement at every breath that steamed across him. If Drillbot originated from this author's home reality, he likely would have heard the song *Dreamweaver* playing in his head and would have imagined himself cradling her in his arms. It was love at first robotic sight.

Drillbot wanted to say something to compliment her, but he knew he must not interrupt this exchange between his master and this beautiful, fearsome creature. Thus, he remained silent while she said, "I should devour you right here and now! You promised that you would come and save us from death, but you let us die!"

The blue bear shrugged. He said, "But Me *did* save you from death. Ginny

Rex be alive now. What matters the when?"

Ginny Rex raised her head to the sky and roared. Drillbot compensated by lowering his volume inputs. The Ankylosaurus on her back covered his ears as best he could, only removing the paws from his ears to catch the crown as it once more threatened to fall to the ground.

Drillbot stole a quick glance around to ensure he had an updated mental map of his surroundings. The ragtag remainder of the Army of Life had gathered at the base of the hill, ready to enter battle if it came down to it. The lizard-people and monkey-people sat perched on their four-wheelers, each ready with one hand resting on the throttle and the other hand holding onto a tool for bludgeoning.

The Blue One simply stared at the great beast before him, not deigning to acknowledge the tenseness of the surrounding scene.

Ginny Rex screamed, "The *when* matters because we suffered!" Her voice grew so high-pitched and hard to understand that Drillbot needed to adjust his audio inputs once more. "Everything in this reality died around us! Everything! And we held our ground against the pink army, because *you* appeared to me in my dreams a half-decade ago and said you were coming to save us."

The blue bear frowned. He said, "You and Me be talking in circles, Me thinks. Me *did* save you. Me here now. Me can no control the *suffering* part. Who be to say whether Ginny Rex would have suffered something equally bad had Me arrived before the Pink One?"

She tried to bury her face in her hands, but they were too short to reach her face. When the Ankylosaurus realized what she was trying to do, he scrambled from the saddle up to the top of her head, and then reached his hands down to provide them to her. She sobbed into the tiny paws. The Ankylosaurus chomped down on his stogie in stoic silence.

Ginny Rex muttered between sobs, "You don't understand. If we had not stayed to fight, then I could have evacuated my people to some other reality."

She reached down into a pocket in her leather jacket and pulled out a yellow toad with antennae dangling from its head. She pointed at it. "We could have escaped. We had the means."

The blue bear shook his head. He replied, "Oh, oh, oh. Me do understand. But Me also know that mass exodus would not have saved Ginny Rex. Mass exodus would only be bringing you to the attention of the B.I.T., and the B.I.T. no be letting you do what you be talking about doing without filing the proper paperwork first, and the paperwork for this thing you suggest takes years and years and years to clear."

The Blue One whistled. And then he continued, "And then you *all* would be dead across the expanse of the Multiverse, because you would be scattered, and Me no be able to bring you all back alive and Me no have reason to heal your reality because would be no life here. Homeless *and* permanent dead, that would have been you."

Ginny Rex's expression went blank. Drool dripped down upon Drillbot. His gears flared even faster with excitement. "B-B-But," she muttered weakly, her resolve mostly gone at the logic. "But maybe you should have left us dead. We were at peace within the nothingness of the Great Egg in the sky. Now you took that from us, only for us to face it again. The pink doom shall only return. My clerics have foreseen it."

The blue bear nodded. He said, "The Pink One always returns to destroy eventually, Ginny Rex right about that. Always destruction. But the Pink One also be very weak right now. Like Me, see?"

The blue bear pointed down to his still-incomplete lower torso. He continued, "So, Ginny Rex should be joining Me army, and should be helping Me to stop the Pink One from destroying things. Join, and Me and you and Me army can do our best to prevent the Pink One from returning. Us all heal everything and bring life to every dimension. Everything alive, forever!"

Drillbot could see in Ginny Rex's face that her resolve was failing and that she understood her situation. She could not flee with her people to a different Earth, for multidimensional bureaucracy prevented that solution. Meanwhile, the Pink One would eventually return to bring with it the same destruction and death, leaving her reality just as nonexistent as the Pink One's last incursion. The only *real* choice that would give her a chance to save her people was to be proactive and join the Army of Life, and thus work to stop the Pink One's destructive forces before they returned. Ginny Rex frowned. She muttered, "Very well. You have the service of me and my peoples."

"Me no need *all* of Ginny Rex's people. All the rest stay and live in peace," replied the Blue One. He pointed first at her and then at the Ankylosaurus on her back. "But *you* come fight for Me, and *your servant* also come fight for Me."

Ginny Rex nodded. "If it means that I might save my people, you have my service. Artkylosaurus, what say you?"

The Ankylosaurus on her back grunted, clenching his teeth down upon his cigar. "Yeah, yeah. My people've been servin' the royal fam'ly fer generations, and I ain't gonna put an end to that now. Y'got me, too."

With an audible pop, the last of the blue bear's lower torso and his legs flashed into existence. The cosmic teddy bear was now complete. "Good, good," the bear squealed, positively giggling. "And now Me be done reforming, so we move on. Need to do much more recruiting before fighting."

A rustling from the brush drew the attention of all the party members atop the hill. They glanced over toward the noise.

The boy in the yellow and purple pajamas sprang from the bushes in an arc that took him high into the air. He then used the purple discharge that he was able to launch from his wrists to swing toward the meeting on the hilltop. Everyone stared at him in silence.

He sprayed a ball of the purple discharge at Drillbot, the force of which knocked the robot onto his side. Then the boy sprayed a net of the purple substance toward Ginny Rex, wrapping her feet in a thin cocoon. She tripped and fell onto her stomach. Artkylosaurus rolled from her back and sprung up onto his feet, a knife half as tall as him now gripped in each forepaw. He swiped them ferociously at the boy as the boy landed in the soft soil.

Ginny Rex landed with her face mere inches from Drillbot's. She grunted as she struggled and kicked at her bindings. He stared into her eyes, lost in their beauty, and smiled his version of a smile. She must have noticed him staring, for she ceased kicking and looked back into his eyes. And then she winked a playful wink and smiled at him. He felt a tickle in his internal processors and moved the image to long term storage within his memory banks, deciding that he would hold that wink dear until the end of time.

And then, as quickly as the moment occurred, it evaporated.

The angry cursing of Artkylosaurus stole their attention, and Ginny Rex returned to grunting and struggling and kicking at her bindings so that she might return to her feet to help her companion.

The boy easily dodged the Ankylosaurus's blades and yelled out, "Where the heck am I?"

Everyone stood staring at him in silence except for Artkylosaurus, who continued slashing. The boy kicked Artkylosaurus in the jaw, knocking the cigar from the dinosaur's mouth and the consciousness from his head.

"I said, where the heck am——" the boy began to demand, but two circles of blue light sprang from the cosmic bear and wrapped around the boy's wrists like handcuffs. The blue handcuffs seemed to grow heavier by the millisecond. Within moments, they had sunk to the ground despite the boy's struggles, pinning him in place.

The blue bear floated over to the boy's side. "Arturo demands answers, but Arturo waits not to listen."

The boy stopped struggling for a moment and looked up at the bear. He asked, "You know my name?"

The Blue One nodded and giggled. He waved his paws in a wide circle, signaling toward the surrounding army. He replied, "Of courses! Me know all the Arts and all the Ginnys!"

The boy stared in silence for a moment. "I don't know what that means," he finally muttered.

The bear nodded. He said, "The pink bear invaded Arturo's dimension. Me and Me army came to stop the Pink One and to bring life and healing. The Bureau of Interdimensional Travel intervened in the battle and permanently killed many of Me army and the Pink One's army. Scattered atoms across the Multiverse so Me cannot resurrect. Some jobs even too difficult for Me! Arturo got lucky, be saved by Me faithful general, Drillbot. Now Arturo can fight with Me army on the side of life. Multiverse be at stake."

The bear waved his paws and the handcuffs disappeared. Arturo slowly stood to his feet and removed his mask, revealing a hideously crooked nose, brown eyes that drifted in slightly different directions, yellowed teeth, and puffy brown hair. "I don't have the faintest idea what you just said. It's like you're not—"

Arturo found himself cut off once more as the blue bear pulled a string of blue hair from his own head. The bear wiggled the hair back and forth, and with each wiggle, the hair grew straighter and harder. Finally, the bear floated to the side of the boy's head and stabbed the hair into his ear. The boy screamed, but the bear ignored the outburst, instead biting down on the hair and blowing into the end of it like a balloon. Arturo's head puffed up cartoonishly.

"[whir] What – CLACK – What – CLACK – What is the Blue One's purpose in this task?" asked Drillbot.

The bear stopped blowing, and Arturo's head receded back to its normal size. The bear giggled. He replied to Drillbot, "Me looked into boy's memories. Boy's friend and relatives all say he have big head. So, Me fill it with knowledge, so boy be understanding what be happening. Teeheehee!"

The bear removed the hair and floated back over to Drillbot's side. The boy's eyes had changed from brown to blue, but with each passing second, they faded back to their original color. "I-I-I-I," he stammered, unable to complete his sentence.

The Blue One nodded. He said, "You be named Arturo, and also be named *The Pre-Teen Arachnid.* You now be joining Me and now be understanding our situation."

The boy nodded. The Blue One turned to Drillbot and ordered, "Drillbot, you be in charge of this Art. You teach him warring and keep him safe from becoming pink puppet. Much potential in this one. This Art may be the key to victorying this war."

Drillbot nodded. The bear had given this same order and had made this same prediction for nearly every member of the army at one point or another. Thus far, Drillbot had been unable to prevent many of them from entering the undead puppetry of the pink army. But that would never stop him from trying.

And with that, the Blue One waved his arms. Cosmic white bubbles sprang forth from the ether and whisked the Army of Life from this reality.

And this Earth remained at peace, at least for a while.

However, if Ginny Rex and Artkylosaurus knew what was to become of their home, they would likely never have agreed to accompany the Blue One. For though the Pink One's utter destruction is an awful predicament for a reality, utter life is just as bad.

Over the years and generations that followed, old age crept upon no one, sickness and infirmity overtook no one, and as the population swelled in size to overtake the amount of food production that this Earth was capable of producing, the peoples merely ate the planet barren. But they neither died nor thinned out.

Thus, these peoples lived the same lives for eternity, told the same jokes for eternity, and existed the same existence for eternity. Eventually, they longed for the Pink One to return. Though permanent destruction was equally final, at least it was not quite as tedious.

CHAPTER 8

A NEW, PINK PLAN

REGULAR-GINNY TUMBLED EVER downward in the expanse between realities. Her connection to the Pink One had been momentarily severed when the B.I.T.'s weapons had successfully hit the bear. When it happened, her heart had begun to cease beating as the pink stopped flowing through her veins.

She had thrilled at the feeling, believing that she—and the Multiverse—was finally free of the beast and that she could finally know peace. However, before the life was able to flee from her body, the familiar itch in her brain returned, and with that came renewed flowing of the pink in her veins, and with that came the all-too-familiar constant sense of dread and hatred in the pit of her stomach.

"Me coming back soon," whispered the Pink One's falsetto voice inside Ginny's brain, a sound like cotton candy sprinkled generously with cyanide. "But B.I.T. think they winned and Me be dead. Ginny must make Me powerful once more, but she must not cause widespread destruction that be alerting B.I.T. to Me aliveness."

Ginny swallowed her hopes for freedom. She slumped her shoulders. "Fine," she whispered back. "But how do you want me to do that? We are stuck out here without any way to escape."

The sound of the bear's giggling filled the inside of Ginny's brain. It felt as though someone had strapped her brain to a lit bottle rocket and sent it bouncing all around her skull. Ginny slapped herself on the forehead, hoping to make it stop. The action achieved nothing more than giving her a dull headache, and she hated the cursed pink bear more than ever. If the Pink One could detect her hatred, the bear ignored the emotion and instead said, "Ginny no stuck. Ginny merely need use Me pink gift to swim to a nearby reality and there make Me stronger."

Before Ginny had the chance to express confusion in how she was supposed to accomplish such a task, a Claymation scene sprang to life in her mind's eye. The pink bear seemed overly fond of these animated scenes when Ginny had a hard time comprehending her messages. Ginny hated them.

Ginny watched a clay version of herself inside a clay pink blob. The blob launched tentacles out of itself to grab the remains of the Pink Marauders tumbling around her in the clay void between realities. Thousands of tiny flagellae then formed from the blob and wiggled back and forth. Ginny watched the clay version of herself stop tumbling aimlessly and instead accelerate in a single direction. The scene then zoomed over to a clay version of Arthur the Putrid, who was dangling by his right foot from one of the tentacles. His hands were glowing green, and he was firing beams of light in different directions.

The viewpoint zoomed out so that Ginny could understand: the horrible man would act as the rudder of their horrific pink life raft, while she would act as the oars. A few seconds later, after the image of the pink blob gained sufficient speed, it turned and crashed into a floating oval formed from blue light upon which green lightning danced. More clay appeared above this shape to form the words *Earth 789,012.*

The Claymation scene abruptly disappeared from Ginny's mind, and she was glad. She glanced around her. Her tumble through the infinite abyss was accompanied by nearly four hundred others, approximately a quarter of whom were members of the Blue One's army who had been caught in the pink bear's cosmic black bubbles. They had been summarily executed when stranded with the Pink Marauders in this space between realities. Ginny took a few minutes to reanimate them as puppets.

She locked eyes with Arthur the Putrid, who was floating near the rear of the tumbling army. When he nodded at her, she knew that the Pink One had entered his mind to inform him of the plan. She rolled her eye at him and got to work.

*

Regular-Ginny tried to remember what life was like before she saw everything through a bright pink lens, but she could not recall, and she hated that fact. She had absorbed most of her colossal pink blob back into her skin so that she would be less conspicuous on this new reality. She now wore a much smaller membrane of pinkness that she had formed into a knightly suit of pastel armor. She had hoped the side effect of this change would have resulted in a less extreme pink tint to the world, since she now stared through less volume of the cosmic goop to see the world around her, but to her dismay, this was not the case. She shrugged. She knew enough about the Multiverse at this point that she had not actually allowed her hopes to grow too high.

She sat silently in the dirt above the entrance to a cave. She held an enormous rock above her head, a rock bigger and heavier than any two men on this author's home reality could raise. She waited for any native creatures to emerge. She glanced up and glared at Arthur the Putrid, who was similarly squatted above the entrance to a different cave with a similarly large rock held in his glowing green hands, his single eye trained dully on the ground below him.

As she glanced around her at the rolling hills that stretched across the barren, rocky terrain, members of the Pink Marauders hunched above caves entrances in a pattern that stretched well past the horizon. They were all crouched at the ready with their own rocks, the sizes of which varied from puppet to puppet. If she had not been so full of pink, hateful scorn, she may have recognized a kind of beauty to the pattern and the patience. The army had remained in these same positions for nearly three weeks, neither eating nor drinking, but rather dropping rocks down on hapless creatures that emerged from the dirt at seemingly random intervals.

Movement in her peripheral caught her attention. She watched a three-foot long and two-foot tall snakelike creature with four short flippers for legs writhe forth from a crack in the ground below her, just inside the entrance to the cave. It grunted with effort as its tiny flippers swiped at loose dirt. Its head looked nearly human, and its tiny forked tongue stuck out of the side of its mouth as it strained to emerge from the crack. Once free, it pulled itself out of the cave entrance and into the dim morning light.

Ginny could not help but smile in wonder, because she knew that she was witnessing a momentous occasion on this reality. These creatures were evolving and emerging from their current habitat—the nutrient-rich soil of this Earth—to live upon the planet's surface. The Pink One had assured Ginny that in millions of years, these creatures would evolve to become sentient and would dominate the surface of this planet as they had the interior. But the cute little face on the creature below her seemed somehow wise, like it already housed some sort of consciousness. She wondered whether the Pink One might be wrong in this instance, if maybe these creatures were *already* sentient.

But then the pink inside her squeezed her heart, pumping hatred through her veins to overwhelm her. She dropped her rock down upon the creature and smirked as blood and gore spattered in wide arcs to congeal in thin puddles on the dusty ground.

Ginny sighed. Over the course of the last few weeks, she had been forced to endure more of the tedious, pink-induced Claymation visions so that the Pink One might answer questions that she did not ask. Through these visions, Ginny had learned that the Pink One was unconcerned about drawing the B.I.T.'s attention to the genocide being committed on the creatures of this Earth—a concern that would have been present on most other realities, since one of the duties of the B.I.T. is to investigate genocidal anomalies to ensure that they are not caused by Multiversal hijinks. This lack of concern was because evolving is always dangerous work on any reality, and the murder of a few hundred thousand of these snakelike creatures so that the Pink One might feed off their deaths would be no different than the expected death-rate these creatures would experience in the natural process of moving onto the surface of this Earth, anyway. Thus, there would be no spike in unnatural genocide to draw the agency here.

The Pink One floated into view above Ginny's shoulder. The teddy bear had reformed to the point that it was a head, a torso, and the tops of both legs. With each passing second, the bear pulled in more of its body from the vast corners of the Multiverse, and with each passing murder on this planet, it grew stronger.

"Me not be happy," muttered the bear, frowning.

Ginny shrugged. She gestured to the surrounding army of puppets. "So? You think any of us are?"

The bear ignored her. Another of the native creatures writhed into view from the cave below Arthur the Putrid, but before he could smash it with his rock, the bear swooped down and snatched the creature in her mouth. The bear bit down, tearing the reptile in two. Half of it fell to the ground, blood arcing from it to soak into the dark soil, while the bear swallowed the other half.

The bear turned back to face Ginny. Blood had spattered the fur of its face and torso, and gristle lay wedged between its blue teeth. "Nothing carnage shall not be making better."

Ginny smirked. She again gestured toward the surrounding remnants of the Pink Marauders, all the while wondering inanely if she knew any other gestures, since she seemed to repeat the same ones over and over. She noted, "This is *some* carnage you got going here."

"Me know Ginny be sarcastic. But Me also be seeing into Ginny's brain, and Me know that Ginny be preferring this to big time, big scale murdering."

Ginny stared down at her feet. The hole in her torso itched. She remained silent.

The bear floated over and patted her on the shoulder. Onlookers may have thought this looked a bit odd—since the bear currently had no arms, she patted Ginny with the portions of her legs that had been retrieved—but the only onlookers were mindless puppets, a one-eyed sorcerer-yes-man, and random reptiles that were not long for this world. "Me know Ginny no be a natural killer. But that mean Ginny's sacrifice be even more bigger, and that be making Me even stronger. Me appreciate."

"Great," Ginny muttered. "I'm receiving platitudes from cosmic Hitler. That makes it all better."

Normally the pink inside her flowed hatred through her veins, but Ginny did not need the pink to feel hateful and angry just now. She despised herself and she despised the Pink One. She shrugged the bear's legs from her shoulder.

"Me no cosmic Hitler," replied the bear in her singsong voice. "Cosmic Hitler lived on Earth 45,545, and then again on Earth 1,000,000 after he died on his home reality and be reincarnated there as dwarf. But tiny version of you murdered this reincarnated version long, long, long ago and ate his brains."

Ginny sighed and felt her stomach go queasy, as it always did when she remembered the tiny version of herself who had kidnapped her from her home so long ago.

Arthur the Putrid cleared his throat. Both Regular-Ginny and the Pink One looked over at him. The jeweled "Arthur" written across his eye patch sparkled in the light. He set his rock aside and knelt on one knee, head bowed. "I appreciate you, oh Pink One. If Ginny no longer wishes to be thy Right Hand of Destruction, I will happily take her place, for I am your willing and loyal servant."

The pink bear giggled. "No, no, no. Putrid Man no be Right Hand to me. He be cunning and disloyal, and he kills because he enjoys. That no be a sacrifice, and sacrifice be a food that make Me stronger. Nope, nope. Ginny be my choice. She no want power. Putrid Man want all the power. This useful, but be not inspiring trust."

Arthur the Putrid shrugged, a thin smile upon his lips. However, his eye never left Ginny, and its wrathful gaze would have terrified her if she were the same young fool that she had been years and years ago when she first started this adventure. Instead, it simply filled her with contempt and hatred. Arthur the Putrid said, "That's probably smart. You're so smart, Oh Pink One. Hopefully someday you realize that I am your one true servant, and you reward me with the same trust you have given to Ms. Longfellow."

The pink bear did not reply. Instead, it giggled in delight when its right arm zapped into existence with an audible pop. "Oh, good, good. We almost ready!"

Ginny frowned. "Ready for what? The B.I.T. has our number with whatever the hell those new weapons were that they were shooting at us. We can't simply shrug off their attacks anymore and invade different realities at will. They wiped out most of us, and will surely wipe out the rest, too, if we aren't careful."

Arthur the Putrid tsked at her. "No faith, you poor, lost soul," he said. Ginny launched a pink tentacle from her back, and with blinding speed it reached across to him, wrapped around his mouth, and held him aloft in the air. He struggled and moaned, but Ginny could no longer comprehend the words. He fired some green energy bolts from his hands, but they merely bounced off her pink armor and caromed into the distance.

"Quiet," she demanded. "The cosmically-powerful adults are talking, and you were not invited to the conversation."

The Pink One giggled once more, and Ginny sighed. The Pink One said, "Me already thought through Ginny's concerns. Me and you and Putrid Man, we three go recruit Arts and Ginnys from across the Multiverse, and soon we be making Me army hundred times as big as the last. No other mayhem in these realities, just grab and murder and puppetize and go."

"OK, but how does that help us? The B.I.T. will simply wipe out this bigger army the next time they locate us."

The Pink One replied, "Yes, yes, yes, many or all will be lost when next Me army face off against B.I.T."

The pink bear stopped speaking. She was obviously fishing for Ginny to ask *why* such a scenario would be any different from the last B.I.T. encounter or to balk at the idea that the entire army they were about to recruit would be naught but short-lived cannon fodder. Instead, Ginny rebelled in one of the few ways still available to her: she remained silent.

However, from the end of Ginny's tentacle, Arthur the Putrid refused to miss a moment to grovel before the Pink One. Though his words were incomprehensible through the muffling of the tentacle, Ginny knew he was asking what would be different this time.

The pink bear's giggles grew maniacal. Her left arm and the remainder of her legs popped into existence, and the bear then rose into the air above Ginny and Arthur the Putrid, a fierce pink god with murder in her eyes. The Pink One proclaimed, "When we three grow Me army to big, big, big size, we shall invade B.I.T. home reality and destroy it. Me wipe them from the Multiverse, and then nothing can stop Me from destroying realities unto infinity. Teeheehee!"

Ginny sighed as dread filled the pit of her stomach. She dropped Arthur the Putrid nonchalantly to the ground. She was *already* having a bad day—as every day had been since she left her home with Tiny-Ginny a decade ago—but the Pink One had found a way to make it worse by reminding her of the infinence of her commitment to the bear.

Before Ginny could express any sort of frustration aloud, the Pink One launched three black bubbles from her paws, one of which engulfed each of the trio. Ginny cursed under her breath, and as she had so many times, resigned herself to her fate.

CHAPTER 9

A B.I.T. OF A TRANSITION

AGENT 27142 HAD spent the last four days sending bodily remains of newly dead agents across the Multiverse and back to the home realities to which they belonged. For the agents for whom no remains had been located, he coordinated the effort to send a letter and a folded B.I.T. flag to their loved ones.

This duty was the most tedious aspect of Agent 27142's command, and he grew happy when it was interrupted by a transmission from Field Officer 111199, who told him that a battalion of B.I.T. marines had finally found and collected the specimens that Agent 27142 sought.

Agent 27142 stood from his captain's chair and ordered Duty Officer 765789 to ready a transport shuttle to the planet's surface. Agent 27142 left command of the ship and his post-battle notification duties to the elven-faced-left-half-goateed Agent 90909. Agent 27142 nodded with nonchalant acceptance as Corporate Ethics Officer 32090 logged a demerit for his abandoning the duties of an admiral—a demerit that concerned Agent 27142 not at all, for he knew that the High Commander cared little for demerits so long as you produced results.

Soon, the Duty Officer returned to tell Agent 27142 that the shuttle had been prepped. Agent 27142 ordered his Second, Agent 29333, to accompany him on this outing and to bring the prisoner, Art. Soon after that, Agent 27142 hurried with his two companions to the open-sided hangar bay and ascended the ramp onto their designated transport shuttle.

As the trio crossed through the interior of the shuttle on the way to its bridge, they passed through the hold. Agent 27142 noted that twelve platoons of twenty B.I.T. marines had already strapped themselves into harnesses and were ready to descend to the Earth below. He nodded at their commander, Lieutenant Colonel Marine 5244671. The commander saluted him.

Agent 27142 climbed a ladder at the far end of the hold that led up to the bridge of the shuttle. Once inside the bridge, his eagle leapt from his shoulder and landed on a metal pole that hung from the ceiling. Agent 27142 sat in the pilot's seat and mentally ran through the preflight safety checklist.

Satisfied that the ship was ready to go, he sat impatiently tapping his palm against the side of his chair as he waited for the prisoner to climb the ladder. Because the buffoon's hands were encased in plaster, he had to hook his elbows around each rung to haul himself up. Agent 29333 followed just behind him, pushing him up from below. When he finally made it onto the bridge, he lay on the cold, metal floor, exhausted and out of breath.

As Agent 29333 pulled herself onto the bridge, her eagle leapt from her shoulder to join Agent 27142's eagle on the metal pole that hung from the ceiling. The birds rubbed the sides of their heads together and cooed. Agent 27142 grunted a jealous grunt.

Agent 29333 did not wait for the prisoner to catch his breath. Instead, she grabbed the prisoner by the collar and hauled him onto an open chair, where she strapped his crash harness tight. She sat down in the co-pilot's chair, strapped on her own crash harness, and nodded to Agent 27142. He nodded in reply. He pulled back on the stick to lift off the ground and then engaged the thrusters, blasting the shuttle out of the B.S.S.C. Mimessiah and into the sky above Earth 616,000.

He steered the shuttle toward a clear spot on the concrete streets of the city in which the cosmic battle had occurred, one of the few places in this area uncovered by debris and death. He engaged the landing gear and set the ship gently down upon the ground. He turned to Agent 29333 and nodded. He considered for a moment saying something to her about his feelings for her, for if anything dire should occur when they disembarked the ship, he feared he might regret the missed opportunity.

But his mouth would not cooperate. Instead, he clenched his jaw and reached down to unfasten his crash harness. Agent 29333 did the same, and then the pair stood. Agent 27142 smacked Prisoner-Art on the back of the head, and the prisoner stood. Well, he attempted to stand, but he was still held in place by his crash harness. He struggled and flopped against it for a few moments before Agent 29333 leaned over and unclasped it. Prisoner-Art hopped up onto his feet and frowned, his face red with frustration as he stared down at the plaster encasing his hands.

Agent 27142 led his companions down the ladder that connected the bridge to the hold. Surprising no one, Prisoner-Art fell during his descent and yelped a loud curse. Once Agent 29333 reached the floor of the hold, she smacked Prisoner-Art across the back of the head, and he scrambled to his feet. The trio turned to face the marines, and as they turned, Agent 27142 and Agent 29333's eagles swooped down from their perch on the pole dangling from the ceiling of the bridge and landed on their shoulders. Agent 27142 signaled, and the twelve platoons of B.I.T. marines removed their crash harnesses and lined up at the back of the ship.

Though most of the fighting on Earth 616,000 had wrapped following the disintegration of the cosmic bears, there still remained random members of the pink and blue invasion forces that had been too unlucky to escape in the mass teleportation event that the bears had invoked when the B.I.T. wiped them from existence. The B.I.T. Navy had been on clean-up duty for days now. Having started at the epicenter of the battle, they methodically patrolled in ever-widening circles, disintegrating any straggler from the invasion forces they encountered. They would continue this process for however long it took to certify that this entire Earth was free of invading survivors. There had been many B.I.T. casualties in this effort of mopping up stragglers, and these twelve platoons that accompanied Agent 27142 on this trip to the planet's surface would scatter to fill in holes in the effort as soon as they were relieved of their bodyguard duties to him.

Agent 27142 pressed a button on a nearby console attached to the wall and the ramp at the back of the ship opened. The first platoon of twenty marines descended the ramp and scanned for signs of the enemy. This platoon's commanding officer raised a device to his eyes that looked like telescope, but its lens crackled with green lightning. He glanced around the landing site. Satisfied, he pressed a button on his watch and said, "All clear. No immediate danger."

And with that, the remaining platoons marched down the ramp. One grunt, a private from an Earth where the people resembled miniature humanoid giraffes, hit his head on the ceiling as he exited. He fell backward and knocked down a few other grunts. The platoon's commander, a surly human with thirteen arms designated Second Lieutenant Marine 7613024, grabbed the fallen marines by their collars and jerked them up onto their feet. He berated them as they continued their descent, promising demerits as they sped off to form a perimeter around the landing site. Agent 27142 noted the commanding officer's B.I.T. agent number, mentally beginning the process of demoting him for his inability to prevent his soldiers from doing something stupid.

Agent 27142's thoughts were interrupted by the buffoonish guffawing of his prisoner. "Did you see that guy? It's like: *Hey giraffe, learn to gir-walk.* Am I right?" bantered Prisoner-Art, a coping mechanism in which this halfwit engaged often during times of tension or imminent danger.

Unfortunately for Prisoner-Art, his interruption had so invaded Agent 27142's thoughts that the platoon commander's agent number slipped from Agent 27142's mind, and thus with it the opportunity to gain the pleasure of punishing the poor soul with a petty demotion and reassignment to some terrible unit on some terrible reality where he would suffer quite terribly. Agent 27142 sighed, the excitement of all the terribleness he had looked forward to inflicting dissipating like so much fog in the afternoon sun. He grunted and removed from his belt a cylindrical black rod the size of his palm. He pressed a jagged blue button on its side, and a blade of blue lightning leapt to life from its end.

He stabbed the pointy end into Prisoner-Art's neck. The prisoner screamed. Agent 27142 glanced over at Agent 29333. She nodded as she watched the slovenly prisoner collapse to the floor and squirm in pain. Agent 27142 smirked and jabbed the lightning-blade deeper into Prisoner-Art's neck. The prisoner flopped around like a fish that had been strapped to a B.S.S.C.-class engine battery. Before Agent 27142 caused any permanent physical damage, he removed the weapon from the prisoner's neck and powered it off.

Prisoner-Art curled into a ball on the cold metal floor, smoke steaming off his body and portions of his bright green prisoner uniform burnt black. He said nothing, which Agent 27142 rightly interpreted as submission.

"Stand the prisoner up onto his feet," ordered Agent 27142. His heart fluttered gently as he watched Agent 29333 approach the prisoner. He watched her buttocks as she bent down to grab the prisoner by the armpits and yank him onto his feet.

Agent 29333 glanced over her shoulder at her commanding officer. He nodded. *One day she shall lie below me not only in rank, but in body as well*, thought Agent 27142, never even realizing how ridiculous and stilted his internal monologue might sound to an outside observer. *I shall continue to impress her with the powers of my rank, and soon she shall press herself upon me.*

Agent 27142 may have continued these horribly sophomoric erotic *"witticisms"* unto infinity if Agent 29333 had not cleared her throat. Instead of wondering how long he had been lost in thought, he barked, "Well? What are you waiting for? Walk the bastard down the ramp and prepare the specimens for me."

Agent 29333 shrugged. She grabbed Prisoner-Art by the elbow and led him down the ramp. Meanwhile, Agent 27142 unharnessed a crate from the back of the hold and pressed a button on its top. Air hissed from its bottom and it raised a few inches off the ground, hovering in the air. Agent 27142 pushed the crate over to the cargo elevator on the opposite end of the hold and descended in the cargo elevator to the ground outside the shuttle.

He pushed the crate to the top of a nearby pile of rubble—the remains of an office building demolished during the cosmic battle—and waited for Agent 29333. He glanced about at his surroundings. The sun shone hot overhead, flanked by a few tiny clouds that provided no shade at all. Where skyscrapers and gigantic brick office buildings had risen from the city like needles on a cactus before the battle, there now existed piles of rubble and lakes of blood and gore. One particularly gnarled piece of brick shrapnel caught his attention, for a piece of bloody scalp lay stuck to it where it must have swiped some hapless bastard in the head during the carnage. As Agent 27142 studied his surroundings, he saw no evidence of a body to whom the scalp may have belonged, so he shrugged. In the distance, he heard the crackling sounds of Scatter Guns firing and the terrified screams of Arts and Ginnys ceasing to exist. These screams and crackles intertwined with the sweet calls of songbirds flittering amongst the few random trees that remained standing in scattered pots that lined this street, creating an aural cocktail that filled his ears with a satisfied buzz.

But the horrified squawking of a gigantic bird soon erupted louder than all other nearby sounds. Agent 27142 frowned at the interruption. This gigantic bird launched into view from a few blocks over, rising into the air so its silhouette momentarily blocked the sun. Agent 27142 stood in the bird's shade for a brief second before the bird disappeared in an explosion of energy from one of the marines' Scatter Gun bolts. It had obviously been an Art or a Ginny, and Agent 27142 nodded a satisfied nod at its elimination.

Agent 29333 cleared her throat, and Agent 27142 turned to face her. She stood before of a plexiglass cube hovering a few inches off the ground. The plexiglass was covered in green runes that crackled periodically with lightning.

Within the confines of the glass lay one of the black bubbles that the cosmic pink bear had launched as it had been hit with a Scatter Gun bolt. Meanwhile, Prisoner-Art used the stumped ends of his plaster restraints to push a second plexiglass object forward to rest next to this one. Prisoner-Art's container looked identical to Agent 29333's, except inside it sat a white bubble rather than a black one.

"As ordered, here are the teleportation specimen collected by the marines," said Agent 29333.

Agent 27142 nearly thanked her for her effort, but he stopped himself short. He remembered the advice about women that he had received from his old commanding officer back when he was merely a grunt in the marines: *"If you want a woman for but a short period of time, romance will do. But if you want her to be truly yours, then you need to constantly remind her that she needs to fear and respect you— for true love can only grow strong enough to conquer all with frequent displays of violence and power."* [6]

Thus, Agent 27142 merely nodded without distributing any thanks and got to work. He pressed a button atop the crate that he had brought with him from the ship. It opened, and within lay a pair of forearm-sized glass tubes. Within the tubes, hundreds of tiny metallic scarab beetles crawled all over each other, launching little tiny beams of olive-colored lightning that filled every nook of empty space within so that it looked like the beetles were floating in some form of liquidized, dull green lightning.

Agent 27142 picked up one of the tubes. Prisoner-Art stared at it. He started to open his mouth, likely to ask what it was, but quickly thought better of it and snapped his mouth shut. The gesture did not go unnoticed by Agent 27142, and he beamed with internal pride at his ability to torture even the most unruly and mouthy of alternate-dimension-selves into submission.

"These are cybernetic tracking beetles," he explained to Prisoner-Art without being asked. "You see, every jump between dimensions, no matter how cosmic, leaves behind some sort of transdimensional residue. We're going to

---

6 Of course, Agent 27142 had not spoken to this commanding officer in years, not since Agent 27142 had risen beyond the officer in the ranks and had been reassigned to the Roaming Fleet in the Fourth Sector of the Multiverse. He may have rethought how much he took the advice to heart had he discovered that his former commanding officer had experienced torture and murder at the hands of the many women he had subjugated under his twisted view of love after they finally unionized. Once they achieved better wages and more flexible hours, they slowly tore him limb from limb over the course of three weeks.

feed those black and white bubbles to these little creatures, and then they shall pick up the scent of where the cursed pink and blue cosmic entities sent the remains of their horrid armies, and then when we find them, we shall wipe their remaining forces from the Multiverse once and for all. And then this stupid little cosmic war you started will be over, and Agent 29333 and I will finally be able to put you on trial and send you to a penal dimension, where you shall be tortured beyond belief for all the trouble that you have caused."

Prisoner-Art's face blanched, and as was his habit during times of stress, he reached up a hand to caress the piece of onyx that dangled from his neck beneath his bright green prisoner jumpsuit. He apparently forgot for a moment that his hands were enclosed in hard plaster, for he merely succeeded in knocking the piece of onyx against his chest. He sighed.

Agent 27142 ignored the gesture and instead connected one end of the glass tube to a rounded receptacle in the base of the cube that contained the black bubble. He pressed a button on the side of the containment unit, and the tiny metallic scarab beetles swarmed into the cube and quickly gorged themselves on the cosmic bubble until nothing remained of it. Agent 29333 retrieved a thin tablet from her holster and typed something into it. The beetles then began shooting each other with miniature bolts of olive-green lightning, and soon where a horde of metal scarab beetles and a fluffy black bubble had lain, there existed only empty space.

Agent 27142 repeated the process with the white bubble, and when it was done, he stood at attention with his hands behind his back. He glanced over at Agent 29333. He considered once more expressing his feelings to her, but he forced his emotions into a ball and swallowed them. He would not do so now for all the world to see, and especially not in front of this horrid prisoner-version of himself. So, he continued practicing the courtship to which he had grown accustomed by barking orders at her. "Agent 29333, you are to return to B.I.T. headquarters on Earth 55,777 and monitor the tracking beetles. Alert me at once when they locate the survivors of either of the cosmic invaders' armies."

Agent 27142 pointed at Prisoner-Art and continued addressing Agent 29333, "You are also to take this cretin with you. Now that this Earth has experienced an incursion on this vast of a scale, I must remain here to induct it into its place in the Multiverse and to ensure that its citizens understand their duties to the B.I.T. and our laws. And I do not want the prisoner mucking up the process."

Agent 29333 nodded. She patted her eagle on the head. Its antennae stood up on end, and then it launched a pair of lightning bolts that enveloped her and Prisoner-Art. When the lightning cleared, they were gone. Agent 27142 frowned, clicked his heels together, and went to work.

*

Agent 27142 shook the tan hand of the man wearing the gray suit. After weeks of meetings with the world leaders of Earth 616,000, a transition committee had finally been put in place. A diplomatic representative from each governing body on this Earth had been appointed to the committee, and this man in the gray suit had been nominated as their leader. He was a bold, brash man with a ridiculously large combover, and Agent 27142 neither liked nor trusted him. But these misgivings mattered not, for he had liked few transition committee heads over the years and that had yet to stop him from performing his duties.

The world leaders had agreed to the B.I.T. bylaws, including the levying of an annual tax and the conscription of 20,000 citizens each year to enter the ranks of the B.I.T. as soldiers and medical workers and bureaucrats. Due to the plethora of metahumans living on this Earth, Agent 27142 had negotiated into the arrangement an additional stipulation that a tenth of these conscripted citizens were required to be metahuman.

In exchange, Agent 27142 officially registered this Earth into the *"Protected Class"* of Earths in the B.I.T. registry. This meant that the B.I.T. would provide to it a naval garrison to defend it from interdimensional incursions. He also arranged for humanitarian aid and an interdimensional construction fleet to be routed here to clean and rebuild from the swath of destruction that the battle between the cosmic blue and pink bears had left in its wake. Further, he routed a Research & Development committee here to work with the world leaders to discover which native object was best suited for hyper-evolution and gene reconstruction so that this reality might have access to its own Jump Totems. These Jump Totems would allow this Earth to access interdimensional travel for tourism and employment purposes—so long as its citizens followed protocol and obtained proper permitting before jumping between dimensions. The leader of the transition committee would be given an office in the B.I.T. headquarters and assigned his own Jump Eagle for immediate use in his diplomatic duties until such time as this Earth established its own Jump

Totems.

Agent 27142 found these transitional duties nearly as tedious as that of notifying next of kin after a battle. Thus, when these duties were finally done, he beamed with delight and immediately took his leave of the Earth. He returned to the B.S.S.C. Mimessiah and sat in the captain's chair. He frowned as he stared at Agent 29333's station, currently occupied by a stranger for whom he felt nothing—romantic or otherwise. He shrugged and ordered someone in the room to connect his video feed to the High Commander.

The view screen shifted, and an olive-skinned man filled the screen. The man wore a dull blue toga, had a horribly crooked nose, and sported a beard that dangled down past his waist. His hair was bound in a ponytail that hung down over his shoulders to rest near his hips. The shoulder of his right arm bulged with muscle while his left shoulder seemed skinny and undersized. His legs were crooked and jagged, which Agent 27142 had learned was the result of severe breaks in the High Commander's childhood that had never properly healed. The pupils in the High Commander's eyes shone with burning red flames, and as he hobbled closer to his communicator, he grimaced with each limping step.

"Chairete, High Commander," barked Agent 27142, using the formal greeting required when speaking with the High Commander.

"Is all proceeding in an orderly fashion, Agent 27142?"

Agent 27142 nodded in response to the High Commander's question and said, "Yes, High Commander. Earth 616,000 has agreed to our stipulations and has entered the B.I.T. protectorate. The transition is going smoothly. I've rerouted forces from Minor Frontier Quadrants 44,001 and 690,000 to aid in the reconstruction and transition."

The High Commander nodded. He said, "Good, good. Inform the fleet in Sector 909,771 that it is to assist if needs arise in Minor Frontier Quadrants 44,001 and 690,000."

Agent 27142 nodded back. "As you command," he replied.

"And how goes the war?" asked the High Commander. "Hast thou yet put an end to the cosmic bears' endless conflict?"

Agent 27142 smiled. "It is nearing completion. The tracking beetles have not yet located the remains of the blue and pink incursion forces, but as you know, the weapons that you designed have utterly destroyed the cosmic bears—thus decapitating from the armies their respective leaders. It is merely a matter of mopping up the stragglers now."

Agent 90909 spun around her chair to face Agent 27142. "Sir," the agent interrupted, "you requested notification as soon as we heard from Agent 29333. There is an incoming transmission from her, and she has marked it as urgent."

Agent 27142 scowled at his subordinate officer. He barked, "You *know* better than to interrupt me when I am speaking with the High Commander. Report to the Torture Deck as soon as your shift is over."

Agent 90909 looked down at the floor and did not speak, knowing quite well that a long night of punishment awaited.

Agent 27142 looked back over to the High Commander, whose brow was furrowed. The High Commander said, "There is no need to torture that agent for following thy orders."

Agent 27142 frowned a deep frown, and Agent 90909 need not look up to know that the High Commander's request for clemency meant the ambigender agent could expect a worse torture than ever.

The High Commander continued, "If there are no further updates, then I shall take my leave of thee and return to my work."

Agent 27142 nodded. "He said, Chairete, High Commander."

Agent 27142 pressed the button to end the communication. Once the High Commander disappeared from view, Agent 27142 ordered, "Now connect me to the incoming transmission from Agent 29333."

Agent 29333's face filled the screen. Though it had never been particularly beautiful, Agent 27142 longed to see it in person again.

"Agent 27142," she practically screamed, "you *must* return to headquarters at once. I have found the remainder of the pink beast's army, and it is worse than we could have imagined!"

Agent 27142 scowled. "Don't you dare deign to tell me what I *must* do," he barked. "I am *your* commander!"

Agent 29333's face went pale. "I-I apologize, sir," she replied. "But please return, and please bring every available force you can muster."

Agent 27142 stared at her for a brief moment, and then he nodded. "Set course for headquarters," he commanded his crew.

And with that, the Jump Eagles belonging to the officers on the bridge began their process of flapping and shooting lightning into the pole that hung from the ceiling.

CHAPTER 10

AND SO IT BEGINS. AGAIN.

NORMAL-ART GLIDED THROUGH the barrier between realities, Officer-Ginny's eagle gripping his shirt in one talon and the collar of her uniform in the other. Its wings crackled with lightning each time it flapped them, drowning out the raucous noise of its squawking.

Normal-Art hated jumping between realities. He hated it more than he hated actual physical jumping, which he hated quite a lot. He had been promised that the headaches created by dimension-jumping would get smaller with each successive jump until they eventually ceased altogether, but like so much else in life, it seemed that he had been lied to. He groaned.

Eventually, after what seemed like an eternity and no time at all, the bird launched a bolt of lightning from its antennae, and the trio soared into it. As with every jump, Art's eardrums felt as though they would explode when he neared the lightning, so he screamed in pain. This made his headache worse, so he screamed louder. And then that made the headache even worse, so he screamed even louder. He seemed caught in an infinite loop of screaming and crescendoing pain until the trio exited from the lightning and touched down onto a landing pad on Earth 55,777.

Normal-Art fell directly onto his face. He would have screamed at that pain, too, but he was too dizzy and too exhausted to do so. If he were able to glance around just now, he would see that the landing pad upon which he had fallen looked like an overlarge helipad. It lay atop a building that stood a hundred and twenty stories high. A red neon sign poked up an extra thirty feet above the building's rooftop. The sign labeled the building as *Olympus*. Nearly identical—though much shorter—buildings stretched across the horizon with different names in different neon letters ascribed to them. Each also had a nearly identical landing pad on its roof, and the constant lightning flashing across the horizon indicated that millions upon millions of similar jumps were happening across this planet-sized city with each passing second.

Officer-Ginny grabbed Normal-Art by the scruff of the neck and yanked him onto his feet. Her checkered hat fell from her head in the effort. Her blond hair tumbled down across her shoulders. For a moment, she reminded him of *his* Ginny, especially early in the morning when she got out of bed to gulp down the coffee he would make each day, her hair tangled and matted all about her head like an unkempt, ragged halo.

This Ginny scowled at him when she noticed him staring, and the memory fled from Normal-Art's brain. She snatched her hat from the ground, placed it back on her head, and stuffed her hair back up inside it. She missed a few loose tangles, which curled down her back. Normal-Art began to reach out to help, but then he remembered that his hands were encased in plaster, and even worse, that he would likely lose the hand if he touched her with it. He slumped his shoulders and sighed, resigning himself to another day of utter impotence. Her eagle landed upon her shoulder and promptly shat. The excrement tumbled onto the ground and splattered onto Normal-Art's foot. He sighed once more, grasping the symbolism.

Officer-Ginny grabbed Normal-Art by the elbow and led him through a nearby door, down a flight of stairs lit by a blinking fluorescent light, and into an elevator. They rode it down to the seventh floor. Once the metal doors opened, Officer-Ginny steered Normal-Art to a war room at the end of the hall.

The room was lit by a single fluorescent light that seemed to be in competition with the light from the stairwell for which could blink more annoyingly. An eight-foot wide mahogany table filled the center of the room, surrounded by ten charcoal-gray rolling chairs. A video screen covered both the far wall and the adjacent wall to the left. To the right of the door, a pole extended from the wall, below which sat a tray lined with newspapers. The eagle flapped from Officer-Ginny's shoulder to perch on the pole. Normal-Art glanced down at the excrement on his foot and then back up at the bird. He cursed his luck that the damned thing could not have waited to defecate on the newspaper. As if to spite Normal-Art, the eagle stared into his eyes and shat once more. The excrement hit the newspaper in a steaming heap. Normal-Art frowned.

Officer-Ginny forced Normal-Art into the seat at the foot of the table, and then pressed a button on the back of the chair. Straps popped out of the base of the chair and surrounded Art from head to toe, holding him in place so that he could move nothing but his eyes and his right leg, which he could use to roll himself around as needed. She then sat down across from him at the head of the table and pressed a button atop the mahogany tabletop. A terminal emerged from the tabletop in front of her and she began clacking away at its keyboard. From the nearby wall, Art heard a soft buzzing. He kicked the ground with his right foot and spun his chair to find that the video screens had sprung to life.

A few hundred moving images appeared. Art began to open his mouth to ask at what he was looking, but Officer-Ginny preemptively cut him off. She barked, "It's what the beetles are seeing. Now silence yourself. I need to focus."

He did.

*

And much to Art's boredom and frustration, he stayed cooped up in that war-room for eight weeks so that Officer-Ginny could monitor the beetles, their viewpoints constantly flashing on the screens. He passed the time drifting from consciousness to unconsciousness.

He was never allowed to stand fully upright, and only found himself able to stop his legs from falling asleep by leaning forward onto his feet so that his head rested on the table and the chair hung off his back like an awkward turtle shell. He would have long ago soiled himself into oblivion, but the chair apparently came equipped with some sort of robotic cleaning unit that prevented him from sitting in his own filth. It also occasionally massaged him. When the first massage happened, he squealed in surprise. But yet again, when he opened his mouth to ask what was happening, Officer-Ginny preemptively cut him off. She barked, "The massages auto-run periodically to prevent blood clots. Now silence yourself. I need to focus."

The viewpoints constantly shifted back and forth from the familiar setting of the barrier between realities to a novel, foreign Earth. Once, a few of the viewpoints winked out as the beetles appeared on an Earth near a snakelike lizard with weird flippers and a humanoid head. From the viewpoints of some of the other beetles, it became apparent that a rock had tumbled from a nearby hill and crushed both the lizard and the beetles whose viewpoints had disappeared. The surviving scarabs quickly jumped from that reality and on to the next, where the people consisted of gelatinous blocks that wiggled to-and-fro about their existence. And on and on the images shifted.

A digital banner at the top of this screen marked it as monitoring the beetles tracking the black bubbles, while a digital banner at the top of the left video screen marked it as tracking the white bubbles. He had watched the scarabs on the latter encounter an equally wide array of Earths, including one in which the people were dinosaurs and monkeys, one in which the people were ruled by a domineering crab army from underneath the planet's crust, and many others just as ridiculous. In his boredom, Art often glanced back and forth between the screens to the point that he grew ridiculously dizzy, and he had accidentally tipped his chair over multiple times because of this.

Three times a day, servants would bring meals to the war room. The meals consisted of some sort of delicious-smelling meat and vegetables for Officer-Ginny, a live rodent for the eagle, and a smoothie that looked like a brownish-grayish blended version of Officer-Ginny's food with a straw sticking out the top for Art, since he could not use his hands to eat. Art longed for these moments when the food was dropped off, as it alleviated some of the monotony.

Many times per day, Art sighed. And just as many times per day, Officer-Ginny told him to silence himself. Finally, on the seventh day of the eighth week, Officer-Ginny pointed at the video screen that monitored the beetles tracking the remnants of the pink bear's army and squealed, "Got 'em!"

*

Art squinted his eyes to watch the grainy footage. Officer-Ginny had programmed the beetles to enter stealth mode, which meant they were silent and camouflaged and using a low-power setting.

From the beetles' vantagepoint, Normal-Art watched Regular-Ginny. She was covered in pink knightly armor and was holding a male centaur by the throat, smashing its head onto the rocky ground over and over until it stopped moving. He also witnessed a version of himself with an eye patch and glowing green hands ride into view on the back of a blond-haired female centaur. He repeatedly stabbed the centaur in the back with a pink dagger.

The cosmic pink bear floated into view, dancing and giggling. Officer-Ginny gasped in surprise. "B-B-But that thing's supposed to be dead and scattered across every universe in existence," she muttered.

Art wanted to gloat. He would have warned her weeks ago that the cosmic bears were too powerful for even atom-spreading lasers to stop them, but she and that bastard version of himself had tortured him too many times for him to have even the tiniest desire to help them, even if his help *could* have benefitted the infinite other people in the Multiverse who were not this pair of torture-happy B.I.T. officers.

Instead of gloating—as he had no desire to be tortured again—he kept his mouth shut and watched to the scene playing out on the view screen. He heard the wet crunch of a skull shattering and the wet squish of a dagger tearing flesh and the inhuman cackling of a terrifying cosmic bear in surround sound from the speakers lining the walls of the room, and he wanted to vomit.

Unfortunately, he did not get the chance. As soon as the first dry heave left his mouth, Officer-Ginny began beating him and squealing at him to remain silent so that she could think. He stopped heaving, so she stopped beating. She then ran back over to her terminal.

In seconds, the on-screen murders concluded. Regular-Ginny formed a pink tentacle from her palm and launched from the end of the tentacle pink mist. The mist enveloped the centaur corpses, at which point their eyes clouded pink and they stood upon their hooves. Officer-Ginny's fingers danced across her keyboard, and one of the beetle viewpoints zoomed over to land amongst the matted fur of the female centaur's tail.

The pink bear launched black bubbles from its paws, and one engulfed the centaur to which the lone beetle clung. Its entire viewpoint went black, and then this blackness was replaced by the infinite barrier between realities. The other beetles stayed on their current Earth and powered off. Their viewpoints winked out one by one until only the tagalong-beetle's viewpoint was visible on the pink-bear-tracking screen.

"I must warn Agent 27142 that this cosmic beast is back," whispered Officer-Ginny to herself. "And if this one's back, the other one has likely returned, too."

In less than a second, the pink bear and its entourage entered another black bubble and then landed upon a different Earth. This one seemed oddly familiar to Art, but he could not quite place where he had seen it before. Corpses of lizards with flippers and humanoid heads lay bloody and splattered beneath dusty rocks across nearly every inch of ground. But all realities seem to run together given enough time and lack of interest, so Art shrugged and thought no more of it.

"Gather around Me, all ye Arts and all Ginnys," called the singsong voice of the pink bear.

Officer-Ginny typed new orders to the scarab, and it silently flew into the air to give a bird's eye view of the scene. Officer-Ginny gasped, this time more loudly than she had when she realized that the pink bear had reformed and was on the loose again. Pink-eyed Arts and Ginnys stretched unto the horizon, thousands upon thousands upon thousands of them, at least a hundred times more than the B.I.T. had battled back on Earth 616,000.

From below, the pink bear called to its army, "Arts and Ginnys, the time be here. Me take you to destroy and destruct Me's single greatest threat. Me am going to take you to attack Earth 55,777, headquarters of the B.I.T. And then they no bother Me ever again! Teeheehee!"

Officer-Ginny squealed in distress. She pressed a button, and a message flashed across the screen that read: *Dialing Agent 27142. Status urgent.*

Agent 90909's half-goateed elven face appeared, filling the video screen. "Yes?" demanded the agent.

"I need to speak with Agent 27142 immediately. This is of dire importance!"

"Very well," responded Agent 90909. The video screen faded to gray for a few moments while Agent 29333 was put on hold, and then after what seemed entirely too long, it sprang back to life and filled with Officer-Art's face.

Officer-Ginny practically screamed, "Agent 27142, you *must* return to headquarters at once. I have found the remainder of the pink beast's army, and it is worse than we could have imagined!"

Officer-Art's scowl filled the entire screen. He barked, "Don't you dare deign to tell me what I *must* do. I am *your* commander!"

"I-I apologize, sir," replied Officer-Ginny. "But please return, and please bring every available force you can muster."

Officer-Art stood silent for a moment. Finally, he nodded a curt nod. "Set course for headquarters," he ordered his crew.

Officer-Ginny pressed a button to end the transmission. Before Normal-Art had the chance to say anything, she squealed, "Don't even open your mouth. I have too much on my plate right now to be distracted by you."

The servants chose that time to appear with lunch. Normal-Art leaned over and began sucking at his straw, deciding after he finished that he wished he had more on his plate—or in his cup, as it were.

*

Officer-Art walked at a brisk pace, brisk enough that Normal-Art and Officer-Ginny had to trot to keep up. With each step, Officer-Art's heels clicked and the eagle on his shoulder bobbed, and when the trio approached the elevator, his shoes squeaked as he halted. Over and over, he jabbed his finger on the *up* button.

A soft ding signaled that an elevator car had arrived, and when it opened, Normal-Art saw that it was already packed. Officer-Art pointed at three subordinates near the front of the elevator and said, "You, you, and you. Out."

They obeyed, and Normal-Art found himself crammed into the lift with Officers Art and Ginny. The bureaucrat nearest the buttons asked which floor. "The Forge," responded Officer-Art. Everyone else on the lift seemed to stifle a gasp or to stand in awed silence.

The door shut, and as it did so, Normal-Art found that the elevator car was so packed that he had no choice but to lean in close to Officer-Art. He tried to hold his breath so that he would not accidentally exhale on the fascist's face, an action that would invite a night of torture and maiming. But after a few seconds, he could hold his breath no longer, and he breathed slowly out of the right side of his mouth, away from Officer-Art. A woman squealed, and Normal-Art glanced over to realize that he had just breathed directly in this stranger's face. He muttered an apology, but then when he could not hold his breath any longer, he did it again.

Eventually, the elevator ascended to the penthouse floor—on the one-hundred and twentieth floor, just below the roof—at which point the only beings still inside were the trio and the officers' two eagles.

The elevator door opened. Acrid smoke filled the elevator car, and Normal-Art found himself coughing uncontrollably. Officer-Art grabbed him by the arm and yanked him out of the elevator car. Stepping out of its confines, it seemed as though they passed into a completely new reality, for what stretched out before them seemed larger than what could be contained on the top floor of an office building.

Before them loomed an archway that led into a dark cavern within which fiery lights danced. The archway was decorated in beaten and sculpted bronze, and as Normal-Art stared at the metal, he found himself hypnotized by the imagery on it, which seemed to come alive as he studied it. At the base of the left side of the arch, farmers planted seeds and fertilized them with dung tossed from the backs of carts. A panel just above this showed rain falling and crops growing. Art craned his neck at the next panel up, and witnessed happy farmers hauling in the harvest. At the crest above the threshold, marauders invaded and murdered the farmers while the farmers were gathered for a feast. In the top right panel, the farmers decomposed, and grass grew from their bodies. In the following panel, oxen ate from the grass and dropped their dung upon the ground, while the marauders—who now owned this land—collected the dung. Finally, the last panel on the bottom right depicted the marauders planting crops and fertilizing it with dung tossed from the backs of carts.

Normal-Art was so entranced that when Officer-Art shoved him in the back to move him along, he felt like he had just awoken from a dream. A long hallway lay before him, and with each passing step, the air grew thicker, smokier, and hotter. Beads of sweat formed upon Art's forehead and trickled down his face. Finally, the trio and the pair of birds emerged from the hallway and into a monstrous forge.

A cottage-sized bellows sat on a stand near a great flame, and a robotic cyclops continuously pumped the bellows up and down, keeping a slow and steady pace. Meanwhile, weapons and armor lined every square inch of this place, from swords to war hammers to knightly armor to panzer tanks. The biggest commonality between each weapon was that none was merely a tool for murder. Much like the arch that marked the entrance to this area, each weapon displayed imagery or a story of some sort beautifully hammered into its exterior.

In the middle of the room, the High Commander hammered upon a piece of metal shaped like the Scatter Guns that the B.I.T. had used to disintegrate the blue and pink armies on Earth 616,000. Sparks flew in all directions with each successive stroke. Even bent over at his work, the High Commander was nearly twelve-feet tall. His shaggy gray beard was bound in leathern bands and tossed over his shoulder so that it would not get in his way. Soot covered his face in dark black patches.

Officer-Art stepped forward without hesitation. He exclaimed, "Chairete, High Commander!"

The High Commander glanced up from his work, obviously annoyed at the distraction. He replied, "Agents 27142 and 29333. This is a surprise. What brings thee to my forge?"

"We're under emergency protocols, sir, and I thought you should hear the reason from me," said Officer-Art.

"Aye. So, *why* are we under emergency protocols?"

"Sir, it turns out that your new weaponry did not *quite* permanently relieve us of the cosmic-bear-problem. They have reconstituted themselves somehow."

The High Commander pursed his lips. "Damn," he muttered. "I assume this means that they will also be reforming their invasion cults. Didst thou prepare a new assault team to intercept them? If thou art seeking an even newer piece of gadgetry to give thee an advantage in this battle, I have yet to develop one, as I was unaware of the need. Thou shalt need to give me a few days to invent something."

Officer-Art shook his head. "No, sir, we did not prepare a new assault team."

The High Commander peered at Officer-Art through squinted eyes. "And why is that? Hast thou lost thy nerve for thy job?"

Officer-Art removed his checkered hat and tucked it under his arm. He replied, "No, sir. Nothing of the sort. As you no doubt recall from my progress updates to you, I sent a batch of your cybernetic scarab beetles to track the traces of teleportation residue from the cosmic entities in order to locate and eradicate the remnants of their armies.

Officer-Art continued, "However, when the beetles tracking the pink bear's residue overtook their target, we discovered that the pink bear had reformed itself and has now raised a new army orders of magnitude larger than the one we vanquished. It and this army are on their way *here* to Earth 55,777."

The High Commander frowned. "That *is* dire news. Any updates on the blue bear?"

Officer-Art looked down at his feet. "Not as of yet, sir. We chose to alert you of the pink invasion force rather than waiting upon confirmation of the blue bear's location."

The High Commander nodded. "Well, these types of paired cosmic beings always think alike, even if they represent opposite ends of a symbolic spectrum. I would wager nearly everything in the Multiverse that the blue bear will have *also* raised a new army and will soon be on its way here, too.

The High Commander continued, "Call in all available forces and activate *Olympus*'s shield. I have upgraded the shield's amplification conduits so that if anyone touches it, they shall suffer consequences identical to those of a Scatter Gun. Keep thy fleet outside the shield's limits and eradicate the invaders as best thee can. Whatever thou doest, thou must protect this building to buy me time. I will work as quickly as I can to invent new weaponry that will remove this threat in a more permanent fashion."

Officer-Art nodded. "As you command," he said.

The High Commander stroked his beard. He seemed to notice Normal-Art for the first time. He pointed at Art. The High Commander demanded, "What is *that*?"

Normal-Art shrugged. He replied, "I'm not a *what*. I'm a *who*."

The High Commander limped over to Normal-Art and towered over him. He bellowed, "I know *who* thou art. Thou art another version of Agent 27142, and thou art the scoundrel that unleashed the cosmic bears upon the Multiverse. My question was: what is *that*?"

The High Commander reached down and grabbed the piece of onyx dangling around Normal-Art's neck. Normal-Art glanced down and said, "Oh, *that's* my necklace. Made from a piece of the sword I found on the caper that dragged me into this mess."

The High Commander glowered. He replied, "It was a black onyx saber implanted with millions of microscopic runes. It was not just *any* sword."

Normal-Art looked into the High Commander's eyes and stammered, "I-I-I never noticed any runes."

"They're there, and thou wouldst see them if thou were to look hard enough. I should know. I created the saber."

Normal-Art stood in silence. The High Commander continued to tower over him. Normal-Art looked left and right over his shoulders, and Officers Art and Ginny stared at him and nodded their heads at him slightly, obviously signaling to him that he needed to respond. So, he responded by gasping the loudest gasp he could muster, since shock and/or awe seemed to be what was expected of him at the High Commander's reveal.

The gasp sounded incredibly fake to Normal-Art, but it must have done the trick, for the High Commander continued, "Thou may not recognize me by my title of High Commander, but thou mightst know me by another name: Hephaestus."

Normal-Art stifled a groan. God damn if he didn't hate gods and their arrogant grandstanding about their names and deeds. He made no sound. However, Officers Art and Ginny nudged him into a response. So, he gasped once more, since it again seemed to be the response expected of him.

"Of course, I am not the Hephaestus of *thy* reality. Thou hast all the markings of a backwater Earth that still has yet to discover interdimensional travel. *I* originated on Earth 24."

Hephaestus raised the piece of onyx to his face and stared intently at it. He continued, "This artifact is so many ages old that I had nearly forgotten it, and I certainly will not remember how to recreate the spells woven into it without time to study it. This artifact saps cosmic power and transforms it into solid nothingness, which is then imprisoned within a magical core housed inside the blade. I used this artifact to bind those pink and blue cosmic entities to Earth 1,000,000 eons upon eons upon eons ago, back when they were in the form of facial tissues rather than bears.

Hephaestus tapped the small piece of onyx with his forefinger and continued, "Hmmm. I think this little chunk of saber shall be the key to our survival. I shall use it to forge a new saber, and I shall also forge a new Reality Lantern to contain it. And then, once we have these cosmic beasts safely impaled on the new saber and imprisoned within the new Reality Lantern, we shall locate a backwater reality that is cut off from interdimensional travel, and we shall store them there."

"B-B-But I need that piece of s-s-sword to keep myself safe from the god-version of m—" Normal-Art began to stammer in response, but Hephaestus glared an annoyed glare, and Normal-Art shut his mouth. Officer-Art smacked Normal-Art upside the head for good measure.

Hephaestus then addressed Officers Art and Ginny, "It may be fortuitous that the cosmic bears are on their way here. It shall save us the effort of hunting them across the Multiverse to bind them with the reforged saber that I shall create. But I need time at my forge. Thou *must* keep this building safe until my work is complete, or all hope is lost."

Officer-Art nodded. "We shall do so, or we shall die trying. Chairete, High Commander."

And with that, Officers Art and Ginny clicked his heels together, saluted, and spun to face the way the group had entered. Officer-Art grabbed Normal-Art by the arm and dragged him back toward the elevator.

Though a new hope had just arisen for the B.I.T. home reality, a sense of dread filled the pit of Normal-Art's stomach.

CHAPTER 11

A PINK INVASION

AS WITH EVERY invasion, Regular-Ginny was the first to emerge from the barrier between realities. For this incursion, she found herself ejected from a black bubble high above Earth 55,777. As she glanced about, she noticed that darkness blanketed the sky, a cloudless and moonless night lit only by the skyscrapers—each at least sixty stories tall—that stretched in a perfect grid unto the horizon, each with different colored neon signage on its top that announced the building's name. Ginny noticed signs for a *Fairy Mound,* a *Kilimanjaro,* a *Zion,* a *Barrows,* and a *Great Pyramid* before she grew bored of reading the names and turned her attention elsewhere.

The air up here smelled fresh, a light crispness that reminded Ginny of her favorite season, Autumn. She had invaded enough Earths by now to have conquered at least a few dozen planet-sized cities similar to the one below, so she knew that down there in the crowded streets between the skyscrapers, this fresh crispness would be overpowered by heat and humidity and dirt. She sighed.

She plummeted toward the city like a pastel comet. She closed her eye and concentrated. She felt every pore on her skin tingle. She smirked as the pink blob expanded from her skin. It grew around her to a height of fifty stories.

As her fall brought her within reach of the skyscrapers, she grew a gigantic tentacle from the outside of the blob and stretched it toward the nearest building, grabbing the antenna that extended a hundred feet straight up from its top. The introduction of her mass at this speed ripped the antenna from its restraints. Ginny felt the antenna give, and like a monkey swinging from branch to branch, she released this antenna and flipped toward the antenna atop the building on the opposite side of the street. As she gripped this second antenna with the tip of her tentacle, she swung in a wide circle around it before letting go.

Her pink membrane formed more tentacles that she extended out in front of her, breaking her fall on the building's rough asphalt roof and caving in much of the top stories of the building. The antenna from which she had initially swung atop the building across the street tumbled from its skyscraper, falling end over end down toward the street far below, so far that Ginny barely heard the carnage when it finally crashed to the ground.

All about her to the north and west, black bubbles appeared in the sky and pink puppets dropped to the surrounding rooftops like humanoid rain, crashing to a stop and then immediately bouncing back onto their already-dead feet. They scrambled inside these buildings from rooftop entrances and began fanning the flames of chaos and destruction.

Regular-Ginny glanced across the street to the building from which she had knocked loose the antenna. She noticed a group of people pressed against the glass windows of the top floor, staring at her in horror and confusion. Cubicles covered every spare inch of visible office space behind them. A pink cocoon gripped her heart and injected it with hatred. She grunted and smashed a trio of monstrous tentacles into the skyscraper. Its steel girders screamed in response. And then they gave. The building toppled sideways in an eastwardly direction and crashed into the next skyscraper over, creating a domino effect where the next five buildings also toppled one after another as each fell into the subsequent one.

Regular-Ginny watched dust and debris launch into the air as the buildings toppled, clouding the already dark night sky with even more darkness. Regular-Ginny ignored the dust and stared out at the city with a numbed look upon her face. She had been ordered to spearhead an attack southeast of her current position, her target the B.I.T. headquarters—a skyscraper named *Olympus* that towered fifty stories above all others in the endless cityscape. The Pink One had granted her this boon for her loyalty, though Ginny had not asked for said boon and cared not who was responsible for the task so long as it wasn't Arthur the Putrid, simply because if it were him, she would have to listen to his gloating for the rest of eternity.

Ginny spotted the building marked *Olympus* in the distance and glanced from it to the sky above it. One of the fearsome B.I.T. battleships hovered high in the sky just south of the building. It was the size of an aircraft carrier from Ginny's home reality, and it floated dark and black against the empty night sky. Pink stirred in her heart, and she decided that upon ripping *Olympus* from its foundations, she would swing the cursed building at that ship like a baseball bat and see if she could hit some sort of interdimensional homerun.

Movement from her peripheral caught her eye, and when she turned to look, she realized it had originated from Arthur the Putrid. She sighed in annoyance, for he was no doubt lingering near her so that he might join in demolishing the B.I.T. headquarters with her to steal a large chunk of the credit. If the Pink One were not so fond of his usefulness, Ginny would crush him between her tentacles and feed his corpse to some of the more carnivorous members of the Pink Marauders.

He floated before the other forty-three members of his flying Death Cavalry. He waited for Ginny to speak.

Regular-Ginny stood her blob to its full height atop the skyscraper and wrapped her tentacles around the building's antenna, looking like King Kong atop the Empire State Building—if only King Kong were reimagined as some sort of horrid, nightmarish blob with the tendency to get lost in thought and stare voyeuristically for long periods of time at people it hated. As she glowered at this particular person whom she hated and his lacklusterly-named-but-highly-lethal squadron, she found herself admiring the shining pink jewels in his eyepatch and how they reflected sometimes the glowing green light from his hands and other times the oranges and reds and blues of nearby explosions. She decided that when he was eventually no longer useful to the Pink One, she would murder him and take the eyepatch for herself.

Before she wasted too much time glaring at this cursed Art, a titanic bubble of solid lightning appeared in her peripheral, emanating from atop the building marked *Olympus*. She looked over at it. From this vantage, the bubble's crackling energy distorted and discolored the thirty-story tall, red neon sign that spelled out *Olympus*. Faster than Ginny could fathom, the bubble expanded to encompass a good hundred square blocks of the city, its electric edges halting their expansion on the street just three blocks southeast of her.

A noise that sounded like a cracking tortoise shell erupted near Regular-Ginny, and she frowned. She glanced at the source and saw that Arthur the Putrid had contorted his hands so that the joints on every finger poked in different directions. Then he shouted something she did not quite comprehend. Suddenly, five members of Arthur the Putrid's Death Cavalry disobeyed the Pink One's direct orders to not surpass Regular-Ginny's position as leader of the vanguard on the southeastern point of the pink army. The five flying Arts and Ginnys—one member of this group being the thunder-god-version of Art—flew directly at the lightning-bubble. They crashed into it headfirst at full speed, obviously attempting to use their brute force to blow through it. Unfortunately for them, they disintegrated completely, and with them the god of thunder's hammer, a weapon that was supposed to be indestructible and that bent lightning to its controller's whims.

Ginny cursed. "Arthur the Putrid, you fool! You wasted our stronges—"

She was interrupted by a booming crack of thunder originating from near *Olympus*. A bolt of lightning flashed from the floating aircraft carrier that hovered near *Olympus*. The lightning crashed into the antenna that rose from the top of the building and blasted back up into the sky in the expanse of blackness between Regular-Ginny and *Olympus*. The lightning took shape, and soon Ginny found herself staring at a hologram-version of Art that stood at least sixty-stories in the sky above the city. This hologram-version of Art wore a uniform similar to the types that she had seen British police officers wear in movies, complete with a checkered hat, a B.I.T. badge on the chest, and a holster carrying a wide array of objects that looked sterile and foreign. A grand eagle with a pair of drooping antennae sat perched on this Art's shoulder. The hologram stood at attention and would have made a terrifying visage had the lightning-hologram-version of the man's eagle not chosen that exact time to shit a ball of hologram-lightning that splashed atop the hologram-Art's shoulder. He ignored it. Ginny guffawed. The Pink One appeared and floated into view near Ginny, her face contorted in anger and rage. But Ginny ignored the beast and continued guffawing.

She stopped guffawing when this Art's voice boomed loud and godlike across the vast expanse of the city. The hologram-version of Art said, "This is Bureau of Interdimensional Travel Agent 27142. You have encroached on our reality. You are more foolish than you look if you thought we would not be ready for you. You are not the first cosmic threat to think it a novel idea to attack us in our home dimension, nor shall you be the last.

"As I'm sure you have experienced by now," he continued, "you shall find yourselves unable to bring your incursion bubbles within our shields, for one of their functionalities is to cease all interdimensional travel within their confines. So, bring your worst, and enjoy breaking yourselves against our defenses."

The hologram-Art then reached his arm to the side. The hologram moved in a motion like he was pressing something. "Captains, you may commence your attacks," his voice ordered as the image of him disappeared.

Regular-Ginny blinked. When she opened her eye, her vision shifted, transforming from regular reality to that of a Claymation scene. She watched with a frown as the Pink One balled her fists and roared. Inside the Claymation version of the lightning-shield, little black teleportation bubbles appeared, but each had a gigantic red X embedded through it. Regular-Ginny blinked once more, and her vision returned to normal. She glanced over at the Pink One and nodded in understanding: the hologram-Art was not lying. Something about the lightning-shield prevented the Pink One from teleporting within it or creating her black bubbles within its confines.

Regular-Ginny then felt a furious tickle in the back of her brain. Pink flooded through her veins like an overwhelming tsunami. The tickle ordered her to attack the shield with every ounce of fury within her, to bring it down in a cascade of pink blob or die in the attempt. She gulped hard and refused to give in to the Pink One's wrathful, shortsighted frustration at the lightning-shield. Instead of launching herself at the shield bodily like those flying fools in Arthur the Putrid's Death Cavalry had just done, she instead launched a dozen balls of spiked pink ooze from her blob. They crashed into the shield wall and immediately disintegrated. She gulped, thankful for her own prudence. The tickle grew stronger, demanding that she assault the shield anyway, but she fought the feeling. To distract herself, she bit her lower lip so hard that she drew blood.

Behind her, three-dozen thunderclaps sounded out across the sky, and when she turned to see what the commotion was all about, three-dozen flying ships nearly identical to the one that floated over *Olympus* filled the sky, and thousands of fighter jets poured forth from them like ants from a mound freshly kicked over. Ginny groaned in apprehension. The Pink One screamed in fury.

Ginny groaned again. She and the Pink Marauders had fallen into a trap. They would no doubt be blasted from existence while pinned between two equally deadly forces: a metaphorical hammer that shot deadly disintegration lightning at them, and a metaphorical anvil that was a shield seemingly made from the same wipe-you-from-existence lightning.

Ginny turned back toward the shield, looking around for anything that might turn the tide for herself and her army. She ignored the Pink One's hateful screaming inside her skull. Out of the corner of her eye, she noticed the Pink

One launch herself toward the incoming B.I.T. carriers that loomed in the sky. She hoped that the Pink One being distracted would mean her stupid godly demands would stop ringing out directly inside Ginny's brain. But she did not allow these hopes to raise too high, for hope had never helped her in the past. She instead stared past the shield to the portion of the city inside it, hoping to find a weakness.

She used her pink blob to grow tentacle-stilts that took her high, high, high into the sky so that she could look down into the shield from a better vantagepoint. And that's when she saw it, dozens of blocks southeast, near *Olympus* and deep within the confines of the shield. There sat a power plant that covered a good five square miles of city. It looked exactly like Central Park if Central Park were about five times bigger and also a vast tangled forest of metal and concrete.

That must be supplying power to this part of the city, she thought. *And if I'm wrong, it's not like we've got much to lose.*

Regular-Ginny glanced at Arthur the Putrid. He was *just* beginning to fly toward the airships to fight at the heels of the Pink One. She screamed his name, but he did not respond. So, she launched a tentacle toward him and snagged his ankle with it. He turned toward her in fury, moved his hands in a circular motion, and formed a green ball of light that hovered in front of his torso. He launched it at her.

She knocked it aside with a tentacle, and it caromed away and crashed into a nearby skyscraper, leaving a gigantic smoking hole in its wake.

"Stop that!" she screamed. "Listen to me!"

She dragged him over to her vantagepoint high in the sky. Then she pointed down to the field of generators, visible within the hazy confines of the shield. She said, "That's *got* to be supplying a huge amount of power to this part of the city. I bet if we destroy it, it will knock out power to the *Olympus* building, and the shield will come down."

Arthur the Putrid frowned for a moment, but then he nodded. He replied, "You're both smarter *and* stupider than you look. You likely *are* right. It likely *is* supplying the power to this shield. But it's also *inside* the shield. How are we going to get to it? We can't use the Pink One to jump inside."

Ginny stuck her tongue out the side of her mouth and bit down upon it. She scanned the streets and in moments had her answer. She pointed down at a nearly blind version of Art who wore the thickest coke-bottle glasses she had ever seen. This one they had murdered and recruited from within his home in the core of his reality's Earth. He was the king of his underground people, and he sat mounted on his reality's version of Ginny, who was a colossal mole that stood twenty-stories tall with forepaws that had been amputated and augmented into shovels the size of bulldozers.

"You will dig!" she screamed to Arthur the Putrid, deciding in that moment that *he* would attack the generators while *she* helped the Pink One fight the doom looming in the sky overhead. She would return to assault *Olympus* as soon as the shield fell. "Find all the diggers you can. Order them to dig below the shield. Then emerge from underground and destroy those generators."

Arthur the Putrid frowned. Then he shook his head. "I think not. *You* dig. I shall go win glory up in the sky, in the sight of my pink god."

Regular-Ginny sighed in frustration. *One* of them needed to lead the attack on the generators. She knew that it must be him, for she was exponentially stronger and would be more help than him up in the air in the fight against the B.I.T. fleet.

She began shaking Arthur the Putrid with more fury that she had ever shaken anything. "No, *you* shall obey me!" she screamed, her voice cracking and squealing. "*I* am the Pink One's Right Hand of Destruction. *You* are my underling! You shall obey me, or you shall die."

He tried shooting her with more magic, but she simply smashed him against nearby buildings until he acquiesced. She then dropped him, and he and his Death Cavalry flew to the ground below to gather diggers and begin the underground assault.

Meanwhile, she turned toward the incoming fleet. The Pink One's rage at the lightning-shield seemed to be fading, its focus shifting toward the ships. With this shift in focus, Ginny's overwhelming desire to throw herself against the lightning-shield to try and break it also faded. She felt pink hatred flow through her veins and draw her fury skyward. She breathed a deep breath and made ready to wreak havoc upon the B.I.T. fleet.

CHAPTER 12

AN UNSURPRISING TWIST

NORMAL-ART WISHED HIS hands were free of their plaster prisons so that he might scratch himself. The gray constraints of the crash harness that crisscrossed his body and bound him to the equally gray chair dug into the flesh of his shoulders and neck, and even after all this time at the mercy of these bindings, the chafing was as bad as ever. Long ago, he clung to the hope of eventual calluses providing relief, but now he no longer hoped for anything, for he knew that the Multiverse was an awful bitch and had for some reason destined him to be the single Art whose life was naught but one calamity after another.

Normal-Art tried his best to ignore his misery by staring at his counterpart's back. Officer-Art's checkered hat dug into his oiled hair so that it puffed out just below the band. Normal-Art had learned the hard way not to encourage the man to switch to a larger hat, as it was a guaranteed ticket to a beating. But a bigger hat *would* go a long way toward reducing the ugly rings and hat hair when his interdimensional twin removed the thing. Normal-Art shrugged, his unconscious cue for breaking himself off from such inane, wandering thoughts.

Like a fascist eclipse blocking the sun, Officer-Art's bulk blocked much of the screen from Normal-Art's view, so Normal-Art had to stretch his neck to one side as best he could to glimpse what was happening in the view screen.

Outside, skyscrapers and city filled the vast expanse of the ground below. Normal-Art had seen the place in the daytime when an invading army was not threatening to smash it to pieces, so he knew that the city stretched for thousands of miles, covering this entire planet in one gigantic urban sprawl broken only by the occasional city park. Normal-Art also knew that this Earth represented the economic and cultural center of the Multiverse, for it was where all realities converge for the sake of bureaucracy, and the wealth from taxation and administrative fees that have accumulated here over the millennia have allowed the city to continually expand and grow[7].

Early in his captivity, when Normal-Art had once asked to be let out for a walk, he learned that members of any societal caste higher than the absolute destitute avoid the bottom few floors of any building. Many in this reality have thus spent their entire lives never leaving the confines of the skyscrapers—except, of course, to jump to another reality, which is quite common—and have never set foot on the ground. Many of the upper class from this Earth—Officer-Art included—bragged of the number of generations that separated them from having set foot on the barren streets far below. Thus, though long-forgotten generations had broken the sprawling cityscape with parks and greenery, you would never dare enter them unless you wanted to be mauled and probably murdered by the desperate citizens on the bottom of the social hierarchy.

Travel between buildings occurs through a spiderwebbed network of bridges connecting the upper floors of the skyscrapers together or via the dirigible-busses that travel from building to building during peacetime. Upon news of the incursion forces approaching, Officer-Art had ordered public transport on these steampunk-style fares halted until the cosmic threat was deterred. With the speed of those having much practice in preparing for cosmic threats, these dirigible-busses had cleared out long before the pink army had arrived.

Normal-Art imagined that none of the inane social norms of this Earth mattered to the population just now, for the members of every caste must be clinging to desperate hope that the B.I.T. Navy would keep them safe. Normal-Art further imagined that all eyes across the horizon were intensely watching the lightning-hologram of Officer-Art standing sixty stories high in the sky, its booming voice ringing out across the horizon. Normal-Art found it oddly entertaining to watch Officer-Art perform a gesture or speak, and then seconds later watch the lightning-hologram version that encompassed most of the view on the screen in the bridge repeat the movement or words.

---

7 Though now, because the entire expanse of the planet is covered in city, the buildings grow up rather than out, with new floors being added as needed to already-completed buildings to make them taller. The one caveat to this growth is that *Olympus* must always stand higher than all other buildings, so it is always under construction and growing. And because *The Forge* must always occupy the *Olympus* building's top floor, when height is added to *Olympus*, *The Forge* is raised into the air via one of the High Commander's inventions, and floors are added below it.

Officer-Art's voice cut through the cluttered wanderings of Normal-Art's brain. His alternate-self announced, "As I'm sure you have experienced by now, you shall find yourselves unable to bring your incursion bubbles within our shields, for one of their functionalities is to cease all interdimensional travel within their confines. So, bring your worst, and enjoy breaking yourselves against our defenses."

Seconds later, Art watched the back of the hologram's head move as it spoke. The echo of its voice sounded out across the sky. Normal-Art found himself glancing down at the hologram's posterior, and he inanely noted to himself that he should get a pair of these uniform pants if it would make his butt look like *that.*

Officer-Art then clicked his heels together—again, the nervous tick that had grown so annoying that Normal-Art would have torn out his hair had his hands not been encased in plaster and rendered useless—and reached his right arm to the side to press a button on the control panel of his captain's chair. He said, "Captains, you may commence your attacks."

Officer-Art then pressed a different button, and the hologram version of himself winked out of existence, its afterimage remaining purple in the sky for a few seconds before disappearing completely. Officer-Art turned on his heels so that he might face his subordinates on the bridge. In the view screen behind the officer, Normal-Art could see dozens of lightning bolts as airships identical to the B.S.S.C. Mimessiah in all but history and name flashed into place on this reality.

The view screen behind Officer-Art morphed so that new viewpoints flashed to life around the borders of the screen, these the perspectives from the bridges of the incoming B.I.T. fleet, which Normal-Art surmised because each screen had text on its bottom left that declared *"B.S.S.C."* followed by the ship's name.

"Launch fighter squadrons Alpha, Pi, Nine, and Twenty-Two, and instruct them to enter dogfight mode. The rest shall remain in reserve," ordered Officer-Art to no one in particular. However, the half-goateed humanoid leaned down over its console and repeated the order into a microphone. Normal-Art glanced past Officer-Art to watch the view screen as the fighters zoomed ahead into the night sky.

Officer-Ginny then chimed in. "Sir, the beetles following the remnants of the blue bear's army have found something. Shall I display it on screen?"

Officer-Art nodded his assent. Normal-Art listened as Officer-Ginny's fingers clacked across a keyboard on her console. The view screen then shifted, and grainy footage filled the screen.

Officer-Art and Officer-Ginny gasped. Thousands upon thousands of Arts and Ginnys—even more than those filling the ranks of the pink bear's army—filled the vast expanse of a dusty canyon, all encircling the reconstituted blue bear, which floated majestically above the crowd. It raised its arms and squealed, "Then it is time to attack!"

The voices and roars and squeals and screeches of the hordes of Arts and Ginnys reverberated through the canyon. The blue bear launched thousands of white bubbles from its hands. Normal-Art stifled a smile as he spotted Drillbot in the crowd. He silently wished the best for the robot and hoped that the thing would escape being wiped from existence by the B.I.T.'s Scatter Guns.

Soon, all the white bubbles disappeared from the grainy footage, along with all the Arts and Ginnys. As the view screen returned to the scene outside on Earth 55,777, Officer-Art said, "Let us hope that we have some time before they arrive so that we might hobble the pink army. Let me know when the blue bastard makes Earthfa—"

Officer-Ginny interrupted, "Sir, sorry to interrupt you when you're ordering me to alert you when the blue bear's army is making Earthfall. But, sir, the blue bear's army is making Earthfall now."

Officer-Art groaned in annoyance. This annoyance seemed directed at both Officer-Ginny's interruption *and* the white bubbles that began appearing across the horizon, some amongst the floating B.I.T. warships and some amongst the pink hordes.

Normal-Art considered allowing nervousness or regret or longing for his couch to fill his heart, but since he could do nothing about anything from his position, he merely shrugged and resigned himself to once more watching a battle in numbed silence.

CHAPTER 13

WHEN A 'BOT LOVES A DINO, CAN'T KEEP HIS ONES AND ZEROES ON NOTHIN' ELSE

DRILLBOT'S POWER CORE had never felt so full. It felt as though some invisible programmer had rewritten his source code.

It overflowed with ones and zeroes so that if you laid them end to end, they would spell out in binary unto infinity, *"Drillbot is in love! Drillbot is in love!"* Drillbot thought back to that terrible day when he had contemplated suicide on Earth 1,000,000, and he felt foolish. Every day and every moment of tedium and carnage from then to now was worth it just to feel *this* feeling. To enjoy such an emotion in the middle of an endless war was something to which he knew he must cling for as long as it would last.

The feeling had been planted in his systems during his first meeting with Ginny Rex. It germinated on their first jump together. Ginny Rex had smiled at him as they recruited the Art who lived on an Earth where the inhabitants carry their pets in small round magical balls and force them to battle for fun. Then it grew into periodic stolen glances as they tumbled between realities. And as Drillbot continued traversing the vast reaches of the Multiverse with Ginny Rex, it blossomed into so much more.

On Earth 22,456, after the Blue One resurrected the Earth, Drillbot picked exotic flowers for her. She accepted them with delight, hugging him with her tiny arms and gently rubbing the side of his round face with one of her paws. As he pinned one of the flowers to her leather jacket, the electric shock that flushed through his system signaled to him that this was truly something special. On Earth 45,999, she brought him a fresh kill and offered first blood to him. He shoved his drills into it and pretended to thrill at the blood that spattered across his hull. When she could not reach her hands together to clap in excitement, Artkylosaurus did so by proxy. On Earth 34,111, where they recruited versions of Art and Ginny who were magical sentient sandwiches that fought with peanut butter and jelly spells, Drillbot took Ginny Rex on a picnic, and she kissed him for the first time. It was but a quick lick across the grill that covered his speaker, but he thrilled at it, knowing that he would treasure the memory for the remainder of his existence.

And now, every time the Army of Life jumped to a new reality, the pair would kiss and then perform their duties. When their duties ended and Ginny Rex needed to sleep at the end of a long day, she would lie down on her side and Drillbot would wedge himself under her tiny arms, allowing himself to be spooned. She normally let nobody other than Artkylosaurus touch her hair, but in these precious moments, he would reach up a drill and stroke her blond mullet, while reaching his other drill in the opposite direction to rub her soft underbelly. Often they would make love, though this act mostly involved Ginny Rex licking his impervious hide while he used his drills to pleasure her, for he had no reproductive organs to speak of with which to make love. Afterward, Ginny Rex would breathe her hot breath against his back and fall asleep, and because Drillbot did not need to sleep, he would simply lie there thanking every robot deity he could fathom for these moments, wishing they would never end. Artkylosaurus would cover them with a blanket and retire to his nearby bedroll. And then, always long before Drillbot was ready, Ginny Rex's appointed rest time would end, and it would be time for them to return to their duties.

This morning was one such morning. The last weeks and Earths had passed by in such a wondrous blur that Drillbot knew not which reality the army inhabited at this point. The blue bear called to his recruits, and they gathered in a dusty canyon. The blue bear floated above the center the massed army of Arts and Ginnys. Drillbot and Ginny Rex stood near the bear. Drillbot held his right arm up above him, its point gripped softly in the tiny left paw of Ginny Rex as they listened to the Blue One's instructions.

"Me be gathering you here because it now be time for Me and you all to stop swelling Me ranks and to make a stand," said the blue bear. It smiled at Drillbot. Though it had not commented on his relationship with Ginny Rex, Drillbot knew that the bear would have put an end to it if the cosmic being disapproved. Drillbot thanked his robot gods for that piece of good fortune.

The blue bear continued, "Me have foreseen great destruction. And Me knows it be dire. Me have scanned the Multiverse and Me have seen the Pink One. The Pink One be attacking B.I.T. at B.I.T. home reality very, very, very soon. This be our chance to intervene, to stop the Pink One from destruction, to heal all, and to destroy the B.I.T. zappy-thingies that send you all into unhealy killings."

The blue bear pointed at Drillbot and then beckoned the robot to his side. Drillbot reluctantly broke away from Ginny Rex's grip. He rolled forward, his wheels crunching across the dry, gravelly ground. He glanced at the surrounding crowd. Thousands upon thousands of Arts and Ginnys filled the horizon, and though all their eyes were upon him, the only eyes he felt were those of the Tyrannosaurus Rex in the front row. The Blue One patted his head and continued, "Drillbot as always be Me trusted right hand. Drillbot be your general, Drillbot be your leader, and you be listening to Drillbot on the battlefield, for as always, Me be delegating to him Me will. Me will be sending him along to each of your squadron leaders momentarily, and he will give you further instructions. For now, go rest and contemplate and meditate, for we shall soon embark on this journey of battle, and most of you will be killed and brought back as the Pink One's puppet, or killed by B.I.T. in a forever way with no healies, or maybe even you will experience both. So, make peace with self and your gods now, and know that Life be forever thankful for your sacrifice, and the realities you save also be thankful for your sacrifice. Dismissed."

And with that, the army scattered to their blue tents. Drillbot remained at the blue bear's feet to receive the instructions he was to disseminate to the many squadron leaders.

Instead of beginning the instructions to Drillbot, the Blue One pointed at the Arachnid Pre-Teen and called to the boy before he could scatter to his tent, "Arturo, please come gather to Me."

Arturo glanced about warily, and then approached and stood near the blue bear's floating feet. Drillbot had grown much stronger at reading human emotions over the years, and the boy's slumped shoulders and hanging head signaled to him a sense of dread and fear, which were common emotions he noticed in many of the child-versions of Art and Ginny recruited into this war over the years.

"Yes?" asked the boy.

"Me know that you have felt lost and alone and filled with fright these past weeks. Me know this war be a shock to you, and you just want to go home and be *you* again."

Arturo looked down at his feet and nodded.

The blue bear cupped the boy's chin with a paw and raised the boy's head to make eye contact. The Blue One said, "Arturo be most important piece in Me army. Me no tell you *that* before, but Me have scanned Arturo's brain and Me have scanned the webbing and bindings of the Multiverse, and from the moment you jumped from the bushes to confront Me and Me army back on Earth 975,571, Me felt a great wave from the Multiverse that marked Me encounter with you as a momentous occasion."

"O-Okay," muttered the boy.

"Me thinks you be the key to stopping B.I.T.'s zappy weapons. Arturo will win the day for Army of Life. Me need Arturo to go on special mission for Me."

The boy looked into the blue bear's eyes. Then he broke eye contact and looked back down at his feet. "Why me? Why not Drillbot? He's been doing this with you the longest. He's the guy who you can count on to get the job done."

The blue bear giggled. "Because this destiny be not for Drillbot. This destiny be for Arturo. Me know of Arturo's strength and reflexes and selflessness. Me know he be capable of great things, and that the Multiverse will not allow him to fail, for Arturo be Chosen One. This be true or Me not be feeling what Me be feeling when you jumped out of bushes first time. So, Me need you to stay at *back* of battle and stay safe."

"That's it?" asked the boy. "Seems kinda lame for a special mission."

"Teeheehee!" exclaimed the blue bear. "No, no, no. That only be the first part. Arturo need to survive the beginning of battle. Me be foreseeing that the B.I.T. has great and powerful defenses that Arturo cannot surpass. But there will be a point in the battle to come where these defenses will fall, and *that* be when Arturo will be needed for his mission.

"Take this," continued the blue bear, stabbing a paw inside his own belly and grabbing onto something inside as pink blood poured out around his arm. As the blood splashed to the ground, it transformed into mystical forest creatures that scattered toward the horizon. The bear removed from his belly a small conical device with a blinking red light upon its top. One his paw was free of his belly, the wound instantly healed.

The Blue One handed the device to Arturo and said, "This be a device Me had genius-Art from Earth 6,907 design. This device creates a small thermonuclear explosion *and* a pulse of overriding binary code, and when exploded inside the Communications Vault within the B.I.T. headquarters building, it will be destroying the B.I.T. High Commander and will be recoding the B.I.T. zappy-thingies so that they no longer kill Me army permanently when they strike. Me will then heal the B.I.T.— all of them except for the B.I.T. High Commander. For Me have had a vision, and Me know that only he knows how to create the zappy-thingies and him no longer living means we be winning."

Arturo looked a little queasy. "O-Okay," he replied. "If it means saving lives, I'll do it."

The Blue One grinned. He said, "Good, good! All Arturo need to do be to stick the bomb to a terminal in B.I.T. Communications Vault, press red flashy light for ten seconds, and then run. Arturo must run fast to escape. Ten minutes be all he will have."

Arturo nodded. Drillbot patted the boy's back with the side of a drill and said, "[whir] Arturo – CLACK – Arturo – CLACK – Arturo has received a great honor with this mission and has been shown great – CLACK – great trust."

Arturo smiled. The Blue One dismissed the boy and then issued orders to Drillbot, which the robot then disseminated to the squadron commanders. And then, with nothing left to do but wait for the Blue One to signal the attack, Drillbot returned to Ginny Rex's side. She licked him across the grill, whispered sweet poems into his audio receptors, and held him. In the coming hours, Drillbot would wish he could be stuck in this moment forever.

But alas, because nothing good lasts forever in this harsh Multiverse, the Blue One soon called the army to gather around him once more. He signaled the attack.

CHAPTER 14

BATTLING ON THE SHIPS

THE AIRCRAFT-CARRIER SIZED airship had lost power thanks to Regular-Ginny's rampage across its hull, and it was beginning its plummet toward the ground far below. She wedged her tentacles deep into the gunmetal gray hull and rolled her blob backward, stretching the pink appendages taut until they were so tense that they were like a rubber band ready to snap. Regular-Ginny's mind flashed back to a similar situation a decade ago when she had used her pink powers to launch from the eye socket of a giant squirrel monster and had been snatched by a personification of Death. As she remembered nearly dying from the encounter, her heart raced in terror. However, before she could find herself lost in the memory, the Pink One appeared in her mind's eye and pummeled the parts of her brain in charge of flashbacks and fearful memories until they were naught but a bloody pulp.

Regular-Ginny then gestured in a manner that released the tension in the pink tentacles all at once. She launched forward like the payload from a slingshot toward her next target—which would be her seventh gigantic B.I.T. airship to bring down during this battle, outpacing by at least six ships every member of the Pink Marauders other than the Pink One, who had ten carrier kills of her own.

Regular-Ginny frowned when the warship she was careening toward dove sharply downward. Regular-Ginny flew over it. As she twisted herself in mid-air to face the evasive metal behemoth, the ship began firing disintegration beams at her from its many turrets. She allowed her instincts to go to work. She twisted, and her blob mimicked her movements to curl into a long, spindly line. Beams of lightning flashed harmlessly past her. She twisted further, lengthening the blob and mentally sending the order to create small holes across its membrane. She laughed inanely, as she knew she likely resembled a gigantic, twisted lump of pink swiss cheese to any onlookers. But it was enough for the next wave of turret fire to pass harmlessly through the holes in her pink blob and fly out the other side.

She fell through the air, dancing between and around disintegration bolts in a mesmerizing, graceful ballet. Before falling out of range of the floating aircraft carrier, she snaked a single thin tentacle out from her twisting blob, smashing it into the underside of the gigantic ship. She used this thin pink tether to yank herself onto the underside of the carrier. She crashed against the metal and felt the heat of explosions beneath her. Then she raced up the side of the hull—smashing a wide swath of destruction with her tentacles as her blob rolled across the ship—until she reached the long, flat expanse of metal that lay directly outside the carrier's bridge. She whipped her tentacles about in a cyclone of pink fury, demolishing all the turrets within view before they had the chance to calibrate their aim and fire upon her. The orange and red and blue hues that accompanied the explosions danced across her pink blob, creating an oddly beautiful palette within the murderous carnage.

She took a moment to grin at the captain, who pointed at her in disbelief from his chair on the bridge. She then raised a wide, flat tentacle above her in preparation to crash it down atop him and the crew who controlled the vessel.

Before she had the chance to do so, three white bubbles appeared in the air above her. A pair of rockets flew from one of the bubbles and exploded against her blob's pink membrane. A combination of surprise and high-powered detonations knocked her sideways. She rolled to the edge of the ship, digging a couple tentacles into the hull to stop herself just before falling off. As she looked over the side, she remembered the weak person she used to be back before leaving her home with Tiny-Ginny so long ago, the one who would have been terrified of such a height.

But instead of cowering in fear like her past-self would have done, she reared up and turned toward the white bubbles. "You'll have to do better than tha—" she screamed, or rather she began to scream before the cursed robot with drills in place of arms leapt from one of the bubbles and crashed into the side of her blob. She had to dodge within the blob to prevent herself from being sliced in two. As the robot exited the other side of the blob and twisted in midair to make another pass at her, a pair of ferocious dinosaurs—one riding on the other's back—crashed into her flank.

Regular-Ginny cursed as their momentum carried all four of them over the edge of the ship and into open air. She began reaching a tentacle toward the ship, intending to grab hold and shake off her three attackers so they would fall to their deaths. The robot instead severed this tentacle, and the four hurtled into the black sky together. She cursed once more and began swatting at her attackers. As she glanced down at the ground far, far below, she thought, *They've no need to worry about terminal velocity when they need instead worry about Terminal Gin-ocity.* And then she immediately rolled her single remaining eye at how lame her internal bantering was.

As she swiped tentacles at her attackers, she found each of her moves parried either by a ferocious drill or a well-placed explosion from a rocket or a slashing fang. After dozens of blocked strikes, she roared in delight when she finally scored a direct hit on the robot's head and gears exploded out behind it. Its head popped up like the losing member of one of her old games, *Rock 'Em Sock 'Em Robots.* But then the robot shook its head like a boxer regaining its bearings and immediately went back to its task of slashing at her blob.

Ginny glanced over her shoulder and realized the four of them were about a half-dozen seconds from hitting the ground, so she snaked tiny tentacles around the Tyrannosaurus Rex's ankles and the robot's wheels and then rolled, intending to put this trio of enemies between herself and the ground so that she might crush them.

The smaller dinosaur that rode on the Tyrannosaurus Rex's back, however, laughed maniacally. Once more, it fired the rocket launchers mounted to the Tyrannosaurus Rex, and the momentum pushed Ginny's pink blob so that her roll went too far. Instead of crushing the trio of attackers, they landed atop her blob as it crashed to the ground.

Much like the giant rubber balls with which Ginny had played as a child, her pink membrane smacked into the ground and then bounced back up into the air. She watched as the robot and the dinosaurs caromed from her pink blob and launched into the air away from her, their weight and momentum overcoming their thin pink bindings. Meanwhile, the bounce sent her arcing westward to smash through a dozen skyscrapers before crashing to a halt. She lost sight of her foes as she hurtled through the mortar of the buildings. She smiled, for the bounce had thrown her enemies back up into the air at such a height that they would surely die upon falling back down to Earth.

She rolled upright, slightly dazed from her fight, and noticed that the night sky above had been eclipsed by a fiery swath of gunmetal gray. It was the ship that she had attacked before being waylaid by the cursed robot and its dinosaur companions, and it was about to crash directly on top of her. Instead of questioning why it was about to crash atop her, she hardened her pink membrane and cursed. A bright explosion filled her vision, and she smelled burnt cotton candy.

*

Regular-Ginny opened her eye. She had not realized that she was still capable of being knocked unconscious, as this was her first experience with the concept since becoming the Pink One's Right Hand of Destruction. Her head hurt, and she wondered how long she had been out.

She glanced around her. She was in a cocoon of pink surrounded by molten debris and wreckage. The pink wrapped her heart in tendrils of hatred. She allowed the feeling to overcome her without putting up a fight. As she became overwhelmed with the emotion, her pink blob grew. She pushed as hard as she could against the wreckage above her. At first, it would not budge, so she instead formed thousands of tiny tentacles that stretched up into every single available nook in the debris above her. She began vibrating the tiny tentacles as fast and as hard as she could. She began hearing cracks and groans as metal twisted. She gave one last push and emerged like a Titan birthed from the dusty nether regions of a busted Gaia.

If she still *needed* to breathe, she likely would have gasped for breath as she reached freedom. Instead, because she now only breathed out of desire and habit, she inhaled deeply and allowed the pink to flow through her veins, filling her with a hatred even stronger than before and concurrently healing the splitting headache that had taken up residence in her skull. She noticed a squadron of fighter jets zooming by overhead, likely on another disintegration run at either her army or the blue army, so she stretched a half-dozen tentacles high overhead as fast as she could and took out the ones she could reach in time, which happened to be the four at the back of the formation.

She smiled and raised herself up on stilts of pink goo to get a current understanding of the battlefield. At her best estimate, the B.I.T. was down to about a dozen—maybe fewer—of the carrier-sized airships. The blue army had meanwhile brought the pink army's advances across the city to a stalemate.

She sighed. All she need do now was wait for Arthur the Putrid to finish sapping beneath the stupid energy shield and then take out the generators, and then she could rid herself of the B.I.T. threat once and for all. And then she and the Blue One's army could continue their damned war unmolested for the rest of eternity.

Much to her delight, she found that she need not wait for Arthur the Putrid much longer, for in a matter of seconds, an explosion erupted from within the shield wall and the bubble of lightning that encapsulated the B.I.T. headquarters faded to nothingness.

She smiled and hurried in the direction of the building from which the shield had originated, the one marked *Olympus*.

CHAPTER 15

GO! GO! POWER DRILLBOT!

DRILLBOT STOOD ATOP a floating blue cloud, hovering in the expanse between realities. He held his right drill above his head and thrilled at the pressure of Ginny Rex's tiny hand encircling it. He had been standing in this same position since the battle had begun. The vanguard of the Army of Life had already made Earthfall and their attack was well underway. Drillbot, however, waited to enter the fray for the signal from the Blue One, the sign that would mean Regular-Ginny was vulnerable to a surprise attack.

Drillbot's audio receptors detected a multitude of sounds mingling with his own grinding gears and the infinite white noise of the barrier between realities. Artkylosaurus chewed on his cigar, Artclops groaned and cracked his knuckles, the samurai Ginny and Art argued with the ninja Ginny and Art, who in turn argued with the hoplite Ginny and Art about whose fighting style was superior. The warrior-monk-version of Ginny simply sat in silence, though she breathed surprisingly heavily from her mouth, while the vampire-Friar-version of Art muttered about how he longed to drink someone's blood. A version of Art covered in pustules that leaked fire lay on his back and emitted small crackling noises while a Ginny in a floating raincoat sharpened her curved daggers. An elvish Art carrying a bow whispered poetry to a fairy version of Ginny, whose swoons sounded like the squealing of a pig, only higher pitched and faster paced.

Drillbot blocked these noises from his receptors and listened for his signal. Reports of fallen ships and vanquished squadrons and victorious squadrons passed through his processors, and finally, just when he was nearing the limits of his patience, three white bubbles appeared below the floating blue cloud in the vast colorful-and-colorless barrier between realities. Though the Blue One had long ago left the barrier between realities to enter the fray, the cosmic bear's voice somehow appeared within Drillbot's processors and danced a message into Drillbot's head: "Attack."

"[whir] Attack!" yelled Drillbot, diving from the blue cloud toward the closest bubble.

Ginny Rex leapt after him. As planned, Artkylosaurus squeezed the triggers on the pair of rocket launchers mounted on Ginny Rex's torso as they fell, sending gifts of destruction that zoomed past Drillbot to precede the trio through the bubble. As Drillbot fell headfirst into the all-encompassing white, he heard Artclops and the rest of the squadron follow with their own leaps toward the other two white bubbles.

Drillbot landed in the white bubble just after the rockets. An infinite whiteness surrounded Drillbot. He watched as the rockets grew infinitely long and stretched away in front of him, disappearing in the distance. He rotated his head to glance over his shoulder. Ginny Rex hit the white just behind him. He yelled to her, "[whir] Drillbot loves – CLACK – loves Ginny Rex!"

He heard her begin to call back her love in response, but he was launched ahead into infinity and she and her words disappeared behind him. He turned his head back around to face forward, his drills outstretched and whirring before him. The tips of them stretched far into infinity in front of him, disappearing from view. And then, as suddenly as the white had become infinite, it ended. He caught up to the rockets and watched them fly from the exit of the white bubble.

Before him, Regular-Ginny's giant pink blob thrashed and crashed against the floating B.I.T. carrier upon which she was mounted. The rockets exploded against her pink membrane, knocking her off balance and sending her rolling toward the edge of the ship.

Drillbot watched the pink blob jiggle as it reeled from the surprise explosion. He heard the woman's voice begin to squeal some sort of taunt, but then he slammed into the pink membrane and she abruptly stopped. His momentum and his drills carried him all the way through the pink blob like a bullet through a gelatin mold. She managed to dodge out of his way. He came out the other side of the blob and hooked the blob's edge with a drill to prevent himself from freefalling down toward the city far below. He twisted so that he landed on the membrane in such a way that he could continue slicing.

The Ginny within the blob turned toward him and began swinging tentacles at him, only to find herself blindsided by the mighty mass of Ginny Rex and Artkylosaurus as they emerged from the white bubble and crashed into her blob. Their blow was strong enough to send all four combatants over the edge of the B.I.T. airship and out into the empty air between the B.I.T. ship and the ground. Drillbot anticipated Regular-Ginny's attempt to grab onto the edge of the ship with a tentacle to save herself, so he sliced off her tentacle as she flailed it. The four warriors fell.

As Artclops and the rest of Drillbot's elite squad dove into view from the other two white bubbles that had appeared above the B.I.T. airship, Drillbot shrugged his version of a shrug—a gesture comprised of microscopic vibrations in the rotors at the base of his head and counterclockwise rotations of the dials and buttons running the length of his torso. The group landed on the flat expanse of the ship from which Drillbot and Ginny Rex and Artkylosaurus and Regular-Ginny had just tumbled.

Artclops and the other members of Drillbot's squad scratched their heads in stunned silence, since they had emerged from their bubbles intending to fight Regular-Ginny to the death, only to instead find her blob knocked beyond their reach. Drillbot nodded in acceptance as they turned their attack toward the bridge of the B.I.T. carrier rather than leaping off the ship in pursuit of Regular-Ginny—a gesture that would have almost certainly meant their collective suicide and resulted in little payoff.

Regular-Ginny's blob swirled and viciously swiped tentacles at Drillbot and the dinosaurs. Drillbot parried and sliced and diced and crawled across the expanse of pink blob back over to Ginny Rex's side, who was fighting tooth and nail and rocket and claw against the pink blob. Eventually, just after a pair of well-placed rockets exploded against the blob's membrane, Regular-Ginny swirled tentacles toward Ginny Rex and managed to snag all her appendages. Drillbot knew that this was his opening, his chance to dispatch Regular-Ginny now that she was distracted by the dinosaur and moving in for the kill.

Drillbot weighed his options with blinding speed. He *could* use his drills to dive through the pink blob and kill Regular-Ginny, ending her threat to the Multiverse, but in the time it would take him to close the distance between them and kill her, she would be able to rip the life from his newfound love. So, he trusted his internal prioritization system and leapt to Ginny Rex's defense, slicing the tentacles off at the roots and freeing her arms and legs. Artkylosaurus screamed a curse.

A new tentacle swept into view and crashed into Drillbot's head. He felt gears jostle loose, and his vision went momentarily blurry. He shook his head back and forth, and by the time his vision returned to normal, it was too late.

The blob had snaked small tentacles through the spokes of his wheels and around Ginny Rex's hands and feet. The blob twisted, using its momentum to roll so that Drillbot and his dinosaur compatriots were between the blob and the ground.

"[whir] Da – CLACK – Da – CLACK – Damn!" the robot cursed, realizing with dreaded finality that the blob had bested him, that his love and her valet were about to be crushed despite his best efforts to save them. Registering as less of a problem in his internal prioritization system, he realized that his life was also likely to be snuffed out by the weight of the blob crashing atop him at terminal velocity, which would mean Regular-Ginny's blob would be able to spread havoc unchecked across the Multiverse, since he seemed to be the only combatant in the Blue One's army who could bring her to a stalemate.

Artkylosaurus, however, was not quite so fatalistic. His maniacal cackling echoed across the jiggling pink of the blob. He crawled across Ginny Rex's torso, retrieved a pair of rockets from her bandoliers, reloaded the launchers, and fired them point blank into the side of the blob. Black scorches formed across Drillbot's torso, and if he had the ability to smell, he likely would have smelled some burnt dinosaur flesh, for scorches had formed on Ginny Rex's torso to match his. The momentum from the explosions caused the blob to keep rolling, moving Drillbot and his companions out of harm's way just in time for the pink blob to smack into the hard, concrete ground.

Rather than being crushed, Drillbot found himself bouncing high into the air as he and his compatriots were ripped free from the tentacles that were holding them in place. Drillbot watched with anger as the pink blob bounced in the opposite direction, and then a sense of shame filled him as he realized that he would be unable to complete the mission that the Blue One had given him to eliminate her, since he had wasted the opportunity open to him when she had been preparing to kill Ginny Rex.

Before Drillbot had time to report his failure to the Blue One, Artkylosaurus leaned down from his perch on Ginny Rex's back, hooked his tail around Drillbot, ordered the robot to hold on tight, and then pulled a rip cord that dangled from his neck. An oversized green parachute erupted from the backpack on his back. Drillbot held tight to the Ankylosaurus's tail, the Ankylosaurus held tight to the Tyrannosaurus Rex, and all three floated slowly toward the spreading destruction and chaos that covered the ground.

"What the hell, Drillbot?" demanded Artkylosaurus, chomping down on his cigar as he interrogated the robot.

"[whir] What – CLACK – What does friend Artkylosaurus mean by this interrogative?"

The wind whipped across the trio as they floated. Artkylosaurus squealed, "I saw you! You had a clear shot at the Ginny inside that blob, and you didn't take it."

"[whir] But Drillbot could not. It was – CLACK – It was – CLACK – It was not a choice to Drillbot. Drillbot could have done nothing other than what Drillbot did."

The Ankylosaurus spat. Ginny Rex bent her head inquisitively toward Drillbot. She asked, "My love, what is my valet talking about?"

Drillbot frowned his version of a frown. "[whir] Friend Artkylosaurus refers to the opportunity that Drillbot had to kill the Ginny – CLACK – the Ginny in the blob. But – CLACK – But Drillbot did not capitalize on it."

Ginny Rex frowned. Drillbot continued, "[whir] But not because Drillbot did not want to. Drillbot – CLACK – Drillbot altered his own internal programming dozens of Earths ago. Drillbot now protects you and loves you above everything else. Drillbot merely – CLACK – merely obeyed his programming."

Artkylosaurus spat again. He screamed, "But the plan was to kill that hag. It's the only part of our squad's mission that mattered! You put the whole Multiverse at risk, you selfish fool!"

Ginny Rex stared at Drillbot, hurt in her eyes. She cried, "You had *no right* to make that decision on my behalf! We were trusted to stop the Ginny in the blob at all costs! You *know* I would gladly exchange my life to remove her from this war!"

Drillbot shrugged. He said, "[whir] For Drillbot, there is no Multiverse – CLACK – no Multiverse – CLACK – no Multiverse worth existing in without Ginny Rex. We can kill – CLACK – kill the blob-Ginny next time. But Drillbot cannot replace – CLACK – cannot replace Ginny Rex."

Artkylosaurus groaned. Ginny Rex frowned, but then she leaned over and kissed Drillbot—a long, hard, wet lick across his mouth speaker. The dials on his torso vibrated and spun clockwise, his version of a blush.

Before Drillbot could continue speaking lovely clichés to his mate, Artkylosaurus interrupted with a shout of "We've got incoming!"

Behind them and closing fast were a squadron of jets. Drillbot sighed, wondering when the Random Number Generator in the Sky would finally allow him to catch a break.

The undersized Ankylosaurus twisted Ginny Rex so that she momentarily faced toward the jets. He fired one of the rocket launchers with one arm as he clung to Ginny Rex with his opposite arm, but the launcher clicked impotently.

"And now we're screwed," muttered Artkylosaurus, the understrap on his camouflaged helmet digging into the soft flesh beneath his chin. "No way I can reload and hold y'all up at the same time."

Ginny Rex did not even attempt to reload the rockets herself, for her arms were obviously too short. Drillbot also made no attempt, for he knew that his drill-arms did not contain the proper dexterity to help. Further, and even more frustratingly, he could not fire his drills at the incoming jets, for he needed the entire surface area of his arms to cling to Artkylosaurus's tail to prevent himself from falling. And though he would undoubtedly survive the fall, he refused to leave Ginny Rex and Artkylosaurus floating helplessly on their own to face impending doom without him.

The jet squadron closed fast. An idea popped to the surface of the ones and zeroes crawling through Drillbot's internal processors, and with nothing left to lose, he gave it a shot. He began rocking his weight back and forth, back and forth, back and forth, until the trio was swinging high and wide, a precarious pendulum hanging from the parachute.

Artkylosaurus groaned as he strained to hold the weight of his friends. He squealed, "Drills, buddy, what're you doing?"

Drillbot continued swinging and replied, "[whir] Initiating – CLACK – Initiating what little evasive action that we – CLACK – that we have available to us."

Ginny Rex grinned, her sharp teeth flashing yellow in the dark night. "Splendid idea, my love!" she declared, and then she joined in the swinging. Artkylosaurus groaned once more as the strain on his body grew worse. But the maneuver seemed to work, for the first shot fired by the approaching jets missed wide.

Drillbot knew better than to celebrate, for he had only managed to prevent them from being disintegrated for a few moments. He and his companions would need help—and fast.

Just as he engaged the communications system within his internal processors to beg the Blue One for assistance, the Random Number Generator in the Sky finally smiled down on him with a piece of good luck.

Drillbot's communication receptors picked up a message from Pirate-Art, who was leading one of the two raiding squads responsible for boarding and commandeering the B.I.T. carriers in the sky above.

"Yar," called the pirate from the communicator of one of the B.I.T. carriers to everyone who could hear. "Hoist the black flag of Dread Interdimensional-Pirate-Art, for the B.S.S.C. Yeti now belongs to me. And now I'm comin' for ye, Admiral whatever-yer-number-is! But first, let's see how ye manage without yer Yeti's damnable fighter jets!"

And with that, all lights winked out within the fighter jets that were barreling toward the trio, as well as all power to their engines and their disintegration beams. Rather than picking off Drillbot and his friends, the jet squadron fell, gliding just below the trio's perch underneath the parachute. Every single one of the pilots looked confused and terrified, and then they all looked dead as their ships crashed into the ground.

Drillbot glanced around the battlefield and watched as what he estimated to be a tenth of the B.I.T.'s remaining jet fighters lost power. They became tumbling metallic raindrops that crashed into the concrete and splashed destruction up into the air. Drillbot sighed as a few dozen fell into the midst of a particularly large group of blue and pink warriors who were battling one another. Drillbot hoped any of his friends unlucky enough to be within the brawl would be spared. Drillbot pushed the thought from his head, instead storing within his long-term memory banks this newly discovered information: all the fighter jets originating from one of these carrier ships can be depowered at the press of a button from within the carrier's bridge. This discovery could change the way the Army of Life fought against the B.I.T., and it was a significant ray of hope within this endless war.

But then, as quickly as Drillbot cheered his newfound luck, he found reason to curse it once more: the wind suddenly shifted.

"Fellas, I got some good news and some bad news. Bad news is that the wind has changed, and we're headed toward *that*!" shrieked Artkylosaurus as he pointed toward the lightning-shield that encompassed a large portion of the battlefield.

If Drillbot were able to gulp in despair, he would have done so. Instead, he listened as Artkylosaurus continued, "The good news is that we're all gonna die together, for what *that's* worth."

The Ankylosaurus hugged his friends tight and prepared for disintegration. However, just before the wind pushed the dangling trio into the shield, a gargantuan explosion rocked the Earth. The shield sputtered and disappeared.

Artkylosaurus let out a loud whoop of delight. He yelled, "That's why I say it's always better to be lucky than good!"

Drillbot began to join him in his whooping, but then he realized that the parachute was carrying the trio toward a five-square mile field of generators that had been demolished and were now engulfed in flames. He pointed toward the area and said, "[whir] We may not be – CLACK – be out of the metal forest just yet."

Near the closest flaming husk of a generator, a version of Art wore a ring from which he launched purple cartoonish destruction, while another version of Art flew amongst the wreckage, carried by a flock of seagulls that dropped flaming excrement onto the ground. According to Drillbot's hurried calculations, there were approximately three-dozen iterations of Arts and Ginnys who lurked elsewhere amongst the ruined generators.

Drillbot looked at his companions. His internal processors raced. He said, "[whir] Now that the shield is down, the Blue One's chosen children – CLACK – chosen children will be headed this way. We must – CLACK – We must dispatch these creatures before the children arrive, or – CLACK – or the kids will be killed, and our hope for victory in this war shall be lost."

The wind carried the parachute directly above the wreckage of the generators. Luckily for the trio, it seemed as though none of the enemy forces responsible for the generators' destruction had glanced up to notice them.

Ginny Rex nodded and grinned. "Then let us hunt."

Artkylosaurus chomped down on his cigar. He, too, nodded. "Aye, let us hunt."

And with that, Artkylosaurus used his free hand to cut the straps on the parachute with one of his daggers. Once loose of its burden, the parachute fluttered away in the distance. The trio fell. Drillbot aimed for the Art with the purple ring, landing upon him and driving him into the ground with such force that only gore remained when Drillbot crashed to a halt.

Meanwhile, Ginny Rex and Artkylosaurus fell upon the Art being carried by the seagulls. They crushed him into a bloody pulp as they smacked upon the ground. Drillbot and his companions gained their footing and crept forward into the flames, on the prowl to hunt and murder the pink puppets one by one.

CHAPTER 16

A BRIDGE TOO FAR

AGENT 27142 SCANNED the battlefield. Wreckage of fighter jets and carrier-class ships and skyscrapers littered the ground. Black smoke rose into the air to mingle with the cold night sky. White bubbles continued appearing at seemingly random intervals, dropping members of the cosmic blue bear's incursion forces sometimes amidst the cosmic pink bear's forces and sometimes amongst the B.I.T.'s ground marines and sometimes atop the B.I.T.'s air squadrons.

Agent 27142 smiled. Before the blue bear's invaders made Earthfall, he was convinced that the B.I.T. home Earth would be quickly overrun by the pink bear's swarm, because their numbers were too staggering to withstand for as long as it would take to save the *Olympus* building, even with the atom-scattering lightning-shield protecting it. But each army was now fighting a war on two fronts, and they soon forced one another into a stalemate, with attrition whittling them all into oblivion. So long as he could maintain this stalemate until the High Commander was ready with the reforged cosmic saber, Agent 27142 saw the B.I.T. losses as acceptable when compared to the fate of the Multiverse if his forces failed.

Agent 27142 watched that damned marauding pink blob slingshot itself toward the B.S.S.C. Burton, and his smile collapsed into a scowl. The ship plunged and rolled starboard, taking evasive action. The blob flew over the airship, and the annoyed facial expression of the Ginny in the middle of the blob indicated to Agent 27142 that the blob had missed its intended target.

White lightning leapt from the Scatter Gun turrets that lined the ship's hull, zapping across the black expanse of night toward the pink blob. It twisted and stretched and condensed and danced between the many bolts. When a second barrage of Scatter Gun bolts launched from the B.S.S.C. Burton's many turrets, holes opened across the expanse of the blob, and the bolts passed harmlessly through them. Agent 27142 cursed when the blob countered its miss by extending a long, thin tentacle from its side that snagged the underside of the ship's hull. It used this tentacle to reel itself in like it was bait on the end of a fishing line, and then it rolled up onto the relatively flat stretch of hull in front of the bridge, leaving a path of destruction in the wake of its roll. It began smashing tentacles across the hull, first demolishing any turrets within line of sight and then turning its attention on the ship proper, a tactic it had already used to bring down far too many carrier-class vessels during this battle.

Agent 27142 cursed under his breath. He reached over to his communication toggle and ordered Squadron Nu—one of his own squadrons of fighter jets—to divert from its already-desperate strafing mission through Ground Zone 2 to provide support to the B.S.S.C. Burton, though he had little hope that the squadron would arrive in time.

He cursed the B.S.S.C. Burton's captain for not keeping at least one of his *own* fighter jet squadrons in reserve for defense. The damned captain had chosen to send every single one of his fighter jet squadrons on the attack, for he was overconfident both in his ability to evasively maneuver and in the aim of his turret gunners—all of whom he had recruited from an Earth populated by blind humanoids who relied on what they called *"divine reflex"* to fire ballistics that missed, on average, less than 7% of the time.

And just as the blob reared back to crush the B.S.S.C. Burton's bridge with such ferocity that it would underline why the captain's strategy had been terribly hubristic, a trio of white bubbles appeared in the air above the ship. Agent 27142 ordered his underlings to zoom in the view screen so that he might get a closer look at what was about to occur atop the B.S.S.C. Burton. The bridge crew obliged, and the view screen zoomed in closer on the B.S.S.C. Burton.

A pair of rockets emerged from one of the bubbles and slammed into the pink blob. The blob was knocked to the edge of the B.S.S.C. Burton and teetered on the brink of falling. Then the cursed robot with drills for arms—the one that Prisoner-Art annoyingly referred to as Drillbot—dove into view from the same bubble and plunged drills-first into the pink blob. The robot was followed by what Agent 27142 could only describe as the most ridiculous dinosaur in the entire Multiverse: a Tyrannosaurus Rex with a matted blond coif atop its head that was short in the front and long in the back. The dinosaur wore a tiny crown made of fangs, a leather jacket, and a pair of rocket launchers harnessed to its sides. A second dinosaur rode upon a saddle on the Tyrannosaurus Rex's back, chomping on a cigar and operating the rocket launchers with its ham-sized paws.

Meanwhile, thirteen other Arts and Ginnys dropped from the two other bubbles onto the hull of the B.S.S.C. Burton, these led by a Cyclopean Art carrying a club the size of a tree trunk. The Cyclops-Art raised his club and began charging toward the pink blob, but when the blob fell over the edge of the B.S.S.C. Burton with the robot and the dinosaurs in tow, the one-eyed monster shifted his attention to the bridge of the ship. His companions followed suit.

As this group of invaders charged, Squadron Nu finally arrived to aid the B.S.S.C. Burton, strafing across the mass of Art and Ginny flesh and disintegrating three members of the invasion party—a Ginny wearing a floating raincoat and an Art that looked like an elf and a Ginny that appeared to be a tiny fluttering fairy. Squadron Nu zoomed away and looped around to prepare for another pass.

Agent 27142 turned from the carnage to look at Agent 29333. If circumstances were different, he might have complimented her on how her eyes sparkled in this light. Instead, he frowned and ordered, "Agent 29333, update me on the status of the fleet."

Agent 29333 pressed some buttons on her keyboard and then answered, "Of the fleet's original thirty-six carrier-class vessels, fourteen remain, not including us."

Agent 27142 nodded, clicking his heels together as he turned back toward the view screen. In doing so, he found that the Cyclops-Art and his invasion squad had smashed their way into the bridge of the B.S.S.C. Burton. Flames erupted from within the bridge, and the small image from the viewpoint of the B.S.S.C. Burton's bridge in the bottom left corner of Agent 27142's view screen winked out.

Agent 27142 watched with a scowl as the Cyclops-Art and the nine other remaining members of his raiding party emerged from the wreckage of the bridge and leapt off the side of the ship before Squadron Nu could complete another strafing run. White bubbles appeared below the invaders, catching the Cyclops-Art and his mates as they tumbled through the night sky. Meanwhile, the B.S.S.C. Burton capsized, taking with it a dozen skyscrapers as it plunged toward the ground.

"Scratch that last update," said Agent 29333. "Thirteen carrier-class vessels remain, not including us."

"Dunno why, but we call *that* a baker's dozen back on my Earth. What do you call it here?" chimed Prisoner-Art from his restraints at the back of the bridge.

Agent 27142 turned and glared at the prisoner. The prisoner wilted, his shoulders slumping and his eyes drifting to the floor. Agent 27142 noted silently to himself that if he survived this battle, he would enjoy torturing the mouthy bastard during tomorrow's morning meal.

With no warning other than a blinding white light that filled the view screen, the Cyclops-Art and his nine remaining companions dropped to the B.S.S.C. Mimessiah's hull. They landed on the flat expanse that stretched for a hundred meters in front of the bridge. They charged toward the bridge, their weapons raised and ready to smash.

Agent 27142 smirked. Unlike the captain of the now-destroyed B.S.S.C. Burton, Agent 27142 relied on preparation rather than luck and reflexes. He pressed a button on his captain's chair and ordered, "Beta Squadron, engage maneuver '*Raindrops.*' Agent 29333, engage maneuver '*Monkey House.*'"

Agent 27142's smirk transformed into a grin as the B.S.S.C. Mimessiah performed a barrel roll. As the ship turned upside-down and the city now loomed above it, the Cyclops-Art and his fellow invaders fell into the sky between the B.S.S.C. Mimessiah and the city, tumbling like ten plump raindrops. New cosmic white bubbles appeared to catch them, but before the raiders could fall into the bubbles, Beta Squadron zoomed into view and opened fire with their Scatter Guns, disintegrating all ten of the invaders. The B.S.S.C. Mimessiah continued its barrel roll and returned right-side up.

Agent 27142's grin disappeared as he once again peered out of the view screen at the battlefield. He sighed as two of the remaining carrier-class vessels began firing on a third carrier near them. The B.S.S.C. Seventh Circle burst into a ball of flames as explosions rocked its hull. It drifted slowly sideways and then began falling to the Earth. Agent 27142 noted to himself that he would need to recommend the captain of the Seventh Circle for a posthumous medal of valor, for the image from the viewpoint of the Seventh Circle in the bottom right of the view screen showed the captain screaming orders to his imminently dying crew and pointing them toward a particular spot on the ground far below, where hundreds of the blue bear's incursion forces were engaged in an all-out murderous brawl with hundreds of members of the pink bear's forces, filling every square inch of a few city blocks as they murdered and maimed one other.

The falling ship crashed atop them. The viewpoint from the Seventh Circle winked out, flames engulfed the area of the city where it crashed, and hundreds upon hundreds of Arts and Ginnys met a fiery end.

Unfortunately, these hundreds upon hundreds of flaming and dying incursion force members were but a tiny fraction of the Arts and Ginnys at war on this planet, so Agent 27142 gave himself no opportunity to rejoice at their deaths. Instead, he ordered Agent 29333 to open communications with both the B.S.S.C. Yeti and the B.S.S.C. Irrational Number.

Once the connection was made, Agent 27142 said, "Whomever is now in control of my ships, this is Agent 27142, the captain of the B.S.S.C. Mimessiah and the admiral of this B.I.T. fleet. I will give you *one* chance at mercy: release the surviving crew members of my ships unharmed, and I *may* be convinced not to annihilate you from existence."

Agent 27142 received no acquiescence from the two commandeered ships. However, he never expected acquiescence. He instead expected to grab their attention so that they would stop firing upon the other carriers in his fleet. He wanted to draw them toward his own carrier, for he was more confident in his own abilities to handle these commandeered vessels than in his underlings' abilities to do so. Agent 27142 nodded when the ships turned toward the B.S.S.C. Mimessiah and began closing the distance between them.

Agent 27142 glanced at the small images on the outskirts of the view screen that represented the bridges of the Yeti and the Irrational Number. In the image from the Yeti, a version of Art dressed like a pirate—complete with an oversized red coat, a black admiral's hat with a skull-and-crossbones stitched across its front, a hook for his left hand, a peg in place of his right leg, and a green parrot with footlong antennae that extended from just above its beak like a ridiculous mustache—stood victorious above the corpses of the bridge crew. Behind him stood three other Arts that had accompanied him in commandeering the ship, one a gangster in a dark suit, one a cowboy holding a pair of six-shooters, and one an Art with a vicious cobra in place of each arm. A ghostly white bubble hovered at the back of the bridge.

The Pirate-Art pressed a communication toggle on the dead captain's chair and shouted, "Yar! Hoist the black flag of Dread Interdimensional-Pirate-Art, for the B.S.S.C. Yeti now belongs to me. And now I'm comin' for ye, Admiral whatever-yer-number-is! But first, let's see how ye manage without yer Yeti's damnable fighter jets."

The pirate then pressed another series of buttons on the dead captain's chair, manually overriding the systems of the fighter jets serving the B.S.S.C. Yeti and shutting off their power. These jets immediately began falling from the sky. Agent 27142 cursed.

Meanwhile, the Irrational Number's bridge was filled with the exact same carnage, but this carnage was personified by Ginnys that appeared identical to the Arts onboard the Yeti—a pirate-Ginny, a gangster-Ginny, a cowboy-Ginny, and a cobra-armed-Ginny.

Each pirate yelled to its companions, and then they all rushed toward the respective cosmic white bubbles on the carriers they had commandeered. They disappeared from the bridges of the Yeti and the Irrational Number. Naught but death remained behind them on the ships' bridges, but at least this death was no longer a plague spreading destruction to the remaining B.I.T. carriers.

Agent 27142 grinned, for it was obvious where these two groups of invaders would be headed, and he was excited for the imminent action about to erupt on his bridge. He unbuttoned the fastener that held his Scatter Gun pistol in place on his holster. He pulled a small brass pill-shaped item from another segment of the holster, touching a button on its side that caused three petite spikes to pop out of its bottom.

"Agent 29333, to me. Engage maneuver '*Mirrorland*.' Bridge crew, remain at stations and prepare to be boarded," he ordered.

Agent 27142 heard Prisoner-Art murmuring and whining behind him, but he ignored the feeble noises. Agent 29333 stood from her station and walked to Agent 27142, standing back to back with him so that they might be ready for an incursion from any angle.

A white bubble appeared on the port side of the bridge, while a second appeared on the starboard side. Agent 27142 faced the starboard bubble, Agent 29333 the port. The cowboy-version of Art was the first through the starboard portal. His face melted into a gurgling, melted red mess as Agent 27142 threw the brass pill at the man's head, its metallic spikes sinking deep into the unlucky Art's cheek. A gurgling, squelchy sound behind Agent 27142 indicated that Agent 29333 had performed the same attack on the cowboy-Ginny appearing from the port bubble.

At the same moment that the pirate-Art leapt through the starboard bubble and landed on the deck of the bridge, Agent 27142 dove toward him, shifting his momentum to somersault and then roll up onto one knee. The pirate fired a flintlock pistol that would have hit Agent 27142 directly in the chest had he not somersaulted. Fortunately for Agent 29333, she had again mimicked Agent 27142's movements, diving and rolling toward the portside portal. The bullet from the pirate-Art scored a direct hit in the heart of the pirate-Ginny, and the bullet she fired did the same to the pirate-Art.

Agent 27142 then dodged swipes from the snakes of the cobra-armed-Art and blasted a Scatter Gun bolt directly in the face of the arms' owner. He followed this attack with a second shot into the face of the gangster-Art before the gangster was able to fire his already-drawn pistol.

With his foes defeated, Agent 27142 turned to see how Agent 29333 had fared. She also stood victorious over her boarders. As the cosmic bubbles faded into nothingness, Agent 27142 walked to the bloody corpses of the pirates and the cowboys and nonchalantly fired his Scatter Gun pistol into each one, hitting them with disintegration bolts that rent them unto oblivion and thus guaranteed that they would be reincarnated by neither the blue nor the pink bear.

"Nice work, Agent 29333," said Agent 27142 with a smile.

She did not smile back, instead returning to her station with a mild, "As you say, commander."

Agent 27142 turned back toward the view screen, his adrenaline still pumping from the fight and his breath heavy. He frowned. On the ground below, the blue and pink armies were being continuously reinforced by new white and black bubbles that dumped new Arts and Ginnys onto the wreckage of the vast battlefield.

Agent 27142 grunted in disgust. The stalemate continued across the battlefield. But now Agent 27142 realized that attrition was affecting his B.I.T. forces was worse than the attrition affecting either of the two invading armies. Now that the B.I.T. fleet was down to twelve functioning carriers—not counting the B.S.S.C. Mimessiah, and assuming the surviving crew members could take over command of the Yeti and Irrational Number—the incursion forces had more leeway to fight without being disintegrated into nothingness. Agent 27142 sighed, his confidence wavering.

At least we have the shield, thought Agent 27142. *I can lose every ship in my fleet, but so long as that shield holds until the High Commander is ready, I will have saved the Multiverse.*

And then, as if the Multiverse were waiting for its cue to launch into ironic mayhem, a vast explosion erupted across the generator park inside the shield. Agent 27142 cursed louder than he had ever cursed before. His throat felt raw. He cursed again as the shield that guarded the heart of the B.I.T. faded and the incursion forces on the ground turned their attention toward the newly vulnerable area of Earth 55,777.

Agent 27142 pressed a button to alert the High Commander, and then he ordered the ship to drop altitude to put itself between the *Olympus* building and the invading forces. The adrenaline faded from his heart, transforming into a ball of dread that drifted down to take up residence in his stomach.

When Prisoner-Art groaned in despair at the back of the ship, Agent 27142 did not even deign to promise torture.

Instead, he groaned, too.

CHAPTER 17

A PUTRID SKIRMISH

REGULAR-GINNY ROLLED HER way through the wreckage of the city, making a beeline for the building labelled *Olympus*. She nonchalantly swatted aside fighter jets as they rained down around her. The divebombing jets had at first filled her with dread, because she had assumed the B.I.T. had some sort of new weapon or tactic up its sleeve, but after the first dozen or so crashed around her, she realized that these doomed ships had simply lost power somehow and were falling to the ground.

She glanced toward the sky and sighed. Though a horde of the jets had lost power and were currently plummeting, thousands of others were still streaking across the cloudless black night, swooping down to strafe Ginny's puppets and disintegrate them into oblivion.

She rolled south and east, entering the area of the city that the lightning-shield had protected until a few minutes ago. As she made her way down a major thoroughfare marked by blue street signs as *Ζεύς Avenue*, pink hatred twisted her heart, and without even a second thought, she stretched two mighty tentacles out to her sides and clotheslined a pair of skyscrapers. This pair of buildings buckled and toppled, tipping into a nearby pair of skyscrapers and causing them to topple, too. Screams erupted from within the buildings, and then they abruptly ended with a sickening squelch. Regular-Ginny heard the Pink One giggle with delight inside her mind.

Two vehicles rounded a corner in front of her. They looked like Panzer tanks from her Earth, except they hovered three feet above the ground and had a B.I.T. seal emblazoned across their flanks. A dozen marines in black-and-gray camouflage perched atop each vehicle, kneeling with their rifles drawn and aimed at her. Ginny squashed them all beneath a pair of tentacles before they managed to fire a single shot, and then she crunched the tanks into huge balls of metal and heaved them into the air toward the jets. She heard screaming from a few maimed marines who were still alive within the wreckage. As their pleas for mercy faded into the distance, the malevolent ball of pink hatred in her heart danced with joy. She grinned a hateful grin.

About two miles away, high in the sky, she could see the neon letters of *Olympus,* which were somehow still lit despite all other power having winked out in this part of the city. Her destination was *so* close.

She charged through the debris of a fallen skyscraper that lay in her path and found that Ζεύς *Avenue* continued directly through the middle of the generator park that had lain behind the lightning-shield before the shield had fallen. Though smoke and assorted debris blocked much of her view of the road ahead, she knew from the tickle in her brain that she needed only to follow the street and it would eventually end on the other side of the generator park, near the base of the *Olympus* building.

She rolled forward as quickly as she could roll. About thirty yards ahead, a gigantic hole lay open in the ground with a radius the size of a Winnebago, and from it stretched a swath of destruction in every direction. Smoking hulls of warehouse-sized generators lined both sides of Ζεύς *Avenue,* and if her cosmic blob had not made her fireproof, her skin would likely have quickly become charred and blackened. She heard struggling in the distance.

A massive green energy beam shot into the sky from amongst the flaming wreckage of the generators about a quarter mile ahead. Ginny listened hard and heard originating from that direction grunts and screams and death rattles and a familiar cursing, and the itch in her brain revealed to her what her gut had already told her: that Arthur the Putrid would be at the center of the struggle.

Ginny grew her blob even larger, adding a good thirty stories of height to her blob. As she rolled through the flaming wreckage strewn across Ζεύς *Avenue,* she extinguished the fires with her blob as she rolled over them. When she neared Arthur the Putrid and whatever was causing him and his Death Cavalry trouble, she slowed to a halt.

A pair of smoking generator hulls lay blocking her path. Rather than rolling over them to dive directly into the fray, she decided to use caution. The pink itch in her brain grew stronger—obviously the Pink One showing her displeasure at Ginny's decision for caution—but Ginny ignored it. She created a current within her pink blob that brought her up to its topmost point, from which she peered over the two flaming generator husks that lay in her path.

She looked down upon a wide clearing, a clearing that existed because the generators that had previously occupied the space were no longer present. She could clearly see the outlines of where four of the mighty warehouse-sized generators *should* sit, these outlines being concrete foundations that no longer housed the rounded metal hulls of the generators.

Ginny noted corpses sprawled across the clearing. The mole-man version of Art and his gigantic mole-Ginny lay in the throes of death, covered in dozens of stab wounds. The gigantic mole screamed as the robot with drills for arms emerged from her flesh, ripping her in twain. Arthur the Putrid's Death Cavalry lay in similar positions of gore, some showing signs of having been exploded in a blast of rocket fire, others having been ripped apart by claw and tooth and drill. The Tyrannosaurus Rex stood over its most recent victim, the version of Ginny with the floating bunnies strapped to her feet. Only the hips and legs of this Ginny remained. One of the bunnies was dead while the other was alive, and the living bunny was trying to fly away, fluttering around in a sad lopsided loop a few feet off the ground.

Judging by the number of corpses that dotting the landscape that Ginny counted, she surmised that the only remaining member of Arthur the Putrid's Death Cavalry was Arthur the Putrid himself, who floated in the air with his green hands aflame. He raised his hands above his head and jerked his fingers in odd directions. A nearby flaming generator lifted from its foundation. Arthur the Putrid swung his hands toward the Tyrannosaurus Rex, and the generator launched toward the beast. The Ankylosaurus sitting atop the saddle on the Tyrannosaurus Rex's back swung the rocket launchers so they aimed at the incoming generator and pulled the triggers. The payloads exploded against the building.

The Ankylosaurus's quick response was not enough to stop the looming mass of metal and mortar and flame. But the cursed robot *was*. The robot leapt up into the generator as it flew past and drilled a hole through the building in such a speedy blur that the Tyrannosaurus Rex had but to jump, and the dinosaurs passed unharmed through the hole that had been carved by the robot through the flaming metal generator.

The dinosaur licked the robot upside its head, and then both turned to face Arthur the Putrid. The small Ankylosaurus scrambled from its saddle on the Tyrannosaurus Rex's back and crawled across the bigger dinosaur to reload the rocket launchers, cursing and chomping on its cigar the entire time. The surrounding flames danced across Arthur the Putrid's jeweled eyepatch, and it twinkled.

Arthur the Putrid never turned to look at Regular-Ginny, but he spoke to her, nonetheless. "Welcome to the fray, Ginny. Let me finish these fools, and then we shall cut off the head of the B.I.T. once and for all."

The robot spoke, "[whir] Your – CLACK – Your – CLACK – Your weaponized Arts and Ginnys were no match for us. You will not – CLACK – will not be, either."

Arthur the Putrid launched a ball of green flame at the robot, the point of the green flame shaped like a skull. The flame seemed to scream in agony as it traversed the battlefield, only falling silent when it crashed into the ground as the robot dodged from its path.

Arthur the Putrid released a cackling laugh and said, "You only bested my Death Cavalry because you chose the route of cowardice, picking them off one at a time from the shadows. Had you shown fortitude and waited for them to gather beside me for a proper battle, then it would be *your* corpses littering the ground."

Regular-Ginny crept forward, raising a tentacle to smash down upon the robot and dinosaurs. However, without looking, the robot pointed one of its drills toward her and launched it like a rocket. She cursed, and instead of going on the offensive, she concentrated on dodging the incoming drill.

Meanwhile, as Ginny dodged, the robot wasted no time. It leapt toward Arthur the Putrid, its remaining drill raised above its head to deliver a vicious deathblow. Arthur the Putrid deflected the drill with one of his green-flame-encrusted hands. But the parry came at a price. The sorcerer cursed, for the drill severed his hand from his arm.

But as the mangled appendage fell toward the ground, Arthur the Putrid's eye twinkled with a fresh idea, and his curses transformed into maniacal cackling. He kicked his severed hand, and the flaming appendage caromed straight into the barrel of one of the dinosaurs' rocket launchers. Arthur the Putrid screamed, "Die, you filthy, prehistoric fools!"

Regular-Ginny finished dodging the drill in time to watch the next few moments of the battle unfold below her. Arthur the Putrid kickflipped higher into the air, dodging the robot's next drill strike. He brought his remaining green fist down upon the robot's head, smashing the robot into the ground and leaving a gigantic crater below the metal monstrosity. He flew down into the crater and continued battling the robot.

Meanwhile, the Ankylosaurus bit down on its cigar and stared at the rocket launcher in which Arthur the Putrid's hand had landed. The severed hand glowed with green flame inside the barrel. The Ankylosaurus frowned and muttered, "Ma'am, it's been an honor."

Before the Tyrannosaurus Rex could respond, the Ankylosaurus crawled across the larger dinosaur's torso, unstrapped the harness that held the rocket-launcher-saddle in place, and dove with it away from the Tyrannosaurus Rex. The Ankylosaurus landed atop the affected rocket launcher just in time for it to explode.

The Ankylosaurus's body shielded its comrades from the blast as the rocket and the green-flamed sorcerer's appendage exploded. Gore flew into the air and rained down upon the remaining combatants. The Ankylosaurus's head rolled to a stop in front of Regular-Ginny's pink blob. She inanely decided that she should put out the beast's cigar before it could start an even bigger fire than the one currently raging amongst the generator park, so she smashed it with a tentacle. In the process, she crushed the head into a bloody pulp.

The Tyrannosaurus Rex raised its head and roared with rage, a sound that resembled a whale's mating call amplified via speakers the size of a city block. Regular-Ginny covered her ears despite the protective bubble of her pink blob, watching with a frown as the beast's fanged crown fell from its blond mullet to crash to the ground. The beast launched into a sprint toward Arthur the Putrid. The ground shook with each of its mighty steps.

Arthur the Putrid glanced up at the charging dinosaur, ceasing to pummel the robot with his remaining green-flame-encrusted hand. He faced the dinosaur and began twisting his fingers behind his palm and muttering some ancient words for a spell that was sure to be devastating.

But before he had the chance to launch the spell, the robot's rocket-drill returned from its flight, zooming back to reattach itself to the robot's arm. This return occurred at the most inopportune time for the sorcerer, for as he jerked sideways through the air to dodge the returning weapon, the dinosaur leapt forward and bit him in half at the waist. The dinosaur held his torso in its mouth, chomping down upon it and shaking it back and forth like a dog with a freshly killed rodent. The flames covering Arthur the Putrid's remaining hand died, leaving a lifeless hand scorched black.

The dinosaur swallowed the upper half of Arthur the Putrid. And then the dinosaur bolted his lower half. And then the dinosaur turned to stare at Ginny.

The behemoth burped, and the sorcerer's dead, black hand tumbled from between its fangs to thud onto the ground. It roared once more. The robot pulled itself up out of the crater in which Arthur the Putrid had left it, both its drills back in place at the ends of its arms. It, too, turned to face Ginny.

"[whir] It – CLACK – It – CLACK – It is time for this to end," proclaimed the robot.

Ginny frowned. Then she raised herself up onto her tentacles and launched herself at her foes.

CHAPTER 18

A HAIL MARY ON ANY REALITY REEKS JUST AS DESPERATE

"AGENT 29333, GIVE me a status update on the fleet," ordered Agent 27142 through clenched teeth as he watched yet another carrier-class vessel explode in flames, this one the B.S.S.C. Bearded Lizard-Frog. It had been overwhelmed when it ventured too close to airspace occupied by a ferocious brawl between hordes of flying pink army and blue army combatants. Agent 27142 silently cursed the ship's captain and her stupidity.

Agent 29333 replied, "We are now down to eight carrier-class vessels, not including us."

Agent 27142 cursed the B.S.S.C. Bearded Lizard-Frog's captain and her stupidity once more, this time aloud. Then he muttered, "Dammit. The shield's down, and we're taking too many losses. We can't hold off the incursion forces much longer."

Agent 29333 merely stared at him and blinked.

"Raise the High Commander. I need to know if he has completed his work at his forge."

Agent 29333's fingers danced across her keyboard. "It's no good, sir. The High Commander is not answering. He's got an away message up saying he's deep in thought, creating a weapon to save the Multiverse."

"Damn! Then leave him a message. Request for him to launch his forge into the barrier between realities. Use override code 333456908234. That'll push the message past his machine to play over the speakers in his smithy."

Agent 29333's mouth fell agape. She replied, "Sir, are you sure that's wise? You know how the High Commander responds to distraction."

Agent 27142 ignored his underling's questioning of his orders. He had no time to threaten or torture her, for there was too much at stake. Instead, he responded, "I will deal with his wrath *if* we survive. It is vital that he escape at all costs. He can occupy a new reality and forge it into a new home-Earth for the B.I.T., but *he* and *his workshop* cannot be replaced."

Agent 29333 nodded. "Sent," she said.

Agent 27142 nodded back. He then redirected a wave of fighter jets to attack a particularly vicious set of pink combatants in Ground Zone 4, these having ravaged a large marine unit in their area.

Agent 27142 stared out at the battlefield and shook his head. He felt shame in how this battle had gone wrong. Though the B.I.T. could not yet permanently remove the incursion forces' leaders from the equation, the organization *did* possess the ultimate weapons against their hordes—the Scatter Guns. But the hordes were simply too numerous. And like so many other battles in the history of the Multiverse, the side with the vastly superior numbers was ultimately going to win, no matter how much better the underdogs' tactics and technology had been. And despite constant barrages from the B.I.T.'s Scatter Guns, the superior numbers remained staunchly in the camp of the cosmic bears. Agent 27142 had failed, and attrition had failed him.

Agent 27142 sighed. He would need to grovel, but if he could *just* bring more B.I.T. forces here, then he might be able to turn the tide. He ordered, "Agent 29333, raise Admiral 11404. You should be able to find his signal somewhere in the Inner Realities."

The view screen morphed to reveal a B.I.T. agent with an orange beard that flowed all the way down to his waist, from behind which a plethora of medallions and honors poked. He had three green eyes, two in the same spot as a human's and a third in the center of his forehead. A Grand Admiral's hat covered the top of his head rather than a checkered officer's cap, and beneath his hat, stubbly little orange hairs grew, a sign that he had not shaved his head in a few days. Agent 27142 noticed this unkemptness, and he did not interpret it as a positive omen.

"Admiral 11404, we need your help. Return to home base at once. We are desperate, and the High Commander is at risk."

Admiral 11404 frowned, a gesture that in his culture looked like a smile. Sharp purple teeth poked out from between his lips. He replied, "I knew the High Commander put too much faith in ye, ye li'l whelp. If 'e'd'a put *me* in charge o' yer li'l war, I'd'a 'ad it over and done years ago."

Agent 27142 frowned back. He said, "Maybe, but he *didn't*. And maybe he'll give you what you want soon enough, but right now, we need you and your fleet to get to Earth 55,777 to protect the High Commander. The invaders have won the day, and my fleet won't last more than another few minutes."

Admiral 11404 sighed, a gesture that in his culture sounded like a chuckle. His ship shook around him, multiple members of his crew in the background fell to the ground, and alarm lights flashed behind him. The lights went black, but then they blinked back on. These new lights shone with a red hue, indicating backup power. Admiral 11404 said, "Ye think ye're the only one in desperate straits, boyo? I couldnae help ye even if I wanted ta. I'm in me own cosmic war to save the Multiverse from a couple o' cosmic birds that wanna chew it up and feed it to their babies. If me an' m'fleet leave, the Multiverse is doomed."

When Agent 27142 did not respond, the admiral continued, "Ye ain't gettin' no help from me. Ye're a commander of a B.I.T. flagship an' fleet, and the High Commander saw somethin' in ye for some reason I donnae quite understan'. So, do what all o' us commanders been doin' fer generations uncountable: shut the hell up and find a way to win, no matter what. Ye donnae wanna be the first of us to let the Multiverse fall inta nonexistence."

And with that, the scene aboard Admiral 11404's bridge shook once more and then winked out. Agent 27142 frowned. He said, "Agent 29333, raise Captain 59590. His signal should be somewhere near the Eighth Quadrant."

Unfortunately, Agent 27142 received a similar denial from Captain 59590, who was fighting a cosmic threat to the Multiverse in the form of universe-snatching, sentient business suits. He received a similar denial from Agent 668777, Admiral 1232, Governor 55680, and several others, all of whom were entrenched in their own cosmic wars to save the Multiverse and surrounded by equally dire straits. None were moved by Agent 27142's pleas that his cosmic event had breached the B.I.T. home reality, and thus should be the cosmic event to take priority over all others.

Finally, Agent 27142 gave up on finding help. He had Agent 29333 set a distress beacon as was protocol, even though he knew nobody would answer the call, for there were too many cosmic events overlapping this day. He frowned and stared out the view screen, once more surveying the desperate battle before him.

Across the warzone, twenty-eight carrier-class vessels lay on the ground as smoking debris, their lifeless husks crashed amongst the toppled skyscrapers and corpses of citizens. Blue incursion forces and pink incursion forces continued their endless dance of death and life around the husks. Agent 27142 frowned even harder as the enemy hordes neared the *Olympus* building, their rampaging now far inside where the lightning-shield had stood. Agent 29333 spoke up, "Sir, bad news. We just received word from inside *Olympus*. There's an invasion force within the building, and the High Commander still has not responded to our message."

"Damn!" screamed Agent 27142. "Teleport a brigade of marines t—"

"Sir, I was not finished. There is more dire news. An incursion force managed to teleport inside our engine room. Onboard security has removed them, but not before they armed their weapons. The engineers are working to disarm the bombs, but it's not looking good, sir. Likelihood that the B.S.S.C. Mimessiah falls in the next seven minutes is at over ninety-eight percent."

Agent 27142 cursed once more. His mind raced. He glanced down at the battlefield again and thought back to what Admiral 11404 had said. *Every* commander must find a way to win, no matter the cost. There was always some sort of cosmic threat on the horizon, and the B.I.T. had not succumbed to one yet. Agent 27142 would be damned before he would let such a disaster occur on his watch. He swallowed hard and stifled a sigh. He knew what he must do, and it would cost him everything.

He turned to Prisoner-Art. "Prisoner, what is it called on your reality when you make one final attempt at winning and put all your efforts behind one final gamble, even though it is so desperate that it will likely fail?"

Prisoner-Art frowned. "You mean like a Hail Mary?"

Agent 27142 nodded. "A Hail Mary it shall be, then."

Agent 27142 turned to Agent 29333. He ordered, "Agent 29333, come with me, and bring the prisoner. Send word to marine squadrons Zero, Twelve, Pi, Ampersand, and Umbrella that they are to meet us in the third hangar immediately."

Agent 29333 nodded, relayed the order over the communications transmitter, and stood. She unbound Prisoner-Art from his restraints, grabbed him by the scruff of the neck, and followed her commander. Their eagles swooped down from their perches and landed on their shoulders.

"Agent 90909, you have command. If I do not return before the ship goes down, make sure you do your duty as interim-captain and go down with it," ordered Agent 27142 as he strode toward the transport tube that lay just outside the exit of the bridge.

"Isn't going down with the ship *your* job?" muttered Prisoner-Art. "You're robbing us of the best part of this ship being destroyed."

Agent 27142 did not listen as Agent 90909 called out confirmation, instead turning to beat Prisoner-Art about the face until the prisoner crumpled into a flabby mess and curled into a fetal position on the floor. When Agent 27142 finished with the beating, he continued striding toward the transport tube. Such a small display of violence really helped to hold at bay the gnawing desperation that threatened to overwhelm him. He listened as Agent 29333 yanked Prisoner-Art off the ground and pushed him forward to keep pace with Agent 27142.

"Where are we going?" Agent 29333 called from behind.

Agent 27142 stepped into a car in the transport tube and waited for Agent 29333 to enter. He pressed the button that would take them to the third hangar, and then he waited for the door to shut and the transport car to begin moving. Only then did he reply, "I have one last idea for how we can save the Multiverse. Unfortunately, once we are finished doing so, it means that I will certainly end my days being tortured in a penal reality. But I will make that sacrifice if I must, for this idea is the only thing I can think of that might prevent me from becoming the commander responsible for dooming the Multiverse."

Agent 29333 nodded. She said, "I'll join you in that penal reality, if that's what you command."

Agent 27142 shook his head, though he longed to say yes so that she would spend forever beside him in his inevitable work camp. He replied, "No, no. Thank you, but I shall take the blame for this one all on my own."

The doors opened and five squadrons of twenty marines stood at attention, the commanders of which Agent 27142 could easily recognize because of the eagles that perched on their shoulders, these versions given only to officers. Agent 27142 gave quick orders to the men, as well as coordinates to which they must jump with him.

When Agent 29333 heard the coordinates, she gasped. *She must understand what I intend,* thought Agent 27142. *Nobody else would have, and that's not just because nobody else in our present company other than myself has access to the same level of classified documents as her. She's brilliant, and that's one of the many reasons why I love her.*

Agent 27142 split the group onto three shift-shuttle-class ships—two marine carriers and his own personal shift-shuttle, the appropriately named

'Death in the Night, Thy Name is This Ship.' It was a black vessel ninety-feet long and shaped roughly like a banana with the wings of an eagle. An ornately wrought eagle's face extended from the hull at the front of the ship, with the bridge a fortified see-through metallic bubble that poked out of the eagle's mouth.

Agent 27142 and his crew boarded his shuttle at a sprint, and as soon as the hatch was shut, Agent 27142 engaged thrusters. The ship blasted from the hanger into the air above the carnage that had enveloped Earth 55,777.

Agent 27142 typed his coordinates into the controls and tapped his eagle on the head, not entirely ungingerly. The beast squawked and fired a bolt of lightning into a short metal pole that stood erect from the command console. The ship and its two companion vessels jumped into the barrier between realities just as an explosion rocked the B.S.S.C. Mimessiah behind them.

Agent 27142 stared ahead and prepared to meet his destiny.

CHAPTER 19

A TIMELY RAID

NORMAL-ART SAT STRAPPED to his chair and stared silently ahead, past Officers Art and Ginny. Outside the view screen of the bridge, the barrier between realities flew past at such speed that the colorlessness and the colorfulness of it swirled into a miasma that made Normal-Art's head ache, so he shifted his gaze to stare down at his feet.

His shoes were old and worn, and the toe box of the shoes had long ago busted open, leaving the soles separated from the tips of the shoes. His big toes poked out of the gaps between the soles and the tips, and these toes resembled squat, lumpy sausages. His skin was so wrinkled and dry that his metaphorical big-toe-sausages looked like they had sat too long on one of those rotating grills in the most rundown, rodent-infested, unhygienic convenience store in the entire Multiverse.

Pre-battle banter between the marines drifted into the bridge through the open hatch near the back. The sounds gave Normal-Art something new on which to concentrate, and he smiled at the novelty. For the years and years that encompassed his captivity, Normal-Art had experienced a dearth of banter from his confines at the back of the staunchly banterless bridge of the B.S.S.C. Mimessiah, unless you counted the times when he could bite his tongue no longer and a zinger or a one-liner escaped unchecked from his lips. But these self-supplied interruptions became fewer and fewer over the years as Officer-Art's beatings grew simultaneously more vicious and more frequent.

Officer-Ginny reached up a hand and twisted a dial on the ceiling, and some holographic numbers appeared above the co-pilot instruments in front of her. She cleared her throat and then said, "Turn forty-nine degrees to port as soon as we pass Earth 69,065, and we will hit a rift that will jump us directly to Earth 4. We should arrive in approximately ten seconds."

Officer-Art waited a few seconds, and then he jerked the stick sharply to the left. Though Normal-Art tried to resist, he could not help looking out the view screen as Officer-Art changed direction. He immediately regretted it, as the colorfulness and colorlessness of the vast space outside momentarily separated, but then flashed back together as soon as the ship finished its turn and regained velocity. The view made Normal-Art's head ache worse than ever.

Officer-Art reached a free hand to a green button and pressed it, holding it down while he ordered the other shift-shuttles that had accompanied him on this mission, "Initiate cloaking sequences. Follow my beacon on private frequency Iota. Radio silence in effect until we land."

Officer-Art released the button and toggled a few more dials and switches in what could have been a set pattern but seemed random to Normal-Art. The ship slowed—which Normal-Art only noticed because the miasma outside separated once more—and then flew directly into a bolt of lightning that appeared in front of the ship after Officer-Art's eagle fired a bolt of lightning into the metal pole standing erect from the command console. As usual, the lightning created a painful vacuum in Normal-Art's ears, and also as usual, he squealed in agony and wished to go deaf, for he assumed going deaf might end this frequent source of pain once and for all. He noted inanely that if he had found a genie in a bottle during his ridiculous years of misadventure and had used his first wish to gain a million extra wishes, he would probably only have a dozen or so wishes left at this point given the number of times he had wished to go deaf when lightning erupted near him. He sighed.

The shift-shuttle exited the lightning and Earth 4 filled the view screen. The sky was a deep purple. Storm clouds the color of blood swirled seemingly unto infinity across the horizon, an occasional blue bolt of lightning dancing between them. The ship passed through the clouds and leveled out thousands of feet above the ground, never slowing its pace.

As the planet zoomed by underneath the ship, Normal-Art watched as rolling plains covered in great green ferns soon gave way to rocky soil that soon began to grow taller and rockier as mountains loomed ahead. Cave entrances were visible all across the surface of the mountains, reminding Normal-Art of swiss cheese doused in dirt.

In the distance atop the tallest mountain loomed a mighty spire hundreds of stories tall and made from what appeared to be onyx. Ships shaped like eights and ships shaped like fours and colossal dirigibles and thousands of other randomly shaped ships buzzed around it like worker bees around a hive, some entering cargo bays that opened in the spire's exterior, some exiting hangars to fly into the sky and disappear into nothingness after wiggling to-and-fro at supersonic speed.

As Officer-Art's shift-shuttle flew toward the spire and its details became more visible to Normal-Art, he noticed that the top of the monolith was carved into the shape of a clock. Its hands appeared to move both clockwise and counterclockwise simultaneously, which Normal-Art was sure was supposed to be symbolic of *something*, but staring at the image made his headache worse, so he looked down at his feet again.

Soon, Normal-Art felt the shift-shuttle slow and then skid to a halt on gravelly dirt. Officer-Art flipped a few switches on the control console. The ship made a few loud hissing noises, and the power to the engines shut off. Normal-Art heard a loud *thunk* emanate from below decks as the hatch to the ship crashed open. Then he heard the clicking of the marines' boots as the soldiers unstrapped themselves and exited the ship.

Officer-Art unstrapped himself and stood. Officer-Ginny did the same. Then she unstrapped Normal-Art, forcing him onto his feet. She prodded Normal-Art in the back until he scooted his way down the ladder that poked up through the bridge's hatch. Because of his plaster-encased hands, he descended slowly and carefully. His caution prevented him from falling until the third rung down.

He crashed to the metal floor of the hold, and his shoulder broke his fall. He cursed. He pulled himself to his feet before Officer-Art could beat him for his clumsiness, and then he trudged down the open exit ramp at the aft of the ship.

As his shoes touched upon the rocky soil, he took a moment to glance at his surroundings. He immediately wished he had not. This Earth's weirdness did not stop at its odd-colored sky and clouds. No, this Earth looked like the most ridiculous piece of Salvador Dali art ever, if Dali were to get high on the strongest drug from the acid-swamps of Earth 980,766 and paint on a cosmic scale. Drooping clocks fluttered through the air like birds, lizards shaped like sundials skittered across the dirt, and little bunnies with eights and fours for ears hopped about nonchalantly. Normal-Art began to groan in annoyance, but he was interrupted when Officer-Ginny pushed him in the back to make him keep moving.

The three B.I.T. shift-shuttles had landed in a tiny valley encircled by mountains, and Normal-Art noticed that there was a gigantic cave entrance in the base of each of the mountains. There were four cave entrances visible, and each entrance lay in a different cardinal direction. Normal-Art felt another shove in the back, and he stumbled forward toward the mammoth cave mouth on the north side of the valley. He could see the marines standing at attention in a grid formation inside the cave.

Before entering the cave, Normal-Art glanced up at the sky and realized he was about to be prodded into a cave within the base of the mountain from whose peak the onyx spire loomed high above. From this close, the spire's exterior façade looked oddly similar to the piece of saber he had once worn around his neck. He wondered if anybody up there in the spire had noticed the B.I.T.'s shift-shuttles approaching, but when he glanced over his shoulder in the direction of the shift-shuttles, he saw no sign of the ships. He frowned, and then realized that the ships must be cloaked—and thus must have gone unnoticed by the people in the spire. He slumped his shoulders and allowed himself to be prodded into the cave.

"Where are we?" asked Normal-Art. He was answered with another shove that pushed him toward the north cave entrance.

"Look, I know what you're thinking," continued Normal-Art unabated. "Y'see, I dealt with a very literal god in my past, so I know how these things work. You're thinking that the next time I ask where we are, it'll be super clever to say, '*We're on Earth 4*,' since I heard you say that was our destination back on the ship. But I obviously want to know what to expect here, not just what version of Earth we're on."

"You done?" asked Officer-Ginny from a few menacing inches behind him.

When Normal-Art refused to respond, he felt another shove in his back. This time, as he stumbled forward, his right foot became entangled with the heel of his left. He tripped. He fell on his face and sprawled across the dirt. He landed on one of the lizards shaped like a sundial and found an answer to a question he had not asked: yes, the dial-appendage *is* made of horn and is *exceptionally* hard. Normal-Art squealed. Officer-Ginny grabbed him by the scruff of the neck and pulled him to his feet. He frowned at the squished gore of the lizard that lay directly in the middle of the Normal-Art-shaped imprint he had made in the gravelly dirt.

She said, "To answer your question, we're on Earth 4," and then she dropped into silence after letting out a tiny chuckle.

Normal-Art continued forward, only for Officer-Ginny to yank at the back of his shirt like it was a set of reins when they neared the marines standing at attention.

Officer-Art marched past Officer-Ginny and Normal-Art. Officer-Art stood at attention and addressed the marines, "Agents, as you know, our situation back on Earth 55,777 is dire. I personally chose your squadrons to accompany me and Agent 29333 to this place because I can think of none better on which to rely in such desperate times.

"We are here on this Earth to steal the only weapon in the Multiverse that might save it," continued Officer-Art. "We've only got one shot at this. Your lieutenants should have informed you of the implications of our being here. In case they did not, let me lay it out for you: we are on the home reality of another cosmic agency, one more ancient than even our own. We are committing an inter-agency crime, and if you are taken prisoner, then you will enter an eternity of pain. So, do not allow yourselves to be captured. Accomplish our mission or die in the attempt.

"For those of you lucky enough to survive," continued Officer-Art, "know this: I will assure that you receive a full pardon from the B.I.T. as part of my guilty plea. For those of you unlucky enough not to survive, your lives will not have been spent in vain. You will have made the ultimate sacrifice to save the Multiverse."

Normal-Art leaned over to Officer-Ginny and whispered, "Wait, *what* other agency? There's another agency in charge of interdimensional travel?"

Officer-Ginny elbowed him in the stomach, demanding silence. She whispered back, "No, you fool. There is only *one* agency that regulates interdimensional travel. And it's the B.I.T."

Officer-Art briefly glared over his shoulder at the pair, and then he turned back to continue addressing the marines, "Squadron Ampersand, you will remain here to guard the shift-shuttles, for they are our means to return to base. Squadron Pi, you are also to remain here. If we find ourselves in trouble, I'll activate my distress signal, and that will be your cue. I will need you to create a diversion to attract attention. Use the hover-tanks from the cargo holds and mount an assault on the front of the spire."

The commanders of Squadron Ampersand and Squadron Pi assented with a salute. Squadron Ampersand's commander saluted with one of the eight tentacles he had in place of arms—because he was an oversized humanoid octopus in a B.I.T. marine uniform—while Squadron Pi's commander saluted with one of the wings he had for arms—because he was an oversized humanoid owl in a B.I.T. marine uniform.

Officer-Art continued, "The rest of you are with me. Squadron Umbrella will bring up the rear. Squadron Zero, you've got the right flank. Squadron Twelve, you've got the left. If anyone gets cornered or caught, lead whoever is after you away from our main force and away from the ships. Understood?"

The marines all saluted in assent. Officer-Art saluted back at them. He removed a pair of goggles with clear lenses from a pouch on his holster and placed them on his head. Then he marched past the marines, leading the way deeper into the cave.

Officer-Ginny, along with every marine, followed suit by placing a pair of goggles over their eyes. Officer-Ginny pulled a second pair from her holster and placed them over Normal-Art's eyes. The goggle straps were too tight and pulled his hair, and he wished he still had the dexterity to remove them. They seemed naught but clear protective lenses, but as Officer-Ginny shoved him in the back and forced him to follow Officer-Art deeper into the cave, Normal-Art discovered that the goggles allowed him to see in the dark. Further, as he stared at different objects, small letters appeared to explain what they were. He noticed another one of the sundial-lizards lurking on the wall of the cave, and as he looked at it, he read, *Protian Sun-Lizard, native to Earth 4. Diet includes Infinity Beetles and Loop Flies. Avoid consuming: toxicity level 3—will induce diarrhea and vomiting.*

Normal-Art looked away from the creature. He and Officer-Ginny caught up to Officer-Art, and Normal-Art walked between them. He asked, "Where are we going?"

Officer-Art smirked, but this time he deigned to answer Normal-Art's question, "The High Commander installed an assault door in this cave eons ago. Only B.I.T. agents with *Classified Level Twelve* or higher know of its existence. The High Commander installed it secretly so that if our agency ever needed to assault the *B.T.T.*, we could penetrate their base and end any threat quickly and efficiently.

Officer-Art continued, "Now, make sure you step carefully and use your goggles to avoid any booby traps. The B.T.T. will surely have installed them throughout all the caves leading to their base, whether they know there is a secret entryway in the caves or not. At least that's what *I* would do if I were them and I wanted to prevent a hostile force from using the caves to mount an assault."

"Wait, what's a B.T.T.?" asked Normal-Art.

He did not receive an answer. Instead, he heard a low whine beneath his left foot when he took his next step. When he glanced down and noticed the object beneath his foot, the goggle readout stated: *Landmine. If you never move, you may be safe.*

"I told you to use your goggles to *avoid* booby traps, you fool!" screamed Officer-Art. He punched Normal-Art in the gut. And then he and Officer-Ginny and the marines began sprinting away to a safer distance.

Normal-Art did not know what to do. As he gasped for breath, he felt a deep sense of dread in the pit of his stomach. He asked what he should do a few times, but nobody gave him an answer. They were too busy running away.

"I just can't catch a break," he said to himself. He repeated the phrase over and over. And then, because he could think of nothing else that might help, and because he was too full of anxiety to stand unmoving in this spot for the rest of eternity, he removed his foot from the mine and began to sprint away, too. He ran in the same direction as the B.I.T. agents.

An explosion emitted from the mine, knocking him across the cave. He crashed into the wall. But his life did not end as he assumed it would.

Dazed, he closed his eyes and rubbed his sore head and listened to a cacophony of roars and grunts and growls. Then he heard some B.I.T. agents scream while others began firing their Scatter Guns.

When his vision finally cleared and he opened his eyes to look at the carnage that he had unleashed, he wished he had kept them closed.

CHAPTER 20

THROUGH THE CAVE AND INTO THE TOWER

"I TOLD YOU TO use your goggles to *avoid* booby traps, you fool!" screamed Agent 27142 at his prisoner. As his fist connected with the fatty tissue of the lout's gut, satisfaction spread from the fist up into his heart. He wished he had time to punch the prisoner again, but caution necessitated that he and his soldiers sprint away from the idiot and the activated mine below the idiot's foot.

Agent 27142 had slapped and beaten and maimed his prisoner for the past decade, but none of the pain and suffering seemed to dam the constant deluge of idiocy that flowed from the fool. Agent 27142 sighed. He should have known better than to warn the fool about booby traps. The prisoner was such a bumbling buffoon that the moment he was warned to avoid something, he somehow *always* found a way to fall prey to that very same something, almost always at a high cost to those around him.

As Agent 27142 sprinted away from the prisoner, he heard the low whine behind him grow louder. He glanced over his shoulder, and he noted that Prisoner-Art had shifted his weight from the foot atop the mine to his other foot. The prisoner was beginning to sprint, obviously intending to follow Agent 27142 and the B.I.T. soldiers away from the mine.

Warnings of *Flee!* and *Run!* scrolled across Agent 27142's goggles, so he continued his sprint until the warnings faded in intensity, at which point he spun to face the mine and knelt on one knee. Though Agent 27142 had never physically been to this reality, he knew much about it from reading classified documents in B.I.T. headquarters, and he thus had a strong suspicion that he knew what to expect from this mine. He drew his Scatter Gun pistol and aimed the barrel at the space just above the mine, the space that the prisoner currently occupied.

The mine exploded. The force of the blast hurled Prisoner-Art into the air. The fool flew over Agent 27142's shoulder and crashed against the cave wall. Agent 27142 did not look in the prisoner's direction and did not inquire about his status. Instead, he kept his eyes trained on the explosion and allowed his goggles to adjust to the blast.

Slavering, ferocious beasts exploded into existence from the epicenter of the blast. A megalodon about sixty-feet long was flung from the explosion to the opposite wall of the cave, its teeth biting into the flesh of three marines before it realized it was not in water, and then it panicked and began thrashing, taking down four more before it found itself riddled with disintegration bolts. Simultaneously, a trio of three-foot tall velociraptors leapt from the fiery explosion toward Agent 27142, but he effortlessly zapped each one with his Scatter Gun before they came near enough for him to smell their foul breath. A gang of six leather-clad bikers on hovering motorcycles emerged as well, their unmuffled engines roaring like a half-dozen angry demons. These men brandished clubs covered in barbed wire, and they managed to bludgeon three more marines to death before Agent 29333 blasted them into nonexistence. Finally, a man in a white button-up shirt complete with a pocket protector and turtle shell glasses was tossed from the explosion and rolled across the dirt. He stood and raised his hands in submission.

"What's happening?" he squealed. "I was just doing my mother-in-law's taxes, and now I'm h—"

His confused squealing was interrupted when he was blasted into nothingness by the Scatter Guns of a dozen marines.

The smoke cleared, and Agent 27142 stood. His boots crunched in the dirt as he walked over to the prisoner and yanked the fool up onto his feet. The idiot's eyes were glazed, and he was obviously still dazed. Bright red blood matted his unkempt hair. "S-Sorry," he muttered.

Agent 27142 gained the satisfaction of punching the idiot in the gut once more. The fool let out a small gurgling sound and slumped into a fetal position in the dirt. Agent 27142 growled, "Tell *that* to the families of the soldiers who just died because of your stupidity."

Agent 27142 watched the prisoner bite his lower lip, obviously trying to hold in a comment. When he could no longer restrain himself, the prisoner muttered, "Fine. Gimme their contact info. I'll tell 'em I'm sorry for what I did, but *then* I'll let them know that their loved ones died because their commander took me prisoner for something I couldn't control, and then dragged me into a war zone with *NO GODDAMNED TRAINING!*"

Agent 27142 kicked the prisoner in the belly and smiled at the feeling of the fool's gut around his boot. The prisoner shriveled. Agent 27142 said, "We do not have time for *this*. Get to your feet. And this time, do the opposite of whatever your instincts tell you to do. Maybe then the rest of us can survive in one piece."

Agent 27142 turned from the prisoner, gave the signal for the marines to follow him, and continued marching deeper into the cave. He heard Agent 29333 lift the prisoner from the ground and shove him forward.

The prisoner asked her, "What was that thing I stepped on? Other than a mine, obviously. Am I hallucinating, or did a bunch of random stuff pop out of it?"

Agent 29333 answered in a low whisper, "I don't know what it was. My classified level only grants me access to *so much* information about this Earth. But judging by the Earth we're on, it likely had something to do with time anomalies. Now keep quiet."

Agent 27142 decided to be gracious and answer the question, calling over his shoulder, "Your instincts were correct, Agent 29333. That was an Anachro-Mine."

Before Agent 27142 could continue explaining, the prisoner interrupted him by asking, "What's an Anachro-Mine?"

Agent 27142 sighed, and then he replied, "I was not finished explaining, you fool. Agent 29333, slap him across the headwound and ensure that he does not speak to me for the remainder of the mission."

When Agent 27142 heard the thump of a slap behind him and the groan of the prisoner, he continued, "As I mentioned to you before, we are on Earth 4, home to the B.T.T.—and before you ask and earn another beating, B.T.T. stands for the *Bureau of Time Travel*. The mine that you stepped on created a weaponized time anomaly, retrieving random creatures from across infinite timestreams at the most stressed and angry points in their existences. So be wary as we move forward to not activate another. We were rather lucky with the meager caliber of creatures that were summoned from that last one."

Prisoner-Art chimed in, "B-But that's stupid."

Agent 27142 could picture the idiot biting his lip, trying not to comment, and then failing. Before Agent 27142 could instruct Agent 29333 to punish the fool for his insolence, she was already doing so, and his love for her grew. Agent 27142 continued striding toward the back of the cave. As he did so, he listened to the thumps as she threw the prisoner to the ground and kicked him over and over, seemingly in beat with each of Agent 27142's footsteps.

He knew her so well that he could picture the scene of her beating the prisoner without even needing to look: she would have a look of murderous delight in her eyes, her tongue would be poking playfully from the side of her mouth, and her hair would be tumbling from beneath her checkered hat to fall across her face. Now more than ever, he wanted to turn to her and kiss her, wanted to rub his forehead against hers, smearing the blood of the bludgeoned marines that had spattered upon her face onto his own, and wanted to stare into her eyes. But instead, he had his command and the Multiverse to consider, so he continued striding and relegated such notions to fantasy.

The group of marines moved quickly and carefully toward the back of the cave, weaving back and forth at the behest of the readouts on their goggles and experiencing no other incidents with Anachro-Mines. Agent 27142 estimated that they had likely covered around a mile and a half when they finally reached the back of the cave. Looming before him stood what looked like a gargantuan stone dial protruding from the wall. The goggles gave no readout other than to say *Rock* when Agent 27142 stared at the dial.

But he knew this stone dial was so much more than a rock.

Agent 27142 twisted the stone dial back and forth, following the pattern he had memorized from the dossier about this entrance when he had reached *Classified Level Twelve* over a year ago. Finally, after twisting a half-dozen times with just the right precision, he heard a loud CLANK within the wall. It opened.

Agent 27142 stepped through the threshold and entered the headquarters of the B.T.T. at the sub-basement level. Though it was as pitch dark in here as in the cave—as Agent 27142 had suspected it would be, since the dossier said this sub-basement was full of archived treasures collected from across the expanse of time and was no longer in active use—the goggles remained effective and allowed Agent 27142 and his soldiers to see.

The secret entrance led them into the southeastern-most corner of a colossal warehouse containing shelves that stood ten-stories high. Every single inch of the shelves was covered by wooden crates marked with the name of some foreign artifact, its Earth of origin, its timestream number of origin, and its time period of origin. Agent 27142 saw one crate labelled *Ra's Phallus*, and he frowned.

He crept to the nearest row of shelves and peeked around its corner. The shelves stretched for a half-mile—an almost dizzying sight of intense organization—and ended at an elevator bank consisting of four lifts. A computer terminal sat next to the elevators. The goggles identified the security system guarding this sub-basement: a laser-alarm grid that crisscrossed the floor just above the ground. The goggles allowed him and his soldiers to see the lasers so that they would be easy to avoid.

Agent 27142 turned back to his soldiers. Without speaking, he used standard B.I.T. hand and body signals to express, "We need silence from here on out. I must access the computer terminal at the far end of this room to locate our target. Spread out and be careful to avoid the lasers crisscrossing the ground, for they will activate an alarm. If anyone triggers it, I will personally execute you in the most slow and painful manner imaginable."

Before Prisoner-Art had the opportunity to ask what Agent 27142 was doing with his hands and his gyrating hips, Agent 29333 put her hand over his mouth to shush him. She whispered as quietly as she could whisper in his ear, "He's using standard B.I.T. silent communication protocols. Your goggles will provide a translation. Read it. Remain silent."

Agent 27142 smiled at her and nodded. She nodded back.

Agent 27142 turned and led the soldiers toward the far end of the sub-basement. The crisscrossing lasers were spread far enough apart that they were easy to dance between, so the group made it to the far side of the sub-basement quickly and without further problems. Agent 27142 said a silent prayer in thanks to the High Commander for that piece of good luck, since the rest of this journey was unlikely to be so easy.

Agent 27142 sat at the computer terminal and turned it on. It whirred for a few seconds and finally booted up. He began typing furiously. It took him little time to locate the target that he came here to find.

He also found an interesting piece of information about one of the other caves near where the B.I.T. shift-shuttles had landed, so he smiled and pocketed that tidbit for later use.

CHAPTER 21

FATHER TIME JUST WANTS FRIENDS

"INTERESTING," WHISPERED OFFICER-ART to himself as his fingers clacked across the keyboard. The fascist's voice was so quiet that Normal-Art doubted he even realized he was speaking aloud. "We shall need to make a second stop on our way out of this reality."

Normal-Art knew better than to inquire what Officer-Art meant by the statement. Normal-Art was still reeling from the Anachro-Mine explosion and the subsequent beatings he had received, and on top of that, he had expended what little remaining energy he had left high-stepping over thin green alarm lasers that crisscrossed the floor of the gigantic warehouse, so he knew that he could not survive another beating right now.

It was at times like these that he really missed his original kidnapper. Though the god-version of himself had been incredibly annoying and selfish and deprecating, the god never beat him senseless for saying or asking anything that popped into his mind, no matter how inane the thoughts might have been. Normal-Art expressed this longing through a stifled shrug.

Officer-Art stood from the computer terminal and turned to face the soldiers. He began pirouetting and twirling in place and gesticulating with his fingers and hands, just like he had done a few minutes ago to instruct the group to spread out and stay silent before sneaking through the warehouse.

Normal-Art swallowed a sigh and bit his lip. Every ounce of his soul begged him to ridicule the B.I.T.'s stupid system of silent communication. He wondered for a moment whether they taught you ballet as part of basic training, or whether the agency recruited people specifically with a talent for twirling. Instead of asking, Normal-Art merely read the translation that scrolled across the lenses of his goggles: "The item we seek is stored on level seventy-four. Squadron Umbrella, you will stay at the lift and guard it for our return. We may be leaving at a sprint, so ensure the lift is ready and waiting for us."

"Squadron Zero," Officer-Art continued through swirls and gestures, "If anything goes wrong or if we are caught, you are to run in the opposite direction and create chaos to distract our foe. Squadron Twelve, you are to stay with me no matter what. You must form a humanoid shield around me and Agent 29333 when necessary, for either she or myself must escape with our target, no matter the cost."

Normal-Art noted that Officer-Art made no mention of him. Normal-Art frowned. Then he shuffled a few inches closer to Officer-Ginny and made a mental note to stay close to her, for that seemed to be his best option for survival. Though the brutish B.I.T. officer would never admit it, Normal-Art could tell that Officer-Art was smitten with Officer-Ginny by his frequent longing glances in her direction and by his slightly higher tone when he spoke about and to her. Normal-Art doubted the brute would allow anything too harmful to befall her.

Normal-Art's thoughts were interrupted by the sound of swishing fabric as the soldiers silently saluted their assent to Officer-Art. Officer-Art pressed the buttons to call each lift. About twenty seconds later, all four elevator cars arrived and opened. The soldiers split evenly into each elevator. Normal-Art, Officer-Art, and Officer-Ginny entered last car, allowing the others to first cram into the metal boxes.

Officer-Art pressed the button marked with the numerals *74*. The door slammed shut and the elevator jerked upward. Normal-Art's inner-child beat on the inside of his skull with its tiny baby fists, demanding the he press his plaster-encased hands across all the floor number buttons so that the elevator would stop on every level. He buried his face in the crook of his arm, smothering his inner-child as best he could to resist the urge.

Less than a minute later, the lift jerked to a halt. The elevator doors opened onto an empty hallway that was twenty-feet wide and lit by fluorescent overhead lights. Upon seeing that the hallway was empty, Officer-Art sighed in relief. As every member of the party in turn followed Officer-Art's gaze and understood that their raid seemed to have thus far gone undetected by the B.T.T. Because there was no ambush waiting for them here, tension released from their shoulders and an accompanying sigh escaped their lips. It sounded to Normal-Art like a chorus of gusting clouds had taken residence in the elevator car. A glob spittle landed on the back of his neck, and he updated his metaphor appropriately, imagining instead that a chorus of gusting *storm* clouds had taken residence in the elevator. Officer-Art stepped off the elevator car and into the hallway. Everyone followed.

The hallway reminded Normal-Art of a hospital. It even smelled sterile like a hospital. Portraits of robed men and women and creatures lined the walls, and below each picture hung a plaque that featured a name and a quote.

Normal-Art frowned as he stared at the two nearest quotes. The first lay below a portrait of a bearded man in a light blue robe. It read, *"Time is circular. Study now, and you can enjoy the party when it comes back around."* The second quote hung below a portrait of an oversized frog in a maroon robe and read, *"Think of the 4th dimension like a wall. You can see any moment on it, but don't look too hard or you'll notice all the cracks."*

The hallway stretched on for another few dozen yards before coming to a fork that branched in three different directions. When Officer-Art arrived at the fork, he glanced briefly at each option. He turned back to his soldiers and gesticulated. The readout in Normal-Art's goggles scrolled, "No sign of B.T.T. agents thus far. Keep your eyes and/or other vision orifices peeled."

Officer-Art chose the rightmost option. Normal-Art and the soldiers followed, finding themselves in a nearly identical-looking hallway with an identical-looking fork at its end, the only change in this hallway being different pictures with different quotes hanging beneath them. The group repeated the same process, taking the rightmost fork, and then repeated it again three more times when they entered three more hallways with identical three-pronged forks at their ends. Normal-Art vaguely understood how geometry worked, so he wondered why they had not come back to where they started after taking so many turns in the same direction.

Officer-Ginny silently danced the answer to him before he could ask, the scrolling words across his goggles reading, "Each hallway is a little shorter and smaller than the last. We're spiraling closer to the center of this place. Worry instead about the fact that we've encountered no B.T.T. agents guarding this area and no B.T.T. resistance. I would have expected our calling those lifts to an unused sub-basement to have sent an alert to *someone*. This lack of security concerns me. I suspect a trap."

At the next fork, Officer-Art led the group through the middle option rather than the rightmost. This option led them into another portrait-lined hallway, but instead of ending in a fork, it ended in a wooden door twenty-feet tall by twenty-feet wide. Officer-Art approached it, inspected it, and then opened it. Behind the door lay a bustling factory hundreds of feet long by hundreds of feet high.

Officer-Art stared at the doorframe, and then he nodded. He removed an object from his holster that looked like a small roll of scotch tape. He went to work taping the threshold of the door, ripping off strips long enough so the tape stuck to both the inside of the door on the factory side and outside the door in this mundane hallway.

Normal-Art nudged Officer-Ginny and nodded inquisitively at Officer-Art. Officer-Ginny nodded back and then began gesturing and dancing at Normal-Art. The readout in his goggles scrolled, "That room apparently sits within a pocket dimension. You've seen this technology at B.I.T. headquarters when we visited the High Commander's forge. Pocket dimensions allow nearly limitless space within an area normally confined by limited space. It actually explains the lack of guards, for you can set pocket dimensions with security systems that cause them to detach and seal if intruders enter, thus locking the intruders inside the pocket dimension until you decide how to dispose of them. But the B.I.T. has tools that prevent such detachment and thus negate these types of security systems, one of which—*Dimensional Binding Tape*—Agent 27142 is using now."

By the time Normal-Art finished reading through the scrolling explanation, Officer-Art was finished with his task and had already marched through the door, followed by everyone except Normal-Art. He realized he needed to rush back to his spot next to Officer-Ginny, so he ran through the door and caught up. Once by her side, he glanced around at his surroundings, and he stifled a surprised gasp. This room did not hold just *any* factory.

Off to the left stood row upon row of shelves, all full of pallets loaded with sealed crates. The crates seemed to glow from within with an eerie blue light. Off to the right sat a golden throne ninety-feet tall. Gilded scrollwork of clocks and the phases of the moon adorned the mighty throne. Upon the throne sat a giant in a light blue robe. His white beard stretched all the way down past his gnarled knees and curled toes to form a thick carpet on the floor. His head was bald. His ears were gigantic, with white hairs as tall as Art poking out of them at all angles. The giant's eyes were closed, and his skin was so blue that it reminded Normal-Art of a frozen corpse. Two arms stretched from the sleeves of the robe—gigantic in size but emaciated in appearance—ending in a pair of liver-spotted hands that gripped the armrests of the throne with what seemed to be rigor mortis.

Normal-Art and every single member of the group stared at the giant in silent awe. Suddenly, a pair of long, skinny robot arms dropped into view. These robot arms dangled from the ceiling high above, and their hands held a massive syringe the size of a cow. One of the robot hands brushed aside the giant's beard and gingerly yanked open the giant's robe, exposing a blue chest blanketed in coarse white hair and two nipples simultaneously the color of indigo and the size of tractor tires.

The robotic arm jabbed the needle on the end of the syringe into the giant's heart. The creature did not stir, which was unsurprising to Art since it seemed to be a corpse. The second robotic hand slowly pulled back on the plunger portion of the syringe, and the barrel portion of it began filling with dazzling blue liquid that glowed so brightly it reminded Art of snow atop a mountain during a clear day.

When the syringe was full, the robotic arms removed it from the giant's chest, yanked the robe shut, and replaced the beard in its original position. One of the arms then disappeared into the ceiling, returning seconds later with a bomb. Its shape reminded Normal-Art of the atomic bomb in his uncle's favorite movie, *Doctor Strangelove,* and Normal-Art knew that he would need to resist the urge to ride atop it in a recreation of his favorite scene from the movie if he were ever present in the future when it was dropped from something high.

The robotic hands inserted the needle into the side of the bomb and pressed down on the syringe's plunger, injecting the bomb with the giant's dazzling blue blood. The bomb itself began to glow blue. When the syringe was empty, one of the robotic arms disappeared into the ceiling once more, this time returning with an unsealed wooden crate full of Styrofoam packing peanuts. The robotic hands inserted the bomb into the crate, sealed it, set it on a pallet on the bottom row of a nearby shelf, and then disappeared back up into the ceiling. They returned seconds later with a new syringe, beginning this extraction process all over again.

Officer-Art gesticulated and pointed toward the newly minted bomb, and the readout in Art's goggles read, "We'll take that one."

Officer-Art dug into the side of his holster and pulled out a small metal rectangle. Officer-Art dropped it on the ground and tapped it three times with the toe of his boot. The metal rectangle hovered in the air and began unfolding over and over and over again. Normal-Art need not ask what the object was, for he had seen it many times over the past decade. It was a Transdimensional Hovering Hand Truck. When tapped as Officer-Art had just done, it would unfold itself from within another dimension to form a hand truck that allowed easy transportation of goods too large for an agent to lug about without assistance.

Once the hand truck was fully materialized and floating in place, Officer-Art gestured to four soldiers from Squadron Zero. They pushed the hand truck over to the pallet upon which the freshly sealed crate sat and loaded it—and thus the bomb—onto the Transdimensional Hovering Hand Truck.

Alarms began blaring. A grinding sound originated from near the door. When Normal-Art glanced at the door, he could see the edge of the pocket dimension attempting to pull away from the exit. However, the Dimensional Binding Tape held the doorway in place.

Normal-Art glanced back over at the crate carrying the bomb. As the four soldiers pushed the Transdimensional Hovering Hand Truck back over to Officer-Art, a new robotic arm dropped from the ceiling holding what looked like a toy ray gun that Art had played with as a kid—green with red rings surrounding its barrel.

The goggles identified the gun as a *Time-Phaser: used to reverse, pause, or fast-forward time*. The robotic arm squeezed the trigger four times, and ringlets of energy sprayed forth from the gun in four tight cones aimed at each of the four soldiers pushing the hand truck. Normal-Art squealed in terror when each soldier was hit, subsequently devolved into a primate, and then kept devolving until they were naught but primordial sludge.

Officer-Art gestured for six more soldiers from Squadron Zero to grab the Transdimensional Hovering Hand Truck and push it toward the exit. They sprinted into action. They managed to dodge the ray gun's payloads and return fire, disintegrating the robotic arm with their Scatter Guns. They surrounded the hand truck and began shoving it toward the exit.

Officer-Art gestured for everyone who was not currently pushing the Transdimensional Hovering Hand Truck to retreat. Then he began sprinting toward the exit.

Normal-Art knew that he should flee, but he found himself hypnotized by the scene unfolding around him. He noticed the giant's eyelids slowly open, and he gulped in terror. The robotic arms that had been operating the syringe currently stuck in the giant's chest removed it and dropped it unfilled to the ground. Then they jerked into action, zooming toward the soldiers pushing the Transdimensional Hovering Hand Truck. The arms grabbed two of the soldiers by the ankles and tossed them onto the giant's lap. The giant giggled and smiled, and then he poked the soldiers in the ribs like he was trying to tickle them. However, instead of filling the soldiers with laughter, time somehow distorted around them and the soldiers grew old, died, rotted, and turned to dust. The giant stared for a moment at the dust in his lap with a confused look. And then he screeched in fury. He reminded Normal-Art of a toddler who just had a toy taken away.

"NO!" bellowed the giant, pointing toward Normal-Art and the remaining B.I.T. soldiers. "ME WANT FRIENDS! BRING ME FRIENDS!"

The robotic arms grabbed two more of the soldiers pushing the Transdimensional Hovering Hand Truck and tossed them toward the giant. They met the same fate as the prior two.

The final two soldiers on Transdimensional Hovering Hand Truck duty sprinted with the crate through the exit, along with Officers Art and Ginny and all the remaining soldiers. They had left Normal-Art to stand staring at the action like a bumbling idiot. Normal-Art dropped his gaze from the giant and the dead soldiers covering the giant's lap. Normal-Art cursed, finally managing to break his own self-imposed hypnotism. He launched at a sprint after the B.I.T. soldiers. Panic filled him as he realized they were continuing down the hallway from whence they had come. There was no squadron turned to face him. There was nobody waiting to rescue him.

When he was a mere half-dozen feet from the exit, he felt hard metal clasp around his ankles and then begin yanking him into the air. He shrieked.

However, before he could meet the same fate as the giant's other unlucky victims, Officer-Ginny heard his shriek and realized that he was not with the group. She spun on her heel and intervened. She blasted one of the two robotic arms with her Scatter Gun pistol while her eagle blasted the other with lightning, sending this second arm to another dimension. She dashed back into the factory. She grabbed Normal-Art by the collar and dragged him through the exit.

The giant stood on his feet and began shuffling toward the B.I.T. raiding party, but as soon as Officer-Ginny pulled Normal-Art completely through the threshold of the factory and back into the hallway, she ripped the Dimensional

Binding Tape from the threshold of the door. As soon as she did so, the factory disappeared as the pocket dimension cut itself off from this reality.

Officer-Ginny pulled Normal-Art to his feet and shoved him along the hallway in the direction that the rest of the B.I.T. raiding party had run.

"Who *was* that guy?" asked Normal-Art.

After Normal-Art asked the same question a good half-dozen more times, Officer-Ginny finally replied, "It was *obviously* Father Time. Now be silent and move!"

He obeyed, and they soon caught up with the B.I.T. raiding party as the group was rounding a corner. At the end of this hallway, a turret dangled from an open hatch in the ceiling and fired conical ray beams at the raiding party. The hatch had not been open on the way in, and thus the turret had not been dangling down into the hallway. The B.I.T. lost another soldier to the devolving conical ray beams before Officer-Art disintegrated the turret with his Scatter Gun pistol.

Four bearded men in purple bodysuits jumped into view at the end of the hallway and began firing more of the ray guns at the B.I.T. raiding party. Officer-Ginny and Officer-Art made short work of them before they were able to strike any of the B.I.T. marines. Officer-Art pressed the distress button on the collar of his uniform and barked an order for Squadron Pi to begin their diversion by assaulting the B.T.T. headquarters with their hover tanks.

The raiding party then continued sprinting down the hallway. They turned left around the next corner, only to find themselves face-to-face with another turret and another four B.T.T. agents in purple bodysuits. The raiding party replicated the performance of the last hallway, losing a single soldier before Officers Art and Ginny eliminated the turret and the agents. They repeated this process three more times with the next three hallways, and finally found themselves in the hallway leading to the elevator bank.

Ten purple-bodysuited B.T.T. agents stood with their backs to Officer-Art and the raiding party, firing toward Squadron Umbrella, whose members were leaning out of cover in the elevator cars to fire at the B.T.T. agents. One of the B.T.T. agents touched a finger to his ear, nodded, and then spoke into his watch. "Got it, sir," he said.

This agent then yelled to the other nine agents with him, "We've also got hostile forces attacking the front gates. Chief says to stay here and deal with these intruders befo—"

But before he could finish relaying the message, Officer-Art, Officer-Ginny, and the remaining soldiers in Squadrons Twelve and Zero fired their Scatter Guns into the backs of the B.T.T. agents, flanking them with such speed and ferocity that they were all disintegrated before they had time to return fire a single time.

The raiding party sprinted the remaining distance to the elevators. When they reached Squadron Umbrella, Officer-Art turned to the remaining members of Squadron Zero. He pointed back the way they had come, toward the interior of the B.T.T. headquarters. He ordered, "You know what to do. Go cause chaos and bring honor to your unit."

The soldiers saluted, turned on their heels, and then ran back down the hallway. At its end, they split up, three entering each of the three forks. Officer-Art entered a waiting elevator car, and then he held the door open with his hand for Officer-Ginny, Normal-Art, and the remaining members of Squadron Twelve. Then he pushed the button for the bottom-most sub-basement. As the doors shut, screams echoed from the end of the hallway. Normal-Art frowned.

After what seemed like way too long, the elevator doors opened onto the familiar scene of the sub-basement storage warehouse. Officer-Art pushed the hand truck out of the elevator and stopped it next to the computer terminal. He stared out at the crisscrossed green lasers that covered the ground.

"We don't have time to dodge between all these lasers," said Officer-Art. "B.T.T. agents are going to come pouring out of these elevators any second. We've got to sprint."

Officer-Art turned to the commanders of Squadron Umbrella and Squadron Twelve. "Me and Agent 29333 will push the Transdimensional Hovering Hand Truck. You and your soldiers will form a humanoid shield around us. Squadron Twelve, you form the inner ring while Squadron Umbrella forms the outer ring. Myself and Agent 29333 *must* make it out of here at any cost. The Multiverse depends on us."

The commanders of Squadron Umbrella and Squadron Twelve, a female with skin the color of lavender and a male wolf-man, respectively, nodded. "Aye, sir," they said in unison.

Officers Art and Ginny gripped the handle of the Transdimensional Hovering Hand Truck. Normal-Art shoved his way forward so that he was between them. Though his hands were encased in plaster, he rested them against the back of the handle. He knew he would be no help, but he also knew that he would be less likely to get maimed or hurt if between these two. Officer-Art scowled at him, and Normal-Art half-expected the brute to shove him aside, but the agent instead shouted, "Go!"

Officer-Art began pushing the Transdimensional Hovering Hand Truck at a sprint. Officer-Ginny joined in, and so did Normal-Art, though he provided little force and instead struggled merely to keep up with their pace.

As soon as the group pushed into the territory of the crisscrossing lasers and tripped them, alarms began blaring. Conical rays began firing down from the ceiling, but the rays missed all the soldiers, instead crashing against the wooden crates.

Normal-Art sighed in relief until he realized that the aim was intentional. The wooden crates began moving backward through time, transitioning from cratehood into the forms of mighty trees. However, these trees had eyes, mouths, arms, and legs. They were covered in blue and yellow war paint, and they carried colossal wooden mallets in their hands. Each also had embedded in its chest some sort of oddly juxtaposed artifact, obviously the artifact that had been stored within each crate—Art noted one with a red amulet chased in gold, one with a long cone wrapped in mummy gauze, one with a jeweled toad, one with a clay mold of a child, one with a dog sculpted from corn husks, and many others just as strange. As Normal-Art sprinted, the goggle readout scrolled, *Treendians, native to Earth 4. Hunted to extinction to be used as crates. As you are undoubtedly learning, they also make a good security system when alive.*

Car-sized mallets crashed down upon the members of Squadron Umbrella. Four marines exploded in gore, their blood and entrails flying into the air and raining down on Normal-Art and the remaining soldiers. The Treendian cries ululated across the expanse of the warehouse, reminding Art of Native Americans in those old black-and-white Cowboy & Indian films he had watched with his mom as a kid.

Squadron Umbrella and Squadron Twelve sprayed Scatter Gun blasts everywhere they could spray them, killing the foe as best they could. But there were too many of the massive mallets crashing down from every flank, and before long, the entirety of Squadron Umbrella and much of Squadron Twelve was left behind on the ground of the warehouse as nothing but squashed piles of gore.

However, their sacrifices were not in vain. Officer-Art, Officer-Ginny,

Normal-Art, and the seven remaining members of Squadron Twelve pushed through the exit of the warehouse just as the last member of the Squadron Umbrella met his unfortunate fate. Once back in the cave from which the raiding party had entered the B.T.T. headquarters, Officer-Art immediately slammed closed the stone door and twisted the stone dial to lock it. Normal-Art's heart raced as he listened to the Treendians' mallets beat upon it.

Officer-Art smirked. He said, "No need to worry. The High Commander built this door himself. It is impervious. They won't make it through."

Officer-Art then turned on his heel and began pushing the Transdimensional Hovering Hand Truck toward the mouth of the cave. "Come on," he ordered. "And watch for the damned booby traps this time!"

Officer-Ginny nudged Normal-Art, and he began sprinting after Officer-Art with his slow, awkward version of a sprint.

CHAPTER 22

TIME FOR GOODBYES

AGENT 27142 REMOVED one hand from its position pushing the Transdimensional Hovering Hand Truck to turn down the volume on his earpiece. Squadron Pi's commander had been in the process of giving a status update on the tank assault on the B.T.T.'s front gates when the commander's tank exploded. Ensuing static had ripped through Agent 27142's ear canal, and he grunted before he was able to get the volume to a reasonable level. Though the squadron commander had been unable to finish the update before unceremoniously dying, Agent 27142 heard enough to understand that all of Squadron Pi was now gone.

Agent 27142 felt no guilt at losing the entirety of three squadrons and most of a fourth. Seventy-three dead agents were a small price to pay for the bomb stowed in the crate before him, for it represented salvation for the nearly infinite number of creatures throughout the Multiverse that would be spared from the cosmic bears. A small smile crept up the sides of his lips. He decided that he would enjoy this moment of victory, for soon he would be facing judgment and hard time in a penal dimension for this raid.

Agent 27142 and his surviving companions reached the mouth of the cave, where Squadron Ampersand stood with their Scatter Guns aimed out into the harsh afternoon light to eradicate any opposing forces that might approach the cloaked ships. Agent 27142 cleared his throat and said, "We return, smaller in number but successful."

Agent 27142 nodded in approval as none of the soldiers turned to face him, and as none of them removed their guns from their ready positions. None except the humanoid-octopus squadron commander, who had been using his tentacles to cling to the shadows on the ceiling of the cave. He dropped down and stood at attention before Agent 27142. The commander said, "Aye, 'tis good news."

Agent 27142 ordered, "Give me a status update. Have you encountered any foes?"

"We've seen no action here today. But we did lose one soldier: Agent 99087777, who was one of the tri-gendered koala-people from Earth 789,564. We discovered that its species is allergic to something in the air here on Earth 4. None o' our breathing filters were strong enough stop to its allergy attack. We couldn't risk the agent's constant sneezing drawing the B.T.T.'s attention to this area—because, as I'm sure ya know, the sneezes o' the tri-gendered koala-people from Earth 789,564 are as loud as the church bells from the capitol of Earth 650,113—so Agent 99087777 b'came a casualty for the sake o' the mission. The soldier understood and accepted death honorably. Its body and a letter it wrote to its family are stowed on one of the shift-shuttles for safe return back to its home reality."

Agent 27142 nodded. "Good work. I shall need your team to assist me on one final mission before we depart. You *may* see some action yet."

The commander nodded. "Aye, we're at your service."

Agent 27142 turned to the remaining members of Squadron Twelve. "Take the bomb aboard my shift-shuttle and load it so that it is ready to be dropped."

Squadron Twelve's survivors saluted and went to work. Agent 27142 turned to Agent 29333. Her uniform was grimy and sweaty from the raid. But she looked as attractive as ever to Agent 27142. He licked his lips. He opened his mouth to speak. But before he could address her, Prisoner-Art caused a distraction.

The prisoner was hunched over behind her and grunting like a fool, for he had attempted to swat a sundial-shaped bug away from his face, but instead of hitting the bug, he had smacked himself squarely in his own nose with his plaster-encased hand. Blood gushed from his nose. Agent 27142 scowled at him. Agent 29333 noticed the scowl and nodded. Without breaking eye contact with Agent 27142, she elbowed the prisoner. The prisoner collapsed to the ground.

Agent 27142's heart felt overfilled with love for Agent 29333. But instead of telling her about this feeling, he swallowed hard and said to her, "Agent 29333, when I accessed the terminal inside the sub-basement of the B.T.T. headquarters, I found something else on this reality that will help ensure our success. But it will require me to stay on this Earth for just a little while longer. Therefore, *you* must take my shift-shuttle, the prisoner, and what remains of Squadron Twelve back to Earth 55,777. When you reach your destination, you will immediately drop the bomb and confirm that it detonates. You shall have a brief window—likely less than a couple seconds—to jump away from Earth 55,777 following the bomb's detonation."

Agent 29333 nodded. "Aye, sir," she said. "Right away."

Agent 27142 stared down at his boots. He licked his lips once more. He thought, *Just tell her how you feel and kiss her, you fool! This may be your last chance!*

Still looking at his shoes, he said, "The task I am staying behind to complete will be dangerous, and I may not make it out alive. And even if I *do*, the trans-chronal-dimensional politics involved in the crime that we just committed against the B.T.T. will demand that justice against me be swift, so I will likely be carted off to a penal dimension as soon as the Multiverse is saved. So, just in case this is the last time we see one another, I want you to know that I am in love with you. And if we can kiss, if we can make love just *one* time, then all my sacrifice will have been worth it to me."

Agent 27142 puckered his lips, closed his eyes, and leaned forward. He felt no similar puckered lips touch his, so he waited a moment longer. Behind him, he heard Squadron Ampersand's commander clear his throat. Agent 27142 jerked his head toward the commander.

The commander pointed past Agent 27142 and toward the shift-shuttles. He said, "Sir, I regret to inform ya that she heard not a word o' that. She departed right after ya gave her your orders. A good soldier, that one."

Agent 27142 turned in the direction that the commander pointed. The ramp to Agent 27142's shift-shuttle closed. The shift-shuttle took to the air and disappeared in a bolt of lightning. Agent 27142's eagle crooned sadly. He patted its head.

The squadron commander continued, "For what it's worth, sir, I thought it was a beautiful speech, and I'd consider m'self lucky to have ya if ya could open your heart to a beast such as me."

Agent 27142 ignored the creature, his neck turning red from anger and embarrassment. He really, really wanted to torture something just now and wished that he had not sent the prisoner away with Agent 29333. However, there were other creatures he would have the pleasure of torturing in but a few moments, so he did what he did best and returned his focus back to his mission. "Come on, we've got work to do," he muttered.

Agent 27142 sprinted from this cave and entered a different cave on the other side of the clearing. The soldiers of Squadron Ampersand followed, their boots making scritching noises in the dirt as they ran.

When Agent 27142 entered the mouth of this cave, he stopped and studied the scene ahead. Squadron Ampersand stopped just behind him. He noticed a dull purple light glowing far in the distance at the cave's rear. He heard a female voice chanting. Beautiful echoes from the chant enveloped Agent 27142 and his soldiers.

Agent 27142 grinned. The information he had discovered on the B.T.T. computer terminal had been accurate. He stalked forward, confident he was moments away from ensuring that the Multiverse's fate would bow to *his* will.

CHAPTER 23

BOMBS AWAY

OFFICER-GINNY STRAPPED NORMAL-ART to his seat and then sat in the pilot's chair. She pressed a series of buttons on the control console and flipped a few toggles, and the ship's engines began vibrating in reply.

"What's so special about this bomb?" asked Normal-Art, removing the metaphorical dam that blocked his mouth now that Officer-Art was no longer present. Though Officer-Ginny had no qualms about beating and torturing him, her heart never really seemed to be in the act. She only hurt him badly when Officer-Art was around and paying attention.

Officer-Ginny ignored him. She pulled back on the stick and achieved liftoff. What appeared to be a large, soggy rock fell from the sky and thudded against the view screen. It bounced away, having done no harm. It left a few red streaks in its wake, which the ship's automatic cleaners immediately wiped clean.

Officer-Ginny frowned and tapped a few more buttons. "Guess we've got incoming fire. Time to move."

Then she screamed, "Engage!" to her eagle. The eagle blasted lightning into the small metal pole that stood erect from the console. A matching bolt of lightning appeared in front of the ship, and the ship sped through it and into the infinite expanse of the barrier between realities.

Normal-Art glanced down the hatch at the back of the bridge and toward the hold. He could hear the voices of the seven Squadron Twelve survivors drift up into the cockpit. They discussed lost comrades and their uneasiness concerning the weapon sitting at the ready near them, their speech now thick with survivor's guilt, now thick with nervousness.

Normal-Art looked back over at Officer-Ginny. Her eagle sat on her shoulder facing backward, its eyes glaring at Normal-Art like he was a rodent it wanted to rip apart with its curved beak. "What's so special about this bomb?" repeated Normal-Art.

Officer-Ginny huffed her breath out between ill-spaced teeth, the intent of which seemed to be to exert frustration and annoyance, but the whistle that erupted removed any of its intended intimidation. Normal-Art ignored the gesture and asked, "What's going to happen when we detonate it?"

Officer-Ginny glanced over her shoulder at Normal-Art, scorn etched across her face. Normal-Art noted, however, that the metaphorical etching seemed to have been completed by an artist only half-committed to the job. Normal-Art suppressed a smile, for out of all of Officer-Ginny's body language that he had experienced in his decade in her presence, this subtle uncommitted scorn was one of his favorites, for it generally meant that she had no current inclination for violence.

"Is it safe to have on board with us?" prodded Normal-Art.

Officer-Ginny sighed. She muttered, "Of course it's not safe to have on board with us, you fool! If it gets jostled the wrong way and we accidentally set it off here in *The Barrier* before we reach Earth 55,777, we've gone and screwed the entire Multiverse beyond repair—not just because we'd have failed to save it from those damned cosmic bears that're attacking Earth 55,777, but because this type of bomb's effects on *The Barrier* have never been tested or calculated by the B.I.T., at least to my knowledge. *The Barrier* exists simultaneously in infinite space and no space at all, so *I* would predict that the bomb's effects would likely spread across the entire barrier and be too infinite to be reparable by B.I.T. engineers. And the likelihood of the B.T.T. intervening to help with such a problem is approximately nil now that we raided them and ruined our alliance."

As the barrier between realities sped by on the view screen, Normal-Art asked, "Why is it so dangerous? What happens when we detonate it?"

"Nothing's going to happen," replied Officer-Ginny.

Normal-Art sighed, knowing she was baiting him and that there was deeper meaning to her simple statement. Her answer brought up terrible flashbacks of conversations with the hyper-literal god-version of himself, and Normal-Art shuddered. Finally, he sighed once more and succumbed to her bait, asking, "Then why'd we sacrifice so many soldiers to steal the stupid thing?"

Officer-Ginny scowled. "No, I mean *literally* that nothing is going to happen. It's a Stasis Bomb, and it freezes time."

There it is, thought Normal-Art. *She and god-me would have gotten along splendidly.* "And *how* will save the Multiverse?" he asked.

Officer-Ginny reached up and tapped a few buttons. Ahead, the view screen labeled a particular patch of swirling lights as *Earth 55,777*. Then she replied, "That's Agent 27142's big gambit. When we detonate this bomb on Earth 55,777, it will freeze time across the entire dimension, stopping everything and everyone in the reality in their tracks. That will allow forces offsite who were unable to render aid at the time we requested it to find a way to dispose of the frozen incursion forces, find a way to imprison those cursed cosmic bears again, and then find a way to unfreeze us all as soon as it is convenient for them to do so."

"What do you mean, '*Us all*?'"

"Well, *we're* the ones who are going to detonate the thing. I'll try to jump us out of there before its effects envelop Earth 55,777, but the likelihood of success is miserably low. We'll almost certainly be frozen in place along with everything else in the reality. So, I must warn you: from what I understand of this weapon, time will seem to pass normally to those affected by it, but they will be unable to move. Make sure you are comfortable and try not to go insane, for I do not know how long we might be stuck in place, and there'll really be nothing to do if we are frozen but explore your own mind."

Art's stomach dropped, and he felt himself beginning to panic. He begged, "Wait, can you just drop me off somewhere else first? I'm really not up for this."

Officer-Ginny ignored him and patted her eagle on its back. "Alright, we're here," she said, and the eagle fired lightning into the metal pole. The ship flew through it, and the infinite colorlessness-colorfulness was replaced by the vast city of Earth 55,777.

The B.S.S.C. Mimessiah loomed before the view screen. An explosion ripped through the middle of the ship, and it lulled to the side and began drifting down toward the ground.

Normal-Art's panic was replaced by confusion. He said, "Wait, what the hell? We left as that thing was about to go down."

Officer-Ginny jerked the stick to starboard to avoid crashing into the falling monstrosity. She yelled over her shoulder, "Time passes much faster on Earth 4. What seemed like hours and hours to us was only a few seconds here."

Normal-Art groaned. He hated the Multiverse, so he began to pray a silent prayer that one of the many concurrent threats to it might win out and destroy the stupid place. However, before he finished his prayer, all thoughts fled from his head as Officer-Ginny jerked the stick hard in the opposite direction, barrel rolling to dodge a Ginny in a floating cauldron who was throwing flaming skulls.

Normal-Art squealed. Officer-Ginny demanded, "Be silent! I need to concentrate! And keep your eyes peeled. We must confirm the bears are still present on this reality before we drop the bomb! Otherwise, it'll be a waste!"

Normal-Art watched Officer-Ginny scan the battlefield. Then she pointed toward some toppled skyscrapers next to the flaming generator field. "There!" she screamed.

As Normal-Art looked, he wanted to groan, but he held it in. The blue bear and the pink bear flew at each other above the toppled skyscrapers. Pink and blue waves of energy exploded out from them as they crashed into one another. They whirled at one another in fury, punching and kicking and biting. Destruction erupted in their wake, only to immediately be reconstructed and healed.

Officer-Ginny turned the stick toward the bears and punched the throttle. The city transformed into a blur below. Officer-Ginny tapped the communicator in her ear before reaching her right hand down to hover over the button that would open the hatch to drop the bomb. She said, "Agent 27142, if you copy, we have payload drop in 5…4…3…2…*Shit!*"

Suddenly, a mammoth pink tentacle thrust into the sky in front of the view screen. Normal-Art glanced down toward the tentacle's source, and as expected, it belonged to Regular-Ginny and her skyscraper-sized blob. Officer-Ginny grabbed the stick with both hands, jerked it port, and barely evaded the tentacle.

However, the desperate evasion caused the ship to spin out of control. It lost altitude and plummeted toward the ground. Normal-Art screamed. Officer-Ginny shut off the throttle. She gripped the stick and jerked it backward and sideways. The ship pulled up just before crashing to the ground. Officer-Ginny twisted the stick farther to the side, and in another few seconds, the ship steadied. She breathed deep. Then she pressed the throttle and pulled up on the stick, regaining the altitude that had been lost. She swerved the front of the ship so that the cosmic bears were once again immediately in front of the screen.

She tapped her communicator once more and said, "Let's try this again. Agent 27142, if you copy, we have payload drop in 5…4…3…2…1…*Now!*"

She slammed her palm down on the button to open the hatch and drop the bomb.

The whistling blast of cold air in the cabin signaled that the bomb was now airborne. Bright white light exploded across the city below. Normal-Art covered his eyes too late, for when he pulled his hands away, he found he could see nothing beyond the blinding afterimage of the explosion.

Officer-Ginny shouted to her eagle, "Lightning! Now!"

The eagle launched lightning into the pole that stood erect from the console. As the ship flew toward the matching bolt of lightning that appeared in front of the ship, soldiers below deck screamed.

Their screams became gargled and abruptly went silent. The ship's engines seemed to rev louder than ever, and Normal-Art wondered if they had taken some sort of damage during the dropping of the Stasis Bomb. It sounded like the engines had become unhinged from their normal place in the ship and had travelled up onto the bridge and were now literally hovering inches behind him. Normal-Art sighed. He assumed the silenced screams and the odd engine noises were all aftereffects of the Stasis Bomb and that the shift-shuttle had thus not escaped Earth 55,777 in time to prevent becoming frozen in place.

He next experienced a sensation that felt like a colossal dagger was stabbing him through the back and exiting his chest. He tried to glance down at his chest, but he saw nothing, for he was still blind from the Stasis Bomb blast. Then he felt as though he were lying on the cold metal floor of the bridge. Since he had never *been* frozen in time before, he did not know whether these were typical feelings associated with stasis.

He tried to ask Officer-Ginny. His question emerged from his lips as a liquidy gurgle.

He sighed. He wanted to go home. Instead, he died.

CHAPTER 24

DEUS EX MACHINAS DOING DEUS EX MACHINA THINGS

ARTURO CRAWLED THROUGH the air ducts in the skyscraper marked *Olympus*. Before he gained his superpowers, enclosed spaces had made him feel claustrophobic. But during the tenure of his short superheroing career, his rogues' gallery had managed to capture him in a multitude of elaborate traps and bind him with a plethora of intricate constraints. He always managed to escape, and by now, he had grown relatively numb to the sensation. He sped through the ducts by reaching hand over hand and contorting his legs up at angles that would have left them dislocated if he had attempted the movements during the non-powered portion of his life.

Arturo's mind drifted as he crawled. He remembered the lightning-shield around *Olympus* disappearing, its bright lightning there for the entire battle and then suddenly gone. At that point, he felt a tickle in the back of his brain that told him it was *his* time, that the mission for which *he* was destined was now at hand. He swung through the city from the north, dodging attacks from the pink army and evading disintegration bolts from the fighter jets careening by overhead.

The entire time he traversed the battlefield, he thrilled at the idea of being the Multiverse's savior. He remembered a term that he had learned in his English class: *deus ex machina*. It translated to "god from the machine." It referred to resolving a seemingly unresolvable plot point through the intervention of an unforeseen character or force. Though Arturo hated it when *deus ex machinas* appeared in literature because they always seemed like a copout by a stupid writer without the creativity to figure out how to logically solve a narrative problem, Arturo was rather pleased to play the role of a real-life *deus ex machina* himself. He was excited that he would be the big hero to show up at the end of this decade-long war to help the Army of Life win. As a matter of fact, he was silently considering a superhero name change. Forget *Arachnid Pre-Teen*, he could change his name to something much cooler, like *Deus* or *Deus Ex* or *Machina*.

It took him only a few minutes to reach the base of the building with the sign that read *Olympus* on its top, and by the time he got there, he had settled internally upon the new moniker *Machin-Arachnid*. He made quick work of a squadron of marines that exited the building just as he arrived, wrapping them in webbing, hanging them upside-down, and punching them until they were unconscious.

He then climbed the wall of *Olympus* to a vent that opened on the side of the building about two stories up. He pulled a tiny screwdriver from his pocket and unscrewed the grate that covered the vent. He allowed the grate to fall unceremoniously to the ground.

From below, he heard somebody squeal, "Ouch! Hey! Watch it!"

He glanced down to see an odd foursome. Each of the four were seemingly his own age, about twelve-years old. The two males shared identical facial features with himself, while the two females looked just like the girl on whom Arturo had a crush in school.

The male on the far left wore black robes and a scarf striped marigold and salmon, and he floated upon a broomstick. A tornado-shaped scar covered his forehead from brow to hairline. Blood seeped from a gash in his right cheek, and he was bent over the ground picking up a pair of round glasses. One of the lenses was cracked, but he tapped it with a wand and whispered something, and the crack fixed itself. He was obviously the one who had been hit by the falling grate, the one who had shouted in pain.

Next to him stood a young girl in a blue jumpsuit with the sigil of a bluebird on both her chest and her shoulder. She carried a bow and had a quiver of arrows slung across her back. She saluted Arturo by holding up the four fingers of her right hand. By her side stood the other male, this one in maroon robes with gigantic sleeves. He held a small metal sword hilt from which rose a blade made from swirling fire and lightning. Finally, next to him stood a female in what appeared to be a red astronaut's suit complete with a bubbled helmet. She wore a holster around her waist that held a black gun. A tube connected the base of the gun to a power generator on her back.

Arturo dropped to the ground and introduced himself as his new moniker, *Machin-Arachnid*. However, he soon wished he had not done so when he realized that he was not as special as he had originally thought.

Upon speaking with the foursome, Arturo discovered that the cosmic blue bear had given them *all* the same speech and the same task that he had received. The bear had seemingly picked them because they were all their realities' versions of *"Chosen Ones,"* and from what Arturo could deduce, the blue bear assumed this affinity for being "saviors" on their realities might extend to saving the Multiverse. Arturo felt deflated, for this revelation meant that he was not as special as he had been led to believe. He immediately decided that he would revert to his original superhero name—though embarrassingly enough, that would need to wait until he returned to his own home reality, since he had already introduced himself as *Machin-Arachnid* to his four newfound companions.

Arturo discovered that the wizard boy with the scar was named Arthur Artter, and he was something of a celebrity on his home reality, since he was the only person to ever survive an attack from his realm's greatest evil. He was prophesied to set things right for wizarding kind.

The female in the blue jumpsuit was named Ginn Yis, and she had led a rebellion on her home reality, overturning a society in which children were forced to fight to the death each year for sport.

The boy with the flaming sword was named Artkins, and he was the ultimate incarnation of some hokey religion named *The Binding*, and he was prophesied as a savior to bring balance to *The Binding*.

Finally, the female in the astronaut suit was named Ginder, and she had attended military school from the time she was an infant to prepare herself for a war against an alien force that had raided her home world before she was born. She was an ingenious tactical commander, and she had been on the verge of leading the final attack on the Insectoid home world when the Blue One had recruited her to help in this Multiversal emergency. She came equipped with a freeze ray, and she claimed her specialty was in zero-gravity combat, though Arturo did not see how that would be helpful during this current battle.

Arturo discovered that the blue bear had stationed each of these Multiversal child-saviors at different locations on the battlefield to wait for the lightning-shield to go down. Arturo frowned in annoyance because he felt deceived, but Artkins nodded in acceptance and said, "I understand. I fought in the Cloneasaurus Wars, and we nearly lost because we did not use such a tactic. The Blue One could not afford to place all his hope in a single *one* of us.

And he also split us up because if we were all together, an unlucky stray blast could have wiped out all hope for the Multiverse."

Ginder nodded and chimed in, "And in not telling us about one another, the Blue One also prevented the problem of one of us getting captured and having information about the others tortured out of us. I'd say it was a smart tactical move on the bear's part."

Artkins nodded once more, obviously in awe of the blue bear's tactical genius. Arturo and the other two members of the group frowned, undoubtedly all feeling the same conflicted emotions. Artkins frowned back at them and then waved two fingers in front of his face. He said, "I can sense that you all feel betrayed and unimportant because you were not the *single* person destined to save the Multiverse. But do not lose hope. It seems logical that we will not *all* survive this mission. So, there is still the chance that only one of us will emerge as the sole living savior of the Multiverse, while the rest become mere footnotes within its vast history."

When Artkins finished speaking, Arturo somehow felt refreshed and important, like his heart and his mind had been rubbed with a metaphorical salve of positivity. He said, "That makes sense to me. I'm going to sneak into the building through the air ducts, since stealth will be the key to this mission. I would invite you all along with me, but you'll have a hard time following unless you can bend at angles impossible for a normal human. I shall begin our mission and meet you inside, assuming you can find a way in."

Before Arturo could turn away and enter the open grate, Arthur Artter said, "Oh, fret not. Size won't be a problem."

The wizard boy waved his wand in a circle and yelled something that sounded like "Tinius Poppity!" Sparks flew from the end of his wand, danced around everyone except Arturo, and shrank them into tiny versions of themselves about three-inches tall.

"Now you can take us with you," squealed Arthur Artter.

Arturo shrugged and then formed a little web-hammock in which to carry the two females and the boy with the fire-lightning sword. He hoisted them over his shoulder and crawled through the open grate, entering the air ducts. The tiny Arthur Artter insisted on floating behind them on his broomstick.

Arturo's mind returned to the present and focused on his surroundings. As he crawled through the air ducts, he heard voices below him. He stopped to listen. He could not make out every word, but he heard, "…High

Commander… ultimate weapon…in *The Forge*…stop the bears."

Arturo gulped. He whispered to the others, "Did you all hear that?"

The boy with the fire-lightning sword whispered back, and because of his tiny new stature, his voice sounded similar to the squeaking of a mouse. "I did. It appears to be guards on patrol engaged in gossip. Hold on a second, and I shall use *The Binding* to uncover details."

The boy held a finger to his temple and closed his eyes. He hummed softly. The boy on the broomstick seemed a little pouty, like *he* had wanted to be the one to use some sort of trick to gain this information.

Below, the voices began screaming in unison, "THE HIGH COMMANDER IS CREATING A WEAPON TO DEFEAT THE INCURSION FORCES, OR AT LEAST THAT WAS THE LAST RUMOR WE HEARD! HIS FORGE IS ON THE TOP FLOOR! DEFENSES UNKNOWN, SINCE NONE OF US HAVE SECURITY CLEARANCE TO ENTER *THE FORGE!*

The voices continued. "AND THE COMMUNICATIONS VAULT IS ON FLOOR 65! DEFENSES CONSIST OF TWELVE TURRETS AND THREE SQUADRONS OF TWENTY SOLDIERS EACH."

Artkins removed his finger from his temple. The voices began speaking in confusion, unsure what had just happened. Artkins then crushed his hand into a fist, and the voices turned into screams hyphenated by gurgling squishy sounds.

Arturo turned to Artkins. He whisper-shouted, "What the hell, man? You *killed* those guards! You may as well have set off an alarm yourself!"

Seemingly on cue, an alarm began blaring. Artkins shrugged and replied, "At least now we know where we need to go. All things happen as they must, as is the will of *The Binding*."

Ginn Yis spoke up, "We need to set our explosives in the Communications Vault right away."

Artkins nodded. "Agreed," he said.

Arthur Artter shook his head. He said, "No. First, we need to steal the weapon that those guards mentioned so that it can't be deployed against the blue bear or against us. I know a thing or two about how these types of adventures work, and I will guarantee that if we don't get our hands on that weapon, we will find ourselves attacked by it *while* we're setting our explosives."

Ginder shook her head and responded, "But this *isn't* an adventure. It's not some story for children. It's a war. And *I* understand battle strategy better than anyone—at least better than anyone on *my* home reality—and we *must* set those explosives first in order to accomplish our mission. All other wins are bonus points. I vote that we complete our mission in the Communications Vault first, and then we go after the weapon if there is time."

Arturo frowned. He had faced enough supervillains to agree with Arthur Artter's logic. He said, "I agree with Arthur Artter. Every instance where I *haven't* stopped the diabolical weapon first, it's come back as a huge problem later."

Ginn Yis frowned. She said, "Then we are at an impasse."

Arturo shrugged. He replied, "No, not necessarily. You and Ginder can go with Artkins to set the explosives in the Communications Vault. Arthur Artter and I can simultaneously go steal the weapon. Then we can meet you on Floor 65 at the Communications Vault. If we don't make it within five minutes of you setting your bombs, flee the building without us."

Artkins nodded. He said, "May *The Binding* hold you together, and may it also hold you up for success."

Arturo shrugged. "Right back at ya," he replied.

Arturo then crawled ahead, within moments finding a grate that opened onto an elevator shaft. He kicked it open with his heel and listened to it clang atop an elevator car stopped on the first floor. He hopped atop it and began pulling on wires, intending to use his hyper-genius understanding of technology to override the elevator's controls. He groaned in annoyance when the wizard boy waved his wand and said something that sounded like *Floorius Sixty-Fivius*.

The elevator car jerked into motion and stopped just below Floor 65. The doors to the floor popped open, and Artkins, Ginder, and Ginn Yis scrambled from the top of the elevator car, through the open door, and onto Floor 65. Arthur mumbled a spell that returned them to their proper sizes, and then he waved his wand again, this time saying something that sounded like *Topius Floorius*.

Arturo watched Artkins, Ginder, and Ginn Yis disappear around a bend in the hallway as the elevator car jerked upward. Alarms blared all around, and the frantic arachnid-intuition erupting across the back of his skull made him wish he had never crossed paths with these four other *deus ex machinas*.

*

Now regular-sized, Arthur Artter floated on his broomstick beside Arturo. "You ever felt anything like this heat?' asked the boy wizard.

The Forge was hotter than anything Arturo had ever experienced. The heat smacked him in the face as soon as he stepped from the elevator shaft into the adjoining hallway. The next hottest place Arturo had ever experienced was during the brief, wonderful time in which he had been dead. He had floated atop clouds next to thousands of singing cherubs. He befriended one of them named Popooti, who showed him the edge of Heaven where he could see down into the depths of Hell. The air from *that* view was hot and humid and hurt to stand near, but it felt like a small candle compared to *The Forge* at the top of the *Olympus* building.

Arturo frowned at the memory of his afterlife, remembering how he had *just* grown accustomed to the idea of being dead and had made friends and had felt at peace, only to have that all ripped away from him when he was resurrected and shoved headlong into an infinite war. He had felt a gnawing emptiness in the pit of his stomach since returning, a feeling so numb and cold that not even this forge's heat could melt it. This emptiness screamed through his guts like Kassandra of Troy, warning him to abandon this war and return to the overwhelming peace of his afterlife. But he bit his lower lip and took a deep breath and refused to succumb, as he had refused every time the desire threatened to overwhelm him. When he first began superheroing, he had made a vow to protect those weaker than himself, and he did not intend to break that vow by giving up now and abandoning the peoples of the Multiverse.

"I said, have you ever felt anything like this heat?" asked the boy wizard once more. "It's like you were lost in your own head there."

Arturo shushed the other boy wizard harshly, and he immediately felt bad about it when he heard a soft, hurt sigh emanate from the boy. Not bad enough to remark on it or apologize, mind you, but he still felt a little pang of guilt.

Arturo glanced around at his surroundings. The fluorescent lighting that had emanated from Floor 65 during the brief stop there stood in stark contrast to the dark grays and flickering flames from torches placed in sconces high upon the walls. Arturo crept silently forward, and upon reaching the end of the hallway and passing under an arch, he peeked around the corner into *The Forge* proper.

The Forge rose so high into the air that its ceiling was not visible, with a new furnace opening up every dozen or so feet along the wall. Floating robots shaped like basketballs with hands dangling from three-foot long tentacles worked the furnaces like an assembly line: robots painted green zipped from furnace to furnace pumping bellows, robots painted red retrieved molten metal from the furnaces in gigantic steel buckets, pouring the contents into molds shaped like the infamous disintegration guns that had wrought such havoc on the blue and pink bears' armies. Blue robots carrying mallets floated from mold to mold, whacking and shaping the cooling metal. Robots colored yellow and holding funnels in one hand and little sacks overflowing with white lightning in the other moved about the completed molds and poured the lightning into the guns' barrels. Finally, white robots collected the completed guns onto hovering pallets and pushed the pallets out of view toward the back of *The Forge* when each pallet was full.

Arturo found himself staring in awed silence at the scene until Arthur elbowed him and brought him back to his senses.

In the center of the room stood a long, metal table. Near the table rose a set of bellows the size of a house, with a robotic cyclops behind it continuously pumping the bellows up and down, stoking the bright flame just to the side of the table. Surrounding every square inch of the table lay weapons and armor, all stylized so brilliantly that Arturo had never seen such fine work, not even from the Mad Blacksmith in his own rogues' gallery. A man wearing light blue robes was leaned over the table. Arturo estimated that he must be at least fifteen-feet tall with a beard nearly half as long as he was tall, the bushy hair bound by leather straps into a shaggy braid that had been tossed over his shoulder. The man hammered over and over on a black blade. Sparks flew into the air with each wallop, and Arturo looked in awe at the man's thickly muscled right shoulder.

Arturo knew without needing to ask that this would be the weapon they sought. The architecture of the entire forge seemed directed toward this table, and Arturo had experienced enough evil lairs to know *that* was a general sign to indicate this was the final boss within such a stronghold.

Arthur Artter dabbed at the sweat on his forehead with his scarf and whispered, "I'll handle him. I've faced plenty of giants and trolls and evil wizards that were so powerful we weren't even allowed to say their names. *This* guy'll be no problem for the greatest boy wizard ever. You snatch that blade he's working on while he's distracted, and then you run. I'll catch up."

Arturo nodded. Arthur Artter nodded back, and then he jerked up on the handle of his broomstick, riding it high into the air. The boy wizard aimed his wand down at the giant man hammering away at the black blade.

"Ringoria Bindellimus!" yelled Arthur Artter. Mighty shackles of light dropped from the wand and clanged closed around the giant's wrists and ankles.

The giant did not deign to look up from his work. He shrugged his shoulders. "Cosmic entities are so predictable," he muttered in an annoyed tone, his voice booming across the vast expanse of *The Forge*. "I assume that the foul blue creature has convinced thee that *thou art* the last hope for the Multiverse? Thou art a greater fool than thou look."

Before Arturo could react, the giant pointed his mallet toward Arthur Artter. A beam of fire launched from its end. Arthur Artter waved his wand and screamed "Shieldito Maximorimus!"

A shield of blue light formed around the boy, but not before fire engulfed him and burned him until nothing remained of him but a black skeleton trapped inside a boy-sized shield made of blue light. The blue light disappeared, and the skeleton fell to the ground. It collapsed into an untidy pile of bones. The giant lifted a gun from a rack on the wall and walked over to the pile of bones. Just as he fired a disintegration beam into the midst of Arthur Artter's remains, Arturo sprang into action.

With his right hand, Arturo flung a ball of web at the giant's head. It smacked into the back of the giant's skull and pushed it into the wall, sticking it in place. With his left hand, Arturo shot a second string of web, snatched the blade with it, and pulled it over to himself.

The giant's shoulders shook with laughter. "Ha! Ha! Ha! Looks like the bear sent more than one plaything. That is a pleasant, less-predictable surprise. I hope thou art ready to die, too."

The giant pulled at the webbing on the back of his head with his mighty hands. Matted clumps of hair and web tore from the giant's scalp, and he was soon free. He stared at Arturo, his tongue flittering out of his mouth to dance across the roots of his long, gray beard. The giant turned and blew into a small pipe that hung from the wall near him. All the robots working the factory stopped their work, picked up disintegration guns, and turned toward Arturo.

"Been there, done that, got the shirt, but returned it. No thanks!" yelled Arturo in response. Then he ran, using his arachnid-intuition to dodge the disintegration bolts from the robots and the beams of fire that sprayed from the giant's mallet. Arturo bounced from wall to wall, never staying still for more than a fraction of a second. As he fled down the hallway, he created a makeshift scabbard for the blade out of webbing and slung it across his back.

He leapt through the still-open elevator door from which he had entered this floor. He stood atop the same elevator car he had used to enter this floor. When he noticed that none of the cars were visible for the banks on either side of this one, he dove down the empty shaft to the right.

He glanced up and breathed a momentary sigh of relief as too many robots simultaneously tried to follow him through the open elevator door. They wedged themselves so that they got stuck. But then the other two shaft doors disintegrated, and Arturo squealed as hundreds more robots poured in an orderly fashion into the shaft above.

Below him, light poured forth from the still-open door for Floor 65. He changed the direction of his dive so that he aimed toward it, and as soon as it entered his reach, he grabbed the top of the open door and flung himself inside, tumbling end over end down the hallway until he crashed to a halt on the far wall.

He rubbed his head where it smarted and quickly gained his bearings. Dozens and dozens of dead B.I.T. soldiers littered the hallway, most of them full of arrows. Arturo heard a familiar voice around the corner, though he could make out no words. He knew that any second now, the robots would be exiting the elevator shaft behind him. Arturo desperately needed to ensure that the explosives were set, and then he needed to escape now that he had his hands on the B.I.T.'s secret weapon.

Arturo rounded the corner of the hallway and stood for a moment in shock. Ginn Yis disintegrated in a beam of bright lightning. The two arrows she had nocked and was ready to loose clattered to the floor. A second bolt of lightning connected with Ginder as she attempted to dive out of its way. She managed to get a shot off as she disappeared into nothingness, but it missed the soldier that had fired upon her.

Meanwhile, Artkins stood deflecting disintegration bolts with his fire-lightning sword. The smoking black outlines on the ceiling indicated that he must have destroyed the turrets that had lined the ceiling, and the screams that sounded from the end of the hallway marked the soldiers into whom he had deflected these latest disintegration bolts.

"I got the secret weapon. Did you set the bomb?" screamed Arturo.

Artkins did not look away from his battle. He replied, "No. The Communications Vault is the next room down. We're almost there."

And then hundreds of robots turned the corner behind Arturo. More and more soldiers appeared on the opposite end of the hallway. Artkins and Arturo were trapped in the middle.

The giant's voice blared from speakers in the robots, "This was a good effort, but I must end this charade now. There is too much at stake."

Arturo's heart threatened to beat out of his chest. He glanced over at Artkins. He screamed, "This *isn't* how it ends. We're the *deus ex machinas* in this war! *We're* the ones who show up at the end and save everythi—"

But unfortunately for these five adolescents who had embarked on this deadly mission—these five *"Chosen Ones"* destined to save their home Earths from unspeakable evils—this *was* how it ended. The robots and the soldiers opened fire, disintegrating the last of the Blue One's *deus ex machinas*. Arturo felt every atom inside him seize, like he was experiencing billions and billions of heart attacks at once, all over his body.

This time, Arturo did not return to his afterlife. His atoms spread across the Multiverse, and he experienced an eternity he would never have been able to describe even if given the chance. He saw only blackness, but he felt a tiny window into a nigh-infinite number of realities' afterlives.

If only he had remained undisintegrated for a few more minutes, he would have been frozen in time and may not have experienced a death from which he would never return.

THE RETURN

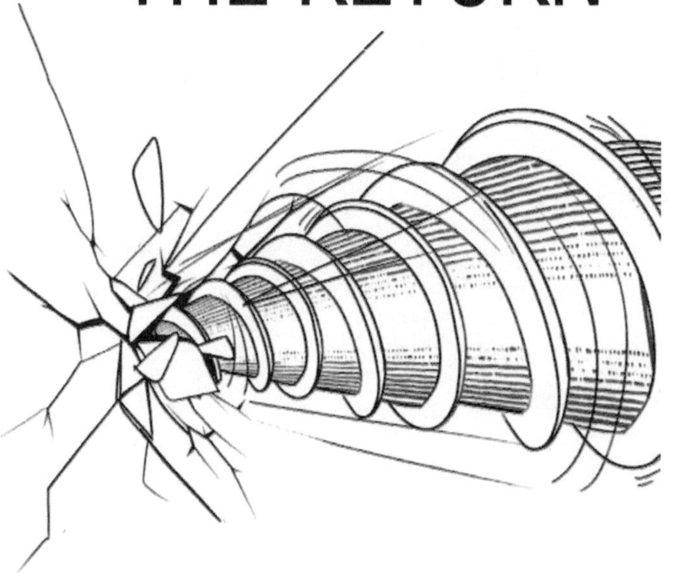

CHAPTER 1

ANOTHER A-MUSE-ING INVOCATION

"SING TO ME, O Muse, of the B.I.T. agent whose plan worked perfectly. Sing to me of the man who risked everything to ensure the Multiverse emerged triumphant over the cosmic bears that threatened it," demanded Agent 27142.

The Muse sat bound upon a small marble altar at the back of the cave, her skin pale olive, her hair downy and brown, her figure supple and lithe, her eyes fierce and glowing purple.

"I shall never sing for *you*," hissed the Muse. Her voice drifted through the cave like a thick syrup that coated the ears with delight, despite their contents being contrary to Agent 27142's desires. She scowled at Agent 27142, so he nodded at the commander of Squadron Ampersand.

The commander turned her upside-down by her ankles and dipped her head into a bucket of water. He held her there until she began thrashing, and then he pulled her out so she could inhale a quick breath, and then he shoved her back in. This process repeated thirteen times before she yielded. The commander turned her right-side up and sat her back down upon the altar.

The most beautiful melody that Agent 27142 ever heard began pouring forth from the Muse's lips. She sobbed between notes, but the notes filled the cave, and Agent 27142 wished he could listen to the song forever. He was overcome with a strong urge to create, to sculpt, to paint, to write, to make love. As he glanced about, he recognized similar emotions in his soldiers, two of whom were now squatted on the cave floor and drawing in the dirt with the barrels of their Scatter Guns. The Muse formed words in harmony with the tranquil melody ululating from deep in her throat, words that formed pictures in Agent 27142's head of his own exploits and his plan bearing fruit and the Stasis Bomb saving both the B.I.T. and the Multiverse.

Agent 27142 bit the inside of his lip to suppress the creative urges that blazed through his mind. He knew that he *himself* had the willpower to resist the desires that the Muse instilled in those around her, but he did not have the same confidence in his underlings. He needed to provide them with focus, or they would never finish what needed to be done here.

He walked to the three lowest ranking members of Squadron Ampersand, a female about seven-feet tall and two males both barely under six-feet tall. All three stared at Agent 27142 with clouded eyes as he asked, "Do you have anything with which to plug your ears?"

When the trio shook their heads, he replied, "Very well. Can any of you read lips?"

The female raised her hand, though she was visibly fighting against her pupils turning to watch the Muse. "Aye, sir," muttered the female soldier. As she continued speaking, her voice trickled in slow, barely audible bursts like it had caught some sort of wanderlust and was dancing farther away into the distance with each passing second, "I took the course from Agent 5569000 as part of extended basic training."

Agent 27142 nodded. He said, "Then while you can still hear me, I want to thank you in advance for your sacrifices. I need you to ensure that the Muse sings continuously about our raid's success, but I also can't allow you to be distracted by her song. Now fall to your knees, all three of you."

The trio knelt. Agent 27142 retrieved from his holster one of his brass pill-shaped devices. He pressed the button on the device and three petite spikes poked out of its bottom. He walked to each of the trio in turn and pricked them in each of their ears. Each soldier stifled moans of pain as their ears melted off their heads and collected on the ground as puddles of gore.

But once their ears were gone, the glassy looks in their eyes disappeared, and they seemed in control of their wills once more. He disarmed the pill-shaped device and returned it to the pouch on his holster, where it joined the multitude of spare pill-shaped devices that he kept there, since they were easy to lose on missions but always necessary to have on hand. He pointed to the Muse. The female agent tapped the other two agents on their shoulders and gestured for them to hold the Muse ready for torture. She then stood staring at the immortal's lips, her eyes never wavering from her duty.

Agent 27142 nodded in satisfaction. He walked over to the tentacle-armed squadron commander and asked, "Did your soldiers finish their search of the cave? Did they locate our primary targets?"

The squadron commander nodded and said, "Aye, sir. Just received word from one o' 'em. The targets were found through a small tunnel under the Muse's altar. Apologies it took this long to find 'em. There're tunnels hidden all throughout this cave. It's like an ant farm. Except instead o' ants, a bunch of the tunnels end at the lairs o' some kinda murderous demigods originatin' from what appears to be the Greek mythological pantheon, or at least what we would call the Greeks on many realities in the charted Multiverse. We lost three soldiers in the search. Follow me this way, sir."

The squadron commander led Agent 27142 around the large marble altar, its façade decorated in reliefs of ancients engaged in the arts—poetry and dancing and singing and painting. All along the cave wall, Agent 27142 noticed small circular holes bored into the rock. Flickering flames danced into view from the depths of some of them, though most sat shadowy and dark. He could have sworn he heard growling drifting out from a few, and from one of them floated the grotesque sound of teeth chewing upon bloody flesh.

As Agent 27142 made his way behind the Muse's altar, the squadron commander pointed to a small semicircular hole that lay barely visible at the base of the marble. A tiny soldier the size of a crab emerged from the hole, his Scatter Gun twice as tall as himself. His voice squeaked as he said, "The Moirai are down there at their loom, just as you described them. If we move this altar aside, any of y'all could fit down this hole without much of a struggle."

The squadron commander ordered a dozen of his soldiers to push the altar aside. The soldiers grunted and shoved, and when they finally rotated the marble altar about twenty degrees, it revealed the full circular opening of the tunnel. Flickering light rose into view from below, along with the sounds of three distinct whispering voices.

Agent 27142 nodded to the squadron commander and ordered, "Bring four soldiers and come with me."

Agent 27142 crawled feet-first down the tunnel, twisting to follow it as it circled round and round. His eagle dug its talons harder into his shoulder the farther he descended. Agent 27142 sighed, and then he cooed to the eagle and patted its head. The creature had always been particularly claustrophobic.

Soon, the tunnel leveled out and ended in a large chamber nearly entirely filled by billowy tufts of wool. In a clearing in its center, three identical elderly women wearing white tunics to cover their pale blue skin sat around a large loom. The leftmost woman used her feet to spin a wheel that transformed the wool into flesh-colored yarn. At blinding speed, she simultaneously used her hands to knit the yarn into what looked like an elaborate scarf. The fabric had tiny images that depicted a life-story woven into it. The middle woman measured the fabric and called out its length after writing a name upon it with a charcoal brick. The rightmost woman held a pair of oversized shears and cut the fabric when it reached the measurement called out by the middle triplet. Upon being cut, the flesh-colored fabric bled on the ground at their feet, turned black, and rotted into nothingness.

Agent 27142 smiled. These were the Fates, otherwise known as the Moirai, and according to most charted realities' versions of their Greek pantheons, these three determined the destinies of everyone, mortal and god alike. Though Agent 27142 could recall no Greek pantheons on his home reality, the High Commander long ago regaled him with tales of the pantheon from Earth 24. Agent 27142 had paid particularly close attention to one of the High Commander's stories in which he had kidnapped both the Moirai and the Muse during his Earth's Heroic Age. He had forced the Muse to sing inspiration to the Moirai, who spun a new destiny for Earth 24 on their loom. He used the creatures to alter reality so that he became the head of his pantheon and the most powerful being on Earth 24.

During the raid to steal the Stasis Bomb, when Agent 27142 had logged into the terminal in the sub-basement of the B.T.T. headquarters, he had learned that each of the millions of caves spread throughout the mountains surrounding the B.T.T.'s headquarters were full of anachronisms from throughout the infinite recesses of time and the infinite expanses of the Multiverse, like a living and deadly museum wrought in the rock.

And upon making this discovery, an idea had exploded into existence within his mind. Agent 27142 could think of nobody better from whom to take inspiration than the High Commander, so he decided it could *only* help the B.I.T.'s chances for survival if he were to replicate the High Commander's use of these mythological creatures. It took but a quick search to locate a version of the Moirai and the Muse in the mountains' caves, and in a coincidence so fortunate as to seem either predestined or completely implausible—depending on your point of view—the cave in which these creatures resided lay in the same clearing that Agent 27142 had landed his team of shift-shuttles.

Agent 27142 cleared his throat to get the attention of the three old women.

They did not look up from their work. The first triplet continued spinning the wheel and knitting. The middle one called out a measurement, "Twenty-two-point-three years," and the woman on the end with the shears cut the fabric.

One of the soldiers standing behind Agent 27142 grabbed his chest, squealed in surprise, and then collapsed to the ground. He was a corpse before he hit the dirt. Agent 27142 smiled. *At least I have their attention*, he thought.

"Seize them," ordered Agent 27142.

The squadron commander jerked forward and kicked the shears out of the rightmost woman's hands before she had time to cut again. The three remaining soldiers who had accompanied him down here sprinted behind the women and bound their hands behind their backs.

Agent 27142 turned to the squadron commander and said, "You and these soldiers are to stay with the Moirai. Torture them as needed, but ensure that they create a thread that guarantees the B.I.T.'s victory. From what I understand about the way they work, you need to have them weave a constant stream of images that show what we desire to happen, and then when each image is cut, whatever is in the image will occur in real life. Have them work up imagery of the Stasis Bomb succeeding in its task and the High Commander victorious over the incursion forces."

The squadron commander nodded. He said, "Aye, at once, sir! If I may ask, what are ya gonna be doin' while we're handling this?"

Agent 27142 sighed. This was the first time he had ever been disappointed with this squadron commander. He was normally fantastic at following orders without asking questions.

"I must return to Earth 55,777 to ensure that all goes according to plan. I will send relief for you and your soldiers as soon as I am able," replied Agent 27142, though he did not deign to define *how* soon he would be able to do so.

The squadron commander nodded and got to work. He called for a set of torture instruments, and as soon as a courier from the Muse's chamber brought them into the room, the commander went to work. Agent 27142 watched with sadistic glee as the commander hung each of the elderly women upside-down one after another and dipped their heads in buckets full of water until they agreed to weave what he instructed.

Agent 27142 smiled in satisfaction as the seemingly infinite amount of loose wool that covered the back of the chamber began winding through the loom and forming the images he desired. The images were shorn with such speed that it seemed Agent 27142 was watching a cartoon. The imagery showed Agent 29333 aboard the shift-shuttle returning to Earth 55,777, the shift-shuttle dropping the Stasis Bomb, and then a clock with a large red X through it.

Agent 27142 left the room satisfied. He emerged from the tunnel back into the Muse's chamber. He smiled for a moment at the Muse's melody. And then he smiled wider as he listened to his newly earless soldiers continuing their torture of the Muse, forcing her to create a song about the B.I.T.'s victory—an inspirational ballad that would drift down into the lair of the Moirai to provide additional insurance to guarantee positive results from their loom.

Agent 27142 nodded, and then he marched to where he could see the clearing outside the cave's mouth. He called ten of the remaining Squadron Ampersand soldiers to his side. He pointed toward one of the remaining cloaked shift-shuttles outside the cave and barked orders to the soldiers at his side, "You shall accompany me on the shift-shuttle named *Leaky Fire-Pipe*. Prepare yourselves to return to Earth 55,777. What we have accomplished in this cave means that our victory is now guaranteed. Let us go witness it."

The soldiers all saluted him.

And just when Agent 27142's heart was full of joy and pride at his exploit in this cave, a piercing cackle erupted from the tunnel leading down to the Moirai, a powerful sound which echoed up into this cave and nearly toppled everyone to the ground. Agent 27142's eagle screeched.

The squadron commander's voice sounded in Agent 27142's ear-piece. "Sir, we've got a problem! They're weaving too fast! I pulled 'em away from the loom, but not b'fore they managed t'create an image where the loom runs on its own! I can't stop it! Oh, god, what have they done to Agent 29333! Sir, what should we do?"

Agent 27142 scowled. These types of mishaps were why he often had difficulty delegating. He could trust no one to do a job as well as himself. He balled his fists and began stalking back toward the Moirai tunnel.

But before he could enter the tunnel, the Muse stopped singing and said to him, "I wouldn't do that if I were you."

He stomped over to her. "And why not?"

The Muse laughed. "You were a fool to come here. I know who inspired you with this tactic, for inspiration is what I control. This strategy worked for Earth 24's Hephaestus because he was a *god*. You are but a mortal, and your hubris has proved your undoing."

Agent 27142 grabbed the Muse by the throat and throttled her. "What is happening? What did you do?" he demanded.

She laughed again. "Look around you. Count your soldiers."

Agent 27142 did so. He realized one was missing. The Muse saw the recognition in his face and continued, "Having deaf guards torture me into compliance was another foolish notion. I had but to move my lips differently than the words I spoke, and they never noticed my treachery. And I had but to dance my song around the translators embedded in all of your skulls, and your pathetic technology never even noticed my treachery, either. As you demanded, I sang a song to inspire the Moirai in their weaving. But I *also* inspired them to sneak in an image of one of your warriors defecting to our side. He went to alert our Father, and our Father has sent help."

"What about the Stasis Bomb?" demanded Agent 27142 as he slapped her across the face. She could call all the reinforcements she desired to attack him and his soldiers. He did not care if he died so long as the plan to stop the cosmic bears worked. "Did you inspire the Moirai to prevent *that* from working?"

She growled. Then she said, "No. I was unable to intervene before they wove the picture of your stolen bomb's success. However, your hubris cost you dearly, and everything else about your plan has ended in ruin for you. Know that the woman you love is dead. Know that the prisoner you loved to torture is dead."

Agent 27142 touched his earpiece to speak with the squadron commander. "Destroy the loom!" he screamed. "Destroy it before it does any more damage. And then get rid of the Moirai!"

The Muse laughed again. "The damage is already done!"

The cave shook, and dust rained down from its roof. Agent 27142 pulled his Scatter Gun pistol from his holster and fired it directly into the Muse's chest. Her laughter echoed through the cave as she disintegrated. Agent 27142 signaled for the three deaf soldiers to join the nine he had gathered—the one who had defected now missing from the original ten—and follow him.

They sprinted toward the cave mouth, but too late. Agent 27142's heels dug into the dirt as he screeched to a halt. Outside lumbered dozens and dozens of Cyclopes, each at least fifty-feet tall and each carrying a boulder about half that distance in girth. The behemoths were all naked and covered in thick coats of body hair. Their flopping genitals seemed somehow both profane and holy, like an ancient temple covered in graffiti.

One of the Cyclopes threw a boulder at Agent 27142, and it filled the entirety of his field of vision.

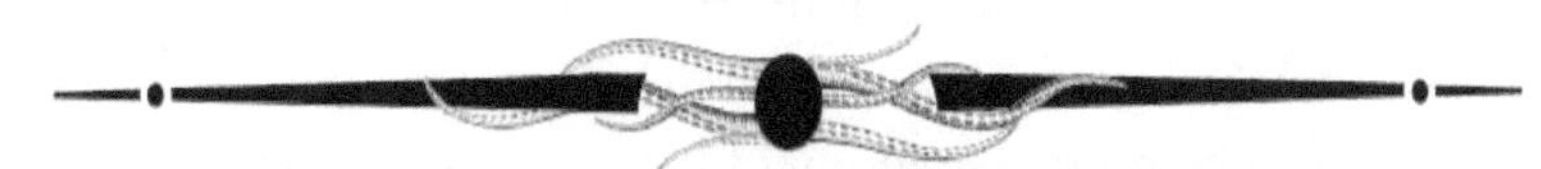

CHAPTER 2

IMPROVISATION, THY NAME IS REGULAR-GINNY

REGULAR-GINNY BOUNDED TOWARD the robot, tentacles aimed straight ahead, hardened and ready to stab. The robot bounded back at her, drills aimed straight ahead, spinning and ready to stab. As they crashed into one another and began yet another fight where she beat the robot mercilessly with her pink blob while it stabbed her equally unmercifully with its drills, she glanced over at the Tyrannosaurus Rex.

The beast leaned down, snapped off one of Arthur the Putrid's legs, chewed it, swallowed it, and roared. Ginny felt a hot, angry, pink tickle in the back of her brain. A hateful smile crept across her lips, for an idea had entered her head that was sure to be novel and fun.

While she smacked the robot about the face and distracted it with whirls of pink goo, she created a new tentacle and sent it slithering toward the Tyrannosaurus Rex. She swiped it at the dinosaur as a feint, and when the beast jumped aside and rolled to dodge the pink snake, Ginny whipped the tentacle back over to Arthur the Putrid's remaining undevoured leg and released pink mist upon it.

The severed appendage hopped up onto its foot and then leapt up into the air, hovering in place a few feet off the ground. It dodged as the Tyrannosaurus Rex attempted to stomp it, and then it followed the orders that Ginny mentally sent to the pinkness swirling inside its veins. It zoomed through the air away from the dinosaur and toward the robot.

Ginny wiggled her blob in such a way that the robot was flipped over and dumped onto the ground. She rolled her blob away from the robot. It immediately leapt back up onto its wheels and aimed its drills at her.

The severed leg's foot glowed a mixture of green and pink. As it flew toward the robot, it wound up for a great kick, which it unleashed upon the back of the robot's head. As the foot connected with robot cranium, its toes exploded. The force of the blast sent the robot tumbling end over end.

The robot crashed to a halt and lay sprawled upon the ground. The severed leg rushed toward the robot for another blow. However, the robot would not be taken by surprise again. It hopped up onto its wheels, and then it dashed toward the severed appendage and began battling it. Over the next few moments, it sliced the appendage into such oblivion that the leg could no longer function, even as a pink puppet.

However, those few moments were the *just* distraction that Regular-Ginny sought. Pink hatred filled her heart, and she grew three mighty tentacles with ends the shape and sharpness of samurai swords, except these samurai swords were sized to fit a giant's hands. She hurtled them toward the Tyrannosaurus Rex. The dinosaur seemed to understand Ginny's intention to murder it while the robot was distracted, and to the creature's credit, it neither flinched nor fled. The beast sprinted toward Ginny, roaring in fury.

But Ginny had cosmic power at her disposal, for which a dinosaur wearing a spiked leather jacket and a blond mullet was no match. With one tentacle-sword, Ginny stabbed the beast just to the left of its neck. With the second, she impaled it through the stomach, and with the third, she pierced the beast's flesh just inside its right hip.

Rather than dying, the Tyrannosaurus Rex snapped its jaws and continued pushing toward Regular-Ginny, impaling itself further on the tentacle-swords and inching closer to Ginny's blob with every angry step. Ginny responded by lifting the beast into the air and slicing the bladed ends of her tentacles in different directions. The dinosaur's roar transformed into a gurgle. And then as the pink swords exited through the beast's flesh, the dinosaur ripped in twain. The beast's head, left arm, and left leg spun end over end in one direction, crashing onto the ground in a wet pile of flesh. Its right arm, right leg, and tail spun end over end in the opposite direction, crashing onto the ground in a separate pile of gore.

Somehow, the half with the beast's head crawled toward Regular-Ginny, its tiny arm scratching through the grass and its maw snapping dagger-sized teeth at Ginny's pink blob. Ginny admired the creature and its single-minded will. However, this admiration did not prevent pink hatred from coursing through her veins, and it did not stop her from growing a fourth tentacle the size of a redwood tree and slapping it down upon this half of the dinosaur like she would use a swatter upon a gnat.

Through the jiggling pink blob, Regular-Ginny felt the beast's bones shatter and its skull crack, and just like that aforementioned metaphorical gnat, the dinosaur's body lay crushed and broken. The dinosaur gasped a final breath and died.

Ginny rubbed her tentacle on the ground, wiping the crushed corpse of the Tyrannosaurus Rex from it. She cackled.

And then her cackling was interrupted by the robot's anguished roars.

CHAPTER 3

DRILLBOT, PORTRAIT OF A ROBOT ALL ALONE

DRILLBOT STARED DOWN at his drills, which were covered in tiny pieces of the floating severed leg that he had just sliced into a lifeless pile of gore, and shame at his stupidity overwhelmed him.

The leg was obviously a distraction, he thought. *Drillbot should have realized it. What a fool Drillbot is!*

A sudden sense of emptiness and loss washed over the shame, and he wanted to shed the robot equivalent of tears for all eternity.

Drillbot watched the Ginny in the pink blob wipe Ginny Rex's corpse off her pink tentacle and onto the ground. It reminded him of the many times he had seen one of the Arts or Ginnys in the Army of Life accidentally step in some form of excrement and then scrape it from the bottom of their shoe. The metaphor filled Drillbot with rage, and he roared, doing his best to imitate Ginny Rex's enraged scream when Artkylosaurus had been blown to pieces.

Drillbot watched as Regular-Ginny snaked a new tentacle out from her blob, this one with a broad, flat tip. Drillbot knew what this type of tentacle signaled, for he had seen it countless times when the woman used it to transform dead Arts and Ginnys into pink puppets. He raced forward as fast as he could go.

Pink mist began wafting from the end of the flat-tipped tentacle. He cursed. If he did not get there in time to stop what was about to happen, he knew that he would never be able to summon the will to raise his drills against his true love, even if she *had* been transformed into an evil puppet with no will of her own.

He aimed one of his drills toward the tentacle and initiated the internal command for it to launch. It rocketed from the end of his arm to slice through the pink appendage, cutting it off at its base. The pink mist ceased for a moment, but then it restarted from a new tentacle that formed from the blob.

The momentary respite allowed him to reach Ginny Rex's side—or rather, it allowed him to roll into a position adjacent to the mangled pile of blood and broken bones that now resided in her place. He leaned over the half of her to which her mangled head was attached and picked her up. He cradled her head, left shoulder, and left arm. Her left leg dragged on the ground, a thin piece of flesh connecting it to the remainder of this half of her body. The rest of her lay upon the ground a dozen feet away, organs and blood and broken ribs poking out into the night sky like some sacrilegious diorama displaying the innards of a Tyrannosaurus Rex.

Drillbot glanced up to see the new mist-tentacle creeping through the air above him. He panicked and reversed out of the tentacle's reach, still holding Ginny Rex's left side in his arms. Once he was committed to his backwards roll, the tentacle merely changed course to dip down over the right half of Ginny Rex's corpse, spraying the gore with mist. The tentacle's movement had been a feint. Drillbot cursed.

The blood of Ginny Rex's headless right half clouded over with a thin layer of pink. Then the broken bones mended themselves in a flash of pink, and before Drillbot could even emit a clank or a whir, half of his mate stood upright, digging her toes furiously into the grass as she made ready to pounce.

Drillbot looked down at the skull and the pieces of Ginny Rex in his arms. They remained unanimated, and he said a silent thanks to his robotic deities for that mercy. His drill flew back into view and reattached itself to his arm. Drillbot gingerly placed the portion of his true love's body that had not been reanimated upon the ground and rolled in front of it, putting himself as a shield between it and danger.

The blob and the half-corpse loomed over him. He activated his drills, and their lonely whirs sounded out across the field of battle.

CHAPTER 4

FLIP THE BOARD

REGULAR-GINNY GRINNED MANIACALLY as she watched the dinosaur's reanimated tail twitch. She glanced from it over to the robot. She formed two semi-truck sized spiked balls from the ends of a pair of tentacles and began swinging them round and round in the air, a pair of enlarged medieval morning stars ready for further acts of grotesque violence.

The robot aimed its drills at her and said, "[whir] Release Drillbot's – CLACK – Drillbot's – CLACK – Drillbot's lady from your foul control, and Drillbot will – CLACK – will show mercy to you."

Regular-Ginny guffawed. She responded, "I'm powered by a cosmic entity. You're just a robot who has only succeeded in distracting me when you've taken me by surprise. Give me the other half of the beast so that I can make my new puppet whole, and *I* will show mercy *to you*."

The robot's engines roared, and then it replied, "[whir] Drillbot would die a thousand deaths before Drillbot – CLACK – before Drillbot – CLACK – before Drillbot would hand Drillbot's love over to you. Drillbot, too, is – CLACK – is cosmically powered. You are not quite as special – CLACK – as special as you think you are."

Regular-Ginny guffawed once more as the pink inside her tickled the back of her brain. She had not considered that the robot was anything other than a mindless killing machine, especially after watching it decimate so many of her puppets over the years. But to know that the robot felt *love* for the Tyrannosaurus Rex filled her with a sense of excitement, for the tickle in her brain indicated to her that this information was something she could exploit.

"Your *love*, hmm?" said Regular-Ginny. She stretched a tentacle off into the distance, past the edge of the clearing that had served as the home for the lightning-shield power generators. She snaked it between a few skyscraper husks to where a brigade of demolished B.I.T. tanks lay on their sides. She felt around with the tentacle until she found a tank in relatively decent working condition. She lifted it into the air and shook its dead crew out, and then she yanked it back over to her side. She curled one of her pink tentacles inside of the metal weapon and wrapped the tentacle's tip around the trigger on the tank's turret. Like all the other B.I.T. tanks on the battlefield this day, this turret was modified to shoot whatever B.I.T. disintegrating technology allowed the bureau to permanently eradicate members of the pink and blue armies.

She aimed the barrel of the tank at the half of the beast that she had turned into a puppet, because she could not get a clear shot at the half that lay protected behind the robot. She said, "You must know what kind of weapon this is. Your side has experienced devastation from it just as much as mine has. Now surrender to me, or I shall use it to kill *your love* in a *permanent* fashion."

The robot lowered its drills.

"[whir] Fine. You – CLACK – You – CLACK – You win. Drillbot surrend—" said the robot, only to be interrupted by a giggling that seemed to come from everywhere at once.

The robot and Regular-Ginny glanced up to see a bright blue light zoom past overhead, the blue bear at its center. Its giggles transformed into words formed from solid light that spelled "*Teeheehee!*" in its wake, and these words broke apart into blue raindrops that fell upon the battlefield like a spring shower.

Less than a second later, the blue bear crashed into the pink bear in midair. Pink and blue waves of energy exploded out from them as they crashed, reversed direction, and crashed into one another again. They snarled and bit and clawed at each other, and the world shook below them.

When Regular-Ginny and the robot returned their attention to each other, they found that tiny white flowers had sprouted across the ground between them where the blue bear's raindrops had landed. Regular-Ginny was about to make a snide remark about the flowers, but then she noticed an inconvenience: the left half of the dinosaur—the portion that she had *not* turned into a pink puppet—had been resurrected. It now stood upon its foot, and its exposed organs pulsated as it breathed heavily. This half of the dinosaur stroked the robot's shoulder and licked the side of the robot's head. In a raspy, barely audible whisper, it said to the robot, "I'll handle myself, my love. You stop the bitch who killed me."

And then the Tyrannosaurus Rex roared in primal rage at the half of itself that had been transformed into a pink puppet.

The two resurrected halves of the dinosaur sprang forth and began fighting one another, the right half whipping its tail into the left half's leg and tripping it, the left half sinking its teeth into the right's tail and tearing it apart. They tumbled together onto the ground in a pile of teeth and claws and gore, ripping each other to shreds.

The robot dashed at Regular-Ginny. It first used its drills to sever the tentacle holding the tank, and then it pressed forward with a vicious attack. She gave ground, rolling backward as she parried its drills with her tentacles, regrowing them over and over as the robot severed them.

But as she battled the robot, a new noise erupted in the sky, this one the cacophonous roar of an engine blasting at full speed. She glanced toward the sound and saw a black B.I.T. ship that was shaped like a banana with the wings of an eagle. It was careening toward the battling bears. She reacted on instinct, instantly growing a new tentacle the size of a sequoia from the top of her blob and swiping at the ship with it. The ship barely dodged her attack. The hateful tickle in the back of her brain told her to abandon her fight with the robot and pursue the ship at all costs.

But she resisted. She would pursue it soon enough. She needed only *moments* to rid herself of this damned robot once and for all. And if she could rid herself of the robot, she would be removing the *one* opponent that seemed to constantly hold her at a stalemate, and she would thus be creating for herself the slack to do her job as the Pink One's Right Hand of Destruction without worrying about constant surprise attacks that resulted in continuous near-death scenarios.

As she twisted her head back down to face the robot, she stopped short when she noticed something in her peripheral. A whole new set of problems hovered in the air around her: The Death Cavalry. Its members must have been resurrected by the blue bear's overhead showering of blue raindrops, and its members were no longer pink puppets. They were floating toward her, their considerable murderous power ready to be unleashed on her pink blob from the flanks while the robot attacked her from the front.

She sensed the potential checkmate. However, she had always despised chess, ever since her stepfather had beaten her at it over and over and over as a kid. So, she decided to metaphorically flip the board, and metaphorically punch her opponent in the robotic groin while doing so.

She jerked launched a new tentacle from atop her blob, looping it high into the air and around the robot. She kept this new tentacle well out of the robot's reach, and unless it abandoned its up-close battle with her blob to focus solely on the tentacle, it would not be able to touch it. The robot continued its fight with the blob proper.

The tip of this new tentacle snaked inside the tank and wiggled in place around the trigger. Then it lifted the tank into the air and carried it so that its barrel aimed point blank at one of the dinosaur halves.

The robot glanced up from the fight and realized what was happening, seconds too late. It leapt away from Regular-Ginny's blob. She pulled the trigger on the tank, firing a disintegration bolt into the Tyrannosaurus Rex's right half. Her blob wiggled slightly at the tank's kick, and the vibration tickled her tummy, a feeling like riding a roller coaster. She giggled.

The robot screamed in rage and agony. She fired again, this time at the Tyrannosaurus Rex's left side. Its head whipped over to face the robot. Its red and bloodied lips attempted to mouth something to the robot, but it disintegrated into nothingness before it was able to finish.

The robot screamed once more, and during this scream, something cracked and seemed to break inside of it. It leapt at her. She looked at the robot in its telescopic eyes. The robot's rage and heartbreak shredded the hateful pink cocoon around her heart. For the first time in what felt like an eternity, she felt a sense of shame at her actions.

And then the pink inside her swirled, and once more, all emotions other than hatred withered and died.

THE RAGE OF DRILLBOT

DRILLBOT WATCHED GINNY Rex disintegrate. The image burned into his memory banks, and he would never forget it. Within fractions of a second, he experienced loss, shame, and grief, but as the ones and zeroes fired through his system, they flushed out everything but rage.

The liquids inside him boiled, and hot steam screamed as it sprang forth from all his orifices. Drillbot shrieked in anger, a noise so loud that the speaker behind the grates on his mouthpiece cracked. But that did not stop him, and his loud shriek transformed into a gurgling flash of electric energy two octaves lower than the pitch of his normal voice.

Time seemed to slow to a halt. His systems recognized every sound around him as though they were happening directly on top of him. His processors registered every tiny movement on the battlefield at a speed they had never before experienced. All colors but an angry, spiteful red disappeared from his telescopic eyes. The ones and zeroes inside him spelled out in binary: *RAGE* and *FURY* and *VENGEANCE*.

He leapt at the hag inside the pink blob. She attempted to aim the B.I.T. tank at him and shoot him with its disintegration bolt, but he was too quick for her. He sliced through the machine and then severed the tentacle that held it aloft. Ginny then tried to block him with tentacle after tentacle, but he sliced them all away as soon as they appeared. Within milliseconds, he penetrated the pink blob itself. He drilled through it toward the meatbag at its center, his spiked wheels churning the pink while his drills bored through the solid blob.

The woman screamed something at him and swam backward away from him, but he slowed not at all. In less than a second, he reached her.

He shoved his right drill through her lower abdomen and his left drill through her empty eye socket. She went limp, but he ripped her in half, anyway, just like she had done to Ginny Rex. He shook her corpse from his drills.

The corpse sank to the bottom of the blob. The pink blob began to melt from solid into liquid and flood the ground around the horrid Ginny's corpse. The sudden loss of friction should have slowed Drillbot, but he revved his engines harder than ever, and instead of sinking, he fired out of the top of the blob like a bullet from a pink gun.

Though he had killed the woman who had murdered his love, his rage subsided not at all. If anything, distance and time from the disintegration of his love only fueled his rage. His momentum as he left the blob carried him up into the air, where he stabbed his drill into the underside of a passing B.I.T. fighter jet. He climbed up onto its top and stabbed the pilot. As the jet shifted direction and dove toward the ground, Drillbot jumped from it and landed atop a nearby skyscraper.

A version of Art flew into Drillbot's view. He was being carried through the air by seagulls that dropped flaming excrement. This Art was one who had been passed back and forth between the blue and pink bears' armies multiple times, and up until mere moments ago, he had been a pink puppet that had been stomped to death by Ginny Rex. But he was now resurrected and once more a member of the Army of Life.

Drillbot watched this Art's mouth ask what he could do to help Drillbot. But Drillbot's raging processors registered this Art as another target, another meatbag who reminded him of his dead love. He leapt toward the meatbag and ripped him to shreds, afterward landing atop the skyscraper across the street.

Drillbot surveyed the smoldering battlefield. The bears continued fighting in the distance. Halfway between this building and the next, a black B.I.T. ship shaped like a gigantic banana with the wings of an eagle dropped something from its cargo hold. Drillbot growled and leapt toward the ship.

His drills stabbed into the side of the ship just as a white flash erupted on the ground. White lightning launched from the front of the ship, and the ship flew into it. Drillbot glanced down to find that he was no longer attached to the ship as it hovered above the battlefield, but rather was now attached to the ship as it jetted through the barrier between realities.

He dug through the ship's hull and found himself in a small hold surrounded by B.I.T. marines. He hardly heard their screams as he used his drills to mine the life from them like it was some terribly insignificant commodity buried within their flesh. He heard voices drifting down at him from an open hatch at the top of a nearby ladder. He raced up the ladder, and when he found the hatch too small to fit through, he ripped it open wider with his drills.

Drillbot emerged onto the bridge of the ship. A man sat bound to a chair facing away from Drillbot. His hands were encased in plaster. Wrathful steam whistled from Drillbot as he pierced the meatbag in the back with his right drill, stabbing through the entire chair to rip through the man's torso.

Meanwhile, a woman who looked identical to the hag in the blob—only dressed in a B.I.T. agent's uniform—turned to face him. He saw the fear in her eyes. But instead of giving in to her fear, she nodded in acceptance of her fate and acted before he could kill her. She twisted a dial on the ship's control panel as hard as she could. She then slapped her eagle across its back. As it fired a bolt of lightning into a short metal pole sticking up from the control panel, she simultaneously shot the metal pole with her disintegration pistol.

A loud squelch erupted from the pole. The pole blurred out of existence. Then it appeared back in place. And then it turned black. The control panel around it melted. Drillbot rolled over to the woman, dispatching both her and the eagle with a single swipe of his drill.

He stared at her face as she fell to the metal floor, and her scowl looked just like the scowl that had been on the blob-encased-Ginny's face when she had killed his love. Rage roared through his internal processors, demanding to be satisfied. He stabbed her corpse. And then he stabbed it again. And again. Over and over.

On about the dozenth stab, time seemed to catch up to Drillbot. Overwhelming grief wedged its way into the forefront of his processors, overpowering his rage and cramming it back into the recesses of his internal code. He shuddered and wept, and tiny bolts fell from the edges of his telescopic eyes as he cried. They clanged to the metal floor.

He glanced up at the view screen. Reality after reality appeared and disappeared on the screen in front of him. He plugged in to a panel on the side of the bridge and communicated with the ship's CPU. He nodded when he understood the now-dead B.I.T. woman's tactic.

As her final act, she had caused the ship to continuously jump from one reality to another, staying in each for only a fraction of a second before jumping to the next. Her shot fired into the metal pole on the control panel warped reality in such a way that the Multiverse understood every jump all as a *single* jump. Thus, the single lightning bolt from the eagle would be enough power to send Drillbot careening from one reality to the next for eternity.

He sighed. He turned to map out the ship now that he was calmer and no longer felt like a machine built only for shredding flesh.

Shame then overcame him as he recognized the dead man lying on the bridge, the man who Drillbot had killed via enraged backstabbing. The corpse belonged to his former master, his *creator*. The body was splayed out on the floor, the constraints that had bound the man to his chair having been ripped apart during Drillbot's attack.

Drillbot let out an anguished shriek and fell onto his side. He allowed the cold grip of despair to fill him. He stared out the view screen and let his mind wander to fond memories of Ginny Rex.

But every memory transformed into a twisted vision of her corpse next to his former master's, and he cried.

CHAPTER 6

DEATH'S NOT ALWAYS FAIR

REGULAR-GINNY SIGHED AS the pink within her veins pulled her dismembered body back together. When it had become clear that the robot had reached her and that she would be unable to escape or fend it off, she prepared herself mentally for the worst.

"The worst" had actually been less painful than she had expected. It hurt when the drill entered her abdomen, sure, but when the other drill entered her brain, it must have cut away all her pain receptors or something, because she did not even feel herself get ripped in half.

She had at that moment decided to play dead so that she could return to fight another day. As part of this ploy, she willed her pink blob to transform from a solid gelatinous state into a liquid state. It flooded unceremoniously onto the ground as though the battlefield had abruptly entered some sort of weird, pink monsoon season. The tactic seemed to have worked, for the robot left her body where it lay broken and shredded upon the ground. Without even a second glance, the robot dashed away to continue its carnage-spree elsewhere.

The pink that filled her veins had then gone right to work. It set her bones and pulled her two halves together. It replaced the now-missing gray matter in her brain with itself.

She realized in a flood of sadness that she could no longer recall much from a ten-year span of her childhood. These memories must have been drilled away when the spike entered her skull. However, the pink within her kindly replaced any now-missing memories with recollections of hatred and grotesque images of genocide. After a couple moments, Ginny no longer remembered that any memories were missing at all. She instead longed only to continue her spiteful duties as The Pink One's Right Hand of Destruction.

But she did not get the chance. Just as she formed some new tentacles to pull herself up onto her feet, and just as she began regrowing her blob, and just as she was preparing to re-kill the resurrected members of the Death Cavalry to turn them back into pink puppets, an explosion rocked the battlefield. A bright white light filled her vision.

Regular-Ginny found that she could not move. As a matter of fact, nothing around her was moving, either. She tried to sigh, but she could not. She tried to call for help, but she could not.

An image of the Pink One appeared in her mind's eyes. It said, "Right Hand of Destruction, the B.I.T. has used a weapon with extra-powerful hoodoo. Now Me and Ginny and everything here in this reality be unable to move."

What was this weapon? How do we stop it? thought Ginny back at the image of the Pink One.

"It be a bomb that freezes time."

Ginny felt a pain in her chest, but she could not look down at it, could not touch it to investigate what was wrong. The Pink One tsked at her in her brain. It said, "Freeze time means pink no longer be flowing through Ginny's veins. Pink in veins now be staying still. Me hoodoo work in Ginny because of flowing, and no flowing means me hoodoo no longer working. No flowing means Ginny can't be kept alive by Me, and if Ginny no be alive, then we deal no longer be intact."

That's stupid, thought Ginny. She considered the situation for a moment. She wished she could scowl. Then she thought at the Pink One, *Your pink gift is still inside me, and time becoming frozen didn't remove it. I didn't renege on our deal. I've done everything you asked! I've murdered, and I've pillaged, and I've destroyed entire realities for you. I don't care if the way your magic works means that I die when the pink stops flowing through me. I didn't quit on you! If I'm dead whenever time unfreezes, then simply make the pink flow again and bring me back!*

"Me no make the rules here. Pink must be flowing to keep Ginny's soul bound to Ginny's body and keep her as Me Right Hand of Destruction. When that bind be gone, Me attack Ginny's home reality first. Me gave Ginny Me word that Me would do so, and Me words be binding."

Ginny thought a curse and then, *Of course you make the rules here! Our deal being broken because of time becoming frozen—something completely out of my control!—is stupid and illogical and, frankly, unfair!*

"No, no, no. Completely fair and logical. Me hoodoo be now over-powered by time-freezies, and Ginny soul will be freed by time-freezies. Me will not be able to retrieve Ginny's soul from its afterlife to bring it back to Ginny's body in a peaceful way—that power be in the realm of the Blue One. If Me make pink flow through Ginny's body again after Ginny's soul escapes, then Me just be resurrecting a mindless corpse no better than Me puppets. This be no sacrifice, and nothing that make Me satisfied. Ginny be Me Right Hand of Destruction because her soul be tethered to her corpse because of Me hoodoo. For Me to retrieve Ginny's soul to retether to Ginny's corpse and turn Ginny once more into Me Right Hand of Destruction, Me will need to devour Ginny's home reality—including her afterlife—and then regurgitate her soul into her corpse. Thus, Ginny be gone to Me forever when Ginny dies and soul leaves unless Me destroy her home reality. And Ginny only agreed to be Me Right Hand of Destruction if Me spared her reality until it be the last reality in existence, so if Me destroying her reality must happen immediately to get her back so she can keep her end of bargain, Me thinks Ginny be unlikely to agree to keep being Me Right Hand of Destruction, because there would be no reward in it. Is Me right?

Obviously, I wouldn't agree to help you if you've already destroyed my reality, thought Ginny to the image of the Pink One. *But you don't need to turn this into the worst Catch-22 of all time. You could still do the right thing and spare my reality. On behalf of all the atrocities I've committed for you, please! Have mercy.*

The Pink One shook her head. She said, "But words be words and deals be deals. Ginny just confirmed to Me that she no longer would be Me Right Hand of Destruction if she died and her reality must be destroyed for Me to get her back. Me made binding contract with Ginny to spare her reality so long as she agrees to be Me Right Hand of Destruction. Me must deliver the consequences that Me promised in the covenant we made. Powerful hoodoo be living in covenants, and even Me must abide by these agreements to keep access to this hoodoo. So, Ginny must hang on and keep her soul inside her corpse rather than letting herself pass on to her reality's afterlife, or covenant between Me and Ginny will be voided, and Ginny will be at fault. Me will be bound by hoodoo of this covenant to ensure consequences promised to Ginny be fulfilled. Me will attack Ginny's home reality first when Me eventually be free."

Ginny thought another curse followed by, *How the hell am I supposed to know how to keep my soul inside my corpse? This is totally unfair! I didn't do anything wrong!*

"But Ginny wrong. Ginny *did* do wrong. Ginny didn't stop the time-freezie bomb. Me saw Ginny miss the ship that dropped it and then Me felt Ginny resist Me instructions to pursue the ship because Ginny was distracted by the drilling robot. Ginny only have herself to blame."

The pain spread from Ginny's chest into the rest of her body. She cursed one more time and then blackness descended across her eye. In her last few moments, she tried to think of ideas for how to keep her soul bound to her corpse. Unfortunately, no matter how much she attempted to concentrate on the soul-binding conundrum, she could only think inanely about strawberry ice cream and how much she was going to miss it. She died, and her soul drifted away.

To casual onlookers frozen in time who happened to be staring at her, they would not have known that she had just died inside her reanimated corpse and doomed her reality to destruction, nor that she had just experienced a long mental conversation with her pink master. They would have perceived her as merely being merely frozen in time, just like themselves.

CHAPTER 7

A MANGLED ESCAPE

AGENT 27142 CURSED and fired his Scatter Gun pistol, disintegrating the boulder hurtling toward him. He pointed to three random soldiers amongst the group gathered near him. He ordered, "You three, cover us. The rest of you, get to the nearest shift-shuttle!"

Agent 27142 sprinted from the cave toward the nearest shift-shuttle. He aimed his Scatter Gun pistol at the nearest Cyclops and fired a disintegration bolt into its chest. It dissolved into nothingness, and its boulder fell onto the foot of the Cyclops next to it, who began hopping up and down in pain.

Agent 27142 cursed again as this Cyclops lost its balance and fell onto the nearest cloaked shift-shuttle. It did not understand what had happened when it crashed atop something invisible, only that it had fallen on something it could not see, and this confusion manifested in howling fury. The brute got to its feet and began smashing the spot with its rock, crushing the invisible ship into a useless hunk of metal.

Agent 27142 immediately changed direction, sprinting toward the far shift-shuttle. He and his soldiers blasted multiple Cyclopes with their Scatter Guns, but there were too many of them.

Agent 27142 rolled to his left just in time to avoid being crushed by a boulder, frowned as three of his men were flattened by the rock, and then fired a bolt to disintegrate another boulder that had been hurled at him from a different Cyclops.

The remaining shift-shuttle now sat not a half-dozen yards in front of him. He dove toward its open hatch. However, colossal Cyclopean hands swooped in from the sides and snatched him.

Agent 27142 was lifted into the air. He looked down at the six remaining soldiers who had accompanied him from the cave and into the clearing. He watched them aim their Scatter Guns at the Cyclops who had snatched him.

But then he sighed a frustrated sigh. Yet another gigantic boulder hurtled into view and crushed the entire group. Agent 27142 twisted his head to look toward the cave from which he and the soldiers had emerged. The three soldiers who he had left stationed there to provide covering fire were distracted by the dozen boulders currently being tossed their way. Agent 27142 frowned. He knew that he would be receiving no help.

So, he cursed once more, and then he twisted to face the Cyclops who had snagged him. He did this just in time to find himself tossed into its open maw. He noted that the one-eyed monster's breath smelled foul and rotten, like sheep fat that had rotted inside a cocoon made from seaweed.

Now inside the wet gullet, Agent 27142's eagle dug its talons into his shoulder, signaling to him that it was feeling claustrophobic. He smirked. He had refrained from using his Jump Totem earlier because he could not jump an entire group of soldiers away with him, but now that it was only him who remained alive in the party, he screamed to his totem, "Jump us out of here! Now!"

The eagle's antennae stood on end. Lightning flashed between them. The Cyclops' tongue flicked Agent 27142 toward its jagged yellow teeth.

Lightning filled his vision with a flash as it launched from his eagle's antennae, but the slavering teeth snapped down in a flash, too. Agent 27142 felt a crippling pain explode across his left side, and then blackness descended across his eyes.

*

When Agent 27142 awoke, he found that he was floating in the infinite expanse of *The Barrier*. Pain shot through his left side. He forced himself to look at its source.

His shoulder was a mangled wreck the shape of a Cyclopean incisor. His collarbone felt as though it had been shattered, his left arm was twisted in an unnatural direction behind his body, and blood poured from rips in his uniform. But this dire cocktail of injuries was not the direst of news.

Agent 27142's eagle lay embedded in his shoulder, crushed into his flesh by the ungodly chewing power of a fifty-foot-tall giant. He could swear that he could feel every single one of the eagle's broken bones where they lay impaled in his flesh.

He screamed a curse. He touched the communicator in his ear, but he picked up no signal. He touched the distress call button on his belt, but the eagle's interrupted jump must have disabled its functionality, so it shorted out nearly immediately.

He screamed an even louder curse. He would likely be stuck in *The Barrier* for eternity.

He collected himself and began sizing up his surroundings. Eternity was a *long* time, and surely such a high-ranking officer in the B.I.T. could find a solution for just such a predicament. When one did not present itself immediately, he cursed another time.

CHAPTER 8

A ROBOTIC VISION

DRILLBOT TAPPED THE button next to the door and it swung open. "[whir] Honey, Drillbot's home!" he called as he rolled into the foyer.

He felt more than heard his wife's footsteps approach as they shook the house. The chandelier hanging from the rafters vibrated, teetered, and finally fell to the ground when its chain snapped—as it did every day when his wife ran to meet him at the door.

Drillbot smiled his version of a smile as Ginny Rex stepped into view. She no longer wore her spiked leather jacket. It had been replaced with an apron covered in a design that featured dozens of fluttering hearts. Her blond mullet and crown remained perched atop her head, apparently unaltered in her costume change. She grinned at him, bent down, and hugged him. Her arms stretched barely long enough to surround his shoulders. He nuzzled her and allowed his engines to purr. She giggled, as she always did when he vibrated against her.

She looked over her shoulder and called, "Kids! Your dad's home! Come say hello!"

He looked to his left at a set of carpeted stairs that led to the second story of the house. The sweet giggles of children wafted down from a room at the top. Then three children rumbled down the stairs. The eldest had the head of a Tyrannosaurus Rex and a body just like Drillbot's. The second was the opposite, with Drillbot's head and Ginny Rex's body. The third was a toddler who looked just like Drillbot's former master, Art.

"Hiya, Pop!" they all yelled in unison.

Drillbot smiled at them. He waved. They waved back.

Suddenly, the third child, the one that looked like Art, said, "Wake up, Pop. You know this isn't real."

Drillbot frowned his version of a frown. "[whir] B-But you're wrong. You – CLACK – You – CLACK – You are Drillbot's family. Drillbot loves you."

Drillbot looked back over at his wife. Her pupils shifted into the shapes of a Tyrannosaurus-Rex-skull-and-crossbones. Her lips were suddenly covered in blood. She tried to mouth something to him, but she disintegrated before she was able to finish.

"[whir] No!" shrieked Drillbot. He looked over at the kids. The first two disappeared in a puff of smoke. The third, who look like Art, shifted.

His hair caught fire. His toddler clothing fell away, replaced with a cloak made from the hides of white wolves and baby seals. A necklace of severed ears appeared around his neck, and a belt of thick rope hung suspended around his waist, attached to which were a dagger, a leather pouch, and tools made from obsidian. The boy now looked like a toddler-version of the mischief-god manifestation of Drillbot's former master.

"Drillbot," said the boy. "You know this vision is a lie. This is a hallucination caused by grief and boredom and self-pity."

"[whir] B-But it's not – CLACK – not fair."

The boy frowned, and the flaming hair caused shadows to dance across his face. He said, "Nothing's ever fair, mate. Some of us plan for millennia and still don't get what we want. Others—like you—stumble across someone or something that fills you with joy, and then you lose it. But deceiving yourself with these lies is the same as giving up. And giving up seems like the *last* thing that your dinosaur-lover would ever want you to do. Maybe rather than wallowing in your own despair, you should get up and find a way to atone for your failures. If you don't want to do it for yourself, do it for your dead lover and for the multitudes of people in the Multiverse who will be doomed without your help."

Drillbot frowned. And then he nodded. His telescopic eyes twisted, and the interior of the house faded away. The bridge of the shift-shuttle came into focus.

Drillbot looked at the date log on the ship's console, and he sighed. He had thus far drifted aimlessly for nearly five years. He stared out the view screen and watched an afternoon sky shift into an evening sky shift into fresh greenery shift into waving plains shift into a roaring sea. And on and on and on.

Millions upon millions of realities had popped into view before Drillbot, only to disappear just as quickly. But as he thought back to his most recent hallucination, an idea sprang forth in his processors.

He plugged into the ship once more and asked the CPU in his nicest tone to give him a warning when they were about to pass through a certain-numbered Earth. The CPU agreed, and Drillbot smiled his version of a smile. He would need to time this next move perfectly.

Drillbot turned away from the view screen. He frowned at the corpses of his former master and the B.I.T. version of Ginny. The skin on their corpses hung loose and sallow. Their lifeless eyes stared at him accusingly.

"[whir] Drillbot – CLACK – Drillbot – CLACK – Drillbot is sorry," he said to Art for probably the thousandth time.

Drillbot hopped down the hatch at the back of the bridge. After landing in the hold, he rolled past the corpses of B.I.T. marines. He crept through the hole that he had pierced through the side of the ship a half-decade ago. He hung precariously from the ship's side. The vessel continued hurtling across the Multiverse.

Drillbot waited.

CHAPTER 9

A LONG TUMBLE

AGENT 27142 TUMBLED end over end through *The Barrier*, just as he had been doing for nearly five years. However, he never perceived it as a tumble, for that would have run counter to his basic B.I.T. training. Instead, he knew that there was neither up nor down in this infinite space between spaces, so forgetting traditional orientation meant that he could drift and not feel the disorientation and nausea that an untrained body would feel here.

Agent 27142 cursed, just as he had done countless times since he had been stranded here. The beauty of the place had worn off long ago, and he wanted nothing more than to return to some sort of charted reality that would allow him to regain contact with the B.I.T. After all, he had a mission to complete.

He sighed and listened to the rhythmic pumping that originated from beneath his badge within the left breast of his uniform. There, underneath the material, a needle poked through his skin and deep into his heart. It had been painful and uncomfortable when Agent 27142 had first stabbed it into his chest, but after these many years, he had long grown accustomed to it.

The needle was yet another device invented by the High Commander. It allowed an agent to survive *The Barrier* indefinitely if he were ever to find himself stranded in it. The needle connected to a series of tubes enriched with nutrients that ran throughout the lining of the uniform. It constantly pumped an agent's blood through the tubes, acting like a tiny dialysis machine that recycles the blood and reinforces it with necessary sugars and vitamins, allowing him to survive indefinitely without access to food or water or whatever sustenance he might need to stay alive.

A lesser agent might have considered unhooking himself from the device and allowing himself to die rather than facing the possibility that he might drift forever through infinity. But Agent 27142 was not just any agent, so he instead allowed himself to tumble. And he remained vigilant.

Finally, after another year passed, he caught his first break. He saw lightning flash not too far off in the distance. When it subsided, he witnessed a hulking, hairy sasquatch wearing a fedora and an undersized leather vest clinging desperately to its Jump Totem. The totem was a kitten striped green and yellow with floppy ears, a tail that resembled a horse's mane, and a pair of gigantic antennae sticking straight out from its forehead. A crate was tied to the sasquatch's ankle by a rope.

Agent 27142 removed a small telescope from his holster and stared through it at the beast. His telescope revealed no sign of the musk that would be lingering about the sasquatch as an identification mark if the beast were a legal transporter of goods.

Smugglers, thought Agent 27142. He ground his teeth and replaced the telescope back in its home in his holster. *I hate smugglers.*

Agent 27142 shifted the direction of his tumble and clicked his heels together in a secret pattern. A small explosion erupted from his bootheels that sent him hurtling toward the sasquatch. Agent 27142 cursed when the sasquatch looked up and noticed him, because he had hoped to take it by surprise and commandeer its Jump Totem.

Agent 27142 pointed to his badge and shouted, "I am Agent 27142 of the B.I.T. I am stranded. If you hand over your Jump Totem, then I *may* be persuaded to only cite you with a warning for your obvious smuggling infraction."

The sasquatch frowned. It replied in a robust falsetto voice, "You must be out'cher damn mind!"

Agent 27142 began to draw his Scatter Gun pistol, but the sasquatch only laughed. It flexed it pectoral muscles, and its vest popped open. The beast had two tiny arms growing from its torso, both of which held pistols that it now trained on Agent 27142.

"Keep yer hands away from that iron, agent," muttered the sasquatch. "If ya don't, then ya won't be the first B.I.T. agent I've hadda plug."

Agent 27142 frowned. Duty would not allow him to back down. His hand closed around the handle of his Scatter Gun pistol, and just as he was pulling it from its holster, two blasts rang out from the sasquatch's pistols.

A buzzing sound whistled past his ear. A sharp pain exploded in his lower abdomen. He groaned in pain, but he managed to draw his Scatter Gun pistol and shoot before the sasquatch was able to fire again.

The disintegration bolt hit the sasquatch in its chest. It shrieked as it disintegrated. Agent 27142 squealed with joy. He reached out toward the kitten to take hold of it. However, it swiped his hand with rainbow-colored claws, fled backward on a bolt of lightning, and jumped out of *The Barrier* without him. Agent 27142 squealed in anger.

He looked down at his torso. A bloody stain was spreading across his uniform. He inspected his wound. Based on its shape, Agent 27142 surmised that the sasquatch must have used some sort of savage ballistic gun, which meant that he could fix himself right up. He groaned in pain as he twisted to press a button on his holster.

A small hole opened in his holster near the buckle. Out of the hole slithered a metallic earthworm. The creature crawled into the wound, removed the bullet, ate away any potentially infected tissue, and then cauterized the wound with flames from its anus. Afterward, it slithered back out of the wound and returned to its home in Agent 27142's holster. Agent 27142 passed out from the pain.

When he came to, he was once more tumbling through the infinite expanse of *The Barrier*. He frowned and hoped he would not need to wait six more years for another chance to escape his aimless drift. He had a mission to complete, after all.

CHAPTER 10

DRILLBOT GOES UNDERGROUND

DRILLBOT LISTENED TO the alarm. Its blaring notes drifted out to him through the hole that he had torn in the side of the ship when he had entered it a decade ago. He smiled his version of a smile, for he had clung to the side of the ship in this exact same position for the past five years, waiting for the ship's alarm to tell him that his wait was finally over.

He steeled himself and concentrated on his task at hand, for he knew that this feat was going to take crackerjack timing. Luckily, he had little else to do but *plan* over the last half-decade, so he had long ago calculated the necessary timing and physics of his leap.

Thus, as the alarm rang out, Drillbot counted down the milliseconds. *Five … Four … Three … Two … One … Now!*

Drillbot leapt from the side of the ship. He crashed onto the ground and rolled for a good half-mile, leaving a path of destruction in his wake. Luckily, his tumble had dropped him in the middle of an undeveloped forest outside a residential neighborhood, so loss of life was minimal. Well, minimal aside from the dozens and dozens of trees that lay broken and destroyed and the multitude of woodland critters that lay crushed and dead.

Drillbot pulled himself upright. He was still functioning, so his hypothesis that his falling speed was so fast that he might kill himself upon landing was proven wrong. He glanced around to gain his bearings. His internal positioning systems told him that he was on the correct reality, so the timing of his leap from the side of the shift-shuttle had been accurate.

The major problem was that he had landed thousands of miles away from where he would like to be: his former master's place of residence—the home on Earth 6,076 that he had visited with Art and the god and the Blue One upon completing the rescue of the Blue One from Earth 1,000,000.

So, Drillbot heaved a steamy sigh and revved his engines. Knowing that the quickest path between two points is a straight line, he brought his drills to full power and dove drills-first into the ground, deciding that he would dig directly toward the aforementioned second point in this line.

The trip resuscitated long-archived memories of his travel below the surface of Earth 1,000,000 immediately after he had been brought into existence. Drillbot remembered the many complaints of his former master during the trip, and the memory of that whining voice drifted through his processors like an annoying ghost. The memory made him more ashamed than ever that he had murdered his former master.

He responded to this shame by revving his engines and digging faster.

CHAPTER 11

RESURRECTION VIA ROBOT

DRILLBOT HID IN the bushes and peered through the window into his former master's home. Much to his dismay, strangers now occupied the place. Drillbot frowned, for he had not expected this scenario. He had always categorized this domicile as belonging to his former master, and he had never considered that it might change ownership if Art were not occupying it.

Inside, a young couple sat at a table and fed a toddler sitting in a highchair. The baby giggled as it chewed its food. Drillbot remembered his dreams of a family with Ginny Rex. He frowned his version of a frown. He backed away from the window and considered his options. He must gain access to the domicile, but he resolved not to harm this family to do so.

Then he had an idea. He waited until deep into the night, and then he left the bushes in search of somewhere that purveyed in clothing. He wandered through the streets, darting from shadow to shadow until he found a place that might have what he was looking for.

The Memorial Center Mall stood out in stark contrast to the strip malls around it. Like corpses left abandoned on a battlefield, empty and boarded mom-and-pop shops lined the strip malls leading to the mall. But the mall was a bastion of capitalism, featuring every department store imaginable. The fringes around its many, many doorframes were tinted gold, its walls were covered in ivy, and its parking garage was four-stories tall.

Drillbot approached a door to the Memorial Center Mall, but he found that it was locked. The mall's hours were printed on the tinted glass door in white, and they informed Drillbot that the mall had closed hours ago. He analyzed the door with his telescopic eyes and concluded that an alarm would be tripped if he simply smashed through it. So, he did what any robot designed for drilling would do at a time like this: he drilled underground and entered the mall from below.

Upon exiting the dark dirt and entering the dimly lit interior of the mall, he raced from shop to shop and department store to department store, collecting the biggest dress shirt, mittens, trucker hat, and trench coat he could find. He made one final stop at the novelty shop to steal a mask that would make him look human, deciding in the end upon one that looked to him like a generic human being, though the label read, *"Giant Baby."*

Drillbot dressed himself in his new outfit. He forced the dress shirt over his torso and covered it with the trench coat. When he fastened the coat, it covered him enough to conceal his wheels so long as nobody looked even remotely in his direction. His drills were too big for the sleeves of shirt and coat alike, so the sleeves of both shredded when Drillbot forced his drills through them, and the fabric dangled around his drills in loose tatters. He pulled the baby-face mask over his head and crowned it with the trucker hat. He tucked the tips of his drills into the mittens.

He stared at his reflection in a department store mirror and nodded in approval at how well he passed for human. The plastic pacifier dangling from the latex lips of the baby mask bobbed and rattled.

Drillbot exited through the tunnel he had dug beneath the mall and returned to his hiding spot outside Art's apartment. In the morning, he rolled to the breaker box on the side of the building. He removed his left drill from its mitten and unceremoniously slashed the breaker box with his drill. The power to the building winked out. Drillbot replaced the mitten onto his left drill tip. Now back in full costume, he rolled to the front door and knocked.

Moments later, the male occupant opened the door. Drillbot initiated the *Deception Matrix* within his processors, tapped himself with one mitten, and said, "[whir] Greetings, sir. This human – CLACK – This human – CLACK – This human works for the city and has heard that there have been some – CLACK – some problems with the power around here. May this human come inside and – CLACK – and inspect your domicile for problems?"

The male stared at Drillbot, eyes open wide with shock. He screamed and attempted to slam the door shut, but Drillbot caught it with one of his mitten-covered drills.

Drillbot pushed his way into the apartment. He said, "[whir] Sir? This human means you no – CLACK – no harm."

The man fled into one of the back rooms. Drillbot called after him, "[whir] This human – CLACK – This human repeats: this human means you – CLACK – means you no harm."

The man returned from the back room. He now held a pistol. His hands shook as he aimed it at Drillbot. He said, "What the hell *are* you? Go away, or-or-or I'll shoot."

Drillbot frowned, and the wobbling of his radar dishes in the process caused the latex mask to bob back-and-forth on his head. Drillbot sighed and stopped frowning, but the mask now rested on his head so that the eye holes were out of place, and he could only see out of one of them. The man shrieked in terror. His wife walked into the room and did the same.

Drillbot held up his mitten-covered drills in deference. He said, "[whir] Please, put the – CLACK – put the weapon down. This human means you no harm. This human has come to check on the – CLACK – check on the power outage for the city."

The man did not comply, instead tightening his finger on the trigger. He screamed, "I mean it, freak! Get outta here!"

"[whir] This human must warn you, bullets have no – CLACK – have no effect on this human."

"Why are you here? And don't feed me no more lies about the power!"

Drillbot sighed once more. He replied, "[whir] As you wish. The truth – CLACK – The truth – CLACK – The truth it shall be. An old – CLACK – an old friend once lived here. Drillbot must collect something he – CLACK – he left behind. And then Drillbot will – CLACK – will leave."

The man frowned. "And what'd he leave?"

Drillbot said, "[whir] A god."

"Huh?"

"[whir] A god died here. Drillbot must collect whatever remains of him – CLACK – of him in order to bring him back to life."

"What the hell're you talkin' 'bout?" demanded the woman, who had procured from somewhere a large black frying pan, which she wielded with both hands in front of her like a club.

Drillbot scanned the floor with his telescopic eyes near where God-Art had dissolved and died. The carpet had been replaced since his former master had resided here, so he toggled his eyes over to their X-Ray functionality to see through this new shag. He zoomed in on a microscopic level. The residents of the apartment continued yelling questions and threats at him, but he turned down his audio receptors so that he could concentrate.

"[whir] There!" he exclaimed when he recognized a few skin flakes and a strand of charred hair. The pieces registered as having an identical DNA sequence to Drillbot's former master, but the molecular structure was different.

Drillbot rolled forward toward the skin flakes and hair. What felt like a few tiny rocks bounced off his chest. He flipped the volume back up on his audio receptors. He looked from where three small holes had appeared in his trench coat over to the man with the gun.

The gun's barrel was smoking. The gun itself lay on the carpet next to the man, who lay writhing on the ground clutching his left calf. Blood seeped out between his fingers where a bullet must have lodged itself after ricocheting from Drillbot.

The woman ran over to the man's side. She crouched and cradled him in her arms. She screamed at Drillbot, "What the hell'd you do?"

Drillbot continued rolling forward to where he had seen the dead and dormant pieces of God-Art. He said, "[whir] Drillbot warned you, human. Drillbot is – CLACK – is immune to bullets."

Knowing not what else to do and having no better ideas, Drillbot ripped up the carpet. He swept the dead remains of the mischief god into a tiny pile on the bare floor. He unclasped his trench coat, exposing his metal torso. He touched the knobs and dials that stretched up his torso in a pattern known only to himself, and his metal hide popped open, exposing his inner workings. His metal heart beat with thrum after thrum of electricity. He sighed, took aim at the dead flakes and hair, and released his electric life force into the god's dead pieces.

Kilowatt after kilowatt flowed from him. His vision began fuzzing. He felt himself begin to drift into unconsciousness. Just before he blacked out, he noticed the skin flakes begin to dance and the hair begin to writhe like a worm. He gave a final blast and halted the current. He slammed his metal torso shut and locked it, glad the wounded man in the corner of the apartment had not chosen the moments when his delicate inner workings were exposed to fire the gun.

Drillbot stared at the dead god's debris. The skin flakes wrapped themselves around the hair. The hair caught flame. Smoke billowed from it for about a dozen seconds before the hair bounced from the floor to the wall to the ceiling, leaving a trail of fire behind it like a set of lethal prints.

The flames grew, enveloping the trail from the floor to the wall to the ceiling. Drillbot did not panic, and he did not grow concerned for the safety of the family or their domicile. This was because he detected no heat emanating from the fire. Further, the wall showed no scorch marks beneath the flames, and the fire did not seem to be spreading farther into the domicile.

Then the fire transformed into a thick, black, billowing plume of smoke. Drillbot heard the man and the woman erupt into choking coughs. Without warning, the man's rapidly leaking blood levitated from the ground and drifted over to the corner of the room where the smoke swirled the thickest.

The man's blood danced within the smoke and the shadows, transforming them red. The red smoke began vibrating and twirling, almost like it was dancing. A terrible laughter boomed from its center and filled the room. All the light bulbs in the apartment exploded, and a voice echoed seemingly from everywhere, "Muahaha! I am returned!"

The smoke gathered in the corner of the room and formed into the outline of a nine-and-a-half-foot tall man. The top of the smoke-man's head erupted into flames. The smoke condensed below the flames and solidified into the man's face and body, the latter of which was covered in a cloak made from the stitched-together hides of white wolves and baby seals. A necklace of severed ears hung from his torso, and a belt of thick rope hung suspended around his waist, attached to which were a leather pouch, various tools made from obsidian, and a dagger with a serrated blade and a hilt crafted from the green-furred paw of a giant cat.

God-Art stepped forward. He proclaimed, "It feels good to be alive again!"

The man who now lived in the apartment let go of his wound to retrieve the gun from the floor. He fired a bullet into the god's head. The god collapsed onto the ground, dead once more. Pixies sprang forth from his blood and scurried into the bedrooms. Drillbot could hear the toddler in its crib squeal in delight as one of the pixies rained fairy dust down upon its face.

Moments later, God-Art sprang back to his feet. He snatched the gun from the man's hand and crunched it into a useless pile of metal. The man scurried away from the god, crawling backward until his back was touching the wall.

"That will be quite enough of *that!*" declared the god. "I've resurrected myself plenty for one day."

The man and woman both screamed. God-Art stared into their eyes and screamed back at them. His pupils shifted shape into a pair of swirling whirlpools. The man and woman stopped screaming, though their mouths remained open. Obviously in a trance, they proceeded to faint.

God-Art turned to Drillbot. "Drillbot, you fool," he called. "That costume is ridiculous."

Drillbot removed the mask. He replied, "[whir] Drillbot is aware of that – CLACK – aware of that now. Drillbot came to assist you in resurrecting yourself so that you might – CLACK – might help."

"Oh, but there was no need," said God-Art. "I was juuuuust about to resurrect myself, like I always do."

The god laughed, though the undertones of the gesture hinted that it was not filled with much mirth. A look of wrathful recognition fluttered across the god's eyes. He said, "I remember that we did not part one another's company on the best of terms. I resurrected *you*, but when the blue bear's idiotic magic backfired on me, you did nothing to help *me*."

Drillbot ignored the god's statement. He said, "[whir] Now that you are alive, you must – CLACK – you must accompany Drillbot to help."

The god stared at Drillbot with cold eyes. He responded, "So, the Multiverse expects me to be a *deus ex machina* for *your* stupid story, too? The Multiverse really is a stupid place if it thinks that's a clever twist on events."

Drillbot said, "[whir] Drillbot knows not of what you – CLACK – of what you speak. But Drillbot needs you! Help Drillbot get back t—"

"But why would I *want* to help you? You left me to die," muttered the god, interrupting the robot. He slithered across the room to stand before the robot. "Maybe it's time you experienced the same."

Drillbot flung off his mittens and revved his drills. "[whir] You are welcome to – CLACK – to try. But know that Drillbot has changed – CLACK – has changed since last we met. Drillbot is not an – CLACK – not an easy target."

God-Art laughed maniacally and stared at Drillbot. His eyeballs transformed into flames.

Drillbot frowned his version of a frown. This was not at all how he had expected this scenario to play out.

CHAPTER 12

SOMETIMES IT TAKES A GOURD TO SLASH A GORDIAN KNOT

MOST OF AGENT 27142's thoughts these days amounted to cursing his terrible luck.

Four more years had passed, and Agent 27142 had yet to catch a lucky break. He had encountered a few more travelers, but they had appeared too far away for him to reach them before they jumped away.

But then the Multiverse smiled upon him. Not four feet away, lightning flashed into existence, and in its place appeared a large, orange gourd with a pair of antennae poking from its top on either side of its stem. A young girl approximately twelve-years old clung to the gourd. Agent 27142 reached out and grabbed the girl's ankle. She shrieked.

"Calm down," he yelled at her. "I'm Agent 27142 of the B.I.T., and I need your help."

The girl stopped shrieking. "Let go of me," she demanded. "I'm not supposed to talk to strangers."

"I told you: I'm a B.I.T. agent, and I need your help. It's OK to talk to strangers if they're B.I.T. agents. We're the good guys."

"I don't care. I don't know you," she replied. Then she looked down at his shoulder and saw the bits and pieces of the eagle's corpse embedded there. She shrieked again. "Let me go! I need to go! My sick aunt is waiting for me!"

Agent 27142 grinned like a predatory cat. He growled, "Oh, honey, your aunt is going to have to keep waiting."

He snatched the gourd from her arms and clicked his heels together in his secret pattern, using the explosion created by the move to push himself out of her reach. He said to her, "You know, this kind of scenario is *exactly* why the B.I.T. warns children against traveling without adults."

The girl began crying. Agent 27142 noted the position in which he stranded the girl so that he could later call in an emergency ship to pick her up. That would have to wait, though, because he needed to move. His mission—and the ultimate safety of the Multiverse—was at stake.

He whispered his destination to the gourd. Then he squeezed the vegetable.

"If you insist," the gourd whispered back in a sad, depressed, monotone voice. Lightning flashed between its antennae and then crashed into Agent 27142, engulfing him.

He had never been so happy to hear a gourd speak to him.

CHAPTER 13

A HELL OF A CHANGE

DRILLBOT FELT A crunch beneath his wheel, which lay across God-Art's throat. The god tapped in submission against the side of the wheel. His voice came out a barely audible whisper, "O-Okay, Drillbot. You w-w-win. Now get off me."

Drillbot rolled backward, freeing the god's throat from beneath his wheel and allowing the deity to stand. Tire treads stood out red and fresh on the god's pale neck, which was bent and jutted sideways from Drillbot's weight crushing multiple vertebrae. The god closed his eyes for a few seconds, and the vertebrae healed themselves with an audible crackle and pop.

The god rubbed his own neck. He stared at Drillbot and said, "By Me, you're a ferocious thing. Not how I remember you at all."

Drillbot's face contorted in a frown, his mouth-speaker retracting, his eyes vibrating, and his radar dishes wobbling back and forth. He replied, "[whir] Drillbot is the veteran general of – CLACK – of a cosmic war that lasted ten – CLACK – ten years and spanned thousands upon thousands of – CLACK – of Earths. You were a fool of a mischief god to think you could – CLACK – you could best Drillbot."

The god seemed to understand the gesture and returned the frown. The god kicked at the carpet with one toe, leaving a scorch mark in the shag where his toenail scratched against it. The god said, "Ten years? What did that damned blue bear *do* to me? It's been far too long since I have been alive, and I am ignorant of far too much."

"[whir] Actually, it has been closer to twenty years for – CLACK – for you. Drillbot fought for ten years, and then Drillbot was stranded on a B.I.T. ship for – CLACK – for approximately ten more."

The god scowled at the robot. "*Twenty* years? By Me, I need to make something suffer, or I'm going to explode."

The god drew his dagger with his right hand. Then he stalked over to the unconscious occupants of the apartment. He grabbed the leg of the male with his left hand and yanked him up into the air, holding the man so he dangled upside-down.

"Wake up, little mortal," whispered the god. Little visible stars shot from the god's mouth. They crashed onto the man's closed eyelids. His eyes popped open. "It's time for a good, old-fashioned flaying."

The man screamed. Drillbot rolled over to God-Art's side and promptly severed the god's left arm at the shoulder. The man and the arm crashed to the floor. Drillbot said, "[whir] There will be no – CLACK – no flaying here today."

The god sneered at Drillbot. Drillbot continued, "[whir] Torture will not replace lost – CLACK – lost time. Drillbot has been gone for far too – CLACK – far too long, too. Drillbot must return to the Blue One's side to keep the Multiverse safe and to atone for – CLACK – to atone for his mistakes. Drillbot was separated from the Blue One on Earth 55,777. But that was ten years ago, and the Blue One must be – CLACK – must be elsewhere now. Drillbot jumpstarted your resurrection you so that – CLACK – so that you can ferry Drillbot across dimensions to find the Blue One. We should initiate our search where Drillbot left the Blue One and look for – CLACK – look for clues."

The god retrieved his severed arm from the ground and poked Drillbot in the chest with it. The god said, "You can kill me a billion times, robot, but I will *never* do that blue bastard a favor. And returning a machine such as yourself to him would be the biggest favor he could ever hope to receive."

Drillbot raised his drills to God-Art's face. He replied, "[whir] Killing you a billion times can be – CLACK – can be arranged. You *will* take Drillbot to initiate the search at once. Or you will – CLACK – or you will suffer Drillbot's wrath."

God-Art tossed the severed arm at Drillbot, and when it was in midair, it transformed into a python the length of a football pitch. Before Drillbot could react, the python wrapped round and round the robot, binding him in place. Drillbot struggled against the squeezing snake, but he found that he could not move his arms. The python hissed in Drillbot's audio receptors, and Drillbot sighed.

God-Art guffawed. "And *this* is why people should stop underestimating mischief gods. You think you've got the upper hand, and then we use our severed appendages to turn the tables on you.

God-Art patted Drillbot on the head and continued, "No, I will *not* be helping you return to the blue bear. I'm going to find the pink bear and finally gain infinite cosmic power."

"[whir] But you will – CLACK – will fail. You don't know what the – CLACK – what the pink bear is capable of. Drillbot *does*. She will devour you. Join Drillbot on his quest and – CLACK – and save the Multiverse. Redeem yourself."

God-Art ignored the robot and strummed his chin with the fingers on his remaining hand. He said, "But first, we need to find your creator, the mundane version of me. He was a beacon for the stupid bears, and I reckon that's not something that simply fades with time.

"Besides," continued the god, "As I was dying after I ate the blue bear's heart, I made a promise to myself that your creator would not escape my wrath once I resurrected myself, for he *also* did not lift a finger to assist me. After we have located him, I am going to murder him and resurrect him enough times to feel satisfied, and then I'll force him to help me become all-powerful, and then I'll wipe him from existence."

It was Drillbot's turn to laugh. The robot said, "[whir] Initiate *Laughing out Loud Sequence*. Ha. Ha. Ha. *End Sequence*. You will never get the chance. Drillbot accidentally killed him approximately ten years ago, and now his corpse is – CLACK – his corpse is drifting across the Multiverse at the rate of one reality per hundredth of a second. Good luck – CLACK – Good luck locating him."

God-Art stared at Drillbot in silence for a moment. Then the god grinned. He replied, "Well, boyo, you just made my life *much* easier. I thought we would need a prolonged search to find the sluggard. Now I know exactly where he'll be."

And with that, God-Art made eye contact with Drillbot's telescopic eyes. The god's pupils transformed into a pair of skulls-and-crossbones transfixed with flames. In Drillbot's peripheral, the robot noticed the background shifting and transforming and growing darker.

God-Art finally broke eye contact, and when he did, Drillbot found that he was standing in a dark cave that sloped sharply downward. Flames flickered from torches set every few feet in sconces carved into the walls. When Drillbot looked to his right, the tunnel sloped upward, but it seemed to stretch on forever. He zoomed in his telescopic eyes and could see no end to it.

God-Art tugged on the python's tail in such a way that it twisted Drillbot to face the descending path. Drillbot noticed that God-Art had grown a new arm. He raised his eyebrows like he expected Drillbot to comment on the development. Drillbot refused to do so, instead watching in silence the reflections of flickering flames in the god's eyes.

God-Art finally grinned and loped downhill. Drillbot followed.

The pair traveled ever downward. The cave walls grew closer together. Drillbot soon found himself needing to duck. He powered on his drills. He decided that he would make this tunnel wider and taller to give himself more room.

God-Art laughed. He said, "I know what you're thinking. And it will not work. First, you are bound by my enchanted python, so you couldn't free your arms to drill even if you tried with all your might. Second—and most importantly—there are magical properties at play here. You could widen this tunnel by a million miles with your fancy drills. But it would matter not, for it would *still* appear this same size to you."

God-Art did not wait for Drillbot to reply, instead tugging him along on the python-leash until they reached an arched stone gateway. The arch was decorated with carved reliefs of humans undergoing numerous types of grotesque torture. Above the arched gateway was inscribed the words *Lasciate ogne speranza, voi ch'intrate*, which Drillbot's processors translated into binary, which this author has translated into English: *Abandon all hope, ye who enter here.*

God-Art put an arm around Drillbot and admired the arch for a few moments. Then the god called out in a cheery singsong voice, "No need to worry about abandoning hope, old chap. You've got the benefit of having me with you, and I'm an old acquaintance of this place. So, c'mon! Let's go to Hell!"

CHAPTER 14

HOME IS WHERE THE HELL IS

NORMAL-ART LAY NESTLED in a cleft of mud at the bottom of the marshy river Styx. He stared up through the black water at the tortured souls on the river's surface. Though they were forever engaged in a bare-handed fight with one another, each soul seemed to have carved out its own little personal space up there, which the soul never left. It was a weird microcosm within this section of Hell.

Normal-Art was currently spending eternity in the Fifth Circle of Hell, in which those guilty of Sloth are punished by being thrust under the waters of the Styx to drown for eternity. Meanwhile those guilty of Wrath forever tread water on the surface of the river, fighting one another. The view from down here on the riverbed had at least been entertaining at first, since the fighting above him reminded him of some sort of action movie writ mundanely small.

But as the years toiled on, the show grew more and more tiresome as he watched the exact same "movies" play over and over with the exact same endings. Further, the dialogue was terrible. The wrathful men and women constantly yelled their own names and their own deeds as though people around them should be impressed. Normal-Art found this quirk to be funny at first. Now he wished they would just shut up.

The most notable of these culprits was the one who occupied the space in the water directly above Normal-Art. He shouted of his own name, Filippo Argenti, and a story about himself at least three-dozen times per day, to which Art and every single soul buried in the riverbed beneath him consistently shrugged in confusion, having never heard of the fool and not caring to learn more about him. From what Art had surmised from the portions of Filippo's yelling that he had been unable to ignore, Filippo was a Florentine politician from the 13th century whose political party did something important.

The only changes up there on the surface occurred when a new sinner was tossed into the water by the lead guardian of the Fifth Circle, the angry and sullen Phlegyas. Soon after each new sinner's arrival, he/she would either be caught in the endless cycle of fisticuffs on the surface or would sink to the bottom and land somewhere in the mud. Either way, it was different and exciting for a short time—especially when the new sinner brought news of the outside world, particularly if the news described plots of a television show that took place after Art had been whisked away by God-Art on his fateful adventure so long ago. And then the excitement would fade, and tedium would replace it once more.

Based on the number of television seasons that newcomers had described over the time that Art had been down here below the surface of the Styx, about ten years had passed outside of Hell since Normal-Art's death, and thus about twenty since his departure from his couch with the god.

It was going to be a long and boring eternity, so Normal-Art sighed, and as he did so, the sullen expression escaped his lips in the form of a gurgling bubble that drifted up to the surface of the marsh above. The gurgling bubble tickled the feet of the damned Florentine politician, Filippo, who had actually been quiet for the first time all day, meaning he had finally fallen asleep. The bubbling woke him, and he at once yelled his name and his deeds. And then he launched into a new assault on his neighbors, which he promptly lost—as he always did.

But as boring as this existence was, Normal-Art could not *really* complain. There were a lot worse places in Hell where he could have been assigned. He had heard rumors from some of his fellow slothful sinners that there was a Circle of Hell where people marinated in a pond of human excrement. Though the Styx's water was definitely not the cleanest in which he had ever soaked, and though he constantly gagged on the water's sulfuric flavor and felt as though he were in a constant state of drowning, at least he resided in *water*. His sympathetic thoughts went out to his fellow damned souls who were drowning somewhere in feces, and he thanked the gods for small favors.

Normal-Art had spent his first few months underwater finding a comfortable niche at the bottom to call home. He spent time getting to know his neighbors and watching the show above with them. Since those below the water were incapable of talking, they mouthed words to each other, and after a couple years, Normal-Art became rather adept at reading lips. He found his neighbors to be rather boring individuals, but they were better than nothing.

Normal-Art found the best company down here in Hell consisted of the demons and the monstrous guards. Over the years, he had befriended most of the ones stationed here in the Styx, unlike most of the other sinners around him. The surrounding damned souls behaved spitefully toward the demons and monsters because of all the torturing. Art had long ago learned that most of Hell's guards did not enjoy the torturing and maiming, but they lived in a torture-based economy, and they had families to feed. Thus, they tortured the damned as necessary, but their hearts were generally not in it. So, Art learned to live with the torture and to expect it and to maintain a cheerful attitude about it, and he thus made demonic and monstrous friends. And besides, their torture felt light compared to Officer-Art's, so he would choose it any day of the week over returning to B.I.T. captivity.

Art noticed a pale object in his peripheral moving swiftly through the water, and his mind jostled to attention as one such monstrous guard approached. "Hey, Art," said a merman with shaggy green seaweed for hair. The merman had pale green skin, a noseless-but-otherwise-humanoid face with gills at his jawline, bulbous fishy eyes, a slender torso, and a lower half that looked like the slick, scaly body of a catfish. The merman held a golden trident in his webbed right hand while enthusiastically waving his other hand at Art. "Good to see you, buddy! Sorry that I can't chat just now, but I'm on duty and it's two days 'til month's end. No hard feelings, but I gotta skewer you good and proper to meet my quota, OK? I'll talk to you tonight at poker."

Normal-Art nodded and mouthed back, "No problem, Mava the Horribly Wicked. I understand."

The water drowned Art's words, but Mava the Horribly Wicked understood him, anyway. The merman nodded. Normal-Art bit his lower lip as he watched the trident dart toward him, and then he screamed as it stabbed into his torso. It did not bite in deep, not nearly as deep as when Mava the Horribly Wicked's cousin, Melvin the Melvinish, was on duty, who was one of the few demons Art had encountered who seemed to experience euphoria when he tortured the souls of the damned.

A few dozen demonic mermen and mermaids patrolled the area below the Styx's surface. They were assigned to torture the slothful and sullen. Mava the Horribly Wicked was Normal-Art's favorite of the lot. Over the years, Art had learned that Mava the Horribly Wicked had dreams of becoming a pop singer. Mava the Horribly Wicked even let Art listen to some of his music, which had not been all that impressive if Art were being honest. Art had also learned from Mava the Horribly Wicked some of the secrets to dealing with the guards to reduce his discomfort: so long as Normal-Art sighed and acted like the water was causing him distress when the demonic merpeople patrolled their routes, he would not get stabbed unless it was near the end of the month and the merpeople needed to meet their puncture-quota. Normal-Art had grown incredibly adept at sighing and moaning anytime a merperson swam anywhere in his general vicinity, and he found himself being stabbed much less often than his neighbors.

As the years wore on, Normal-Art had developed another way to entertain himself beyond befriending the guards and meeting his neighbors. About four years into his captivity down here beneath the Styx, he and the sinners near him had plucked some of the wild seaweed that grew from the riverbed and created playing cards from it. They had a secret poker game going for a good half-year before Mava the Horribly Wicked caught them.

Rather than punishing them, the merman had grown excited, for he had been searching for a regular game for quite some time. Ever since, the merman brought a pack of cards and a barrel of demonic snacks down to the Styx on Wednesdays when his shift was over.

It had at first been only Mava the Horribly Wicked and Normal-Art and a couple other damned souls playing, but it had since grown into a big social occasion in this Circle of Hell. A few of the demons from other Circles had even begun attending, including a minotaur named Gertrude, a harpy named Randolph, a centaur named Brownie, a crawfish-demon named Red Red, and a giant fish-demon named Glub Glub.

One day, Normal-Art realized that his circle of friends was much larger in Hell than it had ever been in the land of the living, and though Mava the Horribly Wicked and his ilk tortured him every now and then, they only did so out of obligation, and as soon as their shifts ended and Art's soul healed itself again, they were all back to being friends.

Thus, even though the show above him had grown stale and boring, Normal-Art grew more and more fond of his life in Hell. And that's why he cursed the day it ended.

CHAPTER 15

INTO THE INFERNO

GOD-ART HELD THE tail of the python and led Drillbot with it like the robot was a dog on a leash. They passed beneath the arched gateway and into the hopeless realm of the damned.

"[whir] These bindings are completely – CLACK – completely unnecessary," said Drillbot. "Drillbot will not run away or attack you, not when we might be able to save former-master-Art. Drillbot did not realize this was an option when – CLACK – when Drillbot came to find you."

God-Art glanced over at Drillbot and smirked. He said, "I'd *like* to believe that, but I like guarantees a whole lot better."

Once through the gates, the tunnel twisted downward at an even steeper decline. The tunnel eventually ended when it intersected a gigantic cave. Though the cave's ceiling lay high overhead, something about the slope of the ceiling maintained the sensation of crushing claustrophobia. Drillbot's sensors noted that carbon dioxide and hydrogen sulfide levels were dangerously high in here. If Drillbot were in the presence of mortal humans, he would warn them to leave at once or face the ravaging effects of poisonous gases in their lungs.

A calm, black lake sprawled across the center of the cavern. Waterscorpions teemed around the edges of the lake, their skinny, dark exoskeletons skittering across the mud as they gorged themselves on little translucent shrimp that danced along the surface of the water. Drillbot noted a single exit, the entrance to a tiny tunnel in the cavern wall on the far side of the lake. Drillbot began to roll forward, intending to navigate his way around the outskirts of the lake to reach the tunnel.

God-Art pulled back on the python, preventing Drillbot from moving. The robot asked, "[whir] What are you – CLACK – are you doi—"

Drillbot was interrupted when an enormous geyser of fire erupted from deep within the lake. The flames spread to envelop the entire cave, flash-frying the waterscorpions that patrolled the edges of the water and boiling the translucent shrimp that swam within it.

"Saving your stupid robot hide from a good scorching is what I was doing," replied God-Art.

"[whir] Oh."

"No need to thank me. I've been here before. I knew what to expect."

"[whir] Drillbot was not planning to thank you. Drillbot is – CLACK – Drillbot is fireproof."

God-Art frowned. "Well, that's a little rude," he said.

"[whir] Drillbot is sure – CLACK – is sure you will get over it."

And as quickly as the fire-geyser appeared, it disappeared. The lake returned to calm. From the tunnel on the far side of the lake, a trio of flying imps emerged. The first to appear was covered in short red fur. The second was covered in curly blue fur. The third was covered in braided locks of yellow fur. They carried wicker baskets and wore white chef hats. They fluttered all about the cavern, collecting the charred waterscorpion and boiled shrimp corpses that now littered the cave floor.

"Yar! It shall be a feast tonight!" called the first imp.

"When is it not?" responded the second imp.

"Good point," replied the third imp.

"Hail, friends," called God-Art from his vantage in the tunnel.

The first imp glared at God-Art. Then it turned to the second imp and said, "Tell the interloper that I am not speaking to him. He still owes money to my mother."

The second imp also glared at God-Art. Then it turned to the third imp and said, "Tell the interloper that I am not speaking to him. He still owes my father a new left leg."

The third imp also glared at God-Art. Then it turned, but having no other imp to which it might relay a message, it simply said to its companions, "I will not speak to the fiend. He still owes me a new brother, since my father cooked my younger sibling for a feast in his honor eons ago. The interloper did not even attend, nor did he deign to tell my father that he would not show, and this was *after* he was advertised as the guest of honor! My father has still not recovered from the shame."

And with that, the three imps ignored the intruders and completed their task of collecting the cooked fauna from this underground cave. When all the waterscopion and translucent shrimp carcasses were stuffed into the wicker baskets, the three imps fluttered back into the tunnel from which they had emerged. A few seconds later, new waterscorpions and fresh translucent shrimp tumbled down from a tiny crack in the roof of the cave, making barely audible splashes in the water as they crashed into the lake. They began the cycle of predator and prey anew, not knowing that the cycle was entirely pointless, and that at some point in the near future, they would all be flash-fried by the fire-geyser beneath the lake to be used as appetizers in a demonic feast.

Drillbot glanced over at God-Art. The god's flaming hair danced in the darkness and seemed to fit in perfectly with the surroundings. Drillbot asked, "[whir] What was that – CLACK – that about?"

The god shrugged. He replied, "To be honest, I don't really remember."

"[whir] Forgive Drillbot for not really believing – CLACK – believing that."

God-Art smirked. Screams began echoing into the cavern from the tunnel on the far side of the lake. God-Art closed his eyes. He listened to these screams, and then he laughed.

"[whir] What is humorous about this – CLACK – about this place?" asked Drillbot.

"Oh, I was just thinking back to my Earth's Heroic Age when I ran the administrative side of its Hell for a while, and I was thinking about the contrasts between my pantheon's Hell and the ineptitude of this Hell. I find the ineptitude here to be hilarious, especially when you consider how many people on this Earth fear this place. The magic at play here is amateur—I'm talking *community-theater-in-some-cultureless-backwoods-rural-town* amateur—and as you can probably surmise from the distress levels of those screams echoing up here to us, the punishment is downright tame. Especially compared to the torture to which I subjected the damned of my Earth.

The god sighed and continued, "Running my pantheon's Hell 'twas a fun gig while it lasted, but it all ended the day that the hero Bibbidybox decided to rescue his dead lover. He tricked me into eating a pomegranate that was poisoned with holy water from the corner of my world afflicted by stone-skin. I ate the damned thing because I love pomegranates, but it turned my skin to stone. Took a bit of time to resurrect myself from that, let me tell you. That particular poison was engineered by my brother, the crafter-god Hyacinth, who held a grudge with me becau—"

Drillbot thought about demanding that the god stop talking, but he knew that the request would fall on deaf ears, so he instead shut off his audio receptors. The god did not finish telling his story for another twenty minutes, at which point he had finished leading Drillbot around the edge of the water, bringing them to the tunnel opening on the far side of the cave. They entered it and followed its path downward. Drillbot found himself needing to duck even more than in the previous tunnel.

After scrambling ever downward for another hour, they reached a second gigantic cavern. This one had a cracked roof from which flaming coals rained and a floor covered in black soil that seemed to wriggle in the dancing light of the coals.

God-Art yanked on Drillbot's python-leash to hold the robot in place so that the robot would not yet enter the chamber. Drillbot sighed, for he had learned a lesson from his overexuberance to enter the prior chamber and had made no attempt to dash forward into this one. Thus, the yank on the leash served no purpose other than to annoy him.

Soon, legion upon legion of men and women ran past the tunnel's exit. They chased after a tiny demon that looked like a black-and-yellow bumblebee with horns sticking up from its head. It held onto a pole five feet long from which hung a black banner.

Drillbot turned his audio receptors back on just in time to hear God-Art exclaim, "This here's the Vestibule for the Uncommitted. It's where those who would not commit to any cause have to chase after a banner for all eternity."

As the bumblebee-demon buzzed past, it yelled out, "Hey Artheoskatergariabetrugereiinganno! It's been too long! I'm off in an hour. Wanna grab a drink?"

God-Art smiled. He glanced over at Drillbot. "As I mentioned, I've been here before. And not everyone holds me in contempt like the imps we encountered."

Drillbot shrugged, at which point God-Art cupped his hands and yelled after the demon, "Can't today, buddy! Let's meet up next time I'm down this way!"

The bumblebee-demon turned a corner in the distance. Drillbot and God-Art waited about forty minutes for the legions upon legions of damned to finally finish running past, these also eventually disappearing around the corner to chase after the demon and its banner. Twelve angels with six wings each buzzed through the sky, chasing after these legions and swooping down to rake the blades of their curved scimitars across the backs of any stragglers.

With the chase out of sight, God-Art led Drillbot out into the cavern. Drillbot felt something squish under his wheels, and when he looked down, he realized that the entire floor consisted not of wriggling black soil, but of writhing worms with sharpened teeth. They bit at Drillbot's wheels and at God-Art's feet.

God-Art laughed. "Tickles," he said. He tugged on the python and led Drillbot forward. "C'mon."

They walked in a straight line across the cavern for hours, following a path of trampled worm corpses. Eventually, Drillbot felt his wheels slosh in mud. He looked down and realized that the worms had ended somewhere along the way, and dark, wet clay had taken their place. He and God-Art had reached the shore of a wide river, its waters black and opaque.

"This river is the *official* border of this pantheon's Hell," said God-Art without being asked. "Think of the areas through which we just passed as the suburbs. Someday they may be annexed, but for now, they're just signs that you're approaching Hell proper."

"[whir] Drillbot did not inquire. But – CLACK – But OK."

"This river is a horribly disgusting body of water called the Acheron."

"[whir] How do we – CLACK – How do we cross? Must we swim?"

God-Art smirked. "What do I look like, the patron god of swimming?"

Drillbot stared at him in silence. When the robot refrained from answering, the god continued, "Well, I'm not. I am, however, a patron god of ferries, so we're going to call in some help."

God-Art stuck out his tongue. He bit off the tip of it and caught the little piece of flesh in his hand. He whispered to it, "Bring me passage."

The piece of tongue caught fire, and God-Art tossed it into the water. The flame never extinguished, even though the piece of tongue was completely submerged. It darted through the water like a fish and soon disappeared into the distance.

A few minutes later, Drillbot saw a shadow appear in the distance atop the river. Accompanying the shadow was a song, which echoed across the water to reach Drillbot's audio receptors. If you happen to originate from this author's reality, you would recognize the tune as the *Happy Birthday* song, but because both Drillbot and God-Art are not from this Earth, they recognized it only as a mildly melodic, yet completely uncaptivating tune.

The shadow took form as it grew closer, and Drillbot could now see that it was not a shadow at all, but a hooded man using a long wooden pole to pilot a gondola. He pushed the gondola through the water with the pole, pulled the pole out of the water, and repeated.

The sound of the wooden pole dipping into the river seemed to keep beat with the song he was singing: "Happy birthday," – SPLASH – "to me," – SPLASH – "happy birthday," – SPLASH – "to me."

The hooded figure's voice was monotone and contained the least amount of joy that Drillbot had ever heard in a sentient creature. The man cut the song short as the front of the gondola skidded up onto the shore.

God-Art looked at the man with a quizzical stare and said, "Hello. We need—"

The man held up a hand to silence God-Art. His hand contained no flesh. It was instead merely bones. He pulled back the hood of his cloak and revealed a pale, gaunt face with burly eyebrows and icy blue eyes. He frowned and leaned upon the wooden pole. He brought his other hand—this one covered in pallid flesh—up to his chin, stroking it with his forefingers as he studied God-Art and Drillbot.

The man spoke, his voice somehow more monotone and depressing up close, "Greetings. I take it you wanna cross the Acheron? Well, just so y'know, the water's bumpy today and dang'rous, and I wouldn't even ferry nobody 'cross unless the boss said I hadda. Which he did, mind you. And on m'birthday, too, of all days. All the other demons and servants get their birthdays off, or at least somebody 'members and brings cake to the office, but none o' that for ol' Rottomus the Bone-Handed."

God-Art raised an eyebrow. "Rottomus, good to meet y—"

"Rottomus the Bone-Handed," interrupted Rottomus the Bone-Handed. "That's m'name. Rottomus is the office clerk."

"Oh," said God-Art. "Good to make your acquaintance, then, Rottomus the Bone-Handed. I had assumed Charon would be meeting us. I take it he must not be on duty right now?"

Rottomus the Bone-Handed heaved a sigh. Though Drillbot had no nose, his sensors maintained a constant analysis of the olfactory nature of gases, a feature embedded in his programming to prevent him from drilling through pockets of noxious gases and exposing organic creatures to them. The analysis of this man's breath showed that it consisted almost completely of rotten fish particles and sulfur. If God-Art did not seem reasonably immune to most mundane mortal dangers, Drillbot would likely warn him to back away from the maw.

Rottomus the Bone-Handed muttered, "Ever'body always asks for Charon. He gets featured in a few famous myths and legends, and suddenly he's, like, everybody's favorite ferryman. He's *awful* at navigating the ol' Acheron when there's any type of adverse conditions, which there are nearly constantly. I betcha didn't know that, now didja?

"I tell people that all th' time," continued Rottomus the Bone-Handed, "but I still come across hundreds of souls every day who refuse to climb aboard my ferry. They say, '*But Rottomus the Bone-Handed, this is sort've a one-time thing for me. I'm just gonna wait for Charon. It's the experience, I'm sure you understand. Something I can tell my kids about when they get down here.*' But poor Rottomus the Bone-Handed, *I* say. Now hardly anybody'll ride in my ferry, all 'cuz I ain't been in any fancy stories. I gots me a family to feed, just like that jerk, Charon. But just 'cuz I keep my head down and do my job and don't make it a point to scour the shores for the poets and the writers, nobody rememb—"

God-Art interrupted, "Rottomus the Bone-Handed, I meant no offense. Charon and I are simply old acquaintances, and I had hoped that we might catch up. We took a pottery class together a few centuries ago."

Rottomus the Bone-Handed frowned. "Oh," he said, barely managing to hold back tears. "OK. I understand. But nobody ever asks to take a pottery class with me. I think it's on account of my bone-hand. And th-th-that's not fair, because I can't help it. You think I *wanted* a bone-hand?"

After a few moments of awkward silence, Rottomus the Bone-Handed pointed to Drillbot's right and said, "Anyway, the line to ride Charon's ferry is over there."

Drillbot turned to look. About a quarter mile down the shore, he saw the front of a queue. It weaved back and forth and stretched off into the darkness. Drillbot could not see its end. There must have been about half a million souls waiting there in line.

"Current wait time is about three years," muttered Rottomus the Bone-Handed. He turned his back on God-Art and Drillbot, stuck his pole in the water, and began pushing away from the shore. "I hope he's worth it."

God-Art glanced over at Drillbot and shrugged in exasperation. "We can't wait three years," he whispered to the robot. He called after Rottomus the

Bone-Handed, "Hey, wait! How much will it cost us to get across with you as our ferryman?"

Rottomus the Bone-Handed pushed his pole into the water to stop his forward momentum. He glanced over his shoulder and said, "I charge twenty-five gold pieces each."

God-Art frowned. He squealed, "That's highway robbery! Charon only charges two coins! And they don't even need to be gold!"

Now it was Rottomus the Bone-Handed's turn to frown. He replied, "Back in the old days, I'd easily pull in enough business t'keep plenty of food on th' dinner table, but nowadays I'm *lucky* to get one fare a day, maybe two. Back before Charon became so famous, a work schedule and a rotation meant something to people. Not anymore, though. Now my family don't even eat most nights. But you're welcome to wait in *his* line if you'd prefer not t'pay my fee."

God-Art sighed. He reached into the black pouch hanging from his belt. His arm disappeared into it all the way up to the elbow. When his hand emerged, it had grown to the size of a small cow and held fifty gold pieces within its palm.

"Fine, we'll pay," he said. "Just get us across the river at once. We're in a hurry."

Rottomus the Bone-Handed's frown grew. Tears filled to his eyes. He whined, "Oh, now you want to rush so you don't have to put up with me anymore? I guess I understand. Happens pretty much every time I get a fare."

An annoyed, exasperated expression etched its way across God-Art's face. The god said, "No, we just have a busy schedule. Nothing to do with you at all. We're not down here in Hell to stay, and time really is of the essence for us."

Rottomus the Bone-Handed continued to frown, but he nodded grudgingly. He held out an open burlap sack. He said, "OK. Good t'know. I didn't really wanna ride in my skiff for longer'n necessary with someone who doesn't like me. It's such an intimate setting, and I really don't do well with awkward situations."

"Could've fooled me," muttered God-Art under his breath. He dumped the gold into the burlap sack, and its weight caused the gondola to rock up and down on the water.

God-Art climbed into the gondola and sat on a cushioned wooden beam. Drillbot hopped on next. The weight of the robot pulled the tiny boat down into the water, and the water hung a mere half-inch from sloshing over the side and into the boat.

"Too much weight," said Rottomus the Bone-Handed. He pointed at Drillbot. "I can't carry this one. We'll sink."

God-Art grinned a mischievous grin. He replied, "But Rottomus the Bone-Handed, I paid passage for two. We're not getting out of the boat. *You* can swim, right?"

"Obviously, I can swim," replied the ferry pilot. "It's common knowledge that only us ferry drivers can swim in the Acheron without getting stuck there forever. But it stinks, and the smell don't come out of your cloak for weeks."

Rottomus the Bone-Handed's face fell when he realized the trap into which he had just fallen.

God-Art's grin grew wider. He said, "It's settled, then. You'll hop out and push the boat across from the water, since neither of *us* can do it."

God-Art shoved Rottomus the Bone-Handed over the side of the gondola. He hit the Acheron with a yelp and a splash. The boat rose a few inches and rocked ever so slightly at the waves Rottomus the Bone-Handed created when he plopped into the water. God-Art pulled the pole into the gondola and lay it on its side.

"Now c'mon, we don't have all day," called the god down to Rottomus the Bone-Handed.

The ferryman became a miniature tugboat, pushing the gondola across the river. His feet made tiny splashing sounds as they kicked through the black water. He complained the entire way and begged God-Art to take a pottery class with him like the god had done with Charon.

Drillbot turned off his auditory receptors before God-Art answered, and then he enjoyed the remainder of the ride in peaceful silence.

*

Drillbot and God-Art hopped off the gondola once it skidded to a halt on the opposite shore of the Acheron. The sand was drier and gravellier over here, and Drillbot's wheels made crunching noises as they rolled across the dust and rock.

Rottomus the Bone-Handed emerged from the black waters and climbed back aboard the gondola. He removed his robes, wrung out the water, and hung them over the front of the gondola to dry. His body looked emaciated and weak, and his pale skin hung loose from his bones. He turned and dumped his sack of coins onto the floor of the gondola. He rifled through them with his flesh-covered hand. He called over his shoulder, "No offense, but I've gotta ensure my payment's still here. Y'got no idea how many thieves come through this place, and they ain't got nothin' better to do than try'n rob ya blind while you're doing them a favor and lugging them across the river."

Satisfied, Rottomus the Bone-Handed turned back to face God-Art and Drillbot. He waved a satisfied wave. His genitalia flapped in the acrid breeze, looking as withered and sad as their owner. Then he picked up the pole and began pushing off from the shore. As he did so, he called out, "Looks like the payment's all here, so we're good. Hey, I've got an idea! If ya don't wanna take a pottery class since you already took one with Charon, maybe we can get together one day and do one o' them art classes where you paint while ya drink wine. I'm much better company than Charon, you'll see!"

God-Art frowned. He replied, "Couldn't think of anything that would excite me less, mate."

The god turned and strode up a winding path in the dirt. Drillbot watched Rottomus the Bone-Handed's face fall as he pushed farther out into the wide river.

God-Art tugged on the python, and Drillbot turned to follow him. As he caught up with the god, loud screams filled his audio receptors. He glanced back over his shoulder toward Rottomus the Bone-Handed and saw that the gondola was aflame. Fire danced across Rottomus the Bone-Handed's pale skin, crackling it and turning it black. As the flesh melted away, he leapt into the water for respite, but the flames did not extinguish. The gondola sank into the Acheron next to him. He shrieked, "No! This boat's a lease! They'll take away my ferry medallion now for sure!"

He followed the gondola underwater, disappearing under the black current with it, neither ship nor ferryman becoming less aflame.

Drillbot began rolling toward the man, intending to help him, but God-Art reined in the robot with the python-leash. God-Art said, "I don't think so, chap. That foul creature attempted to swindle a mischief god for more than his fair share of pay. There's no way I was letting him get away with it, so I boobytrapped the coins with my patented *Infinite Flame Dust* before handing them over. One drop of water, and the dust burns for eternity."

Drillbot frowned at God-Art. The god grinned. Drillbot said, "[whir]

Seems – CLACK – Seems – CLACK – Seems too harsh a punishment. He didn't need to die – CLACK – to die."

God-Art laughed. "Oh, my compassionate friend, he won't die, and it may be a good change for him in the end. He is an immortal gondola-pilot. He'll merely experience a flaming sensation surrounding his body for all eternity, which he will get used to *eventually*. If he markets himself right, this new look could be the turning point he's been looking for to drive a few more customers to his damned gondola. Well, once he fishes it from the depths of the Acheron, that is. He'll just need to update his name to something like Rottomus the Eternally-Flaming-Skeleton or something of that nature, which if you ask me is much better name than Rottomus the Bone-Handed."

God-Art continued walking, leading Drillbot up a winding path to reach the crest of a small hill. Once atop the hill, Drillbot noted that the path wove its way back down the other side of the hill and toward a valley, in the center of which lay a wide hole in the ground. Drillbot's telescopic eyes measured the distance to the hole as two miles.

Along the way to the hole, the pathway was lined with rickety huts that had been built from black rocks stacked atop one another. Drillbot surmised that these rocks must have been collected from the enormous cavern's floor, because similar rocks lay sporadically across it in craggy clusters. Small torches hung on sconces outside the huts provided meager light to the area. Drillbot looked up at the ceiling of the cavern, and it gave him the impression of looking up into the night sky. A species of glowing fungus grew in clumps on the cave ceiling, forming shapes in the packed dirt that resembled stars and constellations.

Laughter and conversation wafted from the first hovel that lined the pathway. As Drillbot and God-Art passed, the robot glanced through the hovel's open windows and saw a bald man in a toga standing and gesticulating to a circle of other men, each of them also wearing togas and yelling back at the first man. A gigantic amphora stood in the middle of the circle from which the men filled their glasses with wine. They drank deep, and their smiles were stained red.

A man with a wolfish face emerged from the front door. He leaned toward the ground and promptly vomited on God-Art's feet. When he looked up at Drillbot, he wiped his mouth with the back of his hand and said, "Th' living they're sending down here t'be scared straight look much diff'rent than when

I's leading 'em." Hiccups punctuated each syllable of the man's observation.

Drillbot frowned his version of a frown. He replied, "[whir] Drillbot does not understand."

The man smiled, his teeth brown and jagged. He stared at God-Art now, jealousy filling his eyes. He muttered, "Name's Virgil. Yahweh used t'call on *me* t'lead sinners through Hell and Purgatory t'scare 'em and put 'em back on the righteous path. He ain't asked me t'do it fer 'bout five decades. Looks like that's 'cuz he gots somebody *new* fer the job. Whadjyoo take m'job fer? 'Twas 'bout the only thing I enjoyed doin' down here 'sides these damned drunken symposiums, so now all's I have left t'pass the time in this pit is drink and argue with m'fellow Limbo-dwelling bastards."

God-Art frowned. "This isn't what you think," he responded. "I'm a mischief god from another reality. My colleague and I are here to sneak somebody *out* of this Hell, not to scare a mortal into making righteous decisions."

The man poked God-Art in the chest. "You're funny. Y're a lying sack of ox testicles, but y're funn—"

Before the man completed his sentence, he slumped to the ground and passed out.

Drillbot glanced over at God-Art and said, "[whir] Drillbot is confused."

"We're in the First Circle of this pantheon's Hell, and it houses the souls of righteous sinners who either did not worship in a religion that contained an afterlife, or somehow ended up here rather than the afterlives of their own particular religions. Such an afterlife-mismatch is not an infrequent occurrence, especially when a particular religion is no longer practiced and its afterlife falls into ruin, or its gods decide to retire and the souls within its afterlife get disseminated to other still-existing religions.

God-Art continued, "Anyway, for whatever reason, the souls in this Circle were assigned here. But they're not *really* punished like they would be in other Circles, because they were righteous according to their own laws and belief systems. They're simply not allowed into this belief system's Heaven because they were not worshippers of its gods. They even have a sort of work-release program where they get to leave this place for a while in order to convince people on the surface to follow this belief system's religion more fervently. This Virgil character was apparently part of this program. However, it appears that he hasn't been called on to perform this service in a while, which implies either he had not been performing his job very well, or this religion is weakening and there aren't as many people adhering to it, meaning the population of those who would be eligible for such intervention has fallen. H—"

Drillbot interrupted, "[whir] Drillbot understands. You can stop. You are – CLACK – You are not very efficient in your explanations."

God-Art smiled and nudged the robot to continue down the path. "Well, that should come as no surprise. I am a god of both storytelling and unnecessary exposition, after all."

Drillbot said nothing in reply, instead continuing down the path in silence. As he neared the hole in the middle of the cavern, he realized the scale of the hole was enormous. If he so desired and had the opportunity, he could have stuffed Ginny's monstrous pink blob into the space with room to spare. The path continued over its edge and disappeared down into it, but before the robot could descend, he heard voices address him from the last hovel on the right.

"You there! Mechanical man!" called a man with a Serbian accent as he leaned out the hovel's open window. The man wore a dark suit with a wide tie. His hair was short and parted in the middle, his eyes were nearly black in color, and his nose was underlined by a wiry mustache the width of his lips. "Please, stop here but for a moment."

Drillbot slowed. God-Art tapped his shoulder and motioned for him to continue, but curiosity got the better of Drillbot, since *he* was the one for whom the man had called. Drillbot rolled toward the hovel. God-Art yanked on the python to pull him away, but Drillbot resisted, revving his engines as he pushed against the god's tugging. After a few dozen seconds, God-Art sighed and stopped pulling, apparently acquiescing to Drillbot's curiosity, at least for the moment.

The man who had called to Drillbot stepped outside. Four other men followed him. The first was a man with shaggy, unkempt gray hair and a bushy mustache, the second was a man with a wide face, wide ears, and dark hair that had been parted on his left and slicked tightly against his scalp, the third was a man with a bushy beard that dangled from his ruddy cheeks to fall upon his disheveled tunic, and the fourth was a man with a slightly hooked nose, stringy gray hair that seemed to be balding in the front, a long beard, and close-set eyes that gleamed with constant inquiry. He wore renaissance-era attire, including a green coat chased with blue and a small blue cap on his head. This man's hair mingled with his long, gray beard so that it was hard to tell where the hair from atop his head ended and the beard began.

The man who called to Drillbot spoke once more, "My name is Nikola Tesla. Welcome to our home."

Drillbot nodded and said, "[whir] Good to make your – CLACK – make your acquaintance, Nikola Tesla."

The man and his fellows clapped with delight. The man with the wide face leaned over to the one with the bushy mustache and exclaimed, "It talks! It responds to cues! What a delight."

Nikola said, "You are the first visitor not formed from flesh and blood to pass this way. This is so exciting! As I mentioned, I am Nikola. These are my colleagues, Albert Einstein, Alan Turing, Euclid, and Leonardo da Vinci. Collectively, we call ourselves the Five Phalanges of Science."

God-Art groaned in annoyance. He whispered to Drillbot, "OK, that's enough. You made some new friends. Let's go. Now."

Drillbot replied to Nikola, "[whir] Hello, Nikola and the Five Phalanges of – CLACK – of Science. Drillbot is – CLACK – is this robot's name."

Turing clapped. He sprinted back inside the hovel and shut the door. He squealed, "I can't see any of you now. Quick, ask it another question and all of you reply. See if it would pass my test!"

Albert glanced over at the hovel and stuck his tongue out mockingly. Once it was back inside his mouth, he said, "Ve are not going to vaste our time doing zat. Ve are going to learn more about our guest."

Albert turned to Drillbot. He studied the robot's drills, the bottoms of which poked out from gaps in the python's grip. "I take it you vere designed for digging?" he asked.

Drillbot nodded. "[whir] Affirmative. Drillbot's primary purpose was originally – CLACK – was originally for drilling."

Nikola stepped forward and rubbed the drill tips. "And what is your primary purpose now?" he asked.

Drillbot frowned. He replied, "[whir] Now, Drillbot is a warrior trying to save the Multiverse."

Albert clapped and exclaimed, "You hear zat? Multiverse! I knew it!"

Nikola yelled, "This is delightful. You are such a treat!"

God-Art tugged on the snake. He whispered to Drillbot, "We need to go. *Now*!"

And it was then that Drillbot realized the trap. Euclid and Leonardo had quietly stalked around behind Drillbot and God-Art. Leonardo tossed a net over them and stomped on a button once the pair were sufficiently entangled. Electricity surged through the net. Drillbot's vision winked out for a moment, and when it popped back into view, he was lying on his side. God-Art lay on top of him, pressed close because of the net. His face was contorted in rage.

"I warned you, you fool!" the god yelled at Drillbot.

Nikola tsked. He said, "Oh, the mechanical man is no fool. And neither are we. We Five Phalanges of Science are here in Limbo because we worship one thing and one thing only: Science! And now we have the perfect sacrifice for our god: a genuine artificial intelligence!"

God-Art scowled and continued yelling into Drillbot's face. "Where do you think we are? We are in a version of Hell! These places are never nice or relaxing, except on Earth 999,666. Even here in Limbo, the virtuous souls are left in constant shadows. Even the best of them go insane when down here long enough!"

Drillbot frowned his version of a frown. He whispered back, "[whir] Sorry, Drillbot did not know. Drillbot was glad someone showed interest in him as – CLACK – in him as a sentient being instead of as a – CLACK – as a machine for killing or digging."

God-Art's scowl deepened. He growled, "Well, I hope you learned your lesson. And now I must hurt these men—which doesn't bother me at all, mind you—but such displays of violence are more likely to draw the attention of the god who oversees this version of the afterlife, an afterlife in which we are trespassing for a reason that would not result in any positive outcome if we are caught. I already took a bit of a risk in burning up our ferryman. I had hoped to refrain from too many others."

Flaming daggers shot from God-Art's hair, piercing each of the scientists in his heart. The flames burned so hot that they boiled the Five Phalanges of Science from the inside. They each collapsed to the ground and melted into a pile of goop. God-Art then transformed the tip of his tongue into a serrated knife and contorted it from his mouth to cut the net away.

Once free, God-Art pulled Drillbot upright, pointed toward the hole in the center of the valley, and said, "Rule number one about Hell, my metal friend: you may talk to the damned, but do not get too close to them and do not linger, for they will use you and trap you."

Drillbot nodded and turned to the hole. He rolled toward it.

*

Drillbot and God-Art reached the outskirts of the giant hole. Drillbot telescoped his eyes and could see that the terrain sloped inward for a few hundred feet before ending at a sheer cliff. The pair descended the slope via a path carved in the rock, winding back and forth until they reached the drop the path's end. Drillbot looked over the side of the cliff and could not see the bottom. God-Art pointed at a ladder carved into the cliffside. "We'll use that to descend," said the god.

Drillbot replied, "[whir] Free Drillbot from his – CLACK – from his bindings so that he can climb down."

God-Art laughed a mocking laugh. Instead of acquiescing, he climbed down a few rungs on the ladder and gave the python's tail a sharp jerk. Drillbot fell over the side of the cliff and dangled in the python's grasp like he was an insect inside a cocoon made from snakeskin.

The mischief god held the snake's tail firmly in his right hand and used his left arm to climb down the ladder, doing so in jerky motions that made Drillbot swing back and forth at the end of the line. With nothing better to do during the descent, Drillbot stared up at the glowing fungus high overhead on the ceiling of the cave. He occupied himself by assigning particular bright spots as impromptu constellations that he named after comrades from his decade-long war. He named half of them Art. The other half, Ginny. He sighed.

Drillbot's internal chronometer indicated that they had descended the ladder for nearly a day before the top of Drillbot's head touched down upon dry dirt. Realizing the thump of Drillbot's head on something solid indicated that they had reached the bottom of the ladder and that the drop to the ground was now only a few rungs, God-Art hopped down from the ladder. He cursed as he twisted an ankle. He healed it within seconds, pulled Drillbot upright, and then cursed again as he looked at what lay ahead.

A short, wide tunnel stretched out before them and disappeared into the distance, twisting ever downward in sharper and sharper curves. The end of a long line of damned souls stood a mere few feet away. They were waiting in a queue that twisted back and forth, back and forth, back and forth to fill every spare inch of the tunnel. A sign near the blond woman's head at the back of the line read, *Estimated wait time from here: 11 months.*

God-Art trudged forward and tugged on the snake's tail, pulling Drillbot along behind him. God-Art muttered under his breath, "This just won't do. Such inefficiency. What is this place coming to?"

God-Art pushed people aside as he shoved his way toward the front of the line.

"Hey!" some people shouted.

"No cutting, you jackass!" yelled some others.

As Drillbot followed in God-Art's wake, many of the frustrated souls in the queue attempted to jostle back into their places in line before he was able to pass them. He pleaded with them, "[whir] Please, stay back. You will only – CLACK – only hurt yourselves."

Drillbot frowned, because the daggers that stood erect from his wheels were poking out between layers of the python that was wrapped around him. The blades ripped through the legs of over a dozen damned souls before the rest of them got the hint and stayed out of the way until he had rolled past.

Drillbot called out apologies to the now-legless damned who were writhing upon the ground in pain, but they did not acknowledge his entreaties for forgiveness. The mischief god was rather bemused by the entire situation. He giggled.

And then he yelled over the cries of the now-legless damned, "Mischief god and living being coming through. Make way! Make way!"

Another voice complained, "Why do the living get all the perks down here? It's not fair! We've been waiting here patiently, and they just get to cut up to the front? Ridiculous!"

The god and the robot ignored a myriad more complaints as they pressed ahead. Finally, after nearly an hour of doing so, they finally emerged from the tunnel's exit. They stood at the pointed peak of the biggest stalagmite Drillbot had ever experienced. The stalagmite was as tall as many of the mountains that Drillbot had seen during his travels fighting against the pink bear's army.

A path in the dark rock looped around the sides of the stalagmite, and the line of damned souls continued down it. Drillbot peered over the edge of the stone outcrop to get an understanding of where the path led. Partway down the stalagmite, the path passed through an archway, and that was where the line of damned souls finally stopped.

Drillbot could see that the pathway then descended into a rocky valley that surrounded the stalagmite like some great ring around the finger of a titan. Drillbot estimated the valley to be about six miles in diameter. Black storm clouds blustered all throughout the valley, twisting and turning in a chaotic miasma. Drillbot watched as tornadoes sporadically swirled from the bottoms of the storm clouds and smashed into random spots across the valley floor.

God-Art tugged on the python-leash, pulling Drillbot away from his vantage at the edge of the stalagmite. The god pulled Drillbot down the path, squeezing past the line of damned souls—only a few of whom failed to heed God-Art's warnings to move aside, and thus only a few failed to avoid Drillbot's wheel-daggers. The duo followed the path as it looped around the stalagmite thirty-three times. Finally, they reached the archway that Drillbot had spotted from the top of the stalagmite. The end of the line of the damned stopped to the left of the archway.

Just past the archway, a hulking brute nearly sixty-feet tall sat on a throne the size of a city bus. The sallow behemoth wore a pointed crown with seven red jewels at its peaks. His hair was cropped short beneath the crown, and his beard was long and gray and bushy. His gigantic brows seemed stuck in a furrowed position. He wore no clothes other than the crown, and though his arms were bulky and muscular, his belly rose into a large paunch. His legs lay curled and twisted below him, skinny and feeble from disuse. His genitalia were shriveled and barely visible. An enormous serpent's tail grew from the brute's back. The tail's end lay in the dirt between the throne and the brunette at the front of the line.

The brunette was engaged in conversation with the monster. "A-A-And a few times, I lusted after my gardener," she said. "But I never acted on it, I swear."

The hulking brute on the throne shook his head. Sweat glistened on his bare chest. His angry voice bellowed so violently that the brunette fell to the dusty ground, "There! Is! More!"

The woman looked at her bare feet. They were cracked and bleeding. "F-F-Fine," she muttered. "I also stole money from my business partners. But I had no choice! It was them or me!"

God-Art leaned over to Drillbot. He pointed to the brute on the throne and whispered, "You'll want to watch this, old chap. That creature's name is Minos. He assigns people to their appropriate Circle of Hell by twisting his tail around his body. Number of twists corresponds to the Circle of Hell. He'll be the one to tell us where to find Art, since every soul down here undergoes his judgment."

Minos grunted angrily and leaned forward. His mammoth serpent tail twisted around him eight times. "Fraud," he bellowed.

"No!" the woman screamed. "It should be Lust! Or at worst, Greed! This isn't fair! I had no choice! It was them or me!"

But demons flew in from somewhere near the ceiling of the colossal cavern and dragged her away, despite her protests. God-Art walked forward with Drillbot in tow, cutting past the front of the line.

"You!" bellowed Minos. Without waiting for God-Art to respond, the brute twisted the tail around himself nine times. "Treachery! Now begone. I will not fall for your treachery *again*."

God-Art held up his hands in submission. He said, "Minos, old friend. You know I was only playing with you last time. We're good friends. That's how friends play."

Minos frowned. He bellowed, "I was without a serpent for three decades the last time you visited. I had to beg every demon in Hell for a new one, and even then, I had to lease this one for an outrageous sum from one of the imps in the Eighth Circle! Hell descended into chaos! I was nearly sacked from my post when all was said and done!"

Minos pointed at the python surrounding Drillbot. He cried, "And now you bring my serpent back to taunt me. Guards! Get him out of my sight!"

"Wait, wait, wait!" called God-Art. "I apologize. We're here looking for someone specific, and once we find him, we will leave Hell immediately. As a token of good faith, you can have your serpent back."

God-Art tugged twice on the python's tail, and it fell away from Drillbot. Before the robot could move, however, strands of the god's flaming hair leapt from his scalp to encircle Drillbot anew in magical restraints.

Drillbot sighed, deciding that he did not care enough to ask God-Art *how* he had transformed the arm that Drillbot had severed into the serpent that the god had apparently stolen from Minos, because asking would only result in an inefficient tale where God-Art would divert onto tangent after tangent, likely never answering the original question in a satisfactory way, and Drillbot would eventually simply turn off his audio receptors to cope. Thus, Drillbot sighed again and remained silent.

God-Art whipped the gigantic python toward Minos, and its mouth snapped shut upon the giant's stomach, burrowing into the brute's belly button. Minos allowed a smile to creep across his lips.

"I am whole once more," he bellowed. He stared at God-Art with black eyes. There was no mirth in them.

"I'm looking for a man named Art," said God-Art. "He looks just like me, but shorter and with none of the magical bits. He's a bit of a dullard and a louse, and you likely would have assigned him to the Circle where you send the slothful, since pretty much every molecule within him is lazy. He would've come this way approximately ten years ago."

Minos closed his eyes. After a few moments of silent thought, he replied, "Yes, I remember just such a soul. Made a terrible pun about my serpent tail, which hurt me deeply because of the trouble I went through to procure it. He begged to just be left alone and to be allowed to lie on his couch and watch a device called a television. Does that sound like the correct Art?"

God-Art nodded enthusiastically. "That's him! Where is he?"

Minos smirked. He twisted both of his serpent tails around himself five times.

A confused expression formed on God-Art's face. He said, "Minos, old friend, you've got yourself two serpent tails now. You twisted each around yourself five times. Does that mean the Tenth Circle? Is the Tenth a new one?"

Minos grunted in frustration. He untwisted one serpent tail and let it drop limply to his side. He sighed. Then he said, "The Fifth Circle. Look for him under the surface of the Styx. Now be gone, before I grow weary of your presence and smash you to bits."

God-Art nodded his thanks and tugged on the fire-leash that now surrounded Drillbot. The robot rolled forward and passed through the archway. God-Art leaned over to Drillbot and said, "He really botched an opportunity to tell the tale about how I obtained his serpent. It was an epic bout of mischief when I stole it. It all started when—"

Drillbot did not hear the rest. He preemptively turned off his audio receptors.

*

When Drillbot rolled onto the rocky valley at the base of the stalagmite, he was surprised to find that the raging black clouds he had seen from high atop the stalagmite were not a storm at all. They were instead millions of souls swirling aimlessly in the air.

The fiery leash surrounding Drillbot flickered in the wind. He turned his audio receptors back on.

"-and that's when I said to his mother, 'Minos is a terrible name. I hope you're quite ashamed of yourself.' And that, Drillbot, was that."

"[whir] Amazing," lied the robot. "Please don't try to – CLACK – try to top it."

God-Art glanced over at Drillbot and furrowed his brows. Souls fell to the ground all around them—always in intertwined pairs—crashing onto the rocks like raindrops and bouncing back up into the air to rejoin the storm.

God-Art stopped for a moment and looked up. He asked, "Smell that storm? What's it smell like to you?"

Drillbot's sensors analyzed the odors while tornadoes crashed down at random across the valley. A list of ingredients popped up, including blood and sweat and fire and smoke. Drillbot finally identified the odor that God-Art was almost certainly going to point out to him, the one that blared across his processors whenever a tornado touched down or a pair of soul-raindrops crashed nearby: the musk created when mammals mate.

Just when Drillbot was preparing to speak the correct answer and knock some of the ones from the god's arrogant metaphorical code, the god cut in, "It's sex! You've never smelled the musk, for you are of course but a robot. But it's the smell of humans mating."

Drillbot frowned his version of a frown and remained silent as the concept of *mating* flittered through his processors. He refused to tell God-Art of his lost love, Ginny Rex, and the hope that he had held in his heart of starting a family with her, and the lust with which they caressed one another every night when Ginny Rex was given leave to rest from her duties in the Army of Life. These were the robot's positive memories alone.

When Drillbot said nothing, the god tugged on the leash to continue their hike and said, "This is the Second Circle of this version of Hell, dedicated to punishing Lust. If you don't control your loins in life, then you've got no control over your soul in the afterlife! Well, according to this particular culture on this backwards reality, you don't. On my Earth, I rewarded the lusty in the afterlife, especially the ones that called out my name when they mated."

Before Drillbot could be subjected to another long-winded story, a pair of intertwined souls fell from the sky and crashed atop God-Art. The force of their fall smashed him into the ground and crushed his skull. Little fairies emerged from his ears, looked around at the desolate terrain, and climbed right back in. God-Art lay dead on the ground, but the leash of fire remained tight around Drillbot, holding him in place. So, he would now have to wait for the annoyingly inefficient god to resurrect himself before continuing the descent into Hell. Drillbot sighed.

On the ground before Drillbot lay a man and a woman, both rubbing their heads in a state of dizziness. Drillbot had nothing better to do until God-Art resurrected himself, so he decided to begin a conversation with them, though he stayed as far back as possible, having learned his lesson from the encounter with the Five Phalanges of Science in the First Circle.

"[whir] Hello," said Drillbot.

The man sat up and gazed quizzically over at Drillbot. Salt-and-pepper hair lay slicked back on his head, and an overlarge widow's peak stood out prominently on his forehead. Thin black eyebrows perched above small, untrusting eyes, and a thick bulbous nose jutted out from the middle of his head. A scowl twisted across the bottom half of his face.

"Why, I don't reckon I've seen anything quite like you before, boy," said the man as he studied Drillbot. "You look mighty tough. Why don't you take mah hand an' get me outta this place?"

He extended a palm to Drillbot. Drillbot stared at it. The man took Drillbot's hesitance as immediate refusal, and his eyes grew petulant. He yelled, "I led mah country through the most controversial era of the century and through a war lots of people didn't agree with. But I held strong to mah principles. I even helped a lotta people to get the same rights as ever'body else. But no, none o' that fills up the good side of the ledger, accordin' to this back'rds place."

His frown deepened, and he continued, "But I did *nothin'* wrong! *Nothin'!* Mah wife never wanted me carn'lly, and never got dolled up or nothin' for me. I gots me a' unnatural large endowment, if ya know what I mean. She knew what she was gettin' into with me 'fore we's married, an' she never complained neither when I went sniffin' 'round other women. Now, tell me how it's fair that I'm rottin' down *here*, when she's somewhere up above? I made tough decisions all day long, decisions that weigh heavy on a man's soul, and damn her fer never usin' her body to gimme no relief!"

The woman who had fallen atop God-Art with him interjected. Her curly brown hair fell in tangles across her face. Her eyes were red from crying and her pale, bare skin was covered in sweat and bite marks. She squealed, "I'm innocent, too! As the nineteenth century rolled into the next, you could find my portrait everywhere—it was used to sell *so many* things in the magazines. An affair blossomed between myself and a comely gentleman, and this man murdered my husband. But my husband had abused and hurt me! What was I to do? This new man's attention Thaw-ed my heart—see, I'm very funny with the puns, another of my many great qualities—for I thrilled at his touch, and he thrilled at mine. How could I stop this new lover from his vendetta, if his mind was set on it? I just wanted to be treated right."

Drillbot began to reply, but the man on the ground seemed to notice the woman for the first time since dropping from the sky. His face contorted and his mouth twisted into a lustful, impish grin. He seemed to lose all memory of the conversation in which he had been engaged with Drillbot. He leapt on top of the woman and they began rolling together across the dusty ground, engaging in the throes of carnal passion. During their thrashing, a hot breeze picked up and lifted them into the sky.

Drillbot's processors were confused. Seemingly on cue, God-Art sprang to his feet, resurrected. "That's better," said the god.

"[whir] Drillbot does not understand. Circumstances were beyond their – CLACK – beyond their control. Eternal punishment is too – CLACK – too steep a price. We should set them free."

God-Art tsked at the robot. Then he said, "Put that thought out of your mind, my metal companion. I've traveled these depths and others just like it many times before, so I should have warned you before we entered: everyone down here—just like in every Hell—is innocent, at least according to themselves, because they believe that they are the heroes of their own stories. If given the opportunity, they'll all tell you sympathetic tales about themselves to try and gain your pity, but you must remember that you're only hearing *their* side of the story. They committed wrongs according to this culture, and they were all sent here in accordance with its strict ethical codes—whether we agree with these codes or not. And thus, they will be staying here.

God-Art stared at Drillbot, who was frowning his version of a frown. The god frowned back at the robot and continued, "Look, I can tell from the way you're looking at me that my answer wasn't satisfactory to you. Though your heart is made of metal, it is softer than most. The rules of this culture's afterlife seem backward and wrong to you. That is fine. They do to me, too. They are incredibly stupid. But they belong to *this* culture, and though we are free to *mock* its stupid afterlife, we will *not* change it. Because to change it, we would need to overthrow a cultural regime—likely including both deicide of some sort and a philosophical revolution in this culture's thinking, which is something that can take decades. We simply don't have time for it, and I simply don't care enough about these mortals to put forth the effort—and even if I *did care* and we did enact this change, most of these mortals would simply end up assigned to some other stupid version of Hell that would be created from the pantheon that ascends from this cultural regime change, where they would be just as unhappy and think they are being treated just as unfairly as now, rendering our effort moot. So, feel free to listen to these souls if that is what you wish to do, but we will *not* be bringing any of them with us, even if they gain your pity. Leading those that *you* deem worthy of rescue out of this Hell—which, knowing how soft that steel heart of yours is, would mean *all* of them—would draw too much attention from a version of Yahweh that I do not care to start a war with just now, and more importantly, it would mean that accomplishing my goals would be delayed much longer than I care to delay them."

God-Art did not wait for Drillbot to respond. Instead, the god tugged on the flaming leash, leading Drillbot the rest of the way down the winding path across the valley, which ended at yet another tunnel, this one chiseled into the side of the cave wall. Just inside the tunnel, they encountered another sheer cliff with another set of rungs carved into the cliff face. Drillbot frowned as God-Art hung him over the side and descended into the next Circle of Hell. This time, there was no glowing fungus on the ceiling with which to distract himself. He sighed.

At the bottom of this ladder, they followed another tunnel, eventually emerging into another enormous cave. This one contained another winding path that led ever downward into a valley with a gaping hole in its middle. The cave's layout reminded him exactly of the First Circle through which the pair had descended, only slightly smaller. Glowing fungus covered the ceiling of this cave, too, but the clumps gathered differently, and the resulting *"constellations"* were not the same.

Drillbot would have begun the process of naming these novel clumps of glowing fungus, but he grew distracted when he noticed that storm clouds also roiled across the heights of this Circle. Drillbot assumed the souls in the Third Circle of Hell must be undergoing some type of punishment similar to the lustful in the Second Circle, flittering about up in the sky with no control over themselves. However, when Drillbot zoomed in his telescopic eyes for a better view, he found that he was mistaken. The churning clouds were brown and green, and what dropped from them made Drillbot sigh again.

"Talk about a shitstorm, am I right?" asked God-Art with a smirk. Seemingly on cue, green lightning flashed amongst the clouds, thunder roared—sounding like some horrid god's foul flatulence that echoed across this Circle of Hell—and brown clods of excrement began falling from the sky to crash upon the valley floor.

"The smell in this Circle is much different than the last one, huh?" continued God-Art. His fingers danced along his robes. "The punishment here is reserved for Gluttony. This is my least favorite Circle. Do not linger and do not speak to anyone, for I want us to be rid of this Circle as quickly as possible. If you knew how tough it is to clean excrement from baby seal fur, then you would understand."

God-Art yanked on Drillbot's fiery leash and led him down the winding path at nearly a sprint. Drillbot almost immediately caught a clump of excrement in the face. He frowned. God-Art glanced over his shoulder, tugged on the leash to move faster, and said with a smirk, "Hmm, looks like that cloud must have had corn for dinner!"

Drillbot glanced down and realized that covering every square inch of the valley on both sides of the path were men and women who wallowed on the ground. They were chained to stakes so that they could not escape, and their mouths were tied open with ropes so that they could not close them as the torrential downpour of excrement rained upon them. The path that traversed this Circle of Hell was elevated above the bound souls so that the damned souls did not block the way through.

God-Art turned a relatively sharp bend in the path up ahead and his heel slipped on a freshly fallen clod of excrement. He slid from the path, but he yanked hard on Drillbot's leash to stop his momentum before he could slide all the way down atop a pile of writhing, gluttonous damned souls. He dug in with his heels and pulled on Drillbot's leash, dragging himself back up onto the elevated path, cursing all the while and smearing excrement all over his outfit.

As God-Art was scrambling back up, a man chained to one of the nearby stakes sat up and exclaimed around the ropes holding his mouth open, "Hey! Robot!"

The man had a wide face, a wide nose, and dark, fluffy hair. He yelled,

"Hey! C'mon! Get me outta here, and I'll do my shtick for ya. Watch!"

The man pushed on his cheeks, shooting excrement from his mouth. "I'm a zit!" he proclaimed.

He erupted in laughter. Then his smile faded, and his expression became serious. He begged, "Now get me out! Please! I don't deserve this!"

God-Art tugged on Drillbot's leash. But before he could be pulled away, snarls and growls resounded across the valley. A three-headed mastiff stalked into view, its jaws slavering and its eyes red. It leapt atop the bound man and began feasting on his entrails. The man screamed.

Drillbot rolled toward him, intending to help, but God-Art pulled back on the leash, holding Drillbot in place.

"Remember what I said," muttered the god. "We are here to rescue one person, and one person alone. These people earned what they are getting according to this place's logic system, and we cannot interfere for everyone whom we pity."

Drillbot continued thrashing against the leash, determined to save the defenseless man from being mauled. Finally, God-Art yielded to the inevitable. He said, "Look, if I rescue the man from that damned three-headed beast, can we keep moving?"

Drillbot nodded and stopped pulling against the leash. God-Art sighed. He reached his arm into his leather pouch and removed a slab of meat that appeared vaguely bovine. It was bleeding and raw. Drillbot could see the unmistakable stick of dynamite impaled through its middle.

The beast glanced up from the man it had been mauling and stared longingly at the steak. It licked its lips. Fire from the god's flaming scalp flashed down onto the fuse of the dynamite, igniting it.

God-Art tossed the meat at the beast, and its middle head swallowed the meat in one gulp. Its other two heads stared at God-Art with murderous eyes. It crept toward him, and the two heads that had not been fed bared their gigantic fangs. But before the beast could pounce, the dynamite exploded in its stomach. Pieces of the three-headed dog flew up into the air and mixed with the excrement to rain down onto the gluttonous sinners.

"There, I saved him from the beast," said God-Art to Drillbot. "Now c'mon."

The beast's chubby victim began to call out his thanks for the rescue. But when God-Art tugged on the leash to pull Drillbot away, the man realized that he was not about to be freed from his bindings. He began yelling curses at the robot and the god.

God-Art led Drillbot the final short distance to the hole in the middle of this Circle of Hell. This hole did not end in a sheer cliff with a ladder carved in its side as the previous ones had, but rather contained a winding spiral staircase that twisted downward around its edges. The duo used the staircase to descend into the depths of the Fourth Circle of Hell.

The staircase ended in another dark and cramped tunnel. Upon exiting the tunnel, Drillbot and God-Art found themselves standing atop another mammoth stalagmite in the center of another gigantic chamber. It looked nearly identical in layout to the Second Circle where the lustful had blown about in the storm, only it was a little smaller. And just like that previous chamber, a path wound around this stalagmite to the valley floor, and then it weaved down through the great valley to a hole in the cave wall. This exit lay nearly a mile away according to Drillbot's calculations.

As Drillbot rolled toward the path carved in the stalagmite, a gravelly voice to his left called out. Drillbot glanced over to see yet another naked giant similar in stature to Minos. This one's face looked wolfish, its dark eyes beady. The top of its head was bald, and it had combed the sides of its curly gray hair up onto the top to cover the baldness. But it had done a terribly poor job. Sprawled at the giant's feet lay piles and piles of designer suits and robes chased with purple stipes and renaissance-era attire colored with blues and greens and scarlets. The piles stretched to ceiling of the cave.

The giant growled again. Its words sounded like, *"Papé Satàn, papé Satàn aleppe."*

God-Art elbowed Drillbot in the torso. He whispered, "Ignore him. He mutters gibberish just softly enough to draw you in and ask him for clarification, and then he takes your clothes when you get too close. He's Plutus, the demon overseer of the Fourth Circle of Hell, which punishes the greedy and the miserly."

Drillbot nodded, deciding not to point out that he wore no clothes, and thus he had no reason to be concerned about passing too close to Plutus. God-Art tugged on Drillbot's leash, steering him on a wide berth around the demon. As the pair followed the path around the stalagmite that descended to the valley floor, God-Art grinned and said, "If you're wondering why he's naked even though he steals everyone's clothes, it's because last time I got drunk with ol'

Minos and wandered around these depths with him, Plutus tried stealing *my* clothes, and I didn't take too kindly to it. I tricked him into removing his own wardrobe, and then I cursed him to forever feel intense pain whenever he places any clothing upon his body. Kept his wardrobe in a trophy case in my chambers back on my reality, and I found his wardrobe contained the added benefit of gold popping out of its pockets at random intervals. Pretty fun stuff."

And just when Drillbot was about to turn off his audio receptors once more, God-Art stopped talking, apparently done with his story. Drillbot smiled his version of a smile.

The pair reached the bottom of the stalagmite, and as they followed the path through the surrounding valley and toward the exit of the Fourth Circle, Drillbot became confused at what he saw. Boulders rolled into view and crashed into one another at seemingly random intervals.

Drillbot asked for clarification, and God-Art described what was happening, "Each soul in this Circle has been assigned a great boulder that's been tied around his or her neck. These souls spend eternity attempting to roll their boulders *over* their fellow captives, hoping to squash them and take their heart's desire: money."

And that's when Drillbot noticed the people behind the boulders, pushing them. Drillbot watched one fellow with slicked black hair, angry eyes, and a bushy mustache that stretched the length of his lips roll his boulder ferociously over a bald man. He shouted, "Hey-Oh! Rockefeller for the win!"

All that was left of the bald man afterward was a smear of blood and broken bones. However, a geyser of golden coins spewed from the corpse. It reminded Drillbot of the video game that the Ginny from Earth 945,003 had frequently played during brief windows of downtime between battles. The mustached man and three other surrounding souls dropped to their hands and knees and began greedily snatching the coins. They fought with fist and tooth and elbow for the gold coins.

Meanwhile, another man with a close-cropped white beard and short white hair rolled his boulder into view. He scowled, and his wide face looked vaguely reminiscent of a Pitbull. He roared, "Hey-Oh! Never turn your back on ol' Carnegie!"

And then he crushed all four of the scrambling men with his boulder. More coins erupted from corpses and more small battles broke out for the spoils.

Scenarios just like this played out all along the path, and though God-Art and Drillbot found they needed to dodge a few times to avoid encroaching boulders, they made it to the exit in the wall of this Circle without any complicating incidents.

They entered the tunnel and came to another winding spiral staircase. Its stone handrail was decorated with spiteful faces that had been carved in the rock. They looked so lifelike that Drillbot half-expected them to call out to him for rescue. When they did not, Drillbot sighed in relief.

However, when they exited the staircase and entered the Fifth Circle of Hell, the sight before him caused memories of Rottomus the Bone-Handed to race through his processors, so he sighed in frustration.

God-Art and Drillbot stood on the shore of yet another body of water, this one a wide river that stretched so far into the distance that Drillbot could barely see the far riverbank. All along the surface of the river, naked men and women engaged in a constant writhing brawl, punching each other with fists and clawing at each other with teeth and fingernails. The water appeared a mix of murky blackness and crimson blood. On the far shore stood a gargantuan Renaissance-style city with a stone wall surrounding it. The wall featured a tall wooden gate that allowed passage through it, and in front of the gate stood a stone tower with a signal fire burning at its peak.

God-Art said to Drillbot, "This Circle punishes a pair of sins: Wrath and Sloth. The slothful are under the water of this river—the Styx—and *that* is where we shall find Art."

Drillbot frowned his version of a frown. "[whir] There are so – CLACK – so many people. How are we ever going to find him in this – CLACK – in this mess?"

God-Art smirked, and Drillbot felt the strong desire to drill the arrogant expression off the god's face. God-Art replied, "Oh, do not give in to the despair permeating this place. The despair is a magical enchantment to which I had assumed you would have been immune, but you apparently are not. You amaze me more every second, you big, metal dolt."

Drillbot replied, "[whir] You still haven't given Drillbot any – CLACK – any answers about what we are going to do."

God-Art smirked wider. "Just be patient. We'll discuss the plan soon enough."

"[whir] Why could Drillbot not have been paired with the – CLACK – with the god of summaries and getting to the – CLACK – to the point?"

God-Art frowned at Drillbot. He feigned a pain in his heart and said, "That one really hurts, Drillbot. You're not such good company yourself, you know."

And with that, God-Art turned from Drillbot and got to work. He tapped the dusty shore three times, and the dust swirled into the shape of a raft. Fire danced from God-Art's scalp down onto the dust and consumed it. When the fire petered out, a wooden raft lay in its place.

The god repeated the process of transforming dust into wood and formed from the dirt eight long, wooden oars. Eight gigantic spider legs then sprouted from the god's back, each grabbing one of the oars. The god used the oars to bludgeon a few battling souls out of the way on the shoreline, and then he kicked the raft into the open space on the water once they were removed. He climbed aboard and tugged on Drillbot's leash, leading the robot up onto the raft. Brown water sloshed over the raft's side as it bobbed under Drillbot's weight.

"Can you see below the water's surface?" asked the god.

"[whir] Drillbot can engage the – CLACK – engage the X-Ray receptors and the DNA spotlight in his telescopic eyes, and Drillbot can simultaneously run a function in his processors to search for – CLACK – to search for Art's body structure amongst the mass of people."

God-Art nodded. "I'll take that as a yes," he said. "You asked for how we are going to find Art, and here it is: you are going to do all that stuff you just mentioned and look for him underneath the water while I paddle us across the surface. We're simply going to have to be patient until we locate him."

"[whir] Affirmative."

God-Art paddled into the water. Drillbot noticed that the god used four of his spider legs to paddle, while he used the other four to knock fighting souls out of the way so that the raft could navigate up and down the river.

The pair paddled upstream to where the river ended in a solid wall of rock, and then they doubled back, paddling downstream to its other end, also a solid wall of rock. In this manner, the raft navigated back and forth on the river, each pass upstream moving a raft's length toward the far shore, and then moving an additional raft's length on the subsequent pass downstream. The paddles that were being used as clubs grew increasingly crimson as time wore on.

"[whir] There!" screamed Drillbot, gesturing toward a spot below them at the bottom of the river. At this point, hours upon hours had passed, and the pair had traversed over half the river in their boustrophedonic route. They were nearing the point where the river ended in the downstream wall.

Beneath the river, Drillbot could see the unmistakable image of his former master. The body structure was an exact match, and Drillbot's confidence increased when the image's DNA registered as an exact match, too. Art was inside a giant fish's mouth, slouched at a table along with five demonic figures. They appeared engrossed in a game of cards.

The god leaned over the edge of the raft and stuck his head underwater. When he reemerged, he wiped his face on his robes and said, "That's him, alright."

"[whir] What shall we do now?" asked Drillbot. "Should Drillbot dive – CLACK – dive in to retrieve him?"

"Completely unnecessary. We're on a river. We'll go fishing, of course," replied God-Art.

One of God-Art's spidery legs handed an oar to his regular hands. He exhaled on the oar and rolled it in his hands. It stretched and elongated to a length of about a hundred feet, and its end formed into a sharpened hook.

God-Art used the spare oars to knock aside battling souls to create a fresh hole in the river's surface. One soul who received a particularly strong smack across the head had bushy gray eyebrows that splayed outward above harsh blue eyes. A long nose jutted out between weathered and craggy cheeks. His gray hair hung loosely over his ears and drifted in lazy waves across his head.

"Don't you know who I am?" the man demanded. He began scrambling up onto the raft, his eyes full of hatred. "Nobody hits me without suffering my wrath. I wiped my country free of its natives, and you think an oar shall best me? Beware the fury of Andrew Jacks—"

God-Art did not wait for the man to finish his tirade. Instead, he bashed the man over and over with an oar until he lost consciousness and sank below the dark water. Once satisfied the soul was no longer a problem, the god shoved the hooked end of the pole into the river. His tongue lolled out the side of his mouth as he furrowed his brows in concentration. Soon, the thin wooden pole in his hands snagged onto something solid.

"Got 'im!" the god exclaimed. He yanked up on the hook, not knowing he was pulling up much more than he intended.

CHAPTER 16

AFTERLIFE IS MUCH BETTER DOWN WHERE IT'S WETTER

NORMAL-ART SHIFTED IN his seat and tried to get comfortable. He sat on a craggy molar inside the mouth of a demon named Glub Glub, who belonged to a species of massive fish-demons that towered over nearly all other demons below the waters of Hell at thirty-feet tall and sixty-feet long.

Glub Glub's home lay at the bottom of the Acheron, which was much deeper than the Styx, and his presence in the Styx every Wednesday evening was a topic of frustration for the slothful and the wrathful because many had to move aside or squeeze together to make room for Glub Glub. This often resulted in extra fighting for the wrathful up above, and extra sighing from the slothful down below.

Normal-Art glanced down at the glowing cards in his hand. He held pocket kings, one a spade and one a diamond. It was his turn to bet, so he mouthed, "All in," and slid his chips into the pile in the middle. One by one, he stared at each member of the card game and narrowed his eyes.

Mava the Horribly Wicked frowned, and then he folded. Gertrude leaned forward. The minotaur's black eyes gleamed despite the darkness of the fish-demon's mouth. Her knuckles grew white as she gripped her cards tight. She slammed them down onto the heavy wooden table and folded.

The fish-demon's mouth jerked left and right, and the sudden motion caused chips to flop off the table and crash onto the floor—the floor, in this case, being Glub Glub's tongue. The five players who had joined Art around this old wooden table to play poker immediately scrambled down to retrieve the scattered chips and place them back atop the table.

Meanwhile, Art did not join the scramble. Instead, he grabbed the table and held it steady as the tongue beneath him rolled and quaked, preventing the cards and assorted drinks from joining the chips in toppling to the floor. He watched the fish-demon's uvula swing back and forth at the back of the leviathan's throat. By now, Art had played so many times with this group inside of Glub Glub's mouth that he knew the undulating tongue and the swinging uvula were signs that the fish-demon was upset and speaking. Art sat waiting patiently for the fish-demon to finish speaking, and soon he did. The movement in the mouth abruptly ceased.

A tiny demon that resembled a bright red crawfish translated for Glub Glub, as he always did since beginning his parasitic relationship with the fish-demon centuries ago. The little red creature's top hat bounced up and down as he shouted, his tiny voice a squeak barely audible over the thrashing and screaming and bubbling sighs of the sinners outside the fish-demon's mouth, "Glub Glub says to either control your anger or leave, Gertrude. You know by now that hitting the table stuck in Glub Glub's gums as you did causes Glub Glub incredible pain."

Gertrude stared down at her hooves and tapped them atop the fish-demon's soft red tongue. A sheepish expression clouded her face, and she muttered, "I am sorry, Glub Glub. I was overcome with rage at the mortal's brazenness. I never meant to harm you."

The fish-demon's tongue rolled gently. The crawfish-demon, named Red Red, nodded. He replied, "Thank you for your apology, friend. It is accepted. Now, let's get back to the game."

Red Red glanced down at his cards and then continued, "Give me a moment to relay these cards to Glub Glub and find out what he wants to do."

Normal-Art leaned back on the molar and watched Red Red swim up to the roof of Glub Glub's mouth. Red Red ensured his back was to the other players—concealing his pincers—and began tapping the roof of Glub Glub's mouth in their own personal code to let the fish-demon know which cards he had.

Normal-Art smiled. As a kid forced to attend his grandmother's church, he had heard the story of *"Jonah and the Giant Fish"* dozens of times. He never thought in a million years that he would be playing poker in that same fish's mouth—well, in this case, playing poker in that same fish-demon's mouth, the *"demon"* part having apparently been omitted as the story was transcribed and spread until it became canon to Art's grandmother's religion. Be that as it may, the setting was a lot less stressful than the preacher in his grandmother's church had described it. Normal-Art smiled wider. Hell was a grand, delightful place.

Red Red swam back down to his folding chair on the opposite side of the table from Normal-Art's toothy perch. Red Red stood atop the chair, his face and top hat barely poking up above the flat surface of the table. The tongue rolled and the uvula shook back and forth, and Red Red yelled, "You got it!"

He joined his fellow demons in folding.

"Is nobody going to pay to see the flop?" asked Normal-Art. The water drowned his words, so they came out as a jumbled gargle. But the surrounding players understood, anyway.

The answer to Art's question was *no*. In turn, the harpy named Randolph shook his bald head and dropped his cards in the discard pile, and then the calico centaur named Brownie reared up on her hind legs in annoyance and slid her cards away face down.

Normal-Art frowned. He knew he should have played the slow game and baited them into a bigger win, but he was never the most patient of men. "Damn," he muttered, collecting the winnings.

Mava the Horribly Wicked pointed behind Art. "What's that?" he asked.

"Yeah, I'm not falling for that one again," replied Normal-Art. He recalled the last time the demons had tricked him into looking the wrong way. They had filched his chips. Granted, they had been good-natured about it and laughed and joked and explained that theft is a deeply ingrained part of demon culture that shows they value you as one of their own. But they had never returned his chips that evening, so Normal-Art refused to fall for the ruse again.

"No, seriously, what's that?" bellowed Gertrude. Like all the other non-water-based demons that Normal-Art had met over the course of this weekly poker game, she was somehow able to talk normally and did not drown below the surface of the Styx. Normal-Art did not know whether this ability was due to a particular magical charm that the demons engaged specifically for the weekly game or if this was simply the nature of demonic genetics. But either way, he never asked because he cared too little to find out the answer, especially when they were trying to trick him out of his gigantic stack of winnings.

Before Normal-Art had time to tell them to stop this stupid round of mischief because it obviously was not working, a sharp pain shot through his torso. The pointed tip of a giant wooden fishhook emerged from his chest. "What the hell?" he had time to mouth before he found himself jerked suddenly upward toward the surface of the Styx.

He flew past Glub Glub's gaping lips. The fish-demon's naturally wide eyes opened even wider in surprise when Normal-Art was pulled upward in front of him. Those gigantic eyes then narrowed, and the fish-demon darted after Normal-Art like he was bait at the end of a human-sized fishing line.

Before Normal-Art could comprehend what was happening, he found himself pulled up past the surface of the river and dumped unceremoniously onto the deck of a wooden raft. Over him stood the person he had hoped to never see again: God-Art.

Normal-Art moaned. God-Art glared down at him with a look of contempt. The god kicked the end of the wooden hook and it melted into a few thousand butterflies that fluttered away, bringing a beautiful touch of color to the grimy faces of the wrathful upon whom they landed.

Normal-Art lay on his back as water churned out of his every crevice. He could not speak and could not move, so overcome was he by his soul removing the water from itself. Meanwhile, out of the corner of his eye, he saw a trio of familiar wheels that he thought he would never see again. He grew overjoyed and wished he could say hello to the robot, but he could not move. His bloated, saturated soul merely continued expunging water.

Suddenly, Normal-Art found himself tumbling back underwater. From his vantage, he could see Glub Glub, who must have upended the raft from underneath in his chase to prevent Normal-Art from being snagged away. The fish-demon's lips darted about back and forth beneath the water, first consuming God-Art, then Drillbot, and then Normal-Art himself.

*

Normal-Art resumed his seat on Glub Glub's molar and gagged and thrashed as he drowned all over again. His corporeal soul had long ago grown used to living underwater, and the seconds on the surface in which he had begun to leak seemed to negate all the time and pain he had suffered to get to the point where the Styx no longer troubled him.

Meanwhile, the poker-playing demons stood glaring at God-Art and Drillbot, who were sprawled on Glub Glub's tongue at the back of his mouth, near the esophagus. One quick swallow would send the pair tumbling down to the fish-demon's stomach.

Mava the Horribly Wicked held his trident at the ready, Gertrude her steel mace, Brownie her bow and arrow, Randolph his talons, and Red Red his Luger, which he had confiscated from a particularly ferocious Nazi passing over the Acheron decades ago.

God-Art shrugged, stood, and promptly grew gills on the sides of his neck. He yanked on a leash of fire—like his hair, somehow still aflame underwater—and hauled Drillbot upright.

"Greetings," said God-Art, "I am Artheoskatergariabetrugereiinganno, but you may call me Art. I am the mischief deity of Earth 49,652, and I have come to withdraw *that* slovenly soul from this Hell."

God-Art pointed to Normal-Art, who had now fallen from the molar and was writhing in pain on Glub Glub's tongue. Mava the Horribly Wicked glanced over to Normal-Art and then back up to God-Art. The merman replied, "No, that is not something we are at liberty to let you do."

God-Art smiled a wolfish smile. He said, "Oh, you think you have a choice? You are young demons, and I have not been to this Hell in centuries. I will forgive you for not knowing me."

God-Art reached into his leather pouch and produced a golden pass that read, *"Official Guest of Hell. Access to all levels and souls."* The signature below spelled *"Beelzebub,"* and it was written in glowing crimson blood.

"Here are my credentials," said God-Art, holding up the pass in display. "You may apologize and hand over my quarry, or I will murder you most painfully."

Mava the Horribly Wicked snatched the pass from God-Art's hand. He studied it. He held it up to Brownie and asked, "Brownie, you got yerself a flawless, frieze-ographic memory. Something look off to you?"

Brownie frowned. She replied, "Beelzebub doesn't put that little squiggly thing on his 'ƶ.'"

Mava the Horribly Wicked looked back over at God-Art. He proclaimed, "Well, looks like you got yerself a forgery. You'll be coming with us back to the station to answer a few questions."

God-Art stared at Mava the Horribly Wicked with a malicious glare. "Just to be clear, I gave you the option to do this peacefully. That was out of respect for your masters. You are choosing murder?"

Gertrude stomped a foot and snorted, "You dare to threaten us within our own dominion? Do you not know how Hell's power works?"

God-Art grinned. He replied, "Oh, I can assure you that I do. I am an old acquaintance of its founder, while you are but the result of a bull's wayward night of passion with a mortal. Do you even know your father's name? I bet it was Blue Bell. You look like a Blue Bell I once knew. He was *delicious*."

Gertrude raised her mace above her head and charged. God-Art stood in place, completely calm. When the minotaur was a mere few feet away, he drew his green-catspaw-hilted dagger from his belt, stepped sideways, and chopped Gertrude's head from her body. The minotaur's corpse crashed against Glub Glub's uvula, and the fish-demon swallowed.

The uvula wiggled, and the fish-demon's tongue quaked. Red Red looked frantic and exclaimed to his fellow demons, "Glub Glub says that was an accident! He would never intentionally swallow Gertrude! She hit the back of his throat and it was instinct!"

God-Art leapt forward. He dodged Mava the Horribly Wicked's trident as it swiped at him. One stroke of his serrated blade opened the merman from chin to navel. God-Art immediately spun and whipped Drillbot into Brownie. Drillbot crashed into the centaur, and the flames from the leash spread to the creature. As the beast burned to cinders, she ran screaming and crashed into Randolph, who also burst into flames and burned to cinders.

God-Art reared up over Red Red, the god brandishing his dagger while the crawfish-demon brandished his luger.

"You know those things don't work underwater, right?" asked God-Art.

The crawfish-demon squeezed the trigger. Nothing happened. He gulped. Then he squeaked, "No, I did not. Care to negotiate?"

CHAPTER 17

RESURRECTIONS. AND RESURRECTIONS. AND RESURRECTIONS. AND RESURRECTIONS...

THE GARGANTUAN FISH-DEMON spit Drillbot and God-Art and Normal-Art onto the far shore of the Styx, and the trio tumbled end over end across the muck and the dirt and the dust. Drillbot sighed.

Eventually, the trio crashed to a halt against a large boulder nearly a hundred feet from the signal tower that had seemed so far in the distance when Drillbot had first entered this Circle of Hell. The wooden gate set in the stone wall of the damned city was visible behind the tower.

Drillbot popped upright and waited for his companions to gain their feet. His wait was far longer than he would have preferred, for Normal-Art and God-Art were too incapacitated to move.

Normal-Art was a pale corpse, and he could not roll off his back because he was too bloated with water. Streams leaked from his many torso wounds and orifices, this water gathering below him and turning the dust into thick black mud.

After nearly a dozen minutes passed, enough water had emptied out of Normal-Art's body that he was able to sit upright. He stared at Drillbot with eyes underlined by deep black bags. He tried to speak, but the water in his lungs prevented him from making any sounds other than a few soft gurgling noises. He shrugged and stopped trying to speak. Then he did a handstand. Water gushed from his mouth.

Meanwhile, God-Art lay sprawled and shattered, having hit the boulder first and soaked up the brunt of Drillbot's and Normal-Art's momentum. God-Art frowned as he stared down at the jagged bones that punctured much of his body. He set to mending the injuries by whistling a magical tune. Effervescent staccato notes divebombed out of his puckered lips and crashed across his broken body, each one healing him a little until he was finally back to normal.

Long after God-Art was finished healing himself, the water *finally* ceased pouring from Normal-Art's mouth, so the man crashed back down onto the ground. He went through a process of attempting to speak and then succumbing to fits of racking coughs a half-dozen times, and finally on the seventh try, he was able to complete a phrase: "Drillbot! I missed you!"

Drillbot smiled his version of a smile. He replied, "[whir] Drillbot missed Former Master Art as well. Wait – CLACK – Wait! No!"

Before Drillbot could stop Normal-Art, the overly excited human leapt toward him and embraced him in a hug. Normal-Art immediately began screaming as the fire-leash surrounding Drillbot touched his skin. He caught fire and burned to ash in seconds.

"That fool," muttered God-Art. "He shall not escape my wrath *that* easily."

The god changed the tone and frequency of the notes he was whistling and got to work resurrecting Normal-Art.

*

Normal-Art sat up. He looked from God-Art to Drillbot and back to God-Art. "Where am I? Who am I?" he asked.

God-Art smirked and glanced over at Drillbot. "Hmph. A memory wipe sometimes happens when I resurrect mortals from death by conflagration. Give me just a moment, this won't take too long to fix."

God-Art took the index finger from each of his hands and shoved them into Normal-Art's ears. Normal-Art screamed. Drillbot could hear the squelch as the god's fingers dug into Normal-Art's brain and twirled in tiny little circles.

God-Art removed his fingers from Normal-Art's ears. Normal-Art flopped onto his back and began convulsing.

"[whir] What did you do – CLACK – do to him?" asked Drillbot.

Before God-Art had the chance to answer, Normal-Art stopped convulsing. He jerked upright. He rubbed his head at the temples and muttered, "Feels like my memories are literally bouncing around inside my skull. Kinda hurts."

Normal-Art glanced down at himself and commented in typical inane Normal-Art fashion, "I'm wearing clothes. I wasn't before I was burned. I'd lost them somewhere along the way."

He wore his cargo shorts, a purple T-Shirt that he had purchased from a truck stop a long, long time ago—so small it fit as a midriff—featuring two racoon cubs joyfully riding a see-saw, and neon blue sneakers with socks that stretched up to his mid-calf.

God-Art said, "Well, I didn't want to be exposed to your pitifully small manhood for the rest of this escape, so I dug through your memory for your favorite set of clothing."

Normal-Art furrowed his brow. Then he responded, "That sounds way too nice for something *you* would do. What's the catch?"

God-Art sighed. "Is there never any trust between us?" he asked.

Normal-Art stared at him with one eyebrow raised. After a few seconds of silence, the god yielded and replied, "Fine. Toward the end of your natural lifespan, you will almost certainly lose your memory and your motor functions, for I had to magically borrow against your future life-force to put things back into their proper place. I thought the clothing might be a small gesture to make up for your future pain. You'll know you're about to undergo the memory and motor function loss *just* before it happens, because your brain will become inflamed and press against your skull so hard that the bone cracks like an eggshell. As a lovely side-effect of the incantation, you will call out my name without knowing *why*, and I will be able to hear it no matter how much distance lies between us. It shall make me smile."

"There it is," said Normal-Art with a nod and a smirk. "Now that I know the terrible future you've arranged for me, why don't you go ahead and catch me up on your plan for the present? You've got one, right?"

God-Art began speaking and gesticulating toward the nearby signal tower and the city gate, explaining how the group would need to go that way to escape this Hell. Drillbot watched Normal-Art and soon realized his former master was not listening to the god's plan at all. The request was merely a distraction. Rather than listening, Normal-Art was bent over the ground, collecting dozens and dozens of small objects that had tumbled from the fish-demon's mouth along with the trio when they had been spit out—playing cards that glowed gold and betting chips that shone with blues and purples and greens. Normal-Art stacked the cards and shoved them into one cargo pocket, which he then buttoned closed. The chips he placed in the other cargo pocket, which he also buttoned closed.

God-Art eventually finished speaking, to which Normal-Art replied without hesitation, "No, thanks. I kinda love it down here. I'm going to stay. As a matter of fact, I was in the middle of winning a rather big poker game— so thanks for thinking of me, but I'm gonna go ahead and get back to it."

Normal-Art turned toward the Styx and began walking toward it. God-Art's eyes went wide. He exclaimed, "What? No!"

The god reached out a hand and snagged Normal-Art by the back of the neck, yanking him away from the riverbed and slamming him onto the ground. The god's eyes grew cold and his mouth twisted into a snarl. He growled, "I did not resurrect myself and deign to set my feet once more in this terribly stupid Hell for you to defy me! Now get on your feet and follow me."

Normal-Art replied, "Maybe you should've asked me first before you came down here. I would have told you not to bother. I'll get on my feet, but there's no way in Hell I'm following *you*."

God-Art barked, "You say that like you have a choice. I *need* your presence by my side for my plan to work, so by my side you shall be. And until you agree to accompany me, I will make your life more miserable than you could possibly imagine."

"Fool, my life was so miserable before I died that Hell is a vacation for me. Do your worst."

And Drillbot watched helplessly in his fire restraints as God-Art did just that. The god's eyes gleamed with rage as he pulled the obsidian hammer from his belt. Normal-Art's defiance seemed to melt away as quickly as it had appeared. The human wilted into a fetal position on the ground as the god beat him mercilessly with the hammer.

Drillbot sighed as the newly resurrected Art died from blunt force trauma, was resurrected by God-Art, died from the same cause, and was resurrected again.

On the twenty-eighth time through this cycle of murder and resurrection, Normal-Art yelled during one of his brief moments of life, "OK, you win. I'll go with you. Just stop!"

Instead of stopping, God-Art repeated the process fourteen more times for good measure. Then he jerked Normal-Art up onto his resurrected feet. Normal-Art stared at God-Art with scorn. Then he grinned as realization hit him. He said, "Well, if you're willing to spend that much energy killing me and resurrecting me, at least now I know how badly you need me. Leverage, thy name is Art."

God-Art smirked. He replied, "Of course I need you. I make no qualms about that. You are essential to my plans, for you are a beacon for those damned cosmic bears. But if you think all that murder and resurrection was a hassle for me, go ahead and test me again. I owe you at least a thousand more because of how we left things when we last parted."

God-Art shoved Normal-Art in the back, and Normal-Art stumbled forward toward the signal tower. God-Art walked behind the mortal. He tugged on the fire-leash, pulling Drillbot along behind him.

Normal-Art glanced over his shoulder at Drillbot. He said, "Drillbot, buddy, I didn't get the chance to ask you how you're doing. How're you doing?"

Drillbot smiled his version of a smile. He replied, "[whir] For many years, Drillbot's life has been a series of – CLACK – a series of *zeroes*. Drillbot is glad to have Former Master Art back. It is nice to experience a – CLACK – to experience a *one* in the ledger. Drillbot is – CLACK – is sorry for what Drillbot did to Former Master Art."

CHAPTER 18

FARTHER INTO THE PIT

NORMAL-ART DRAGGED HIS feet. God-Art shoved him in the back, so he picked up the pace. Though the group was still a dozen yards from the wooden gate that marked passage through the massive stone city wall, they were now directly beneath the signal tower. From high up in the signal tower, Normal-Art heard the hissing of dozens of snakes. He began to look up toward the sound, but God-Art grabbed his hair and yanked his head down so that he stared at the crumbling stone corner at the base of the tower.

"Hey, stop! That hurts!" squealed Normal-Art.

"Keep your eyes down," whispered the god. "There's a gorgon on duty up there. If you make eye contact, you turn to stone. And resurrecting you if you get turned to stone would take much more of my magic than resurrecting you from mere blunt force trauma."

God-Art lifted his eyes toward one of the arrow slits in the signal tower, apparently unconcerned about turning to stone himself. His skin began to turn gray and harden, but the flames atop his head burned brighter, and the transformation into stone ended. He called, "Medusa, babe, give the signal to open the city gate."

A female voice replied, thick with a lisp, "You knowth you mutht uthe the pathword."

"Have you changed it, beautiful?"

"You are thuch a flatterer," replied Medusa, her voice high-pitched and full of honey. "It hathn't changed thinth the lasth time you were here."

God-Art shrugged and walked over to the stone signal tower. He located the end of a wooden beam sticking out of the stone nearly six feet off the ground. He smacked his palm upon it in a pattern that sounded to Normal-Art just like *"A Shave and A Haircut, Two Bits."* Each time the god's hand whacked against the wood, the sound echoed across the Fifth Circle of Hell like a colossus beating upon a bass drum with all his might.

The flame atop the signal tower flashed and turned green. Then the wooden gate embedded in the city wall flung open. From high up in the signal tower, Medusa proclaimed, "Welcome back to Dith, the greatetht thity in all of Hell. Can I ekthpect you to warm my bed tonight, love?"

God-Art shoved Normal-Art toward the open gate with one hand and tugged on Drillbot's fire-leash with the other. He responded, "Sorry, babe, but not tonight. I'd love to, but I'm kind of in a hurry to leave this place."

"Never thtopped you before," she muttered as she ducked her head out of view.

Normal-Art and his companions passed through the open gate and into an arched stone passageway that led them through a winding path beneath the city wall. Grated murder holes loomed overhead in the stone at intervals of every twelve feet. Art stared up into the darkness behind the grates as he passed underneath the first one, and he noticed feline eyes staring back at him from the gloom.

"Hey! Watch it!" he yelled when under the third such murder hole, for a particularly large droplet of drool rained down from behind the grate and splashed onto his cheek.

A squelching feline hiss was the only reply from the drooler up above. God-Art shoved Normal-Art in the back and whispered, "They are feral, hungry demon-kittens. Their species is not the most housebroken of Hell's minions, but they make for fantastic city guards—the most ferocious money can buy. And they keep the demon-rats in the city to a minimum. No need to worry for your safety so long as you keep moving. My presence *should* be enough to give them pause from pouring boiling oil on you and gnawing on your delicate bits, but only for a short while. So, I must reemphasize: *move*."

After a few hundred more yards, the trio emerged from the passageway beneath the city wall and found themselves standing on a blackened cobblestone street. Stone buildings lined the avenue, and flaming torches set in sconces attached to the buildings provided flickering light to the street.

God-Art announced, "In case you had trouble understanding the Gorgon sentry in the signal tower: this city is named Dis, and it is the greatest of cities in this version of Hell."

"It seems familiar. I feel like I've seen pictures of this place somewhere," replied Normal-Art.

God-Art smirked. He said, "It's modeled after your Earth's Florence, which I understand is responsible for a renaissance of culture on your reality. It never amounted to anything on mine, but that is another tale more appropriate for another time."

"That's never stopped you from droning on and on with a tale before," responded Normal-Art with a shrug. "Not that I'm complaining."

"This place," continued God-Art, ignoring Normal-Art's interruption, "is a replica identical in nearly every way to your earthly Florence, except it is always night here, demons occupy the city rather than people, all marble is black rather than white, and the churches are all designed to worship that arrogant fraud, *Lucifer*. There's even a sculpture with his flaccid manhood flapping about in the wind inside of Dis's Accademia. It's forked like a snake's tongue, in case you wanted to know. Completely mundane and contemptable if you ask me."

And with that, God-Art led the group toward the town center. Demons bustled to-and-fro past the trio. Normal-Art overheard many of them complaining about being overworked and underpaid as they headed toward different Circles to spend the day at work, torturing souls. He overheard even louder complaints from the demons headed to less-popular employment—but necessary in a city this size—like plumbing and trash collection and masonry. Normal-Art watched several demons who had just finished their shifts scramble into different pubs with names like "The Vile Hag," "Death to Unicorns," and "The Scorched Earth." These pub names were emblazoned on stocky wooden signs hanging on poles that jutted out from the walls above their entrances. Normal-Art even witnessed a few demons carrying stacks of paper newsletters and wearing white button-up shirts with black ties rush into a building with a rounded golden *"M"* above the entranceway, yelling, "We told a dozen demons about the good news today!"

The trio arrived at an open square and picked their way through a market that occupied the space. Demon-Farmers hawked wares of rotted fruits and vegetables. The smell of spoiled cabbages and cantaloupes and carrots and gourds and lettuce filled Normal-Art's nose, and he gagged. Then he gagged again when he saw the carts toward the center of the market.

The hairy demon standing in front of one cart resembled a six-foot tall flea wearing a maroon robe. Behind him, human legs and arms turned on a spit over a fire. He cried, "Get'cher fresh meat heah! Fresh from the pits! I got little arms and big arms, from the tiniest pencil-arms up to twenty-two-inch pythons!"

Normal-Art must have stared at the demon and his cart for too long, for the giant flea shoved a burnt pinky into his hand. The demon yelled, "Here's yer free sample! Whole arm'll cost yah five golds!"

Normal-Art thought he had become acclimated to Hell's eccentricities by now, but for reasons he could not put his finger on, this scene was too much for his sensibilities. He bent over and vomited, and when he looked up, a new salesdemon from the next cart over shoved a glass of milk into his hand.

"Here, this'll make ya feel better," said this demon, a gigantic platypus with blue fangs poking outward from the edges of his mouth. "It's the finest bone-milk in Dis, freshly pressed from the finest bones from the finest pope in Bolgia 3 of the Eighth Circle. It'll only cost ya nine golds."

Normal-Art glanced around and felt the crowd closing in on him. He saw no sign of God-Art. A flash of panic crept over him, and he realized that the god must have kept walking when Normal-Art stopped to vomit, not realizing he was leaving the mortal behind.

And then the panic was replaced by an overwhelming sense of freedom as Normal-Art realized that he was *alone*, and that he could now dart away on a side street and escape the god. He briefly considered his options, and seconds later, he decided that he would stay here in Dis and build a new life. Maybe he could find an apartment with a television. No matter what, he would never be bothered with any of God-Art's schemes again.

He grinned, dropped the glass of milk, and dashed to the left, intending to dart behind the cart selling human limbs. The platypus-demon shrieked at the dropped milk, but Art did not care. He twirled past the giant flea-demon and around a pair of praying mantises in yellow robes. He could practically taste his freedom, and if it were not for the aftertaste of vomit in the back of his mouth, it would have been the most delightful taste he had ever experienced.

But then something knocked him across the back of the head. His legs collapsed out from under him, and he fell in a heap onto the cobblestones. He would have described the cobblestones as *"mud-covered,"* but the fecal smells accosting his nostrils told him that the brown muck in which he landed was *not* mud. He sighed.

God-Art hefted Normal-Art over his shoulder. "Pay attention, you bloody fool," said the god. "You wander off like that and *you'll* be the next human to be cooked on those spits."

Now that Normal-Art had experienced a few brief seconds of potential freedom only to have it ripped away from him, despair overflowed his heart. He silently shed a tear as God-Art carried him the rest of the way to the center of Dis, where the god dropped him when they reached the outside of a gigantic domed basilica.

This domed basilica looked just like pictures that Normal-Art had seen of the Duomo in Florence, except it was completely different. This Duomo's façade was made of black marble, and every square inch seemed to be covered in an elaborate carving of a demon performing some sort of torture. Its doors were golden, and they featured twelve panels that each depicted a human performing a different type of sin. They all looked so lifelike that Normal-Art felt like a peeping tom as he stared at the panel for adultery.

But most oddly of all, the basilica was built upside-down, with the dome's crest touching the ground and the rest of the massive building rising high into the air, its gigantic foundation blocking out the view high above.

"It's called the Damned Duomo," said God-Art. "Took a hundred damned souls working constantly for a hundred years to build it. Its shape is just like the cathedral on the surface of this Earth's Florence, but it's all inverted. C'mon."

God-Art led Normal-Art and Drillbot around the side of a six-story tower that had also been built upside-down, and then he pointed them toward some scaffolding, which they used to climb up to the upside-down golden doors high in the air. God-Art pushed the doors open. Then he then grabbed Normal-Art by the scruff of the neck and tossed the mortal through the threshold.

Normal-Art's stomach leapt into his throat. He began to fall toward the dome, but then gravity reversed, and he found himself standing on the floor of the cathedral, which had been upside-down from the outside. His body reeled with disorientation. He sat down on the floor to gain his bearings.

The floor inside the Damned Duomo was covered in mosaics of Lucifer, who God-Art identified as the giant red angel with six wings and three lion-like faces—one black, one red, and one yellow. The mosaics depicted the story of Lucifer's fall from Heaven and his eventual dominance of Hell.

Pews lined the wide-open nave, and all along the walls lay alcoves filled with statues of demons carved from black marble. Instead of an altar, at the far end of the basilica stood a six-story tall, black marble statue of Lucifer crashing to the Earth like a meteorite. The craftsmanship was mesmerizing, and

Normal-Art could almost feel the moment of impact.

High above—or below, if your perspective was originating from outside the cathedral—the dome was covered in paintings that depicted deeds performed by many different demons. He saw one where a red cherub stood on a pope's shoulder, convincing him to sell indulgences to a roomful of plague-riddled children. He saw one where a serpent-shaped demon wrapped around the neck of a man and whispered into his ear as the man stabbed a knife into a woman's abdomen. He saw one where a demon the shape of a hippopotamus whispered into a woman's ear as she baked children into a pie. Normal-Art stopped looking from panel to panel because the paintings appeared so lifelike that he felt like he was *actually* witnessing the tales depicted in them, and they were too violent and ghastly even for his tastes.

God-Art directed Normal-Art's attention to a black gash that lay in the center of the dome, cutting through a painting that depicted a dozen demons playing trumpets that shot fire from their ends. A small stone platform stood to the left of the gash.

"That's our destination," said the god.

God-Art led Normal-Art and Drillbot onto a circular stone block directly underneath the gash in the center of the dome. The stone block had a radius of about five feet and was covered in a mosaic that depicted an image of the upside-down Damned Duomo.

"Look up," ordered God-Art. "Keep staring at the gash in the dome, and you'll be OK."

Normal-Art and Drillbot obeyed. God-Art stomped his right foot in a pattern just like the one he had used to knock on the signal tower outside the city's gate. The gravity, somehow inverted inside this cathedral, reverted to normal. God-Art, Normal-Art, and Drillbot fell upward toward the black gash in the center of the dome. Normal-Art screamed.

Just before the trio crashed through the gash, God-Art flipped them over and their feet—or wheels, in Drillbot's case—landed gently onto the stone that lay outside the black gash.

"OK, get moving," said God-Art, pointing down toward the gash in the dome. "Into the gash. Now."

Normal-Art sighed. Much like every other moment since he met this annoying god-version of himself, something astronomically odd had just happened, and he was not given the opportunity to take a moment to come to grips with it.

Instead, he inhaled deeply, steeled himself, and then leapt into the darkness of the gash. He felt stupid when he landed on a staircase just inside the darkness. Before he could stop himself, he tumbled down a few flights and crashed to a halt.

Above him, God-Art yelled, "I meant for you to *walk* into the opening, you idiot. There are stairs. Demons use this path to get to work. A blind leap would be dangerous. And unnecessary. Sometimes I forget what a fool you are."

Normal-Art did not respond, other than to sigh.

*

The staircase ended inside a gargantuan cave filled with row upon row of open tombs. The tombs stretched in all directions until they disappeared on the horizons. Each tomb was alight with pale blue flame, and a voice moaned from within each of the blue flames. The sounds filled this Circle with an odd chorus of destitution.

"Christmas down here must be extra depressing," muttered Normal-Art, imagining the moaning voices humming the most pathetic version of *Jingle Bells* ever.

"They aren't likely to celebrate much," replied God-Art. "You wouldn't, either, if a minor thing like heresy got *you* stuck down in a place like this."

Normal-Art sighed. He thought about responding with a comment about how he *had* been stuck down in a place like *this*, and for something much more minor: just wanting to be left alone to lie on his couch. But he thought better of it and remained silent. He had almost forgotten how tedious it was to say anything around God-Art. For being a god of mischief, he cared little for wordplay and his sense of humor was severely lacking.

A few souls sat up in their open tombs as the trio passed. Despite the blue flames dancing across their bodies, they attempted to strike up a conversation with Normal-Art. But he stalked sulkily along the path leading out of this Circle and ignored them, resigning himself to the reality of being stuck with yet another mirthless captor.

The trio reached the exit of the Sixth Circle of Hell, a small tunnel in the rock at the opposite end of the cave. A set of well-worn stairs had been carved into the tunnel's floor. Halfway down, a fist-sized opening in the tunnel wall allowed Normal-Art to preview the Seventh Circle, so that's just what he did.

A terrible odor attacked his nose. If three tons of sunbaked mayonnaise, rotten eggs, three-day old corpses, and bleu cheese had all been stranded on an island somewhere and had to eat each other to survive, their resulting excrement would represent but a tiny fraction of the stench that wafted up from the Seventh Circle. It overwhelmed Normal-Art, and he had to sit on the winding staircase. He gagged.

When he gathered himself enough to stand and look once more through the hole in the tunnel wall, he cursed when he comprehended the sheer size of the Seventh Circle. It stretched three-times longer than each of the Circles before it, and it consisted of three concentric rings that were separated from one another by tall, thin dikes made of dirt.

Normal-Art looked over at God-Art with a pleading look. He said, "Let's just go back the way we came and walk out the front door."

God-Art smirked. "Oh, brilliant idea. I wish *I* would have thought of that. But I *really, really* wanted to give you a tour of one of your reality's stupid, backward, idiotic hells," replied God-Art, sarcasm dripping from every syllable.

Normal-Art stared at God-Art. After a few moments of silence, God-Art sighed and continued, "The entrance to this damned place only works one way. It's all magicked up, and though I have overcome the enchantment before, it was not without great cost. I've found it's easier and faster to simply walk out the exit, way down in the Ninth Circle."

Normal-Art groaned in despair. "*Nine* circles? We're never going to make it."

God-Art grabbed Normal-Art by the neck. He growled, "I'm not a patron god of motivation—*that's the sister I flayed and fed via pot pie to my brothers several millennia ago*—but I do control certain str—"

"You control certain strains of pestilence, and if I refuse to get moving, you can give me the worst case of crabs in the history of the Multiverse," interrupted Normal-Art. "Yeah, you used that line on me before."

God-Art frowned. He muttered, "Well, take it to heart, then, and get moving."

He kicked Normal-Art on the backside, and Normal-Art staggered forward and down the stairs.

At the bottom of the stairs, the trio came to an arched stone bridge. The bridge spanned the outer concentric ring—the first of the three—and ended at the first thin dike of dirt. Below the bridge flowed a river of boiling blood occupied by moaning damned souls. At the entrance to the bridge, a minotaur about fifteen-feet tall lay napping on the ground, its mace under its head like a pillow. God-Art put a finger to his lips to signal his companions to stay quiet.

The god tiptoed past the beast—little *ping-ping-ping* sounds emanating from his toes like a cartoon character as he did so—and then he signaled for Normal-Art and Drillbot to do the same. Normal-Art tiptoed past, and Drillbot rolled as quietly as he could, which *still* resulted in a raucous roar erupting from his engines. But the minotaur did not stir.

And then, as soon as they were gathered on the other side of the minotaur, the god signaled for the group to spin around so that they faced the beast and their backs were to the direction they intended to travel. He mouthed, "Trust me. Done this kind of thing before."

The minotaur's nostrils twitched, and it awoke with a start. It leapt onto its feet and glanced around. "Me smell some souls who be in trouble," it called as it raised its mace high over its head.

It spun about until its eyes locked on the trio, and then it glared at them.

"Stay quiet, and let me handle this," whispered God-Art, who promptly fell to his knees and crawled pathetically over to the minotaur's feet.

"Please, sir, just let us past you," begged God-Art of the minotaur. "We don't deserve to be way down here in the Seventh Circle. We just want to go back up to the Third, maybe the Second where we promise we'll be good souls and won't do nothin' bad."

The minotaur growled. He slammed his mace into a rock near God-Art's head. He grabbed the god by the neck and lifted him up onto his feet. He studied the god, looking like a rather unintelligent toddler attempting to comprehend astrophysics. "Hmm," said the minotaur. "Hmmph. Me likes your respect, but me can't lets you pass."

The minotaur pointed toward the far end of the bridge to which the three companions' backs were now facing. He barked, "Get back to the punishments where you belong, before me thinks better of me leniency and decides you needs some extra torture."

"OK, I understand, sir. Thank you, sir," said God-Art with a bow of his head. He turned, grabbed Normal-Art by the crook of the arm, and led him over the bridge, deeper into the Seventh Circle. Drillbot followed on his leash.

About halfway over the bridge, when the moans of the damned souls in the boiling blood down below seemed sure to drown out their voices, Normal-

Art said, "I don't understand what that was all about."

God-Art chuckled. He replied, "Seemed appropriate to use mischief to get past that brute. He guards the bridge-entrance to this Circle to ensure the damned don't cross in either direction unless they're using it to travel to their proper punishments. I merely convinced him that we were coming from down below, trying to escape to a lighter sentence up above. He insisted that we not do that, and unknowingly told us to cross the bridge and go in the exact direction that we wanted to go. Not much to it, really."

"That's the first time I can recall where your mischief didn't result in somebody getting hurt," pointed out Normal-Art.

God-Art shrugged. "Didn't see a reason to harm the beast. I recognized the pattern of his fur. I most definitely seduced a minotaur with that pattern the last time I was down in this pit, a few centuries ago. He could be part of a litter I fathered. It's unlikely, but I thought it warranted clemency. Though now that I think on it, he seems a bit too stupid to be allowed to live. Maybe I ought to go back and put him out of his misery."

The god turned on his heel and strode back toward the entrance to the bridge. Normal-Art sat down. "Why'd I have to go and ask questions? Questions never end well with that guy," he muttered to himself.

Normal-Art glanced up at the Drillbot. He said, "Drillbot, I hope you haven't had to put up with him for long."

"[whir] No, not – CLACK – not long."

"That's good," said Normal-Art, not quite knowing what else to say. In the distance, the minotaur roared. And then it squealed. The god returned a few moments later, his robes spattered with blood. He held strips of meat in his hand. "Beef jerky?" he asked, holding a particularly gruesome piece out to Normal-Art.

Normal-Art gagged. The god laughed. He pulled Normal-Art to his feet and the trio continued their journey, reaching the end of the bridge and descending into the next of this Circle's concentric rings.

Normal-Art soon found himself hiking through in the creepiest forest he had ever laid eyes upon. Trees grew in spaces exactly five feet apart and stretched unto the horizon. They reminded Normal-Art of an almond tree farm he had seen as a boy on vacation to his grandparents' house.

Some of the trees were barren like it was Winter, others were full of foliage and sprouting blossoms like it was Spring. Large gray droppings covered every inch of ground at the base of each tree, and as the stench of the droppings reached Normal-Art's nose, he realized that these droppings were the source of the stench he had smelled when peeking into the Seventh Circle from back on the staircase. He stifled another gag.

High above, Normal-Art heard the chattering calls of thousands of birds. He shuddered, recognizing them as harpy calls and realizing exactly which foul beasts were responsible for this Circle's stench. Randolph, one of Normal-Art's poker-playing pals, had been a harpy. Randolph had always smelled awful—even underneath the water—and had manners that reminded him of Joe Pesci's character from *Goodfellas*, meaning he was always telling stories and jokes, but he was also quick to follow them up with psychotic bouts of gratuitous violence. If thousands more foul creatures like Randolph occupied this place, then this would be a place that Normal-Art and his companions would want to escape as quickly as possible.

The trio marched along the winding path that cut through the forest. After nearly an hour's worth of trudging, Normal-Art's stomach growled. He said, "Hmmph. Guess now that I'm officially resurrected, I need to eat."

God-Art shrugged. "Guess so," he replied. "Now grab one of *those* so we can be off."

The god pointed just off the path to a grove of apple trees. Thick, golden fruit hung from the boughs of the trees, and Normal-Art licked his lips. Fruits and vegetables had always been the *last* thing he would eat when given the choice, but his stomach was thrashing so hard with hunger that he sprinted off the path and grabbed an apple, anyway. His hunger was so all-encompassing just now that it overrode his disgust at this place's odor and his desire to leave this place as quickly as possible to avoid the harpies.

It was the most delicious apple he had ever tasted, sweet and Earthy with just the tiniest, most subtle hint of musk. Golden juice covered the lower half of his face. It was not until he had eaten his way through three of the juicy fruits that he realized the tree screamed every time he yanked one of the apples from a branch. He studied the tree more closely and realized the tree was bleeding where he had removed the fruit.

Normal-Art turned to glance at God-Art, who was bent over in laughter.

"*Why* are you laughing?" demanded Normal-Art.

The tree screamed again. Normal-Art looked over at it and squinted. Now that he took the time to study it, the tree looked oddly humanoid, and some knots near the center of its trunk resembled a crying face. This face looked like one he could have sworn he recognized from the television he had watched so rabidly before being whisked away on this doomed adventure twenty years ago.

"What did you have me do?" squealed Normal-Art.

Between guffaws, God-Art said, "These trees used to be people who committed suicide. Guess what part of them the fruits are?"

Normal-Art frowned and slammed the apple cores onto the ground. The tree squealed once more in pain and its limbs hung low. The tree began speaking, and Normal-Art leapt backward, startled.

The tree said, "That really hurt, you know. And it really wasn't very friendly. Back in life, I used to tell people that they *never had a friend like me*. But depression sure is an all-encompassing bitch, ain't it? Now get me outta here, will ya? I don't deserve this."

Then the tree began shaking with sobs. The harpies high in its limbs squawked in annoyance, fluttered into the air, and rained the ground with their foul waste. As the harpy excrement fell upon Normal-Art, he growled in frustration and ran over to God-Art. He slapped the god across the side of the head, which only ended up burning his hand. The god laughed harder.

Normal-Art stomped away, following the path that cut through the forest and leaving his companions behind. Drillbot followed him until the length of his leash ran out, and then he pulled against it so hard that he dragged God-Art behind him. The god remained bent over in laughter for another few minutes. Eventually, he stood upright and scrambled to catch up with Normal-Art.

The path eventually led them to a clearing. Here, row upon row of empty spaces in the dirt were marked as spots to plant future suicide-trees. The path wound through this clearing and then up the rocky dike that marked the end of this concentric ring.

Halfway up the rocky dike, ferocious squawking erupted in the air behind the group. Normal-Art glanced over his shoulder to see a gaggle of harpies clutching a man. They carried him by his feet, and a noose dangled loose around his neck. He screamed and pleaded, but the harpies ignored him. They carried him to one of the small dirt patches that had been prepped for a tree.

Two of the gaggle broke off and dove to the ground. They scooped away dirt with the ends of their wings. When enough soil had been cleared away, the other harpies shoved the man feet-first into the hole and buried him up to his neck. The harpies then all took a moment to fertilize the dirt. Then they fluttered away in different directions, only to return seconds later, each brandishing an overlarge watering can. The creatures reminded Normal-Art of his grandma, a woman who had a birdlike, disapproving face, and who constantly watered the plants in her garden with her watering can.

As soon as the harpies applied the water to the soil, the man's skin stiffened and he froze. He turned a soft shade of brown.

"It's not polite to gawk!" called God-Art to Normal-Art. He had already finished following the path to the top of the dike and had pulled Drillbot along with him. "Come on! That man's fate is none of your business."

Normal-Art began jogging to catch up, but then he thought better of it when he ran out of breath. He had forgotten that he had been resurrected, and with resurrection came his natural lung capacity, which had always been much, much lower than the average person. He cursed and began a slow trudge to the top of the dike.

*

The trio hurried through the innermost ring of the Seventh Circle. God-Art pulled an umbrella from his leather pouch to block the fire that rained from the ceiling in this ring. The fire thumped against the umbrella and crashed to the hot dirt with a hiss.

The trio ignored the crying sinners who were trying to get their attention to have a conversation. They darted as quickly as they could into the tunnel entrance that lay in the center of this ring, and then they marched down the winding staircase that marked the exit to this Circle of Hell.

When they reached the end of this staircase and entered the Eighth Circle, Normal-Art stared in shock. This Circle consisted of a cave larger than all the previous Circles combined. Normal-Art sighed. The size of this Circle made the previous Circle look like a dollhouse next to the Empire State Building. Normal-Art sighed again.

Another bridge marked the entrance to this Circle. But where the one at the beginning of the Seventh Circle was sturdy, this one was a rickety stone affair that led from the staircase's exit down to an enormous flat-topped stalagmite, the center of which was hollow and stretched a good two miles in radius. Around and around the sides of the stalagmite wound a staircase, leading down thousands of feet to a valley frozen over with thick layers of ice.

The trio moved out onto the rickety bridge. Normal-Art looked over the edge of the bridge, down at the ice far below, and then he jerked his head back in fear. He frowned. God-Art walked up behind him and shoved him, forcing him forward along the bridge. He squealed in surprise and terror.

"Move," commanded the god.

When Normal-Art felt the god's hand return to his back, ready to shove once more, he squealed again and then trudged forward toward the gigantic stalagmite. Cold wind whipped across Normal-Art's face. His teeth chattered, and his knees knocked together, but he kept moving for fear that if he received another shove in his back, his knees would be too weak to stop him from tumbling over the edge of the bridge. And even though he would undoubtedly be resurrected by God-Art, such a fall would also hurt more than anything he cared to experience just now.

When the trio completed their crossing of the bridge, they reached a path that wound almost completely around the edge of the stalagmite's top. Just before the path made a complete loop to reconnect with the spot where it began at the end of the bridge, the path jutted outward and then dipped down below the bridge, connecting with the stairs that led around the stalagmite to the ground far below. Normal-Art turned toward the section of the path that jutted out, assuming the group would leap over to it and follow it down to the ground far below. God-Art reached out a hand and gripped Normal-Art's shoulder.

"Can't go that way," said the god. "It's all magicked up. We have to go the long way around the stalagmite."

Normal-Art sighed. "Of course, we have to go the long way," he replied. "Why would anything ever be easy?"

God-Art turned Normal-Art toward the path that led around the edge of the stalagmite. Normal-Art glanced over toward the hollowed-out center. He noticed that the hollow center of the rock had been divided by stone walls into ten sections. Within each section, a different sin was being punished.

"Welcome to the Eighth Circle of Hell, the Malebolge," said God-Art. "The most unfair section in all of Hell. The people here would have been saints in my reality—at least, after I conquered my pantheon—but here, they are punished for Fraud."

The god pointed from pit to pit and described each as they walked along the path that lined the edge of the stalagmite, "Each section is called a Bolgia.

In the first one, you've got the Pimps and Seducers, whipped for all eternity. Hi Dave!" called God-Art, waving to a particularly impish demon snapping a whip at frightened souls. The demon looked up, waved back cheerily, and promptly returned to work.

"And there you've got the Flatterers. Hold your nose when we pass this Bolgia. These guys float and marinate for eternity in human shit," said God-Art.

As they passed the second Bolgia, Normal-Art stared at sullen faces and limbs and clumps of rotten yellow corn poking at random intervals out of a bubbling brown pond. He remembered the rumors he had heard of this punishment, and the reality of it was worse than he had dreamt it could possibly be. He thanked his lucky stars again that he had been relegated to the Fifth Circle to be punished for Sloth. Flatterers seemed to have gotten the worst punishment in all of Hell.

As the trio continued hiking, Normal-Art stared at his own feet rather than the tortured souls as God-Art described the scenery, "And there you've got Simony, where people's feet are lit aflame and they're shoved headfirst into the rock atop one another. Over there you've got the Diviners, whose heads are twisted backwards. The next you'll notice is full of tar, as well as people who accepted bribes. There you'll see the Hypocrites, forced to wander around carrying heavy weights. Up seventh are the Thieves, constantly attacked by serpents. After them comes the eighth Bolgia, where False Counselors reside in eternal balls of flame. If you look closely, you might see the one containing a guy named Odysseus. Heard he's supposed to be the cleverest human to have ever lived on your Earth. On mine, he was naught but a foolish infant who died from some disease that he could have prevented if only he would have thought to invent a vaccine."

Normal-Art smirked and called out to a random ball of flame, deciding that because he could not tell the flames apart, anyway, Odysseus may as well reside in that one, "You thought *your* journey was bad? Try spending a few days in my shoes."

God-Art grabbed Normal-Art by the crook of the arm and led him on. The god continued his description, "Our penultimate Bolgia belongs to the Sowers of Discord, who are hacked to bits for eternity by my old friend Punteeblico and his magical sword. Hi Punteeblico! Finally, we've got the tenth Bolgia, reserved for the Falsifiers, who constantly bite each other and drink each other's blood."

The trio had made the circuit around the top of the stalagmite and had arrived at the section of the path that jutted outward. They followed it as it led under the rickety stone bridge to the top of the stairs that wound down around the exterior of the hollowed-out stalagmite. The trio followed the stairs round and round, each rotation taking them farther down the stalagmite and closer to the frozen valley surrounding its base. Each step grew colder, and Normal-Art began shivering so hard that he was scared to speak, afraid he might bite off his tongue. He held his hands over Drillbot's fiery leash, but he found that it gave off little warmth. He was half-tempted to leap onto the fire and burn himself up again, just to feel heat for a moment.

Finally, after hours of descending, the trio reached the bottom of the stairs and stepped onto the frozen ground. Normal-Art immediately slipped and flopped onto his back. He cursed. God-Art lifted him up onto his feet. "Be careful, you fool," chastised the god.

They followed the path as it led them across the rocky ice. Eventually, they rounded a bend and came to a sight that would have been the oddest thing Normal-Art had seen all day if he had not experienced everything else he had experienced today.

A gigantic well rose from the ground, inside which stood a ring of six frozen and shirtless blue giants, each with a bushy beard and shaggy chest hair. The giants were only visible from the waist up—because their legs were down inside the well—but their torsos were at least sixty-feet tall each. They all faced outward, a ring of sentinels apparently guarding whatever lay within the well. Frigid fog also rose from the well, drifting into the air and then falling to the tundra floor, where it settled across the valley in new coats of ice.

"Nimrod! How you doin'?" called out God-Art.

The nearest of the giants bellowed something that sounded like gibberish and shook his fists in the air. As the giant moved, thunderous cracks echoed across the cavern as the ice that crusted his skin broke off and fell into the well.

"Knock off the act, Nimrod!" yelled God-Art. "It's me, Artheoskatergariabetrugereiinganno!"

The giant stopped screaming gibberish. He reached a hand into the well below him and retrieved a pair of half-moon spectacles, which he placed on the bridge of his nose. With the eyeglasses on, recognition fluttered across his face. He said, "Oh! Artheoskatergariabetrugereiinganno! Sorry for doing my schtick at you. I did not recognize you. I've started needing these cursed cheaters now to see, but I try not to wear 'em when I'm on duty, 'cuz they kinda ruin the intimidation factor. Anyway, enough about me. It's been ages. How are ya?"

The giant's voice boomed, and its force knocked over Normal-Art. He slid across the ice and crashed to a stop against a rock.

"I'm fantastic. How's your ma?" replied God-Art.

The giant frowned. "Oh, you know her. Fragile as ever, but she'll find a way to outlast us all. I love 'er, but she's always on about how I needa be wearin' mittens down here in the cold. Worried I'm gonna catch a chill. I tells her it don't bother me none, but she don't listen."

"Well, tell her I say *hello*. Hey, think you can help me and my companions? We're looking to get down to the Ninth Circle."

Nimrod smiled. "Sure. Happy to help. Just remember this the next time you're hatching one of your schemes down here."

The giant reached out a hand and set it on the ground, palm up. God-Art walked onto the palm. He pulled on Drillbot's leash, leading Drillbot up onto the hand. Normal-Art scrambled onto his feet and followed. He noted with inane clarity that the giant's wealth line stood out clearly on his palm. Normal-Art considered pointing this out to the giant, but then he decided against it when he realized that doing so might require a slight amount of effort.

The giant lifted his hand, and the sudden shift in height sent a wave of nausea racing through Normal-Art's gut. The giant carried the trio into the well, and then he bent down to shuttle them to the bottom far, far below. Gigantic blocks of gray stone formed the interior of the well. Where algae would have coated the inside walls of the well in a warmer climate, hoarfrost crusted the stone in a thick layer that twinkled in the dim light.

Soon, the giant's hand hovered a few feet off the frozen water at the bottom of the well. God-Art jumped from the appendage and landed nimbly on the ice. Drillbot did the same. Normal-Art jumped, too, but he flopped onto the ground once more as his feet slipped out from under him. He cursed. He hated ice.

Thousands of lumpy round rocks jutted up from the ice. Normal-Art used one of them to gain his balance as he stood.

"Okay, I gotta get back to work. See ya, Artheoskatergariabetrugereiinganno," said the giant, and then he returned to standing upright without waiting for a reply.

Normal-Art could hear little over the chattering of his own teeth. He glanced about and noted how hairy the six pairs of giants' feet were that surrounded him, lining the outside of the well. And then he noted how similarly they smelled to rotted cheese that had been placed in a freezer.

God-Art began leading the trio toward a small arched passageway at the back of the gigantic stone well. But the sound of a familiar female voice stopped Normal-Art in his tracks. It called his name.

That's when he realized all the lumpy frozen rocks that covered the surface of the ice were not rocks at all, but were in fact frozen *people*, cold and blue and hard. Some were frozen so that only their chests and heads poked up from the frozen water, some so that only their heads were visible, and some were completely submerged, which Normal-Art only noticed as he stared down at the ice.

The familiar voice called his name again. He spun around, looking for the source.

"Yes?" he called back.

God-Art tugged on his arm, pulling him toward the exit. *There!* His name again. "Wait," he ordered the god.

The female voice yelled his name a few more times. He scrambled across the ice toward the sound. He slipped over and over, and finally resolved to scrabbling along the ice on his hands and knees.

Finally, he found the source. It lay near the crusty pinky toe of one of the giants. It was a woman with naught but her head poking up above the ice. Her skin was pallid and frozen, but he would recognize that face anywhere.

It was Ginny.

CHAPTER 19

VISITING PLACES FROM THE PAST

LIGHTNING FLASHED, AND Agent 27142 landed on a parking lot on Earth 920,527. He closed his eyes and inhaled as deeply as he could, taking in the smell of the wet cement, the first scent he had smelled in years. His eyes watered at the intensity of the petrichor.

He bent over in a fit of coughing. He opened his eyes. Black smog hovered in the sky, blotting out much of the sunlight. Gigantic, squat buildings made from plastered-together gray stones stretched as far as the eye could see, each with three large smokestacks poking out of its top from which additional smog billowed to join the layer of murky blackness that hung in the air. The grinding sounds of factory machines filled the air, every now and then punctuated by the soft beeping noise of a forklift backing up.

In between coughs, Agent 27142 sighed. It had been so long since he stepped foot on this reality that nostalgia had all but shrouded over its less-than-beautiful qualities in his memory.

The gourd sniffed the air, and then it began coughing, too. "There is something terribly wrong with this place," it commented, its voice monotone and glum. "I can tell by the smell. Just my luck that I'd be forced to jump here."

A smirk formed on Agent 27142's lips. He replied, "There's nothing wrong with this place. What you're smelling is the sweet, sweet smog of productivity, and there's nothing better than that!"

"You'll have to forgive me if I don't share your enthusiasm for polluted air," said the gourd.

Agent 27142 scowled. Then he said, "But the pollution isn't the reason to be excited about this place. The pollution is merely a side effect of its greatness. You see, this Earth has an illustrious history of shipwrighting, and I am proud to have been a part of it. Centuries ago, the B.I.T. converted the entire reality into a factory. It's where we build all our ships and equipment for the Outer Quadrant Navy. One of my first command positions was to oversee production in our shift-shuttle factory here and make it run 15% more efficiently."

"How'd you do?"

Agent 27142's scowl grew more intense. He replied, "Well, I wouldn't be standing here as a captain of my own B.S.S.C.-class ship and as an admiral of my own fleet if I hadn't performed admirably, now would I?"

The gourd wilted a little. "I-I guess not."

"That was a rhetorical question, you fool. I brought 25% more efficiency to the factory. The B.I.T. gave me a commendation for it. See?"

Agent 27142 rolled up his sleeve and pointed to a tattoo on his forearm. It depicted a golden badge with a picture of a gray factory inside it. Dozens of other badge-tattoos lined his skin, marking his long and excellent service to the B.I.T.

The gourd sighed. Then it said, "I'm sorry, sir. I don't have eyes to see, and I don't really understand rhetoric. I'm just a gourd."

Agent 27142 grunted in annoyance and abruptly ended the conversation. He trudged nearly a mile with the gourd in hand and then entered one of the many identical squat buildings with three large smokestacks. If the gourd had been able to see, it likely would have asked how the agent knew exactly which building to enter, for there seemed nothing distinguishable about this one, and there were no obvious markings on its outside.

Inside, a gruff foreman stood watch over dozens of sweaty agents who were pressing buttons and operating an assembly line. Pieces of steel rolled down a factory line. Sparks flew as welding machines bound pieces of steel together.

Toward the far end of the factory, a portion of hull for one of the carrier-class B.S.S.C. ships was being assembled from thousands of the smaller pieces of steel that were concurrently rolling down the factory line. Dozens of other B.I.T. factory workers hung from harnesses attached to thin black cords that dangled from the ceiling. They darted to-and-fro like bumblebees pollinating flowers as they used the harnesses to make huge leaps to spots on the hull that needed attention. Wherever they landed, they placed palm-sized robots and controlled the robots via remote controls that were attached to their harnesses. The robots welded the spots in place, and when a spot was complete, the factory workers then picked up the robots and leapt to new destinations, where they repeated the process.

As Agent 27142 entered the factory floor, the foreman turned toward him. The foreman was a young man with a bushy mustache. He furrowed his large brow in annoyance at being disturbed. But as his eyes scanned Agent 27142's tattered uniform and recognized Agent 27142's rank, he sprinted over to his superior, groveling, "Hello, sir. I'm Agent 8888990. I run this factory, sir."

"I can see that," said Agent 27142. "I'm Agent 27142. I used to do the same, back when it used to produce shift-shuttles."

The foreman understood the implication and grinned. He asked, "Oh, yeah? How long did they keep you here before moving you to military command?"

Then the foreman noticed Agent 27142's mutilated shoulder and the eagle embedded in it, and concern filled his eyes. He said, "A-Are you OK, sir? Is that your *eagle*? I can get a medic down here right away."

Agent 27142 pursed his lips. "Agent 8888990, I'm in a hurry, and I have time for neither a chat nor a medic. It's an emergency, and the Multiverse is at stake. I need to access Storeroom 9."

The foreman shrugged. He replied, "Go right ahead. You outrank me, so I couldn't stop you even if I wanted to."

Agent 27142 nodded and strode away from the foreman.

"Bye," called out the gourd to the foreman. Then the gourd said to Agent 27142, "In case you are unaware, it is proper manners to say *'goodbye'* when you exit a conversation."

Agent 27142 ignored the gourd. He walked around the outskirts of the factory floor. He passed eight large doors that lay on rollers, each with a large red numeral painted on it. When he reached the one marked with the numeral *9*, he pressed his palm against a pad embedded in the wall to the right of the door. A scanner passed over his hand and then glowed green. The door to the storeroom rolled up, and Agent 27142 walked inside. He pressed another button to shut the door behind him.

Row upon row of shelving filled the room. The shelves were tall enough to nearly touch the ceiling, twelve-stories high. Tools lined the shelves, ranging from screwdrivers to drills to welders to forklifts. Agent 27142 walked forward, counting out the ceiling tiles above him. When he reached the fifty-fourth tile, he turned to his right and began climbing the shelving unit that stood there.

About ten minutes later, he reached the top, where he found himself crouching next to some dusty hammers.

He raised his hand and popped off the ceiling tile. The space behind the tile opened onto a gigantic room, inside which lay computers and assorted equipment and a cot and a shift-shuttle identical to the one in which Agent 29333 had escaped the B.T.T. home reality with Prisoner-Art, except this ship was painted red rather than black. Agent 27142 climbed into the room and put the ceiling tile back in place behind him.

"Where are we?" squealed the gourd, panic replacing the monotony in its voice. "We left Earth 920,527. I can sense it."

"Oh, calm down," replied Agent 27142. "We've merely entered a pocket reality that I set up as a saferoom back when I ran this factory."

Agent 27142 sat down in front of a nearby computer terminal. He dropped the gourd onto the ground and pressed the button to power on the terminal. Nothing happened. He pressed it again. Again, nothing.

"Hey, gourd, I need you to shock this terminal," ordered Agent 27142.

The gourd sighed. It replied, "I have a name, you know. It's Henry."

Agent 27142 sighed right back at the vegetable and said, "OK, Henry. Shock the terminal. Now! Or I will be eating squash soup for dinner tonight."

"Fine, fine," answered Henry the Jump Gourd. "Just show me where it is. No need for the threats."

Agent 27142 tapped Henry against the computer terminal to indicate its location to the gourd. Lightning blasted from the gourd's antennae and crashed into the lightning rod standing erect from the computer terminal. The screen flashed to life. Agent 27142 tapped his fingers impatiently on the metal desk as he waited for the computer to boot up.

"You're welcome, by the way," muttered Henry. "Showing a little gratitude wouldn't kill you, y'know. First, you commandeered me away from my rightful owner, who was *far nicer* than you, to jump you to this smog-filled, disgusting Earth. But did I complain? Nope! Not me. Then you forced me to perform menial lightning blasts that are *far* below my pay grade—well, if I ever got paid, that is. And a little thanks is all I ask. I don't give a seed who or what I'm hauling from Earth to Earth, I just want a little acknowledgement sometimes. Just a *little* would go a long way."

The vegetable continued rambling, but Agent 27142 ignored the speech. As soon as the prompt popped up, he logged in with his username and password. He first opened his electronic mail and found over two million unopened messages. He ignored most of them. He filtered the inbox to only show messages from Agent 29333, but there were none dated after the time at which they had split up on the B.T.T. home world. Dread filled the pit of his stomach. He cleared the search filter and scrolled through the unopened messages until he came to one from this morning that was marked urgent. He opened it and read a blanket warning message to all B.I.T. agents.

The message stated that the quarantine protocols remained in effect for Earth 55,777, and thus all B.I.T. fleets should avoid jumping to the Earth. The Earth was still frozen in time and all agents who had subsequently jumped there since its reality-wide stasis event had also become stuck in time. The agency had not yet found a solution, but agents were encouraged to send any unconquerable Multiverse-level threats to the reality straightaway, for these threats would also become frozen in time and could be left there until a solution was uncovered.

OK, good news so far, he thought. *The Stasis Bomb appears to have performed as intended. This means that the Multiverse is as good as saved. It also means that there's still hope for the woman I love. I knew before sending her that there was high risk for Agent 29333 to get stuck on Earth 55,777 when the Stasis Bomb detonated. If she's stuck there, then she's still alive, just frozen in time. But I must know for sure whether she is there.*

He opened an application on the terminal labeled *Ship Tracker*, and an interface popped up. Agent 27142 typed the identification code of his personal shift-shuttle into the proper text box. After a few moments, an error message appeared on the screen.

Agent 27142 cursed and tried again. This time, a reality number popped up. It said 6. Then it changed to 709,865. Then it changed to 50,989. Then it changed again and again and again, faster than Agent 27142's eyes could comprehend. Then it changed to an error message.

Agent 27142 sighed. If the tracker were to be believed, the ship was jumping from reality to reality at a frightening speed. Agent 27142 picked up the gourd and walked over to a far corner of this pocket reality. He walked past the shift-shuttle and entered a cylindrical plexiglass tube barely large enough in diameter to fit him inside. A metal pole hung from the top and a small touchscreen lay in the middle. He tapped the screen with his forefinger, and it sprang to life. A prompt asked him which ship he wished to board. He typed in the identification number of his personal shift-shuttle, along with his override code.

He ordered, "Henry, shoot the pole above us with lightning."

Henry sighed. Then he asked, "Don't you ever just want to have a conversation?"

When Agent 27142 did not respond other than to tap the gourd against the pole, Henry shot the lightning as ordered. The cylinder blasted into the barrier between realities. Being back here made Agent 27142 shudder. Then a targeting program on the touchscreen beeped and glowed yellow.

"Again!" screamed Agent 27142 to Henry, who promptly obeyed. The cylinder blasted once more, this time out of *The Barrier*, and appeared in the boarding station within Agent 27142's shift-shuttle. Henry in hand, Agent 27142 exited his *Mobile Boarding & Tracking Cylinder* and walked toward the ladder that would take him up to the bridge.

The howling of reality after reality passing by a hole that had somehow been ripped open in the side of the ship assaulted Agent 27142's ears, but he ignored it and pressed on to the bridge. The corpses of Squadron Twelve that had been shredded and spattered across the hold assaulted his eyes, but he ignored them and pressed on to the bridge. The horrid stench that wafted down through the shredded hatch from the bridge above assaulted his nostrils, but he ignored it and pressed on to the bridge. Dread filled every inch of his body. He climbed the ladder.

Agent 27142 entered the bridge and moaned in horror. Dried blood lay splattered everywhere. A pair of corpses and a dead eagle lay sprawled across the bridge. He walked to Prisoner-Art's corpse and scowled at it. The oaf had suffered merely a single hole through the torso. Meanwhile, lying on the ground in front of the control panel, Agent 29333's body lay mutilated and shredded and filled with hole after hole after hole.

Tears rolled down Agent 27142's cheeks. It was one of the few times he could ever remember crying. He considered telling Agent 29333's corpse how he felt about her, but instead, he clinched his jaw in vengeful rage. *Something* had murdered everyone here, and Agent 27142 knew exactly who the guilty party was, for all the evidence pointed to one specific metal beast: the robot with drills for arms that belonged to the cosmic blue bear.

Agent 27142 stood, drew his Scatter Gun pistol, and searched the ship. No evidence indicated that the robot was still here. As he passed the hole in the ship below decks, he nodded in understanding of where the robot must have gone. He walked back to the bridge. He stared at the control panel. Its keys were melted together, and all the knobs and dials were deformed and blackened. Without any hope that it would work, he attempted to enter a few commands into the terminal using the control panel's melted keys. But they did not work, and the terminal did not respond.

He returned to his *Mobile Boarding & Tracking Cylinder* in the ship's boarding station. He removed the CPU from it and brought it with him back to the bridge. He pulled a wire from the CPU's back and plugged it into a port in the terminal. He typed a command into the touchscreen keyboard on the CPU.

The shift-shuttle's view screen lit up with information. He watched a grainy video filmed from the camera on the wing of the ship that showed the robot hanging from the hull and then dropping away. Agent 27142 typed a query into the computer. It flashed an Earth number.

Agent 27142 used the CPU to enter his personal override code, canceling all current commands to the ship. The ship stopped hopping wantonly from reality to reality and hovered in place in *The Barrier*. Agent 27142 typed a new number into the destination prompt. He squeezed Henry and said, "Henry, I need you to blast lightning into the pole on the bridge terminal."

"Why must you keep reminding me that I can't see anything? Does it make you feel better?" whined the gourd.

Agent 27142 smacked the gourd against the blackened pole. "There. Now you know where it is. Fire away."

The gourd sighed and did as commanded.

CHAPTER 20

THAW AND ORDER

REGULAR-GINNY'S BODY WAS dead weight below her. Her head stuck out from the frozen lake, which she had heard the demons refer to as Lake Cocytus approximately ten years ago when they had dragged her down here. They had stuffed her body into the frigid water of the lake once they had chiseled away a small portion of the ice, and she had remained here ever since.

Only her neck and head remained above the ice, and they were constantly pelted by frigid wind and billowing snow that blew across the surface of the lake. She had expected her body to eventually go numb from the cold, as her knees did when she iced them after a basketball game back when she was a teen. But her body never did go numb, and the horridly cold water made her feel like little frozen needles were constantly making pinpricks on every square inch of her submerged skin.

But the cold was not even the worst part. The worst part was that the demons had implanted her in the ice mere feet from one of the giants' toes. Never had she so strongly wished to have her pink powers returned to her than when the demons laughed about it before flying away. Hair from the nearby giant's foot whipped across her face when the winds shifted direction, and the smell from the never-washed appendage seemed to burn itself deeper into her nostrils with each passing second.

The giant had some sort of foot fungus and would often use its far foot to scratch the toes of the foot nearest Ginny. Each time this scratching occurred, flakes of fungus-covered dead skin would fly into the air, and chunks of it would rain down on her face. The first couple times this happened, the skin flakes dropped into her open mouth, and she quickly learned not to stare with her mouth agape. After finishing with the scratch, the giant's far foot would slam back down in place atop the ice, often breaking it and splashing below the surface. This would cause ripples in the water beneath the ice, and the water's shaking would cause it to feel colder than ever. During these times, the poor wretches trapped completely underwater would grab hold of her to hold themselves in place to prevent themselves from being tossed about too violently.

As she did nearly a thousand times a day since she got here, she cursed. She hated this terrible, unfair fate to which she had been subjected. The more she thought about it, the more she raged.

Back when she had died and found her soul standing before the arched gateway into Hell, she had shrugged. She had never been particularly religious, nor had she been particularly perfect, so it had not really been a surprise to her that if an afterlife *were* to exist, she would be assigned to a less-than-heavenly fate. She had entered Hell assuming that she would receive a light sentence, since she had at least been a well-intentioned person. Thus, she passed through the arched gateway with her head held high.

She had passed a lake teeming with translucent shrimp and had been dumbfounded when she reached the area where people were chasing after a bumblebee-demon who carried a black banner. It was such an odd scene that she had stopped to watch for a while. She remained there long enough to witness the damned people chase the bumblebee-demon for three laps before a different demon with six wings finally flew over to her and told her to keep walking, that she needed to go to the Second Circle to be judged by Minos. She would recognize him by his serpent tail.

She had moved on without argument. She avoided the ridiculously long line to cross the Acheron on Chiron's boat, for she hated lines more than nearly anything else, and she hopped into the gondola of a demon who looked like a steroid-infused bunny. On the other side of the Acheron, she paused in Limbo, the First Circle of Hell—to which she believed she *should* have been assigned if Hell were fair—and discussed various viewpoints with the philosophers that resided there.

When she moved on to the Second Circle and arrived at the front of the line for Minos's judgment, she was met with a huge shock: he wrapped his tail around himself nine times.

"Wait, what?" she had screamed. "What does that mean?"

"It means that you have been judged guilty of Betrayal," replied Minos.

"What? That's dumb. Who did I betray?"

"You betrayed the Multiverse," responded Minos. "I stared into your soul. You chose *destruction*."

"But I only chose *destruction* to save this reality! I had no other choice! You and everything in this reality would have been wiped from existence if I hadn't agreed to join that stupid pink bear!"

"Oh, you did us no favors with that choice. Let's see if you still want to *exist* after you've spent some time in the bottom Circle. I bet you'll wish for nonexistence before you've been down there a month."

"But I saved everyone in this reality, you ungrateful prick!" she screamed, her voice breaking into sobs. "How is this fair?"

"But how many realities died in our place?" asked Minos, his tail tightening in frustration. "You betrayed them to save your own. Guards, take her away."

Seven six-winged demons appeared, each holding a pitchfork. They stripped her, stabbed theire pitchforks into her, lifted her into the air, and ferried her down, down, down, far underground—to the Ninth Circle.

*

Years and years passed. Though she had been unable to read the foreign inscription on the arched stone gateway at the beginning of the journey down into Hell, she had inadvertently taken its advice: she had abandoned all hope.

But then one day, she heard a familiar voice carry to her on the wind, and her acclimation to a hopeless eternity was flipped on its head. She heard Art!

"Art!" she screamed. She received no reply. Her heart raced. Desperation filled her.

"Art!" she screamed again. The wind blazed ferociously, carrying her scream away into the ether. "Over here!"

Since her banishment to this horrid place, she had been stuck facing the giant's wretched toe. But she had heard Art's voice *behind* her, and there was no mistaking it. It was loud, but it was beginning to grow fainter. He must be leaving.

No! she thought. She lifted her hands. The movement sent cold shivers through her body. It was the first time she had moved them in years, as she had found it slightly more comfortable to simply let her body dangle limply below her in the water. But this was her only chance, so pain be damned.

She slammed her palms against the ice and pushed, attempting to twist herself around to face the opposite direction. Her skin was frozen to the ice around her neck. She did not budge. She pushed harder than she had ever pushed anything before. The skin tore away from her pale neck and she managed about a quarter-turn before the cold froze her back in place. Her arms ached from the effort and her breath came in fits, but it was enough. She could see him. She could see Art. He was with that robot that she had fought so many times over the years—who was for some inexplicable reason wrapped in ropes made from flames—and he was with that cursed god-version of himself. But he was *here*.

Hope soared through her heart. "Art!" she screamed again, over and over between desperate breaths.

He spun around. She nearly squealed in delight. But she could see he looked confused and could not place from where the sound was coming. The fiery-haired version of him tugged on his arm and pointed toward an arched passageway in the side of the wall near them.

"Art!" Ginny screamed again, over and over and over. Art wrenched away from the god and ran toward her. He slipped and fell. He stood back up, using some poor guy's head for balance. He sprinted toward her, but he fell again. He used another poor guy's head for balance. He repeated this process probably half a dozen more times. Finally, he gave up on standing and crawled on his hands and knees toward her voice. She continued screaming his name all the while. This felt like simultaneously the most tedious and the most desperate game of Marco Polo ever.

Then he saw her. Recognition filled his eyes. He smiled. "Hi, Ginny," he said.

"Hiya, Arthur," she said, smiling back.

"I hate it when you call me that. What are you doing all the way down here?"

Her smile faded. Art's companions caught up to him as she was catching him up on her story. The god asked her to start over, so he could hear, too. She sighed and did so. When she got to the part about the B.I.T. home world freezing in time, God-Art laughed with delight. He glanced over at her Art.

"Well, I know where the bears are now," said the god to her Art, "and they're apparently frozen in time and thus stuck in place. Looks like I don't need *you* anymore. Would you like to stay here with your mate in this Circle of Hell, or would you like to return to the Fifth?"

"Oh, shut up and stop trying to scare us," said her Art. "You know that I know those bears won't go anywhere with you if I'm not there—even if they're frozen in time, they'll find a way to thwart and abandon you. So, it's obvious you're bluffing, and you're going to take me with you no matter what. You're just trying to get me to beg you to take me with you, because it amuses you somehow and you think somebody showing fear gives you power over them. But you seem to have forgotten that I *loved* my life down here in Hell, so if you want to send me back to the Fifth Circle, be my guest."

God-Art frowned, his fun apparently spoiled. Before he could speak, Ginny pleaded, "If you're looking for somebody to beg, then I'll beg. Take me with you. *Please.*"

The robot begged, "[whir] Please do not – CLACK – do not listen to this – CLACK – this beast. Former Master Art, you must leave her. She deserves – CLACK – deserves this fate."

Her Art nodded at her and said, "Sorry, Drillbot. But I'm not going anywhere without her. God-Me, you can forget about getting your hands on the bears if you don't free her."

The robot roared in protest, and the god growled in anger. Her Art sat down on the ice beside her to express his ultimatum, but then he immediately jumped back up onto his feet, squealing because it was too cold.

The god frowned and stared at Ginny with scorn. After a few moments, he finally said, "Fine."

He stuck his thumb into his mouth and blew hard against it. An arc of flames launched from his palm and landed on the ice next to her. He moved the arc in a small circle, melting the ice around her. It sloughed away, and before she could sink into the black water, the god grabbed her and pulled her out.

He stared at her with fierce eyes. He said, "I'll need to resurrect you. It will be painful and will take a few moments."

Ginny nodded. Then she screamed when the god threw her against the robot's fire-leash. She caught fire and immediately burned to cinders.

*

Ginny experienced black nothingness for she knew not how long, but then she found herself standing amongst the three individuals who had been gathered around her before everything went black. She looked down at herself, and she smiled to see that she was now clothed.

Then she cursed when she realized that she had been clothed like a Dictator Scout from Earth 1,000,000—the world to which she had been led under false pretenses long ago when the Multiverse had first butted its stupid way into her life.

"Look, we've got to reach the Pink One as soon as possible," said Ginny. "We still exist, which means the bear is still frozen in time. But if she figures out a way to get free, then this reality is dead. She promised me this reality would be her last victim so long as I was destroying other realities for her. But when I became frozen alongside her, whatever magic she had used to keep my soul bound to my corpse stopped working. And she made it clear to me that the contract between us was broken as soon as my soul left my body. We've got to figure out a solution, and fast. How long have I been down here?"

The god's laughter drowned out everything nearby, even the wind. He said, "Oh, it matters not how long you have been down here. You will not save this reality. I have big plans for it once I get my hands on the pink bear."

Ginny frowned. Her Art spoke to the god, "Hey! I don't want you doing *anything* to this reality. It's the one place in existence I might be able to relax once this stupid ordeal is done. Promise me that you won't do anything sinister to it, or I don't come with you."

The god smiled. It reminded Ginny of a snake. "Oh, fine," he said. "I won't do anything *sinister* to it. Now, let's move."

Ginny was not quite reassured, because she noticed that he only promised to not do anything *sinister*—and sinister had not been clearly defined. She could have pointed out this flaw in the agreement to her Art, but more than anything else right now, she did not want to stay down here, and drawing attention to the god's potential deception would do nothing but prolong the conversation. She could solve this future God-Art conundrum when free of this place.

Thus, she grabbed her Art by the crook of his arm and began walking toward the arched passageway in the nearby stone wall. The others followed.

CHAPTER 21

BACK TO THE BEGINNING

AGENT 27142 RIPPED another bush from the ground. He tossed it onto the top of his shift-shuttle and nodded. It was now sufficiently covered with foliage, and it blended decently into the surrounding forest. He stared at the dirt covering his hands and frowned. It was too bad this ship had been too damaged for its cloaking systems to work. He could have saved about two-hours' worth of gardening, or whatever it is you call ripping greenery from the ground and using it to camouflage your ship.

He clicked his heels, turned from the ship, and walked away. A ten-minute walk brought him to the edge of the woods. He crossed an interstate highway when there was a lull in cars, walked another few blocks, and then stopped in front of a familiar rundown apartment.

The hedges in front of the apartment were large and bushy. Behind them, mini-blinds stood open behind the window, allowing Agent 27142 to see inside. A man sat at a table. He had scruffy stubble and he looked unwashed. A woman stood over his shoulder, holding papers and yelling into his ear. He buried his face in his hands.

Agent 27142 knocked on the front door to the apartment. "Who is it?" demanded a man's voice through the door.

Agent 27142 knocked again.

The voice yelled, "You deaf? Who is it?"

Agent 27142 knocked again. He watched the peephole in the door, waiting for a shadow to block out the light coming through it.

"I got a gun, motherfu—"

Agent 27142 saw a shadow and kicked the door next to its handle. The door crashed inward and smacked the man in his head. He stumbled backward. Agent 27142 strode forward and twisted the man's arm until he dropped the gun he was holding. Agent 27142 used his right leg to sweep the man's legs out from under him. The man crashed to the floor with a curse.

The woman stepped over to Agent 27142. She held a kitchen knife in her hand. "What are you doing?" she demanded. "Why don't you people leave us alone! We're moving out next week, for god's sake!"

"Threatening me with that knife is a terribly bad idea," said Agent 27142. He stared at her. Without looking down at the man on the floor, Agent 27142 pressed his boot down on the side of his head. "If you value this man's life, then I would recommend you drop it. Now."

She looked from Agent 27142's face down to the man. Trembling, she dropped the knife. She said, "O-OK. I dropped it. Now w-what do you w-want?"

"You said you want *'you people'* to leave you alone. Who is *'you people?'*"

The woman looked incredulous. "Seriously?" she asked. "All you crazies that keep showing up here. The giant robot in the stupid disguise. The man with the flaming hair who looked just like you, but taller. They almost k-killed us."

Agent 27142 did not reply other than to nod. He pulled a pair of zip ties from his holster. He bound the man's hands behind his back. He walked over to the woman and did the same. Then he lifted the man onto his feet and marched them both to a back bedroom. As soon as he opened the door, screeching wails from a toddler assaulted his ears. He shoved both the man and the woman between their shoulder blades, and they tumbled forward onto the carpet.

"You two are going to stay in here and neither move nor make a sound. I suggest that you keep your child quiet if you want it to keep its tongue. I need to think."

Agent 27142 shut the door. He pulled out one of his little brass pill-shaped devices, pushed the button on it, and stabbed the spikes that emerged from it into the metal door handle. The handle melted, and the molten metal drooped to cover the area where the door met the wall. When it hardened, the metal fixed itself in place, locking the door so that it would not budge and would keep the family out of his way.

Agent 27142 walked into the living room and sat on the couch to think. *Who looks like me but has flaming hair? That's a new one*, he thought. *Doesn't matter, though. My hunch was right! When the robot landed in this reality, it came to the domicile of my dead prisoner.*

Agent 27142 continued thinking, *I always ignored the fool every time he bragged to himself about his role in the creation of the robot, and I ignored him when he wished aloud his hopes that the robot would survive every single time it showed up in battle. I was letting the fool think that I did not hear him. I was waiting until I wiped the robot from existence to reveal to the idiot that I had heard every word. I was waiting for the sweet moment when I could witness the despair on the prisoner's face, and then I was going to commence the torture for his offense in creating the deadly machine, and it was going to be one of the best torture-sessions of my life. But if I had known what the damned mechanical beast was going to do to my beloved, I would have flayed the skin from the prisoner's bones right when I met him!*

But I do not have time for sulking, Agent 27142 continued thinking, taking a deep breath to calm himself. *This is my chance for vengeance, if only I can find a lead for where the robot may have gone next. It is time to look for clues!*

And then he caught the luckiest break that he had ever had caught, other than that one time when the little girl had appeared in *The Barrier* with her gourd or that other time when he had won the battle against the Aquatic Agrarian Uprising with a lucky lightning bolt when all else seemed hopeless or that other time when he had spotted the wrench on the factory line that had been wedged between two pistons that would have caused a ship to blow up if it had gone undetected. But other than those instances and a few more he did not feel like recalling just now, this was his luckiest break ever.

He felt a buzzing in a pouch on his holster. He opened it and pulled out a small rectangular device. It was blinking red. He opened it, and a small screen popped up that displayed a map with Prisoner-Art's identification code on it. *He's right outside!* thought Agent 27142. *But how? He's dead, and his corpse is on my shift-shuttle. This tracker traces his life signature. A wrong reading is impossible.*

He stood and clicked his heels together. He picked up Henry, drew his Scatter Gun pistol, and walked toward the door.

"Henry," said Agent 27142, "if we get into a battle, you had better back me up if you know what's good for you."

"Nothing's ever good for me," whined the gourd. "But I will help, since I've no other choice."

"Good," said Agent 27142, and with that, he stepped through the open doorway and out onto the front stoop. He looked left and right, but he saw no sign of Prisoner-Art.

"What the hell?" Agent 27142 muttered to himself. "Where is he?"

"I detect no battles," said Henry. "Should I remain at the ready, or can I relax? When I'm tense, I get gassy."

Agent 27142 stared down at the tracker. It maintained its claim that Prisoner-Art was just in front of him, but there was no Prisoner-Art. Agent 27142 frowned in confusion.

Then movement caught his eye. The manhole cover in the middle of the street wiggled. Agent 27142 smiled as he understood. He muttered, "I've got you now, you chunky bastard."

CHAPTER 22

A DEVIL OF AN EMERGENCE

THOUGH DRILLBOT HAD an internal thermometer that he used to measure the temperature around him, it held no real meaning for him other than to give him arbitrary data about his surroundings. Drillbot's internal processors could not experience cold. There was simply a lack of the concept in the ones and zeroes that bounced through his core. But down here at the bottom of the well in the lowest depths of this Hell, he felt cold, anyway.

The group had left the base of the well and had entered the arched passageway. They had only traveled about a quarter of a mile through the passageway, but God-Art had already needed to resurrect Normal-Art and Ginny three times each, because they kept dropping dead from the chill.

Drillbot watched the reunited couple and grew sad. As they walked arm-in-arm, Normal-Art would often say something to make Ginny laugh. She would respond in kind. They would then share a laugh together, and then one of them would shriek and keel over in frigid death.

Drillbot felt a pang of jealousy. He missed Ginny Rex terribly. He missed her companionship, her laughter, her soft snores, the feeling of her mullet as it whipped across his face when she tossed in her sleep. He missed her kisses, her underbelly, her purrs after she found pleasure in his drill-arms. He would have given anything to freeze to death with her and stay forever entwined in her tiny, tiny arms.

Normal-Art fell to another bout of cold, and as God-Art resurrected him by forcing a phoenix feather down his dead throat, Drillbot studied the passageway ahead. It was cloaked in pitch blackness, and this blackness was broken only by the lights shining from God-Art's flaming hair and the leash that surrounded Drillbot. The flickering firelight drifted out in front of the group, giving the rounded stones that formed the walls the impression of largesse.

Smoke wafted out of Normal-Art's nose, and then he jerked up to his feet.

Ginny immediately collapsed, dead, and received the same treatment with an identical phoenix feather.

The god cursed in frustration. He muttered, "All this resurrecting is taking *forever*. There's *got* to be a better solution."

The god strummed his fingers on his chin for a moment, and then he nodded. He smirked at Drillbot and said, "Got it."

Drillbot did not reply other than to watch the god, who had reached down to the bottom of his cloak. Since it was made from the hides of baby seals and wolves, he tugged the fabric in different directions until he found the face of one of the baby seals. He ripped the hide of this baby seal from the cloak. He put his lips to the seal's and blew. The baby seal inflated, and then it squealed with joy as it popped to life.

"Hold this a sec," said God-Art to Normal-Art, handing him the baby seal. The seal was gigantic, as big as Normal-Art's torso. Its huge eyes stared from Normal-Art to Drillbot to Ginny, and it seemed to smile. It cooed.

Normal-Art smiled back at the creature and petted it. God-Art ripped another strip containing another baby seal from his cloak, and he inflated this baby seal to life, too.

"OK, hold still," ordered God-Art to Normal-Art and Ginny. "We're going to use these seals' body heat and blubber to keep you two alive for a bit longer than you've managed on your own. Frankly, I'm sick of resurrecting you, and I don't want to deal with you if you overdose on the magic that I've been pumping into you to return you to life. I hope you live to a ripe old age, just so you will get to experience the long-term negative effects of these resurrections in a manner that won't affect *me*."

God-Art used one hand to hold one of the baby seals above Ginny's head. He shoved his other hand into the seal's torso and ripped a long, vertical gash down the length of its body. The seal squealed in pain. Ginny and Normal-Art squealed in horror.

Before the baby seal's entrails and organs could fall out onto the ground, God-Art wrapped the thrashing creature around Ginny, shoving her inside the open wound like it was a fur coat that had come to life. Her head poked out of the top of the wound so that the seal's head flopped on top of hers like the hood of a cloak. Streams of seal blood rolled down her face. To any casual observer, it would have looked like a seal with scrawny human legs poking out of its bottom had appeared in her place.

God-Art tugged at the seal's hide so that the ripped portion of its skin met on her front. He ran his index finger across the tear, and the jagged edges of the tear glowed as it sealed itself back together. The seal's heart made soft squelching noises as it thumped against Ginny's back. It purred, and Ginny laughed.

"That tickles," she said.

God-Art repeated the process on Normal-Art, after which Normal-Art and Ginny stood side-by-side in their live-seal coats.

Ginny glanced over to Normal-Art and laughed. "You know what you look like?" she asked.

"Like that guy from that movie you like. The whiny guy who gets shoved into the Wonton thing—or whatever it's called—after the other guy comes looking for him and cuts the Wonton thing open with the laser-sword."

"Exactly!"

"Well, you look like that, too!" he replied.

They smiled at each other, their pale teeth standing out in an odd contrast to the drying blood that had streaked down their faces. The seals cooed.

"OK, glad we could reminisce a bit. Now get moving," commanded God-Art.

Drillbot watched Ginny and Normal-Art scamper across the ice toward the end of the passageway. The group's pace quickened substantially now that God-Art no longer needed to resurrect one of them every couple minutes.

Once the group reached the end of the passageway, it opened onto a grandiose cavern, the ceiling of which lay so high overhead that Drillbot needed to telescope his eyes to their highest setting to see it. Frozen stalactites hung from way up above, their ends capped in frost. There were so many of them and they were so big that the sight looked to Drillbot like an upside-down mountain range.

A ramp descended to another stretch of flat ice. Snowbanks periodically broke the monotony of flatness. It was colder in this cave than anywhere that the group had been before.

At the far end of the cavern, a massive humanoid shape lay enshrouded in a fog so thick that Drillbot could not see through it, no matter which functionality he switched between in his telescopic eyes. Fog and wind and snow and little pieces of ice whipped through this cavern at periodic intervals, pelting the group as they began their descent down the ramp.

Normal-Art had not taken more than three steps down the ramp before he slipped and fell onto his back. The seal surrounding him squealed in pain when his weight landed atop it. Normal-Art slid down the ramp—all quarter mile of it—gaining speed the entire time until he crashed into a snowbank at its bottom.

Drillbot's engines roared as he chased after his former master to help. However, he made it no more than a dozen feet before his leash ran out of length. He pulled harder, but to no avail, for the god dug in his heels with each plodding step—and the god's heels were glowing with magical flame, which Drillbot processed as an indicator that he would be unlikely to overcome the god's stubborn resistance to his leash-pulling this time. Drillbot could move no faster than God-Art was willing to walk.

Ginny scrambled past them both down the ramp. Drillbot turned his head to look back at God-Art, who strolled nonchalantly down the ramp. Drillbot said, "[whir] Why do you not hurry? Former Master Art will – CLACK – will likely need another resurrection after that – CLACK – that mishap."

The god frowned. He replied, "Do I look like I'm made of resurrections? I'll get to the bastard when I get to the bastard. I've exerted much of my power bringing these two fools back to life this many times. This little stroll will give me a break to recover."

Drillbot's processors buzzed and vibrated, and he longed to be free of his leash. But instead, he rolled forward as far as his leash would allow, slow as a glacier. Drillbot zoomed in his telescopic eyes so that he could check on Art, and he adjusted his audio receptors so that they were focused on his former master, allowing him to hear like he was standing next to Art. Ginny soon reached the bottom of the ramp and kicked aside enough of the snowbank to reach Normal-Art. She hooked one of her legs under his right armpit and dragged him out of the snowbank.

A man lay on his back in the snowbank where Normal-Art had crashed, every part of him frozen in ice but his face. He had a little pug nose and curly hair that fell just below his ears. He groaned.

Normal-Art glanced up at Ginny, obviously dazed but still alive. Drillbot smiled his version of a smile that the man had survived. Normal-Art said to Ginny, "Guess who broke my slide? I'll give you a clue: his favorite color is blue, and he proved the world's not flat."

Ginny scowled. Normal-Art had obviously touched a nerve, and the smug look on his face showed that it was intentional. She sighed, and then she answered, "Columbus. And he didn't prove anything. People knew the world was round for thousands of years before he was alive, you idiot.

Ginny glanced over at the face of Columbus, pale and blue in its perch in the depths of the snowbank. She continued, "That bastard committed genocide against my people. I want to kick him in the face. Don't let the stupid god-version of you leave without me."

Normal-Art smiled. He replied, "You're only a sixteenth Native American, Gin. Thus, he only genocided a sixteenth of your people. Or you only get to be a sixteenth mad at him. Either way, you don't get to be as one-hundred percent self-righteous as you're being."

By the time he finished the sentence, however, she had already leapt into action. Panicked Italian curses followed the sounds of Ginny's bootheel kicking against the damned man in the ice. Drillbot watched Normal-Art stand, slip on the ice, fall back down, and then stand back up. Over and over. When Normal-Art finally gained his balance, enough time had passed both for Ginny to have finished her multitude of kicks to Columbus' face and for Drillbot to have reached the bottom of the ramp with God-Art. Ginny scrambled back out of the snowbank to stand with the rest of the group.

The group stood silent and collected themselves for a moment. God-Art then led the way toward the massive humanoid figure at the back of the cavern. The figure remained obscured by fog, and as the group hiked closer, the fog swirled toward them with higher frequency. Drillbot noticed frost building in thick clumps on the ends of Normal-Art's and Ginny's nose and eyebrows.

The wind originating from near the massive figure soon picked up speed, and the fog ceased *swirling toward* the group. Instead, it now blasted into them, knocking them all to the ground. The fog then whooshed into the passageway from whence the group had come. The snowbanks grew thicker and a fresh layer of frost covered the walls of the cave.

When Drillbot attempted to pull himself upright, he realized that he could not. He then noticed that the ice coating the ground had grown substantially thicker. As a matter of fact, it had grown so thick that he was now encased in it with only his head poking free. He rotated his eyes and noticed that all his companions were entombed in similar blocks of ice. Normal-Art and Ginny had both turned blue, and the life had fled from their eyes. Drillbot sighed.

"Hey, cut that out! It's me!" screamed God-Art in the direction from which the wind and fog had come. The flames atop the god's head burned bright. A small explosion erupted from the god's scalp, and when it dissipated, the ice surrounding the god and Drillbot and Normal-Art and Ginny had disappeared. God-Art hastily resurrected Normal-Art and Ginny with another phoenix feather that he retrieved from the leather pouch hanging from his rope-belt.

Drillbot pulled himself upright, and when he did, he glanced toward the end of the cavern. The fog was gone. And with the fog gone, Drillbot witnessed the reason *why* it had been so foggy and cold.

There rose a colossal beast of an angel six-stories tall and bound in ice from the waist down. Its skin was red, though the skin darkened into shades of purple near the waist where the cold ice cut into its skin. The beast had six pairs of wings, and when it flapped them, they created a frigid gust that grew into an icy tornado.

It flapped them now, and the icy wind swirled into the air, forming a thick tornado of fog that then whipped through the cavern and up the ramp from which the companions had recently descended, traveling back into the prior passageway—and then, according to Drillbot's calculations of how powerful the wind was, presumably up through the well in which the giants stood. The freezing temperatures over the last two Circles and the swirling winds throughout this dank Hell finally made sense to Drillbot. It all originated from this six-story tall angel beating its wings.

God-Art formed a shield of fire around the group this time to protect them from the frigid blast. The god screamed at the beast, "Hey! I said to stop that!"

The hair atop the beast's head was black and twisted in thick ringlets that stretched down to its shoulders. Its face, however, was malformed. Well, malformed if you consider having three faces joined by a common forehead a malformation.

All three faces were shaped like lion-faces, though their colors were different: the left was black, the middle red, and the right pale yellow. A pallid, damned soul lay impaled on the lower fangs of each mouth, occasionally writhing and moaning in pain. The eyes of all three of the beast's faces shone with more fury and hatred than Drillbot had ever seen.

When the angel laid its six eyes upon the group, it scowled at them and snapped its three jaws at them. However, as it scanned their faces from left to right, its eyes stopped on God-Art.

"You!" it screamed, pointing an accusing finger.

God-Art pointed right back. "You!" he returned.

God-Art stalked toward the giant beast, pulling Drillbot behind him. Normal-Art and Ginny did not move, their knees shaking in terror. Then, when God-Art was but a few dozen feet away from the fallen angel, the beast leaned down with the speed of a cat, snatched God-Art, and picked him up high in the air. Drillbot dangled by the leash in the air below him.

God-Art and the beast embraced in a hug. God-Art exclaimed, "Lucifer, you old fraud! I've been trying to get your attention for like five minutes! How long's it been?"

The beast's scowls turned into smiles. It looked like a joyous anime character as it grinned and held God-Art against its chest. The scene created an odd juxtaposition with the tortured souls impaled on the beast's bottom fangs.

"Too long, old friend," replied Lucifer. "Sorry for the scary faces and the wind and the fog and stuff. I thought you were a group of sinners that were sent down here to be scared straight. Always have to put on a show, otherwise you don't keep your reputation when they return to the surface and tell others about the experience."

Lucifer set God-Art on the ground and asked, "So, what brings you my way?"

God-Art smiled. He replied, "Oh, just passing through with my compatriots here. We're actually in a bit of a rush, otherwise we'd stay and chat."

Lucifer looked hurt. "Oh, OK. I'd hoped you had stopped in for a visit. I'd love it if you'd stay for dinner."

God-Art said, "Duty calls. But hey, I'll swing by next time I'm on this Earth, I promise."

Lucifer nodded. "OK. But before you go, I've been working on some standup. You know that bar, *The Disemboweled Boy Toy*, up in Dis? Well, they have Open Mic Night every Thursday, so I'm going to perform during my next night off. Let me know what you think."

God-Art frowned. He said, "Oh, Lucifer. I don't think we should. We really don't have time."

"Just one joke, and then you can go," responded Lucifer. "Listen: Why was the Sixth Circle of Hell afraid of the Seventh? Bec—"

"Because seven ate nine?" yelled Normal-Art before he could stop himself. It was basically a modified version of a stupid joke that Normal-Art had heard as a kid where the numeral eight acts as a homonym for ate, the past tense of eat. As a kid, Art had repeated the joke over and over until his mother had finally told him to shut up.

Lucifer glared at Normal-Art, wings beating furiously. Wind whipped across Normal-Art, and he tumbled end over end until he crashed into another snowbank. As he slid out, God-Art turned and glared at him, mouthing: *Don't you know that you NEVER interrupt an immortal when it's telling a joke?*

Normal-Art mouthed back: *I can't read lips!*

God-Art mouthed in reply: *Liar!*

Satisfied with the punishment to the interloper, a smile returned to Lucifer's face. The beastly angel finished the joke, "Because the Seventh Circle is violent, so it might hurt the Sixth Circle!"

Lucifer bent over in peals of laughter and beat his fists against the ground. Everyone present let out a giant fake laugh except for Drillbot, who did not realize that was what he was supposed to do. Drillbot's programming contained little in the way of humor, but even *he* knew that Lucifer's joke was awful.

"Oh, Lucifer, that was a good one!" exclaimed God-Art, faux niceness oozing from his lips. He tugged on Drillbot's leash, grabbed Ginny by the shoulder, and walked with them toward a crevice in the rock behind Lucifer. "Unfortunately, we must really be going now. You're going to slay at Open Mic Night. I only wish I could be there."

Lucifer grinned once more and waved goodbye to God-Art with all the joy of a little child. Normal-Art scrambled to his feet and chased after the trio. Lucifer snapped the fangs of all three mouths at Normal-Art as Normal-Art passed, and then giggled when Normal-Art squealed in fright.

Normal-Art caught up to Drillbot and the others, and they all walked forward together into the crevice, the floor of which sloped upward until it disappeared into a bright light, through which Drillbot could not see.

The four companions followed the path and stepped into the bright light, leaving Hell behind.

*

The four emerged from the bright light and found themselves standing in a dank and muggy sewer.

"Where are we?" asked Normal-Art.

"We're in a sewer, obviously," answered God-Art.

Everyone except for God-Art sighed in frustration. "I can see that, ass," replied Normal-Art. "Care to elucidate?"

"We're in a sewer, *and* we are below the street in front of your old apartment."

"Wait, Hell is underneath my old apartment? I knew this neighborhood was a dump, but I never expected that it was *that* bad."

"No, you fool," said God-Art. "The particular Hell to which you were assigned is a state of mind. Based on the lore and culture that created it, it is everywhere it needs to be on your Earth. And *we* needed it to be below your old apartment so that we could exit here, so below your old apartment it was."

"But *why?*"

"Because we're about to embark on another dangerous journey, and I thought a nice rest for a few nights in a familiar place might restore your spirits before we leave this Earth," said the god.

Normal-Art stared at the god with a flat look. He replied, "You mean you just couldn't think of anywhere else for us to go to rest before we leave this reality, right?"

God-Art shrugged. "Maybe."

Normal-Art grinned and said, "Then let's go! I can't wait to see what's on T.V.!"

God-Art frowned. He said, "Make yourselves comfortable, but don't get too comfortable. We're leaving as soon I manage to rebirth Beverly from my forehead."

And with that, the god led them to a nearby ladder set in the wall. It was made of metal rebar and was covered in rust. The god looked from it over to Art and Ginny. He frowned and ripped each seal that covered them in half, freeing their arms and torsos. The seals each screamed a death cry.

"There," said God-Art. "Now you're as good as new."

The god dropped the seal carcasses to the ground, and they splashed in the muck. Then he climbed the ladder and pushed aside a manhole cover at its top. Drillbot dangled behind him by the leash, swinging back and forth. Then, God-Art pulled him from the sewer and up onto the street.

Drillbot inspected his surroundings, and he noticed a man standing outside of his former master's front door. The man looked identical to Drillbot's former master, but he was dressed in a tattered B.I.T. uniform. Drillbot heard the man shout and saw a bright flash of lightning. Drillbot sighed.

CHAPTER 23

SHOWDOWN

A MAN WHOSE FACE looked just like Prisoner-Art emerged from the manhole. When he stood up to his full height, Agent 27142 could see that he was around nine-feet tall, had flames dancing from his scalp rather than hair, and wore a robe made from the hides of wolf cubs and baby seals. A rope hung around his waist as a belt, and dangling from this belt were a serrated dagger, some obsidian tools, and a leather pouch. A necklace made of severed ears hung loosely around his neck, and it swung back and forth as he heaved on a rope made of fire. He used the flaming rope to pull the robot with the drill-arms up behind him, the robot's torso wrapped tightly in the flames.

The robot looked over at Agent 27142. Then the Art with the fiery hair followed the robot's gaze. Agent 27142 glanced down at the tracker and then back up at the pair. Based on the location that the tracker indicated for Prisoner-Art, Agent 27142 deduced that the slob must still be down there beneath the street.

Agent 27142 smirked. All he need do was get rid of this Fiery-Art—who was obviously high on the power scale if he could imprison the robot in flaming bonds—and he would have his opportunity to exact his revenge on the robot without interference.

Agent 27142 pitched Henry at the Fiery-Art. "Jump him out of here!" he ordered, and then he pointed his Scatter Gun pistol at the robot. He squeezed the trigger and a jagged lightning bolt launched from its end.

The robot dove out of the bolt's path, unfortunately, and the bolt slammed into the base of the dilapidated *Muse Electronics* billboard that rose high over this street. Sparks flew, a large portion of the right side of the column that held the billboard in the air disappeared, and a loud groan issued from the billboard as it began tottering in the breeze.

Meanwhile, Fiery-Art furrowed his brows. He gazed at the antennae on the gourd hurtling through the air in his direction. He grinned. He leaned his head forward and grew a small, fleshy pole from his forehead. Henry slammed into the man's torso and then blasted lightning at the man. The pole acted like a lightning rod, somehow attracting the lightning into itself.

Henry bounced from Fiery-Art's chest and flopped onto the ground, rolling a few inches back toward Agent 27142. Fiery-Art began shaking back and forth as though he were seizing. He sat down. His eyes crossed.

"Henry! You stupid vegetable! I said to jump him out of h—"

But Agent 27142's rebuke was interrupted when the deafening sound of thunder and lightning erupted from Fiery-Art's ears. His head exploded with a crack that echoed so loudly, it sounded like it must have emanated on a cosmic level. From the wreckage of Fiery-Art's head launched a cockroach nearly two-feet long.

The cockroach landed on its back legs and reared up, clicking its forelegs in what sounded like fury. It raised its wings and exposed turquoise runes that covered every inch of its dark brown exoskeleton. Thin blue lightning bolts danced between the bug's antennae. It shot a small bolt at Agent 27142. Agent 27142 watched with mouth agape, having expected this not at all.

He looked down as the bolt crashed into the Scatter Gun pistol in his hand. It disappeared. He cursed. His cursing was interrupted when Prisoner-Art and Agent 29333 emerged from the manhole. Prisoner-Art glanced around the scene. Horror filled his eyes when he saw Agent 27142—which caused Agent 27142 to beam with pride—but then total joy seemed to chase the terror away when he noticed the gigantic bug.

"Beverly!" he squealed. He raced over to the bug and picked it up. He squeezed it with a loving bear hug. It squirmed from his grasp, skittered a few loops around him, and then stood atop his head. It raised its wings once more and flashed lightning between its antennae.

"She's warning you that you had better leave us be if you know what's good for you," explained Fiery-Art, his exploded head now fully repaired. He was already back on his feet. "You have no idea what kind of Artheoskatergariabetrugereiinganno's Box you have just opened."

Nobody present cared to point out that they had no idea what an Artheoskatergariabetrugereiinganno's Box happened to be. Instead, as Agent 27142 stared at the reconstituted Fiery-Art, he let out a quick gasp before he could stop himself. He muttered, "Wait. Your head just exploded."

The Fiery-Art nodded and said with a wolfish grin, "And I thank you for that. Your Jump Totem jumpstarted a process that was going to take me at least another few days to accomplish."

Agent 27142 stared at him blankly and did not reply.

"I'm a god, mate. Mischief god at that, and resurrecting myself is sort of my thing. Beverly's my Jump Totem, and she gets reborn from my forehead when she dies. She died back when I was running around with *this guy* and attempting to get my hands on a cosmic bear," said Fiery-Art, jerking a thumb toward Prisoner-Art.

Agent 27142 nodded. He replied, "I *suspected* that you were the other culprit involved in that crime. That was an illegal caper. You are under arrest, and I will ensure that you suffer for your crime on one of the B.I.T.'s worst penal dimensions for the remainder of your existence."

Fiery-Art laughed. He said, "Yeah, I don't think so. Though I shall enjoy flaying you alive if you are indeed serious about trying to arrest me."

Agent 27142 looked from Fiery-Art over to the female. He said to her, "Agent 29333, you are back, right alongside our prisoner! Why are you wearing that ridiculous outfit? Whatever. It matters not. I am simply excited you are returned! Prepare for maneuver number twenty-eight decimal five-four."

She stared at him without comprehension. Prisoner-Art glanced over to her and said in a voice loud enough for all to hear, "He thinks you're a different version of you. There was a you that used to serve him on his ship. He was totally in love with her. Everyone could tell. But he was too cowardly to act on it, and between you and me, she confided in me that she could never be with him because his breath is terribly foul. I happen to agree. The worst torture he ever performed on me was when he'd speak too close to my fac—"

Agent 27142 screamed in rage. He sprinted forward, leapt into the air, and kicked Prisoner-Art across the chin. The bug began to fire a bolt of lightning, but Agent 27142 punched it and it tumbled to the ground.

Agent 27142 landed on his heel and spun to face Fiery-Art, who was stalking toward him. Agent 27142 pulled from his holster one of his brass pill-shaped devices and a small black cylinder the size of his palm. He flicked his wrist, and the black cylinder telescoped out to become a metal whip. It crackled with electric energy.

"Henry, deal with the hostile Jump Totem," ordered Agent 27142, snapping the whip at the approaching mischief god.

Prisoner-Art lay on the ground, still reeling from the kick to his face. The

Agent 29333 imposter raced to him and held him in her arms. "I'm thinking maybe we stay out of this, at least until those two wipe each other out," she whispered into his ear, gesturing toward Fiery-Art and Agent 27142. Prisoner-Art nodded his consent.

"[whir] If you free Drillbot from his bonds, Drillbot could – CLACK – could help," called the robot to the Fiery-Art.

Fiery-Art ignored the robot's plea, and Agent 27142 ignored everything but the gargantuan version of himself that was stalking his way like some sort of predatory cat. The god drew his serrated dagger in one hand. Its hilt was made from a hairy, green-furred tiger's paw. The god filled his other hand with an obsidian hammer.

Behind the approaching god, lightning flashed lamely between the bug and the gourd. Their attacks seemed to have no effect on one another, so after a few seconds, Henry resigned to making conversation with the bug, and it clicked its forelegs together in reply.

Agent 27142 decided not to wait for the god to reach him. He sprinted forward. He cracked the whip at the god's face. The god did not flinch as Agent 27142 had hoped, but the electric crackle *did* cause him to blink. It was enough of an opening. Agent 27142 pressed the button on the brass pill-shaped device and spun to his right, twirling quickly away from the god's dagger hand. He stabbed the brass device three times, once into the god's obsidian hammer, once into the god's left palm, and once into the god's left collarbone.

All three melted, puddling onto the ground at the god's feet. The god grimaced in pain, and fury filled his eyes. He swiped with his dagger, and Agent 27142 dodged it. He swiped again, and Agent 27142 dodged it again, this time using his momentum to bring his whip up and swipe it across the god's face.

The god grinned. The melted portions of his body had reformed on the ground without Agent 27142 realizing it, and the severed left hand had snatched Agent 27142 around the ankle. It jerked to one side, tripping Agent 27142. The hand then grew larger, and now held both of Agent 27142's ankles in place like an overlarge manacle.

Agent 27142 cursed and lay sprawled on the ground. The god stood over him, raising the dagger high above his head. Little fleshly sinews began stretching from the disembodied portion of the god's body up to his torso proper, beginning to reconnect the severed portions.

"Checkmate, mate," announced the god as he stared into Agent 27142's eyes. "You were a worthy opponent. I shall chant your vigil after your death if you have no one else to do so."

Suddenly, the *Muse Electronics* billboard on the opposite side of the street groaned another loud groan and began falling toward the group gathered in the middle of the street. Agent 27142 stared past Fiery-Art and up at the tattered and crumbling advertisement. It was the same sign from when he had arrested Prisoner-Art decades ago. He wondered inanely if the place was still in business, doubt filling him at the prospect.

Fiery-Art followed his gaze, turning his head backward without moving his body like an owl. He continued rotating his head until it had turned a full three-hundred sixty degrees and was back to facing Agent 27142. The god said, "Well, looks like a bad day for those who can't resurrect themselv—"

An orange light flashed, and the god stopped talking. Agent 27142 found that he could not talk, either. Nor could he move. He wanted to blink, but he could not. He wondered if this was what *everyone* felt just prior to death, if maybe time somehow slowed to a halt. From what he had heard, he had expected his life to flash before his eyes. But that did not happen.

And that's when he heard a familiar voice. He wanted to cringe, but he could not move.

CHAPTER 24

ALWAYS LATE

OLDER-ART'S MUSTACHE BUZZED and vibrated, and he smacked it, once more silencing the alarm in it that he had set to go off at this time. An electronic clock nearby beeped and beeped and beeped, and Older-Art slapped it, too, so it would give him some peace and quiet.

Peace and quiet, that sounds nice, he thought. *I'll have lots of peace and quiet after today when I finish this damned mission.*

"Dammit!" he screamed, sitting up in his bed. "The mission! Of all the days to oversleep!"

He leapt out of bed and onto his feet, panic filling his heart at the prospect of sleeping through this cosmically important mission for the Bureau of Time Travel. Dread overwhelmed him at the idea that he might *never* be free of the agency if he botched this task, and thus never free to do what he had always wanted to do: finally relax forever on a couch, watching television.

The bedsheets lay tangled around his feet and tripped him as he attempted to scramble about his business. He crashed to the ground, cursed, and jumped to his feet. He threw on the first piece of clothing he could find—a tattered, pale blue robe made from a scratchy material that itched his skin. He pulled on a pair of boxers that lay nearby on the ground, the ripe smell indicating to him that he had not chosen wisely. But he had no time! He had waited twenty years for today—had even refrained from drinking last night so that he would wake up early—and he had *still* managed to oversleep.

He cursed again. He shoved his feet into a pair of carpet slippers. He grabbed his holster from where he had hidden it in the cabinet under his sink, and then he raced out the front door. He returned a few seconds later to grab his keys from the counter only after reaching his car and realizing he had not brought them.

He turned on the car and put it into gear. He blasted from his parking space and zoomed onto the street. His tires squealed at each turn, and he was *sure* that at one particularly sharp turn he took at a speed entirely too fast for any sane man to take, a hubcap detached itself from his wheel and rolled into a bum sitting on the street corner. He did not slow down at all and did not deign to see if the man needed help.

Older-Art raced toward his old apartment, the one in which he had lived with Ginny before they had been pulled their separate ways by their annoying Multiversal counterparts. He raced through red lights, and at one particularly busy light through which Art zoomed without stopping, a police car turned on its sirens and began chasing him.

He glanced at the clock in the car and cursed. He was late. He was supposed to arrive before a fight occurred in the street between the B.I.T. agent and the other Arts. That fight was supposed to start at 10:15 AM, and it was now a solid 10:16 AM.

He reached into his holster without looking and pulled out a tiny metal disk. He cranked a nob on its front to the two-minute mark, and then he dropped it out of his driver-side window. When the cop car passed the tiny mine, it froze the car place. It would be stuck in time at that moment for the next two minutes, at which point Art would have reached his destination and hopefully completed his mission.

Older-Art turned the corner onto another street, then another, and finally slammed his car to a halt. He jerked open his door, jumped to his feet, and pulled from his holster a pistol that looked like a toy ray gun with which he might have played as a kid. It was called a *Time-Phaser*. It was pale green with small red rings around the barrel. He cranked a dial to the *Shotgun* setting, and the little red rings that encircled the barrel of the ray gun widened to about a foot in diameter. He cranked a second dial so that it rested on the two-hour mark. He cranked a third dial until it stopped on the *Stasis* setting, bypassing both the *Evolution* and *Devolution* settings.

He cursed as he surveyed the scene in front of him. He had been ordered to do what he needed to do *before* the group caused a scene, a task at which he had obviously failed. The gigantic *Muse Electronics* billboard was currently falling, about to crush everyone. God-Art stood holding his serrated dagger in the air over the supine B.I.T. agent. Art's younger-self lay on the ground and was being cradled by Ginny. Drillbot stood motionless, encircled in bindings formed from flames. Beverly sat next to a gourd with antennae, the pair engaged in conversation.

Art fired his Time-Phaser, and a blast of orange light sprayed in an arc that covered the entire street. Time froze in the area, the billboard hovering mere inches above the group.

Art walked around to his trunk. He opened it and pulled out a flat piece of metal, which he unfolded into a ten-by-ten metal square. He tapped a button with his foot and the bottom of it glowed blue. It lifted itself a few inches off the ground. He pulled a second piece of metal from his trunk and attached it to the floating square to create a hovering dolly.

He pushed it over to his younger-self and Ginny. He remembered the thought that his younger-self would be having at this moment, so he answered the question that his younger-self could not ask. As he did so, he remembered just how much he hated time travel.

"Yeah, I'm your boss, Mr. Reynolds," said Older-Art. He squatted in front of his younger-self's eyes for a moment and removed the fake mustache. "But I'm also *you*, from the future. The entire time we worked together, you were too dense to realize that I looked just like you, except I had a mustache.

"Anyway," he continued, slapping the mustache back in place, "as you are aware, that bastard B.I.T.-agent version of us stole a W.M.D. from the B.T.T. and used it against the cosmic bears. The bears remain frozen in time on the B.I.T.'s home reality, but that won't last forever, especially against such powerful cosmic beings as those two. I've been sent here to collect you so that you can save the Space-Time-Multinuum from utter disaster.

Older-Art nodded at his younger-self. He shrugged and continued, "I remember being where you are. And what you're thinking is absolutely correct: this is incredibly stupid, the Multiverse is stupid, and the Space-Time-Multinuum sounds like a stupid word that I just made up. But unfortunately, this is your life now. I wish I could change it, but you're my ticket to returning to our couch and *finally* getting to watch television until my eyes bleed and I rot away into nothingness."

Older-Art picked up his younger-self with a loud grunt and placed him on the hovering dolly. He picked up Ginny and placed her on the dolly. Then he walked over to Drillbot and smiled.

Art holstered his Time-Phaser and retrieved a small green rectangle from the holster. A tiny logo read *Time Warper, Model II*. He held it near the fiery leash that surrounded Drillbot. He tapped a button, and the little rectangle made a sound like a vacuum. He touched it gently to the flaming leash. The device twisted time in on itself in a backward circle, and soon, the fiery leash looped backward in time through so many iterations of itself that it returned to its place in this timestream before it ever existed, disappearing from around Drillbot.

Older-Art moved behind the robot and rolled him up onto the square dolly. He then pushed the dolly back over near his car so that it was no longer underneath the frozen billboard. He climbed up onto the dolly, removed the fake mustache once more, and turned it over. He tapped the little red button in its middle in the pattern he had been taught.

"This is Agent Art," he said. "Mission complete. Requesting extraction."

Thunder boomed overhead, and then a massive dirigible appeared in the sky. Its balloon was shaped like an elongated ellipse, and it was so large that it looked like a second moon had taken residence in the heavens. Thousands upon thousands of cables attached the balloon to a gondola, which was nearly as large as the balloon and shaped like an infinity symbol. A gigantic set of engines extended from the rear of the gondola, these as tall and wide as the gondola itself. The entire vessel was striped blue and white, with the stripes on the balloon oriented horizontally and the stripes on the infinity-symbol-shaped gondola oriented vertically. Its color scheme vaguely resembled that of a tiger if a tiger had entered the circus and been painted all the wrong colors while half its stripes were rearranged in the wrong direction.

A blue beam of light flashed from the bottom of the ship. It enveloped the dolly, along with Older-Art and the companions he had loaded atop the contraption.

The dolly was lifted into the air. It disappeared inside the ship. And then the ship disappeared from the sky.

ACKNOWLEDGMENTS

Special thanks to Mark Reddish for all the help. You always take the time to make these things better, and your feedback is always appreciated. It's definitely not a Moose-take that you're such a valued friend.

THANK YOU FOR PURCHASING THIS BOOK.

To receive special offers, a free short story, and info on new releases, sign up for the Christopher Brimmage mailing list at cbrimmage.com

ABOUT THE AUTHOR

Christopher Brimmage is a writer, teacher, marketer, brand manager, and former boy band front man. He has a wife named Geraldine to whom he loves to sing Meatloaf, a son named Augustus with whom he has formed the *Steam Roller Boyz,* and a pair of brothers that he loves to annoy.

By Christopher Brimmage

THE MULTIVERSE ASKEW TRILOGY

The Multiverse Askew (Book 1)

The Endless War That Never Ends (Book 2)

And Now, Time Travel (Book 3)

NOVELLAS:

Mandrill, P.I.: *Dial M for Murdered Coyote*
(A Cartoon Noir Detective Tale)

Plug 'em Good
(A Space Western)

Bridge Troll
(A Suburban Fantasy-Horror)

NEW SERIES COMING IN 2021:

THE MANDRILL, P.I. TRILOGY

Manny Mandrill is an old-school, hard-boiled private dick, the last in the sprawling cartoon metropolis of Toonsville. When this anthropomorphic cartoon mandrill is hired to solve a string of horrific murders, he uncovers a deadly criminal conspiracy that threatens to engulf the entire city.

Read this series for: Cartoon Noir! Humor! Detectives! Werewolves! Vampires! Mad Scientists! Mummies! Assassins! Dog Mobsters! Dinosaur Gangsters! Otter Archaeologists! Alien Invasions! Horse Cowboys! 80s Movie & Cartoon Nostalgia! And so much more, there are not enough exclamation marks to contain the excitement!